Berkley titles by Piper Maitland

ACQUAINTED WITH THE NIGHT

HUNTING DAYLIGHT

continued . . .

HUNTING DAYLIGHT

PIPER MAITLAND

BERKLEY BOOKS, NEW YORK

THE BERKLEY PUBLISHING GROUP
Published by the Penguin Group
Penguin Group (USA) Inc.
375 Hudson Street, New York, New York 10014, USA
Penguin Group (Canada), 90 Eglinton Avenue East, Suite 700, Toronto, Ontario M4P 2Y3, Canada
(a division of Pearson Penguin Canada Inc.) • Penguin Books Ltd., 80 Strand, London WC2R 0RL,
England • Penguin Ireland, 25 St. Stephen's Green, Dublin 2, Ireland (a division of Penguin
Books Ltd.) • Penguin Group (Australia), 707 Collins Street, Melbourne, Victoria 3008, Australia
(a division of Pearson Australia Group Pty. Ltd.) • Penguin Books India Pvt. Ltd., 11 Community
Centre, Panchsheel Park, New Delhi—110 017, India • Penguin Group (NZ), 67 Apollo Drive,
Rosedale, Auckland 0632, New Zealand (a division of Pearson New Zealand Ltd.) • Penguin Books
(South Africa), Rosebank Office Park, 181 Jan Smuts Avenue, Parktown North 2193, South Africa •
Penguin China, B7 Jiaming Center, 27 East Third Ring Road North, Chaoyang District,
Beijing 100020, China

Penguin Books Ltd., Registered Offices: 80 Strand, London WC2R 0RL, England

This is a work of fiction. Names, characters, places, and incidents either are the product of the author's
imagination or are used fictitiously, and any resemblance to actual persons, living or dead, business
establishments, events, or locales is entirely coincidental. The publisher does not have any control over
and does not assume any responsibility for author or third-party websites or their content.

HUNTING DAYLIGHT

A Berkley Book / published by arrangement with the author

PUBLISHING HISTORY
Berkley premium edition / February 2013

Copyright © 2013 by Michael Lee West.
Cover design by Rita Frangie. Photo composition by S. Miroque.
Sinister Eyes copyright © Dundanim / Shutterstock.
Interior text design by Kristin del Rosario.

ISBN: 978-0-425-25069-3

BERKLEY®
Berkley Books are published by The Berkley Publishing Group,
a division of Penguin Group (USA) Inc.,
375 Hudson Street, New York, New York 10014.
BERKLEY® is a registered trademark of Penguin Group (USA) Inc.
The "B" design is a trademark of Penguin Group (USA) Inc.

PRINTED IN THE UNITED STATES OF AMERICA

10 9 8 7 6 5 4 3 2 1

PROLOGUE

THE FIRST

EXPEDITION

The first time Dr. Ray-Bob Campbell died, he was fifty-two years old, a tenured zoology professor at Auburn University, a big-shot bat expert who resembled the creatures he studied. The jocks called him Dr. Squeak. They made fun of his gangly arms, tapered ears, and wide-set eyes, each one no bigger than a raisin.

Probably he'd still look that way if he hadn't taught that night class and squabbled with a skinny Goth co-ed. Jesus, what a bitch. He'd given her an F; she'd turned him into a vampire.

Actually, Campbell didn't mind being undead. That little catch in his right knee had gone away, and his blood pressure returned to normal. His face seemed different, too, just this side of handsome, and women were always calling his house now, suggesting dinner or more tooth-some activities.

He might have stayed in Alabama forever if he hadn't taken a job with the Al-Dîn Corporation. They'd offered him fifty thousand dollars just to poke around in an African rain forest and study bats. Not bad for a thirty-day gig, he bragged to his girlfriends. Not bad at all. The expedition started on January tenth, and he'd be home by Valentine's Day.

On a chilly January night, the company jet flew Campbell to Franceville, Gabon, first class all the way, right down to the blacked-out windows and plush layovers. When he arrived, he was given an English-speaking Baka guide and a cooler with A negative blood. That night, he and the guide took a dirt logging road to Birougou National Park. The truck rattled over potholes, bugs splattering against the windshield, bushes clawing at the tires.

The red dirt path ended in the forest, and the guide unloaded the gear. Campbell strode ahead, moths swarming around his lantern, primates shrieking alarm calls from the dark trees. He felt like a man of the jungle, but with a conservationist twist. If Tarzan and Al Gore had a baby, it would be Campbell.

He was supposed to hook up with the expedition team just beyond the Ngounie waterfalls, but like he told the guide, he'd get there when he got there. It wasn't like he was dawdling. This part of the Birougou wetlands hadn't been mapped, and it was impossible to see a damn thing because the rain kept falling in punishing torrents. Twice he skidded in elephant dung, but he pressed on. As he hacked through vines and leathery bushes, he thought about those fifty thousand dollars. He'd buy a red BMW and find a big-titted woman.

On Campbell's fifteenth night in the bush, he heard the rushing sound of the Nyanga River. He stepped into a narrow clearing. The moon glowed through tangled limbs, and far below, luminous ripples cut across the black water. He heard a scrabbling sound and raised the lantern. Light spilled over the bank, past rustling weeds and darting shadows.

Nothing was out there. Nothing he couldn't handle.

The guide loaded equipment into a small boat, then waded around to the bow and held it steady while Campbell climbed aboard. He heard a loud splash and hoisted the lantern. A sixteen-foot crocodile punched through the water, and its jaws crunched down on the guide's shoulder. The man screamed, the kind of sound dogs make when they get hit by a truck. Blood jetted across the front of Campbell's shirt. He felt disoriented as he breathed in the coppery tang.

The croc threw itself onto the starboard bow, and the stern jerked out of the water. Campbell skidded down the port side, his lantern swinging in his fist, bright arcs cutting over the flailing guide.

Screw this, Campbell thought. He hadn't come to Africa to get bitten by a handbag. He clambered backward, moving aft, his boots ringing against the boat's metal bottom. The croc wiggled off the bow and hung in the air for a moment, then pulled the wailing guide under the water. The stern clapped back down against the surface, and the boat rocked violently. The lantern flew from Campbell's grasp. He jumped out of the boat, landed on the dark, weedy bank, and crouched for a moment, gulping the muddy air. He'd avoided death for a second time, death by crocodile, and nothing would destroy his ass.

But where there was one crocodile, there were more. He scrambled to his feet and raced along the tree line. He didn't see crocodiles or hippos, just bones; some looked human. The air had a dank, weighted feel, like the crypts in a New Orleans graveyard, but he kept running.

Three klicks past the waterfalls, he saw lights at the edge of a grassy *bai*. The wide clearing should have been filled with hulking shapes of antelopes and forest elephants, but it was empty. By the time Campbell got to the camp, he had a bad feeling, nothing he could pinpoint, just a crawly sensation on his spine. He moved past tents, spotlights, and a roaring generator. Off in the shadows, he saw a man sucking a guide's neck. Near the back of the camp, he found the supervisor's tent. A redheaded man came out, zipping his trousers. He was short and wiry, built like a boy. His name was stitched over his shirt pocket: DR. G. O'DONNELL.

"I'm looking for Kaskov," Campbell said. "Or is this the latrine?"

"You could say that." O'Donnell's gaze swept over Campbell's bloody shirt, and then he pointed at the tent. "Kaskov's in there. Good luck."

Campbell walked through the flap. Inside, halogen lanterns hung from wire hooks, spilling light over a cot, a dartboard, and a satcom on a tripod. A blond-haired woman sat behind a metal desk. The surface was astringently neat, except for an ashtray, where smoke curled up from a cigar. A wooden plaque read TATIANA KASKOV.

He clamped his lips together, trying not to smile. This pretty little gal was Kaskov? Her hair was cut just below her chin, and her bangs were shot through with platinum highlights.

She reached for the cigar and looked up. Her eyes were an electric blue, and something flickered behind them as she stared at Campbell. "Are you the bat expert?" she asked.

"Actually the term is *chiropterologist*." He glanced at her pale, toned arms. She had a tattoo above her left wrist, a green snake curling around a black infinity sign.

How long has she been a vampire? he wondered. She appeared to be in her early thirties. Not a girly-girl, but damn cute. Just his kind of babe.

She rose from her chair and sat on the edge of the desk, puffing the cigar. Her khakis were tight, showing the outline of her thighs. "We expected you two days ago," she said. "Did you stop for coffee?"

Campbell sighed. Okay, maybe he wasn't her type, but she didn't have to hassle him. "I've been in the jungle two weeks," he said. "My socks are wet. I've got blisters."

"News flash," she said. "You're not in a resort. You're in an African rain forest."

"You don't have to be condescending." He plucked at his shirt. "See this blood? A crocodile killed my guide."

"That's a relief. I thought you ate him. The guide, I mean." Her voice was cold, but her eyebrows moved in a teasing arch.

Maybe she does like me, he thought. First, he needed to

change clothes and find some blood. Then he'd put the moves on her.

She swept her bangs to the side. "Is this your first trip to the Gabonese Republic?"

"Yeah. I've never been out of the U.S."

"Urban rules don't apply in the bush, Dr. Campbell. Abandon all ye know." She puffed her cigar, smoke curling around her ears. "Did the Al-Dîn rep explain the situation with the bats?"

"Not really." Campbell shrugged. "I'm supposed to observe them."

She blew a smoke ring. "These bats have an eight-foot wingspan. Our last chiropterologist thought they were an unclassified vampire species."

The last chiropterologist? How many have they had? Campbell cleared his throat. "Vampire bats aren't indigenous to this continent. Well, except for false vampire bats, but they're small. A three-inch wingspan, max. The bats you're referencing are probably flying foxes. Better known as fruit bats."

Tatiana pointed to a red welt on her forearm. "See this? Some kind of lizard bit me. The little bastard had wings. It's an undiscovered species. No family or genus. Why can't a vampire bat exist in Gabon?"

He clasped his hands behind his back. Was she a nut job? The kind who believed in UFOs and Sasquatch? You couldn't reason with those types, but he wanted to try.

"If they're as big as you say, why hasn't anybody noticed them by now?" he asked.

"Oh, we've got a specimen. Mr. Al-Dîn shot one a month ago."

Campbell felt a prickle of excitement. "Did you preserve it?"

"The remains went back to South Africa with Mr. Al-Dîn. But not before he touched the disgusting thing. He came down with Marburg Virus."

Campbell's mouth went dry. He stepped back, tucking his arms closer to his body. Fruit bats were vectors for hemorrhagic fevers. Marburg had a six percent mortality rate in vampires. Not that risky, but still. His gaze swept over Tatiana. Her eyes were clear. No jaundice or bleeding.

"Don't panic. Mr. Al-Dîn was the only one who got sick, and he recovered. Somewhat." She stubbed out the cigar. "Let's find your tent. When dawn hits, it isn't pretty."

She grabbed a halogen lantern and walked out of the tent. Her light swept over the ground, where driver ants ripped apart a millipede. The redheaded man walked by and gave her a thumbs-up, then he waded into the grassy field.

"You'll meet Greg O'Donnell later," she said. "He's our smartass biochemist. We have a latrine, but he likes to piss in the wild. He's bunking with me tonight, so you can have his tent."

A whirring noise made Campbell glance at the clearing. A dark cloud raced across the brightening sky. The cloud broke apart into hundreds of black smudges, and then the smudges spun off into dots. A breeze rushed by him, carrying faint echolocation clicks.

Bats. Hundreds of them.

"Move!" Tatiana pushed him toward a tent. "Get under a cot and stay there."

"Are you kidding? I'm gonna watch."

"You'd better find a gun."

Campbell frowned. A gun? Was she kidding? "These are bats," he said.

"I know." She sprinted over to a group of Congolese mercenaries. Above her, slate-colored blotches whizzed through the camp, knocking over spotlights. Campbell felt confused. Bats were superb navigators, but these creatures were crashing into everything.

At the other end of the camp, shouts rose up, followed by the *tat-tat-tat* of an AK-47. Campbell's scalp tightened—a bullet would cause a real death. He dove into a tent, zipped the flap, and crawled on his belly to the small mesh window. His legs trembled as he inched up. The air had begun to pale, and he saw obsidian slabs plunge through the camp. What the hell were they? Further out, in the *bai*, he heard a scream. It was coming from O'Donnell. The little guy raced across the field, punching his fists at the bats. Right before he reached the edge of the camp, amorphous shapes engulfed him. He shrieked, twisting from side to side. Then he was lifted into the air and carried toward the cliffs.

Campbell pissed himself. He sank to the tent floor and put his hands over his head. *Bats had picked up a man?* O'Donnell was a small fellow, but still. A Martial Eagle had a 2.6-meter wingspan, but it didn't carry prey into the trees, didn't hunt in groups, and didn't live in rain forests.

For the next twelve hours, Campbell huddled in the tent, trapped by daylight. Fatigue and nerves pulled him under, and when he awoke, the sun had just gone down. He stepped out of the tent. Spotlights were broken, and the mess pavilion lay in a heap. Tatiana stood in the clearing, organizing a team. She grouped Campbell with two other scientists: Dr. Nick Parnell, a blond entomologist who gave off a 1960s surfer vibe, and Dr. Emmett Walpole, a middle-aged, round-faced British virologist who kept babbling about hemorrhagic fevers.

Campbell walked up to Tatiana. "We need more guns," he said.

She skewered him with a glance. "Why?"

"To rescue Dr. O'Donnell."

She shrugged. "He's dead."

"You can't be sure. He's a vampire."

"He's history. I'll find another biochemist."

Campbell stiffened. They weren't going after O'Donnell? "Then what are we fixing to do?"

"It's a good time to hunt bats," she said. "They've just fed."

"Wait, no." He licked his lips. "It wasn't bats that took O'Donnell."

"Get back in line, you dumb fuck." She shoved past Campbell and turned into the clearing. Five Congolese mercenaries followed her.

Campbell fell back with the others and aimed his flashlight over the tall grass. The beam picked out white chunks. Femurs and rib cages. That's why there were no animals in the *bai*, he thought. It was a killing field.

Dr. Walpole veered into the shadowy clearing. "No, it

wasn't Ebola," he muttered. "Possibly could be a strain of Marburg. Or a new filovirus."

Tatiana glanced over her shoulder and nodded at the blond entomologist. "Nick, take care of your buddy."

Nick Parnell pulled the older man back in line. "Pipe down, Emmett," he said. "You've cracked. Too many days in the bush will do that."

"It isn't the bush, Nick. It's *her*."

"Come on, dude," Parnell said. "Be quiet or she'll hear you."

Emmett put two fingers to his lips and turned them back and forth, as if using a key.

An hour later, the team reached the cliffs. Campbell followed the stink of guano to a shelf of rock. From this height, the moon shone down on a split in the rain forest, where the Ngounie waterfalls poured into a black ravine. *Someone should post a danger sign by those falls*, Campbell thought. They were a demarcation point, a place where life morphed into death.

The team filed through an arched opening into the cave and held up their lanterns. As the halogen beams washed over Stone Age drawings, the images seemed to lunge out of the rocks. Campbell saw disjointed pictures of fanged men; skeletons; a baby in a cage. He dragged his light over a rock table. Pottery shards lay on the ground.

"What's that for?" he asked Tatiana. "A ritual of some kind?"

"Who cares?" She pulled out a Glock and led the team into a twisty passage. Their lights shimmered on the blood-streaked walls. The stench of decomposing tissue waved over Campbell. One of the Congolese mercenaries vomited. Another soldier broke away from the group and ran toward the cave opening.

Tatiana shoved her way around the scientists. She aimed her Glock and fired. The soldier's head jerked. Red sludge hit the wall in front of him and ran down.

"Anyone else?" she asked.

The other mercenaries backed against the passage wall. Campbell's ears rang, and he smelled gunpowder. *What the hell. This is insane.*

Tatiana began to pace, her pants riding low on her hips.

"They'll run the first chance they get," Nick Parnell told her.

Tatiana nodded. "Seize their weapons."

She aimed the Glock at the mercenaries, waiting for Parnell to collect their rifles. Tatiana turned back to Campbell. "Why are you still here?" she shouted. "Bring me a specimen."

Get it yourself, Campbell thought, and folded his arms. The Al-Dîn Corporation wasn't paying him enough. But Dr. Walpole had already started down the passage, muttering about RNA replication and incubation periods.

Parnell set the guns next to Tatiana, then nudged Campbell's arm. "Get moving."

They walked into a chamber. A fetid smell rushed up Campbell's nose, and he pinched his nostrils. Gunfire blasted from the chamber they'd just left, followed by muffled yells. Dr. Walpole darted back into the corridor, his boots scraping over gravel. Campbell repressed an urge to follow him. He glanced at Parnell. "Should we go back?"

"Nope. Tatiana wants a specimen. Let's push on."

Campbell shuffled into the gloom. His boots made a sticky swish as he waded through guano. His light picked out a bundle of rags. Then he saw a human hand, the fingers chewed at the edges. Dear God, he'd found O'Donnell. A stain oozed from the body, and bats had gathered around the edges to drink. They resembled bald, toothed ravens.

Parnell backed up. "These things looked bigger at the camp. How did they lift O'Donnell?"

Campbell's heartbeat pushed against his eardrums. "These are pups," he said. "Just babies."

He angled his light toward the roof of the cave. It was arched like the interior of a cathedral. Rows of silhouettes hung upside-down between the stalactites, and far above them, a colossal mass began to stir.

Parnell spun around and bolted into the corridor. Campbell ran after him. His boots skidded in guano, and he lost his balance. His flashlight sprang out of his hand and clattered to the ground several feet away. As he waded through the muck, a dank breeze stirred his hair. Above him, rhythmic clicks sped up, so loud that they seemed part of the air, part of the rocks, part of him. He stretched his hand for the halogen.

Almost there, buddy. One more inch.

The din invaded his skull. Barbed, leaden objects thronged around him, drilling into his shoulders, buttocks, the backs of his thighs. A force wrenched him off the ground, and he kicked out his leg, hoping to snag his boot on a rock. His foot sliced through air. Bodies surged and rippled around him. He shoved his hands through the warm, squirming mass and created a wedge. When he looked down, he saw just how high they'd taken him. And they were still moving.

Air rushed into his mouth and clogged his windpipe, as if a dirty sock had been jammed down his throat. He was going to die, really and truly die. Far below, his flashlight got smaller and smaller. A dank wind scraped around him, flattening his hair, pushing him up into blackness, past blade-sharp stalactites.

Then he saw what was waiting. A high-pitched noise burst out of his throat and ricocheted through the chamber, then morphed into an inhuman sound, nothing he'd ever heard before, as if the darkness itself were screaming.

PART ONE

JUDE AND CARO

CHAPTER 1

Caro

All I ever really wanted was true love and a calm life, but those things are mutually exclusive when you're married to a vampire. In many ways, Jude and I are a typical couple, except that my grocery list includes fresh blood. And I shop in dodgy places, not a supermarket.

It was late afternoon when I turned my Jeep into the deserted parking lot at the São Tomé port. The muggy February air hinted that a cooling rain was on the way, bringing a reprieve from the sweltering tropical heat. I hoped it would also lighten the turmoil and anxiety that dominated our lives.

I got out of the Jeep, pulled a thick envelope from the glove compartment, then walked toward the pier. A small cargo boat had already docked, and two men unloaded containers to the platform. Behind the vessel, the shallow blue waters of Ana Chaves Bay spread out like a wrinkled ball gown.

A lovely day to buy black market groceries, I told myself.

Months ago, right after my twenty-ninth birthday, Jude and I had fled to this little island off the coast of West Africa. We thought São Tomé would be safe, especially since it hovered right above the equator. Twelve hours of daylight would surely act as a deterrent to the sun-hating vampires who'd hunted us.

This ship's captain, Stefanov, veered around a tall metal container, his sandy hair ruffling in the breeze. He was a lean, weather-beaten man, dressed in a white cotton uniform. His forearms were tanned and vascular, sheened with perspiration. The sharp pleats on his trousers suggested a passion for order and an inner inflexibility.

"I have your goods," he called.

Come on, Caro, I firmly told myself. *Give him a confident, don't-bullshit-me smile.*

My lips remained in a firm line as I handed him a thick envelope. "Your payment."

He opened the flap and counted the banknotes, then looked up, his pale blue eyes narrowing. "This is only fifteen hundred euros."

I frowned. "That's what we agreed on."

"No, no." He shook his head. "It's two thousand euros."

"The last time you were here, you wrote down the price," I said. "The notepad is in my car. Shall I get it?"

"I have expenses from my end." He shrugged. "If you want the shipment, bring the rest of the money."

"But I don't have more."

"You bring all the money, or the cargo stays on the ship."

As I looked up at him, something fell inside me. I'd promised Jude that I wouldn't call Raphael again, a wealthy Italian vampire, and the godfather to my three-year-old daughter. But I was perilously close to breaking that promise.

"I'll pay you next time," I told Stefanov.

"No." He shook his head.

I started to make a fuss when the port official walked up, a hard-boned man in khakis and an orange vest. Stefanov pulled a wad of banknotes and handed them to the official. The man's aloof gaze passed from Stefanov to me.

My heart pushed against my ribs. Bribery was common in Africa, but I didn't want to be caught in the middle of it. I cast a longing glance at the boat. The massive hull was scabbed with barnacles, rust bleeding through the call sign's white letters. Inside that clunker was my husband's only source of nourishment: a foam chest that contained dry ice and B negative bags, each one plump and frosted, like shrink-wrapped beefsteaks. Each unit of packed red blood cells cost a small fortune. Jude needed one bag a day, but he was struggling to get by with less.

The port official strolled off, stuffing the notes into his hip pocket. I jerked my envelope out of Stefanov's hand, then slogged toward my Jeep. I had no choice but to phone Raphael. He would FedEx a few units to São Tomé, and Jude wouldn't have to know.

"Lady, wait," Stefanov called. "We can still cut a deal."

I turned, and the wind sent my hair flying. I pushed it back, and long blond strands wrapped around my elbow. "What?" I said irritably.

"I like your necklace," he said. "Give it to me, and we shall be even."

My hand closed on the gold chain. Dangling at the end was a small charm, a diamond-encrusted baby shoe. Jude had put it around my neck three years ago, the night Vivi was born. She'd been premature, and her little heart valve wouldn't close. Emergency surgery had saved our daughter, but I still thought of the necklace as a talisman.

"No way," I told Stefanov. "This was a gift from my husband."

"And now you give him a gift, yes?"

Fifteen minutes later, I drove back to Praia Lagarto Beach and parked in front of our pink stucco cottage. I carried the cooler toward the veranda, wondering how much longer we could afford to buy blood.

As I walked beneath the cacao trees, the limbs shook violently, and raucous shrieks pierced the air. Somehow the turmoil in our lives had invaded our yard. It wasn't a tranquil place, because a colony of fruit bats had roosted in our trees. During the day, they picked fights with each other. The flying fur rarely stopped before dusk, at which point the colony would rise from the trees, and as the echolocation clicks faded, a blessed hush would engulf our cottage.

Gripping my arms around the cooler, I pushed open the screen door with my hip, then went straight to Vivi's room. She was sleeping, curled up like a baby shrimp, her arm flung around her stuffed elephant. She always slept during the day so she could spend more time with her father. Jude was in the windowless bathroom, the only spot in the cottage where he was safe from daylight. Until sunset, he took refuge in the huge claw-foot tub, nestled with blankets and pillows and books. When I wasn't running errands, I stayed with him, but neither of us got much sleep.

I turned into the kitchen and set the cooler on the table. It was a cozy room, the shelves crammed with yellow pottery dishes, and the window over the sink overlooked the sparkling Gulf of Guinea. The last occupant had been a diplomat, and he'd left a blender, an espresso machine, and a set of copper cookware. I'd added less appealing touches. Next to the blender lay a pile of unpaid bills. Then I saw a thick book, *The Survival Guide to Illumination*. It was the heaviest volume in Jude's library, roughly the size and weight of a waffle iron.

My throat tightened as I stepped closer. He'd been reading about the dangers of zero latitude. Here on the equator, the light fell straight down, blasting twelve hours a day. Because it passed through less atmosphere, ultraviolet rays were brutal, even during the rainy season. Dusk and dawn fell frighteningly fast. An early-morning swim could end in scorched flesh, blindness, or death.

I smoothed my hand down the page, feeling the indentions where Jude had made notes in ink. He'd bought this manual after we were married, and whenever we moved, which was all the time, the book went with us.

At the last airport, the Lufthansa ticket agent had frowned at Jude's bulging backpack, but it had met the requirements for carry-on luggage. That was fortunate, because Jude would never have allowed baggage handlers near his backpack, mainly because he wanted to protect the book. Not only had it gone out of print, it could be dangerous in the wrong hands.

I remembered that night in the airport so clearly. In Jude's human life he'd been a rugby player, and immortality had made him even stronger. But as he moved down the corridor, the bag dropped lower, as if it had attracted more than poundage, his shoulder dipping to one side, as if he were carrying daylight itself.

At dusk, I was still staring down at the book. Why had Jude been reading it? He only pulled it out when we got ready to move to a new place, to study the region's lighting quirks and conditions.

I heard noises on the other side of the wall, which meant he was getting out of the bathtub. A few minutes later, the door creaked open, followed by the distinct tap-*tap*-tap of his footsteps in the hallway.

I turned. Jude walked toward me, smiling. When he was mortal, he'd been a biochemist with pallid, British skin. Now he was even paler. His eyes were butane blue and so hypnotic, I forgot that he'd been reading the survival guide.

"Caro," he said, whispering my name like a prayer. "I missed you."

I drew in a breath when his hand slid inside the collar of my dress, and his cool fingers brushed over my collarbone. Then his smile dimmed. Some vampires have telepathy—I have a smidgen because I'm half-immortal—but Jude never developed it. However, he has a photographic tactile memory, and he knows every detail of my body, from the half-moon scar on my palm to the mole on my right shoulder.

As his fingers slid around my throat, I knew he was looking for the necklace.

"It's gone," I said. "Captain Stefanov raised the price of the blood."

Jude frowned. "That bastard."

I glanced at the cooler. "We should find another supplier."

"That won't help." He sighed. "We're broke. I'm taking that job in Gabon."

The Al-Dîn Corporation had offered Jude a thirty-day job in the Birougou rain forest. The expedition was high tech and high pay. I drew in a breath. Now I knew why Jude had been reading his survival guide. He'd been studying about lighting conditions in an equatorial rain forest.

"Don't do it, Jude," I whispered. "We'll get by."

"I'd be crazy to turn down one hundred thousand euros."

I shook my head. "That's just it. Why so much?"

"I don't have a choice. We have enough cash for two more months on this island. And that's not including blood." He paused. "I'll have to live on rodents—or worse."

From outside, the chattering noise stopped, and the bats rose from the cacao trees, swarming up into the leaden dusk, leaving behind a strange calmness. It pressed in around me, dense and smothering, as if I were caught beneath a shroud.

Jude

Two weeks had come and gone since Jude signed on with the Al-Dîn Corporation. In just a few hours, right after dusk, the company jet would pick him up at the São Tomé airport and fly him to Gabon.

Jude sank down in the claw-foot tub and folded a pillow behind his head, trying to shake the feeling that he'd left something undone. Al-Dîn's first payout had already been deposited in his and Caro's joint account at the Swiss Volksbank in Berne. Now if anything happened to him—not that it would—she wouldn't be broke. Because it had been impossible for him, a fugitive vampire, to get life insurance.

A pulse thrummed in his neck as he listened to her move around the kitchen. He wanted to press his mouth against the nape of her neck and smell the powdery sweetness that always lingered in her hairline; but he couldn't go to her just yet. The sun would not set for another two hours, and the equatorial light was dangerous.

He knew this all too well. Shortly after they'd arrived in São Tomé, he'd come out of the bathroom too soon, and the light had blinded him for three hours. But it had been worth it. He'd walked through the sunny living room and squinted through the arched windows. His wife and daughter were playing on the beach. The sun cast a bronze patina on Vivi's pigtails as she skipped along the water. Caro was hunkered in the sand, the wind tugging her long blond hair, her turquoise dress churning around her knees. She lifted a shell, her palms cupped as if she held a baby dove.

He'd forgotten how pretty his wife looked in sunlight. He watched her rise from the sand, dress billowing around her long legs. She'd gotten pregnant before he'd become a vampire, and their baby was the very last part of him that was human. Caro had loved him enough to embrace the night. Not once had she mentioned the cost of procuring his blood. Nor had she complained about the shabby dresses she and Vivi wore. A burning sensation moved behind his eyelids, but he had stared at Caro until his vision narrowed to a pinpoint. He'd groped his way back to the bathroom. Even though he hadn't been able to see a bloody thing, he'd released a breath that he hadn't known he was holding, and something had eased inside him.

Now he stretched out in the tub and listened to the small, irreplaceable sounds that made up their lives. The distant grind of a diesel generator. Wind chimes on the veranda.

The clink of pottery and silver in the plastic drainer as Caro washed dishes.

The kitchen stove was on the other side of the bathroom wall, and he smelled buttered prawns and *matata*, a peanutty clam stew. Cinnamon drenched the air, and he knew she'd made a green maize pudding, Vivi's favorite. He caught another scent, metallic and salty—Caro had prepared him a going-away drink, blood ice frappé.

He heard footsteps in the hall, and a moment later the bathroom door opened. Caro walked in, blond hair tumbling over her shoulders, her cotton dress backlit from the hall sconce. Jude's gaze swept over the faint outline of her legs, and then he looked up at her face. God, those cheekbones. She had never looked more beautiful.

"I'm worried about the generator," she said. "It's making that funny noise again."

"I'll check it before I leave." He got out of the tub. "Where's Vivi?"

"Napping." Caro lit a candle and set it on the counter. The flame cast a burnished glow over her hair, sending up a dazzle of gold light. "We've got a little time before she wakes."

He was hoping she'd say that. He lifted a pile of blankets and pillows, dropped them on the floor, then turned on the faucets. While the tub filled, he gently pressed Caro against the wall and kissed her. She tasted of salt and mango. He cupped the back of her head, his fingers sliding through her hair. Her body pushed against him, making his breath come faster and faster.

In the candlelight, her pupils were huge, showing an edge of silver-blue irises.

He looked down at her. "Are you still my girl?"

"For now," she said, a hint of a smile in her voice.

Since they'd gotten married, this question and answer had become a teasing invocation, a lighthearted litany that moved between them like music.

He helped her undress, and then his clothes came off just as fast. They climbed into the tub, water sloshing around them, and eased down into the steam. Low inside him, a tight knot of pleasure loosened.

She reached for the soap. "I packed you some sunblock and—"

He silenced her with another kiss, and the soap she was holding thumped against the porcelain bottom of the tub. The heat from her body seeped into his chest and surged into his belly. A small humming sound began in her throat, and her breath hit his shoulder in warm spurts. He wasn't inside her, but she was already coming, the way she always did. One of the lovelier side effects of his vampirism—and her hybridism—was the one Caro loved best: transcendent sex.

She pulled back a little, her breasts bobbing in the water, nipples taut. "A bathtub has so many functions," she said a little breathlessly. "It's a place to wash. And a place to sleep."

"That's true, lass," he said, emphasizing the last word, a Yorkshire endearment that never failed to make her smile.

"A tub is also a place to make love." Her lips curved as she slipped her hand under the water and found him. A tingle rippled through his flanks. He shut his eyes, concentrating on the pressure of her fingertips. He loved how she gave her full attention to a task, whether it was making love, squeezing a lemon, or theorizing about heretics in the medieval church; history had been her passion before she'd gotten mixed up with vampires.

She dipped her shoulders under the water, and her damp hair floated around him like gilded seaweed. She was a mermaid who'd slipped out of her glossy sheath, her legs long and graceful, beckoning him to swim inside her. When he entered her, she drew in a mouthful of air, as if she were learning to breathe for the first time.

A long while later, while the tub refilled, Jude's keen hearing picked up sounds in Vivi's room. He heard her whimper, and then the mattress squeaked beneath her tiny body.

"Vivi's having another nightmare," he said.

"Poor baby." Caro got out of the tub and dried off.

"Why is she having so many bad dreams?" Jude asked.

Caro didn't answer. As she slipped on her dress, three lines cut across her forehead. Then she hurried out of the bathroom. A few moments later, Vivi settled down.

Jude pulled the stopper out of the drain and lay back, listening to the water swirl down the pipe. Vivi's nightmares had begun two weeks ago, right after he accepted that job. Was there a connection? Many hybrids had prescient dreams, including Caro, but it was impossible to know if Vivi had inherited this alarming talent.

When Caro had gotten pregnant, her half-immortal chromosomes had collided with Jude's then-mortal ones, and they'd produced a quarter-vampire baby. Some immortals believed that a hybrid baby was mixed up in an eighth-century prophecy. Images had been found in worldwide frescoes and cave drawings, all of which had been created hundreds of years apart. The art was always the same: a war between humans and skeletons and a baby in a gilded cage. Ancient codices, including one that had been excluded from the Bible, predicted that a one-quarter-vampire baby would be instrumental in the salvation or destruction of the immortals. A small, fanatic group of vampires believed that Vivi was this child.

One baby, two opposing concepts, two possible outcomes. Either way, Jude couldn't decide if this prophecy referred to God's judgment on a subspecies or if it meant that a subspecies would pass judgment on an innocent child.

No parent wanted to hear this. Jude and Caro certainly hadn't. Three years ago, on a sweltering night in Manhattan, Vivi had been born prematurely. She'd been rushed into the neonatal intensive care unit at Lenox Hill Hospital. A valve in her heart wouldn't close, and each time she cried, her blood flowed in the opposite direction, turning her body a dusky purple-blue.

Jude and Caro had stood next to the NICU window, watching their baby scream in the oxygen tank, her fists and feet the color of ripe plums. Wires and tubes snaked around her tiny body. Jude had already received death threats from a group of immortal Egyptian monks—the brothers of the Sinai Cabal had turned Jude into a vampire, and in return, they'd forced him to belong to their guild. But they'd really wanted to steal his then-unborn child.

The nurses had let Caro hold Vivi for a moment. "She can't be the only quarter-vampire in diapers," Caro had whispered, her hand caught around the baby-shoe necklace.

"Let's hope not," he'd whispered back. But he wasn't sure; hybrids were so rare.

"Did my genes cause the heart defect?" Caro's eyes filmed with tears.

"No, honey." He put his arm around her, trying to think of a nonscientific way to explain Vivi's condition. Patent ductus arteriosis wasn't all that uncommon. Before birth, the fetus's blood flows in one direction, thanks to a valve that stays open. This valve closes within three days after the baby is born. But Vivi's hadn't. Her blood flowed the wrong way when she cried, and that was why she was so blue.

After a moment, he said, "A valve in our baby's heart was supposed to close after birth. Sometimes it takes longer with preemies. Let's don't give up yet."

That night, their vampire friend, Raphael Della Rocca, flew in from Italy to be with them. He was tall, blond, and fine looking. Richer than the pope. As Vivi's godfather, Raphael had brought in security guards and a world-famous pediatric cardiologist. Dr. Attenburg had admitting privileges at Lenox Hill, and he was sympathetic to the Barretts' need for privacy.

But Vivi's heart valve didn't close. When she was six days old, she underwent open-heart surgery, followed by an extended stay in the neonatal unit. Vivi's blood showed an increased amount of monoclonal antibodies, a protein that acts like warriors in the immune system. The human pediatricians fretted over various diseases, but Dr. Attenburg told Jude not to worry.

"Hybrid children often have benign blood conditions," he said. "Besides, Vivi's hematocrit and white blood cell count values are normal. She'll be fine."

A few weeks later, Jude and Caro brought home a pink, healthy baby and an astronomical hospital bill—it is nearly impossible for vampires to obtain health insurance, since the forms require sensitive information. However, Jude and Caro had started their marriage with several million euros, and they'd settled the bill. Far more worrisome was the Sinai Cabal. Jude always expected an undead version of Rumpelstiltskin to appear at his and Caro's Upper East Side apartment, demanding they surrender *l'enfant terrible*, the cabal's rude dysphemism for Vivi.

The Barretts left New York and flew to Prague, where they stayed with Caro's beloved uncle Nigel, an undead archaeologist. Uncle Nigel was jovial and sensible. He never failed to make Caro laugh, and he was the only one who could soothe Vivi's colic.

But a few months later, threatening letters from the Sinai Cabal started to jam Uncle Nigel's mailbox. The Barretts moved to Amsterdam. A few months later they flew to Brussels.

They always traveled at night, and sometimes the airports and cities ran together. Madrid, Lisbon, Santiago, Auckland, Kyoto, Stockholm, Vienna, San Francisco, Zürich. Caro spoke all of the Romance languages, including some Bulgarian, and Jude knew enough German and Russian to get by, so they could negotiate with landlords and taxi drivers. However, it required money to be fugitives, especially when one of them required expensive black market blood. The Barretts had literally flown into a financial maelstrom. Jude couldn't shake the feeling that they were moving in other ways, too, further and further from the tranquillity that Caro had craved.

For now the money problems are over, he told himself, sinking lower into the claw-foot tub, *thanks to the Al-Dīn Corporation.*

The bathroom door opened again, and Caro tiptoed inside.

"Vivi's fine," she said. "She was dreaming about bats. I wish they wouldn't roost outside her window."

He frowned. "Is she all right?"

"Yes. She went right back to sleep."

Jude switched off the taps. Then he opened his arms. "Come here, beautiful."

CHAPTER 2

Caro

While the water splashed around us, I snuggled against Jude. A tiny ribbon of blood trailed down my neck and curved around my breast.

"Are you all right, lass?" Jude asked, pulling me closer.

"Mmm-hmm." I smoothed my finger over his throat, where scabs were already starting to form around the tooth marks I'd made. Sometimes when we made love, he couldn't resist giving me a nip. And sometimes I bit him. There's just an undeniably erotic connection between vampires and teeth.

There's one catch, though: Vamps and hybrids are allergic to each other.

Just to be clear, this is not a widely known fact. Jude says that many scientists haven't made the connection, mainly because hybrids are uncommon. A few years ago, a pharmaceutical company was doing research on this very subject, but its maniacal CEO, Harry Wilkerson, died in an Egyptian prison. His company went bankrupt. A fire wiped out his laboratory in Romania, and the research was scattered into the Carpathian Mountains.

I'm skimming over a lot of history, but I don't allow myself to think about Wilkerson. Ever. As a result, few people know what lurks in a hybrid's blood: an antigen.

A vampire will not have a physical reaction the first time he or she bites a hybrid; but the immortal's super immune system will immediately start building antibodies to a hybrid's antigen. The second bite will cause the vamp to suffer an allergic reaction. Small amounts of blood will cause respiratory distress, flushing, and hives. However, if the vampire drinks a lot of hybrid blood, it can cause a fatal anaphylactic reaction.

Conversely, vampires possess a neurotoxin that causes an allergic reaction in hybrids—if bitten, the hybrid will experience a fleeting numbness and paralysis. The vampy neurotoxin that causes trouble for hybrids is excreted in semen as well. Fortunately, when Jude was first transformed, his blood had zero toxins. It took a long time for them to build up in his system. That gave me time to develop a resistance to the neurotoxin. As Jude always said, "Hybrid-vampire immunity works on the same principle as allergy shots. But you were inoculated with a penis, not a needle."

Now if I ever got attacked and bitten by a homicidal vampire—and they do exist—the vamp would turn blue and gasp for air, if, of course, he'd been exposed to my antigens. Thanks to my resistance to the vamp neuro-toxin, though, I wouldn't go numb. It's like a built-in defense system. Which would give me time to run.

However, the second time Jude bit me, I almost had to take him to the emergency room. We were so caught up in the moment that we forgot about the antigen in my blood or how it would affect him. At first, we didn't know anything was wrong; after all, heavy breathing and flushed skin are symptoms of intense sexual arousal. But he was in mild anaphylactic shock. Until he developed antibodies to my blood, he took fifty milligrams of Benadryl prior to sex.

As the steamy water plunged into the tub, I rinsed the dried blood off my neck and gave silent thanks that Jude no longer required antihistamines.

Life is good, I thought. But I wished he hadn't taken that job.

Jude leaned back in the tub, and I rested against him. I traced my finger over his wedding band. We'd bought it when he was thinner. In recent years he'd filled out, and he couldn't move the band over his knuckle. Not that he would try, but I missed seeing the inscription: *To J love the Lass.*

"Do you remember the night we got married?" I asked.

"Every detail." He put his arms around me. "We were in Monaco. Raphael must have bought a case of white rice. I think it's still in my hair."

"And mine."

Jude wrapped my hair around his wrist. "I drove slowly down the road. Cars were honking and passing us."

"But you had to drive carefully. The Moyenne Cor-niche is notoriously twisty. All those drop-offs."

"It was a lovely night, wasn't it?" Jude smiled. "Clear

and starry. You put a Sinatra CD into the player. A snappy tune—"

" 'Luck Be a Lady,' " I said, finishing his sentence, the way we so often did. "Perfect for romance on the Riviera, considering we'd just left the casino."

"Until I tried to turn up the volume on the CD player," he said. "But I accidentally pressed the wrong button and—"

"The sun roof zoomed open."

He laughed. "Your veil flowed up and out of the car. It streamed through the darkness like an angel."

"Or a tablecloth," I said.

Jude hugged me closer. "Oh, Caro, I'm going to miss you."

A trembly place moved in my chest. "Tell me about this expedition."

"The Al-Dîn rep made me swear that I wouldn't discuss it." Jude's mouth turned up at the edges, and I could tell that he was holding back a smile.

I traced my finger over his bottom lip. "But you'll tell *me* everything, right?"

He playfully bit my finger. "It's a scientific mission. Archaeologists, chiropterologists, a virologist, entomologist, microbiologist. Some of the scientists are already in the bush."

I dropped my hand to his neck, feeling his pulse thump against my finger. "Doing what?"

"They're looking for a way for vampires to walk in daylight."

"Is that even possible?"

"Probably not. But Al-Dîn thinks so. Their archaeologists are studying the Lolutus—that's an extinct tribe of day-walking vampires. I'll be working with bats."

"Seriously? You don't have to leave home to study them."

"Yes, but Al-Dîn isn't paying me to analyze the DNA of loud, quarrelsome fruit bats. Apparently the team found a new species in Gabon, one that has the RH1 gene. Better known as the dim-light vision gene."

"A what?"

"The bats we're looking for aren't nocturnal."

"How can Al-Dîn afford to hire all of these experts?"

"Apparently, the corp owns diamond mines in South Africa. An expedition is spare change."

I fell silent. The last few nights, I'd dreamed about bats, carnivorous fish, and flying wolves. Had those images also invaded Vivi's dreams? Sometimes my dreams are laden with portents, but the imagery can be confusing. Jude usually talks me through them, but I didn't want to worry him. He was leaving that night, facing God knew what in the bush.

I found the soap and began washing his chest, spreading bubbles along his black, glossy hairs. "What if I need to reach you?" I said. "Will your cell phone work in the jungle?"

"Al-Dîn advised me not to bring it. But they'll issue a netbook. I'll e-mail."

I glanced away, hoping he hadn't seen my quick frown, and put the soap in the dish. Our budget didn't include wireless Internet, but the island's motels and cafés offered free Wi-Fi, so I could take our laptop to a hotel lobby or Café Companhia.

Jude splashed water over his chest. "Al-Dîn has your cell phone number if there's a problem. I also gave them Father dos Santos's number as a backup."

"But he's a local priest." I turned back to him. "Shouldn't you have given them Uncle Nigel's number? Or Raphael's?"

"Isn't Nigel excavating relics in Ecuador? And Raphael would think I was mad. He'd arrive with a bucketful of money and ten thousand lawyers to get me out of this expedition."

"You're right." I smiled, picturing Raphael. He was a charming blend of old-world ethics and modernity. No, he wouldn't approve of Jude leaving me and Vivi for a day, much less a month.

"Nothing will go wrong." Jude slid his palm over my midriff. "But if it does, don't linger too long in São Tomé. Avoid seasonal places where vampires congregate. Don't go to Peru in July. Spend the summer in Denmark. Raphael will help you. He understands the vampire culture better than both of us."

My belly tightened as I remembered the toothed fish from my dream, and something else, something just beyond memory. I forced myself to smile. "Vivi's already planning your welcome home party."

"I won't be late." He pulled me on top of him, and we plunged under the water.

CHAPTER 3

Jude

Jude spread his hands on the veranda railing and faced the ocean. Most of the time he couldn't see the beach, but tonight it was illuminated by a full moon. A glittering wedge of light fanned across the water, and a tugboat moved across the horizon, leaving behind a foamy wake. Above it, frayed clouds spread across the sky like tire tracks.

He didn't want to leave Caro and Vivi alone in São Tomé, but what else could he do?

He walked back inside the house and turned into his study. An old Tiffany lamp sat on his desk, and honeyed light spilled over heaps of books and papers. At the edge of his blotter he found a blue satin ribbon. It smelled like Caro, and a deep ache opened inside him. He tucked the ribbon into his pocket, then opened his leather backpack. Caro had already added his rubber shoes, straight-leg pants, a drizzle-repellent jacket, insect spray, and moleskin strips for his heels. He squeezed in a map of the Birougou rain forest.

Then he sank down in his chair and cradled his head in his hands.

Too much to take, he thought. *Too much to leave behind*.

Footsteps pattered down the hall, and then Vivi appeared in the doorway, clutching a stuffed elephant. Her pink dress had been washed so many times, the pattern had faded. A trembly feeling caught the edges of Jude's mouth, but he smiled around it.

"Hey, Meep," he said.

Vivi put her finger in her mouth and grinned. She'd given herself that nickname when she was a year old and she started to imitate the noise. At first, Jude had thought she'd somehow seen reruns of Road Runner cartoons, but she had latched onto the *meep-meep* sound that emanates from electric carts in airports, the ones that transport ill and elderly passengers. Jude had begun calling her Meep, and the nickname had stuck.

She scooted to his desk, sliding her feet over the tile, and spread her arms, the elephant's tusk dangling in her small hand. "Pick me up, Daddy."

He lifted her—gosh, she was getting so big—and put her in his lap. She smelled like milk and buttered rice. As he smoothed her dark pigtails, she stared up at him. For a moment, he felt a curious sense of doubling, as if he'd looked into his own eyes—blue, with tiny brown chips in the left iris.

"What's up, Meep?" he asked.

"Bad dreams," she said. "The awfulest ever. You got losted. Mommy was crying." Her small hand flew away from the stuffed elephant and she clutched Jude's arm, a surprising grip for a three-year-old.

"Remember what your mum and I told you? Dreams aren't real."

She let go of his arm and looked down at her knees, which poked up through the nightgown. Her long dark eyelashes fanned against her cheek like paintbrushes. "Why're you going away?"

A sharp wire twisted in his stomach. "Don't you want Daddy to work?" he said, keeping his voice light.

She glanced up, staring at him from under her eyebrows. "No. Don't work."

"I'll be home soon."

"Okay, Daddy."

He exhaled, and the wire in his belly loosened. "Let me show you where I'm going."

He shuffled through his bag, lifted a colorful map of Africa, and spread it across his desk. He put Vivi's small finger on São Tomé Island. "You're right here."

"Uh-huh." She nodded.

He slid her finger across the Gulf of Guinea, to the coast of Gabon, and angled down to the southeastern part of Gabon, near the Congo border. "And I'll be here. In a rain forest."

Vivi whispered the word to herself. "Will it have monkeys?"

"Sure. All kinds." He turned back to the map and pointed to a mountain chain. "I'll be in caves near the

Chaillu Massif. You know what caves are? They're rocks—"

"Bad ones." Vivi's eyes widened. "Don't go there."

He was taken aback by the urgency in her voice. He lifted her stuffed animal and gave it a little squeak. "Do you want me to take pictures of real elephants?"

Vivi nodded. Then she sucked in air, pigtails trembling, and dove against his chest. Her shoulders shook violently, and a moment later, he felt a cool, wet place spread across his shirt.

"It's all right, Meep," he whispered, hugging her close. "It's all right."

She wrenched away, tears streaming down her cheeks. Her hand clamped down on his arm again, and a vein bulged on her forehead. "Don't go."

Jude's head tipped back, as if someone had thrown an unripe guava in his face. A throbbing pain moved through his sinuses, and his ears popped.

A sick feeling washed over him. He turned sideways, put his elbows on the desk, and rested his face in his cupped hands.

"Daddy?" Vivi's voice seemed to be coming from another room, yet he could feel her warm breath hitting his arm in sharp bursts.

Don't worry, Meep. I'll be fine in a minute, he said, or thought he said. *Just a minute more, and I'll be fine.*

A drop of blood slid out of his nose and hit the map. He stared down incredulously. *What the hell.* He'd never had a nosebleed, not even when he'd been a kid. A second drop struck the map, then another and another, faster and faster, as if dark red roses were blooming out of the paper.

Vivi slid off his lap, ran out of the room, and screeched for Caro. Jude pinched his nostrils, but the blood drummed onto the map. He was bleeding all over Africa.

CHAPTER 4

Caro

Five days after Jude left, I tucked my laptop under my arm
and led Vivi into the cool, vanilla-scented air of Café
Companhia. I ordered fresh-squeezed pineapple juice and
a granola muffin for her; a *galão* with extra milk for
myself.

We found a table next to the window, and I plugged
in the laptop. I scanned the messages in my inbox, searching through the e-mails. Nothing from Jude. He was in
the bush, not the Athenaeum Hotel in London. I tried
not to worry.

"Daddy send pictures?" Vivi asked, pushing against
my elbow.

I chewed the edge of my lip. I'd been raised by my uncle
Nigel, a loving old archaeologist who'd mixed half-truths

and falsehoods. He'd given me a nickname, Dame Doom, because I'd been such a fretful child. I hadn't found out about my hybridism until I was a grown woman, and I'd been determined that my child would always hear the facts. But I hadn't understood the complexities of motherhood or the fragile simplicity of a child's question.

"Not yet, Meep," I said, forcing myself to smile. "We'll check back tomorrow, okay?"

"Okay." Vivi held out her muffin, offering me a bite.

When we got home, the cottage hummed with noon light. I had left the shutters open, and humid air pushed through the screens, carrying the bite of salt. Vivi stretched out on the sea grass rug with her Disney coloring book. I walked around the corner into the green-tiled kitchen and began chopping onions for bean soup.

I remembered the night Jude had left São Tomé, how the wind had stirred his hair as he'd climbed into the Al-Dîn jet, then turned back to wave good-bye. I'd almost raced over to him and begged him not to go. Then I reminded myself that he was trying to do the right thing, to provide for his family; I couldn't take that away from him just because I'd dreamed about fanged fish. I'd held my breath as the jet had taxied down the runway, dust churning around the wheels, then the plane curved over the Atlantic and he was gone.

"Mommy, can we go to the ocean?" Vivi called.

I wiped my cheeks, then peeked around the corner. She held a pink crayon in her pudgy fingers. Her expression was so intense, she reminded me of Jude—he always got the same look when he put a slide under a microscope: eyebrows raised, mouth slightly open, head tilted.

I smiled. "Sure, Meep. After your nap."

Vivi put down the crayon, scrambled onto the sofa, and closed her eyes. "I'm ready to sleep."

After I made the soup, I tidied the kitchen—I liked everything just so. I folded a stack of tea towels, straightened the silverware drawer, then scrubbed the counters.

Vampires are prone to OCD. As a hybrid, I had a mild case. Jude's was stronger. He made hundreds of to-do lists and even more Don't-Do lists. Sometimes he felt the need to count the tiles in the kitchen floor—aloud, mind you. He checked and rechecked his stash of blood bags. He charted sunrises and sunsets, not that they varied much on the equator. When the compulsions took hold, I brought him a glass of blood-tinged scotch and rubbed his shoulders with coconut oil until the kinks loosened inside him.

I was feeling rather knotty myself as I walked out of the kitchen. I checked my cell phone. No one from Al-Dîn had called, but I had a message from Uncle Nigel. A few years earlier, he had been accidentally transformed into a vampire while digging for artifacts in Bulgaria. Now, as I listened to his voice message, I smiled. He'd arrived in Ecuador with two other archaeologists; all three vampires were heading to a dig site at Japotó. He sounded jovial, as always.

Which is more than I could say for myself. Jude's absence was a solid thing. I couldn't seem to pull enough oxygen into my lungs, as if I were pinned down by the weight of silence.

———

Like any mother, I worry. Sometimes I think I am making the same mistakes that my parents made, and if I have, that doesn't bode well. Because my family was murdered.

I know little about the events that drove my parents into hiding. Before I was born, a British pharmaceutical magnate had stalked my parents. Apparently my mother, Vivienne, purloined some historical artifacts from the magnate's safe. She was only trying to return the objects to their rightful owner, a blond, curly-haired, thousand-year-old vampire named Philippe Grimaldi—her lover.

My mother wasn't a thief. She was a soft-spoken British woman, a highly educated, law-abiding manuscript curator, and her grandfather had served in the House of Lords. My mother's crime never made the news. If it had, the headline would have read, BIG-HEARTED WOMAN STEALS A RICH ASSHOLE'S TOYS. And the asshole was furious.

Philippe and Vivienne left Europe. They moved around the world and finally ended up in Crab Orchard, Tennessee, a small town ringed by the Appalachian Mountains. I was born a few months later.

We lived in a quaint, two-story white clapboard house, with sweeping views of the mountains. Our driveway sloped down to a solar-powered gate. My family seemed perfectly normal. On warm summer nights, Philippe and Vivienne drank wine on the front porch, wind chimes tinkling in the background.

I loved hearing their voices. My father spoke English with a French lilt, and my mother talked with a cut-glass British accent. Me, I sounded like a strummed hairpin, but it suited the harsh landscape, a raw, rocky place with copperheads and coal mines, and no doctor for miles.

One evening, I was playing in the yard, and I stepped

on a wasp's nest. The ball of my foot swelled until it was as red and big as a pomegranate. My parents rushed me to a hospital in Knoxville. The doctors wrapped my foot in ice and stuck needles in my rear end. I was taken to the pediatric ward, and my mother read Beatrix Potter stories until her voice gave out. After she went to the cafeteria for hot tea, my father opened a copy of *Pride and Prejudice.*

He began to read, and his voice poured over me like warm syrup on a biscuit. At first, I was confused—I'd expected to hear a story about talking bunnies. But as my childish brain soaked up images of characters in the book, Elizabeth and Darcy, I forgot about my sore foot and fell asleep.

The next morning, my foot had almost healed, but my father was gone. Sunlight streamed through the window and fell across the bed. Out in the hall, I heard my mother arguing with the nurses. "Caro has always been a fast healer," she told them.

I held back tears. *Fast healer* sounded bad. When I got home, my father was in the kitchen, a ruffled apron tied low on his waist, and he was cooking my favorite meal— pan-fried rainbow trout, garlic mashed potatoes, and cloverleaf rolls all slathered with butter. There was even chocolate cake for dessert.

I spent the rest of the summer trying to avoid wasps and rattlesnakes, but my vigilance turned out to be use- less. One night thieves broke through the security gate at the bottom of the hill, then crept up the long gravel driveway and set our house on fire. My mother ran through the smoky dining room, shoving items into a backpack. I held still while she hooked the straps over my shoulders.

"Hide behind the waterfall," she said. "No matter what you hear, don't come out until morning. I'll find you later, I promise."

She guided me out the back door. I raced into the shadowy woods, my backpack slamming between my shoulders. Then I started to worry about my parents, and I circled back to the house. Flames leaped behind the windows. Men were dragging my father up the porch steps. I waited till they got inside, then ran after them. There was so much smoke, it hurt to breathe. When I tried to open my parents' bedroom door, the knob burned my hand.

The door opened, and a tall, pale man with black, bushy hair stepped out. I spun around and bolted through the haze, down the hall and out the door.

Hide behind the waterfall, Caro.

I skidded down an embankment and ran to the cave. The cool air felt good on my cheeks. I walked toward the sound of rushing water. Just a few more steps, I told myself. Almost there. I pulled off the backpack and crouched in a dry place, cradling my burned hand, waiting for my mother to fetch me.

Those bad men came instead, calling out to each other in strange, sharp voices, as if knives were trapped inside their words. I opened my mouth wide, struggling to pull in a breath, but I couldn't get enough air.

I waited until the sky turned ashy and the men were gone. With my good hand, I lifted my backpack, crept out of the cave, and slogged toward the charred house. A wall of heat pushed me back. I stumbled down the driveway, through the open gate, into the highway. I ended up in the same Knoxville hospital, but this time a grayhaired, barrel-chested man showed up, claiming he was my mother's cousin.

"Just call me Uncle Nigel," he said, and he brought me to a stone house in Oxford, England. I soon discovered that he was an archaeologist, skilled at piecing together broken things. Uncle Nigel put salve on my burns, fed me candy for breakfast, and brushed the knots from my incorrigible hair.

My backpack had disappeared, along with everything inside it, except for an old Byzantine icon that had belonged to my parents. It wasn't the sort of art a child would hang on her wall, but I liked it. The images were mesmerizing: a female saint in a burgundy robe, an ostrich egg, a gilt-edged book, a castle, and a vineyard. A bleeding man lay on the ground, while a monk hovered in the distance.

Three mornings a week, Uncle Nigel taught a class at King's College, and I went with him. He strode ahead of me, his black gown swirling around his shoes, chalk dust clinging to his sleeves. Every few minutes, he'd glance over his shoulder to make sure I was still there, and then he'd turn back to the throng of students that always followed him, and he'd begin quizzing them about Bronze Age artifacts.

I was still pretty much an emotional wreck. Despite my uncle's kindness, my throat would clamp down, and I would be unable to breathe. When these spells hit, I locked myself in Uncle Nigel's library and found his copy of *Pride and Prejudice*. I stood in the middle of the room and faced the diamond-paned windows that overlooked the garden. Hands shaking, I opened the book and read out loud, forcing air in and out of my lungs.

My Appalachian twang always drew Dinah the cat, an elderly tabby with a distinct M on her forehead. I couldn't decide if Dinah was fascinated or repelled by my odd American accent; whatever the reason, the cat would sit outside the library door and yowl. Part of me wanted to let her in, but another, bigger part was embarrassed to read aloud in front of a cat.

When the mewling reached a crescendo, I put down the book and squatted beside the door. "Please go away, Dinah. I can't hear myself read."

The cat let out an earsplitting bawl. I pressed my lips to the keyhole and shouted, "It's a truth universally recognized that a cat in want of a girl will go to extremes. That's you, Dinah."

The cat screeched louder, as if to say, *Orphans in want of parents will hyperventilate.*

The human and feline caterwauling brought Uncle Nigel. He tapped against the door. "Sorry to interrupt you, Caro darling, but I just made an apple tart."

I chewed my bottom lip, tempted to ignore him, but I'd already caught the scent of cinnamon and browning crust. I cracked open the door, and Dinah shot into the room, tail crooked. Uncle Nigel was right behind her.

"Do you like cream on your tart?" he asked.

I set down the Austen novel and followed him to the kitchen. It was a sunny room with floral dishes lined up in a Welsh cupboard. A teakettle simmered on the Aga.

Herbs grew in pots beside the sink. Uncle Nigel found a knife and a jar of cream. He cut the tart down the middle.

"Half for you," he said, lifting a hunk and setting it onto my plate. He put the other piece onto his plate. "And half for me."

In many ways, my troubles were cured by time and apple tarts. The broken places inside me solidified, streaking here and there like dark veins in a marble slab. But I wanted to learn more about my parents.

I already knew that my mother had been a manuscript curator, and her specialty was illustrated Psalters. My father knew every Cole Porter song, subscribed to *Cook's Illustrated* (but never ate), and had a talent for winemaking. So I badgered Uncle Nigel for details.

"What was my mother's favorite color?" I asked. "Was my dad a chef? Why did my parents choose to live in Appalachia? Why did thieves pick our farm? Did they know we weren't wealthy? Why did they set our house on fire?"

"Vivienne's favorite color was ochre," Uncle Nigel said. He reached into a high kitchen cupboard, pulled out a yellow cat mug, and handed it to me. "This belonged to her."

I held the mug with both hands, trying to imagine my mother's long, delicate fingers gripping the curved handle.

"Your father had a way with sauces," Uncle Nigel continued. "But he wasn't a chef."

I glanced away from the mug. "Why did my parents die?"

He folded his arms around me, taking care not to jostle

the mug, then he lifted a shaggy eyebrow. "I'll try to explain. If you look at the Bible, you'll notice that God uses one word more than others. Do you know that word?"

I thought a minute. "Sheep?"

"No, my dear. God's favorite word is *time*. I'm not talking about clocks. I'm talking about a continuum in which everything happens. Ecclesiastes 3:1 says it all. Just count how many times the word *time* is used. There's a time for weeping and laughing. Mourning and dancing. And all that lot. Basically this means that life is a great wheel. As it passes by you, it will bring different things. It depends where you are in the wheel. Joy, weeping, dancing, sorrow. All of it is moving around and around little Caro."

"I don't understand," I said.

"Let's forget the wheel for a moment," he said, rubbing his beard. "Do you remember the day we went to Glastonbury Abbey?"

I nodded.

"It took the builders a long time to build that monastery. Some people believed the Holy Grail was hidden there."

"Why did it fall down?"

"A king decided that he wanted all of the nice books and treasures in the abbey. His soldiers removed the goodies, then they wrecked Glastonbury. Some accounts say it was burned. Some say that it was torn down. And bits of it were sold."

I drew in a breath. "That was mean."

"But that's what happens in the great continuum of time. Some men build cathedrals. Others burn them." Uncle Nigel drew a circle in the air. "The great wheel keeps moving. A time to build. A time to tear down."

I'd never heard such craziness, except in *Alice's Adventures in Wonderland*. I frowned. "The king didn't have to hurt Glastonbury."

"I agree. You might say that Glastonbury was in the right place at the wrong time. A different king might have had a different reaction. And Glastonbury wouldn't be a ruin. Each time the great wheel turns, we don't know what it will bring. To quote one of my colleagues, 'Timing is everything.'"

"I bet the abbey people were sad," I said.

"I'm sure they were. It was an insurmountable loss. Yet parts of the monastery were so durable, they refused to crumble. They withstood fire and pillaging. Those soaring Gothic arches are still standing." He paused. "You see, Caro. A fire can't take everything."

Uncle Nigel's summer fieldwork called him away from England, but he refused to leave me with a nanny. He took me on digs to Corfu, Yaxta, Tatul, Innisfallen Abbey, and Hadrian's Wall. At night he wove history into bedtime stories, and by the time I started primary school, I had a firm understanding of the past. Well, everyone's past but my own. To misquote Dickens, I knew a "smattering of everything and possessed a knowledge of nothing."

Eventually, I discovered a few things: My father had been a vampire, and my mother had left everything to be with him. The night of the fire, she'd stashed an icon and ten pages of an eighth-century illustrated manuscript into my backpack, along with a note to my uncle Nigel.

Years later, Jude and Raphael had helped me retrieve the rest of the manuscript. My old Byzantine icon turned out to be part of a triptych, one that was mixed up in that appalling prophecy.

I didn't let myself dwell on those days. They were over. But I knew that Jude and I would be hunted for the rest of our days if I hid those artifacts the way my parents had. Both relics possessed a dangerous kinetic energy. I didn't want any part of that chaos, but at the same time, I wanted the objects to be safe.

Before Vivi was born, I gave everything to the Salucard Foundation. This powerful organization was dedicated to the preservation of the immortals' history, and they would keep the manuscript and the triptych in a guarded, temperature-controlled vault. The president of the organization was a distant relative of my father's, and I knew I'd done the right thing. However, he warned me to take care, that he could not control their cabals.

I thought the absence of those relics would bring calmness, but the Sinai Cabal continued to dispatch alarming threats, though no monk ever appeared at our apartment.

Jude and I were determined to protect our daughter, so we went into hiding. We couldn't take chances. Now I realized that we'd unwittingly blundered down the same perilous route that my parents had taken. Except for one critical difference. Jude and I weren't hiding historical objects—we were trying to protect the key player in an apocalypse. As Jude always said, if the prophecies were true, then it didn't matter who triumphed—humans or vampires. A war would mean annihilation.

———

Ten days later, I still hadn't heard from Jude. I looked on his desk for the Al-Dîn Corporation's toll-free number. A clipped, automated voice answered in Turkish and didn't offer an option for other languages. I punched in 0, hoping it would connect me to an operator. It didn't.

I put down my cell phone and dropped my head into my hands. Where could I find someone who spoke Turkish? Was Jude all right? Why hadn't he e-mailed?

A knock at the door made me jump. I edged into the sunny living room, as if too much movement would splinter the glass knot that had suddenly formed inside my chest.

Father dos Santos stood behind the screen, the breeze kicking up the hem of his dark cassock. I felt sick to my stomach. This wasn't a social call. The priest had come to tell me that Jude was injured—or worse. I pulled in a breath and opened the door.

"I have anguishing news," Father dos Santos said.

Angústia. He'd spoken in Portuguese, and the word summoned images of the Inquisition. Heresy, dungeons, burning flesh. I sat down abruptly on the rattan sofa and clenched my hands in my lap. "Is Jude hurt?"

"No, no," Father dos Santos said. "He is missing."

I blinked, trying to make sense of the world. Missing as opposed to injured. The knot in my chest hardened. No, I couldn't panic. People went missing all the time, and they were found. Jude wasn't an ordinary person. He had a superior immune system. He was trim, fit, and tough,

190 pounds of muscle on a six-two frame. He wouldn't be missing long, and he would come back to me.

"The corporation has lost contact with your husband's team, and it is feared that harm may have come to them," Father dos Santos said. He explained that a representative from the Al-Dîn Corporation had phoned Our Lady of Grace Cathedral early that morning. Apparently the rep had called my cell phone but kept getting a busy signal. That seemed odd, but I tried to keep an open mind. Maybe the priest had misunderstood.

Father dos Santos kept talking, but his words flew past me like metal shavings. A rescue party was looking for Jude and the other scientists, but the party had been hampered by Gabon's terrible infrastructure. The Birougou National Park was a come-as-you-dare place, no park officials, no roads, just paths that dead-ended into rivers.

Perspiration slid down my forehead. I opened my hands and rubbed my palms against the sofa, leaving wet smears on the cotton fabric. A headache stabbed through my skull, and then I felt sick.

I vaulted off the sofa, ran out the front door, and hurried down the veranda steps. The fruit bats began to chatter when I leaned against a cacao tree and gagged. My morning coffee splashed onto the grass.

The sky whirled around me as I walked across the yard and lay down in the red dirt road. I squeezed my hands, and the bones felt like chicken gristle.

No, Jude can't be missing. He will walk down that road. My tears will summon him.

Beneath the din of the bats, I could almost hear the tap-*tap*-tap of Jude's shoes, each step distinct and irreplaceable. The wind carried his voice, the words stamped with a Yorkshire accent, curled and burred, a noise that brushed so sweetly against my ears. I didn't want those sounds to leave this world. I didn't want *him* to leave.

My throat closed, and spit trickled down the corner of my mouth. It tasted bitter and metallic. Maybe I'd had a stroke. Maybe I'd die right here. Uncle Nigel and Raphael would have to raise Vivi.

The sun pricked against my flesh, as if bugs were crawling over me. Then I realized that something *was* crawling on my neck, shoulders, and ankles. I lifted my hand, and a black ant moved across my palm.

Father dos Santos's footsteps clapped over on the veranda. "Caro, would you like me to call a family member?" he shouted over the screeching bats.

My family were all dead, except for the few who were undead. No need to explain that to the priest.

"Could you call Raphael Della Rocca?" I called in a tiny voice. If an ant could speak, it would sound just like me. "His number is on my cell phone," I added. "It's on the kitchen counter."

I heard him shuffle back into the house. I was tired of talking. Tired of thinking. Tired of breathing. I didn't believe in fate, I believed in choices. If I'd told Jude about my nightmares, he wouldn't have gone on that expedition. I could have stopped this from happening. But I hadn't said a word. I'd let him go.

My fingers tunneled into the packed dirt and I felt myself slide into chaos. Jude was all around me, welling up behind my eyes, a wavering shadow just beyond reach.

PART TWO

HUNTING DAYLIGHT

CHAPTER 5

———

Jude

BIROUGOU RAIN FOREST
GABON, AFRICA

It was Jude's tenth night in the bush, and he was halfway to hell.

Stinging insects converged on his face as he moved through the darkness. His Babongo guide strode ahead, his unbuttoned shirt whipping behind him in the damp air. As they passed near a troop of sleeping gorillas, the guide put his finger to his lips and gazed up at a tree, where the harem and babies slept in a twiggy nest. Then he pointed at the ground. The males were hunkered on a thick layer of vines and torn branches.

"Do not look," the guide whispered. "If the silverback wakes, get on your knees. Lower your head. And maybe he will not kill us."

Two kilometers beyond past the Ngounie falls, the

guide stopped at the edge of a lush, treeless *bai*. The moon cut through the clouds, brightening the distant, razored cliffs of the Chaillu Massif mountains. Across the clearing, lights spangled in the trees.

The guide led Jude through the tall grass. The camp began at the edge of the *bai*, where hardwoods had been cleared to make room for the tents.

That's odd, Jude thought. *Why go to all that trouble?* The big field would have been a logical choice to pitch a human camp. Then he remembered what *The Survival Guide to Illumination* had said about the dangers of a rain forest. The canopy provided some protection from the brutal equatorial glare, but ultraviolet rays still penetrated. A *bai* would receive twelve hours of scorching daylight. That was why the camp had been pushed back into the trees. Vampires needed maximum coverage.

A man with bushy red hair came out to meet Jude. His thin, boyish frame was engulfed by his baggy white T-shirt and camouflage pants.

"Are you Dr. Barrett?" he asked. A port-wine birthmark spilled across his right cheek.

"Call me Jude."

"Great. I'm Lenny. One of the team leaders." He offered a feeble handshake, his palm moist and cool, a diamond cluster ring sparkling on his finger. "So, Jude. Did you run into problems getting here?"

"A few."

"Did you lose your guide?"

"No, he's—" Jude broke off. The grass was tamped down where the guide had been standing.

"He probably ran off," Lenny said. "That happens. Come on, I'll give you the grand tour."

They walked through the brightly lit camp. Spotlights hung down from metal poles, shining on the forked paths, pushing back the darkness. The layers of sound felt invasive—trilling, buzzing insects; wind creaking through the branches; laughter rising from tents; the rhythmic hammering of generators.

"Few people see this part of the Birougou," Lenny said. "No planes fly overhead. No poachers. It's nature's biochemistry lab. Thousands of flora and fauna and other organisms. Many haven't been classified."

Jude nodded.

"You can get bottled blood over there." Lenny pointed at a large mess pavilion. It was crowded and noisy, men jammed around metal tables, lanterns hanging from the domed roof.

"These guys are getting ready to head out to the caves," Lenny said. "A different team goes every night."

Jude turned in a circle, trying to take it all in.

"Field lab is over there." Lenny waved at a long, tubular canvas tent.

They walked down the well-lit path, past tents that were covered with a foil-like material. A pretty woman stepped out of the trees, gripping a Playmate cooler. Her platinum-streaked bangs fell past her eyebrows. Her lips were pursed, as if she were getting ready to whistle. Her breasts filled out the white T-shirt, and the khaki pants hugged her narrow hips.

Lenny thumped Jude's arm. "That's Tatiana Kaskov,"

he said. "The other team leader. A Russian linguist. But don't let her looks fool you. She can handle herself in the bush."

"That's good to know," Jude said.

"Tatiana?" Lenny called. "Dr. Barrett is here. You want to brief him?"

"Not now. After the poker game." Her gaze locked onto Jude. Her eyes resembled aquamarine chips, like something in an exotic cocktail, shaved ice and blue curaçao. "You play poker, Barrett?"

Jude hesitated. "I didn't bring any money."

"We use blood. Not money."

"Another time," he said.

"All right. See you later." She headed up the path, swinging her cooler.

"Let's find your tent," Lenny said. "You're bunking with a guy from Texas."

"When will I get my netbook?" Jude asked. "Because I need to send an e-mail."

"I'll try to find you one. But there's no Internet access right now. Our satcom has been down for a week." Lenny stopped in front of a domed tent and banged on the door flap. "Dr. Hamilton? You decent?"

"Hell, yes," a deep voice said. The zipper came down and a tall, beefy man stepped out. A long, bulbous nose dominated Hamilton's square face. His white-blond hair was clipped short at the sides and swooped down in the back, flipping over his collar.

"What's up, buddy?" Hamilton said, his bright green eyes shifting from Lenny to Jude. His quick smile projected the charisma of a political candidate.

Lenny seemed immune to the man's Southern charm. He introduced the two scientists and almost fled down the path, his hair bobbing around his ears.

Hamilton clapped Jude on the back. "Make yourself at home. Your cot is by the window."

Jude stepped inside the tent. It was set up like a dorm room, a bed and a metal desk at each end. Hamilton's gear was heaped on the left side, clothes and digging tools spread out on the wooden floor, as if he were identifying his territory the way a dog marks bushes and trees.

Jude walked toward his cot and set down his gear. Dr. Hamilton hadn't moved from the door, craning his neck. His massive shoulders filled out his khaki shirt, and each time he took a breath, the seams gave off an audible creak, as if the fabric could barely contain his grit and girth. Every pore in his body exuded a feral masculinity. Suddenly Jude understood how the Neanderthal had disappeared—someone like Dr. Hamilton had gotten rid of them.

Jude opened his backpack, lifted the photo of Caro and Vivi, and set it on his desk. *Only twenty-nine more days, and I'll be home*, he told himself.

Hamilton stepped away from the door. "That your family?" he asked, nodding at the picture.

"Yes." Jude smiled.

Hamilton rubbed his forehead. His fingers were broad and tapered at the end. "Your wife is real pretty," he said. "But I didn't think Al-Dîn hired married men."

Jude shrugged. "What would that matter?"

"The bush can be deadly." Hamilton paused.

Jude nodded. He had the feeling that Hamilton was

sizing him up. But why? Maybe he didn't want a roommate.

Hamilton pointed to a cooler. "You want some blood? It's good with ice and whiskey. I brought a fifth of bourbon. Found me some honey and wild mint earlier this evening. Let me fix you a drink."

"Thanks," Jude said.

Hamilton walked to his side of the tent and opened the ice chest. As he made their beverages, he kept glancing at Jude. "Some weird stuff has been going down."

Jude frowned. He seriously didn't want to hear this.

Hamilton carried two plastic cups to Jude's cot. He handed one to Jude, holding his gaze. "Nobody told you about the attacks?"

"What?"

"Bats. Big sons of bitches. They been picking off the team." Hamilton spread his hands apart, ice clinking in his glass. "I'm not lying. I saw them. Out here, bats are at the top of the food chain."

Was this guy crazy? Jude tilted his cup, a fragrant green sprig bobbing in the blood and whiskey. Was that really mint or some type of hallucinogen?

Hamilton swallowed his drink in one gulp. "You don't believe me."

Jude thought a moment before he spoke. "Lenny didn't mention the attacks."

"If he had, would you have come to Gabon?" Hamilton shrugged. "I wouldn't have."

Jude let that remark slide. He'd just met Hamilton. Vampirism occasionally brought out psychotic tendencies, such as paranoia. He took another sip of his drink. It cooled the back of his throat.

"I know this must sound crazy," Hamilton said. "But it's true."

"Why would bats attack a camp?" Jude asked.

"For dinner."

"Bats aren't carnivorous."

"These are." Hamilton's eyes held a fierce gleam. "You should've seen the carnage."

"And you're sure they're bats?"

"Yeah. I'm a cave archaeologist." Hamilton tossed the cup on the floor, and walked back to his cot. "So, what's your field, buddy?"

"Biochemistry."

"What area?"

"DNA sequencing and synthesis."

Hamilton whistled. "Bet you're real smart. How long you been a vampire?"

"Almost four years," Jude said.

"I been one since 1938." He lifted his hand, dismissing those years with a broad sweep. "I got a few more decades kicking in me. I don't want to die here. Do you?"

"No."

"If you look out for me, I'll look out for you. Deal?"

"Okay."

Hamilton's eyes glistened. "Us scientists need to look out for one another."

Jude finished his drink, pouring the bloody ice melt into his mouth. He set the empty cup on the desk, then stripped to his T-shirt and boxers and got into bed. He could feel a shift in the outside temperature, a sudden coolness as the wind broke through the canopy, setting tree limbs to creaking. The weight of the air seemed to push into the tent and settle against Jude's sternum, the same feeling that he'd experienced the night he'd been turned into a vampire.

Four years earlier, he and Caro had gone to an Egyptian monastery to look for artifacts. Jude had still been human, and Caro had just found out that she was pregnant. She'd told him about the baby at the top of Mount Sinai. The next morning, they'd returned to the monastery, feeling safe among the monks—some were human, some were immortal. That night, a crazed human had breached the thick, fourth-century walls and attacked Caro. When Jude tried to rescue her, he'd gotten shot. Raphael and his men had saved her and they'd brought down the shooter, but Jude had been mortally wounded. Caro told the monks to transform him into a vampire. The following day, Jude awoke in a dark room, his head shaved, a crushing force moving through his chest. He'd sensed that something worse was about to befall him and Caro—and it almost had. The cabal had planned to put Jude into a rehab program for novice vampires and keep Caro alive until the baby was born. But Raphael had saved them again. He'd helped them escape into the Sinai Desert, and for a while they'd been safe. However, immortality had not put an end to their problems.

Now, all these years later, he was deep in a rain forest, and he had the same unbearable weight in his chest and the unshakable feeling that he was about to lose something irreplaceable.

Before dawn, Jude and Hamilton got dressed and walked to the mess pavilion.

"Something is wrong with this part of the bush," Hamilton said. "It's too quiet."

Jude hated to agree, but the air was still and empty. No primates chattered in the trees. No birds flitted between the branches. No elephants stood in the *bai*.

Hamilton pointed to a tall, rangy middle-aged man who stood outside a tent. He wore a disposable surgical mask and gloves. "That's Walpole. A veteran from an earlier expedition. He's British like you. A virologist. Obsessed with Ebola."

"How long has he been in the bush?" Jude asked.

"Too long," Hamilton said.

They stepped into the mess pavilion and got in line for the bottled blood. Hamilton gestured at a younger man who stood a few feet away. "He's another veteran," Hamilton whispered. "Nick Parnell. A California entomologist. Parnell must've gotten his neck bitten in the sixties. Maybe a surfer vampire got him. He calls everyone *dude*. I don't know how a slick fella like him ended up in purgatory."

Nick Parnell shuffled forward in the line. His long blond hair was pulled back into a club, tied with multi-colored beads. He wore a red Hawaiian shirt, denim cut-offs, and acid green flip-flops.

Gunfire boomed in the distance. Jude glanced out of the tent, toward the clearing. A black cloud streaked across the grainy sky. The mercenaries stood at the edge of the clearing, firing AK-47s at the cloud.

The mess hall emptied. Vampires raced across the path, running into tents. Jude looked around for Hamilton—he was gone.

"You might want to take cover," Parnell called. He stood by the cooler, holding a half-empty blood bottle.

"What's going on?" Jude asked.

"The Batmobile has arrived," Parnell said, then drained the bottle.

A massive creature flew by the mess pavilion, its body the size of a goat, its leathery wings broad as a sofa. Jude ducked.

The bat whizzed over a path and knocked down a bald-headed man. The chap scrambled to his feet, and the bat pursued him into the trees. More gunfire discharged.

Cries rose up as the bald man raced out of the trees and headed toward the mess pavilion. Two bats chased him, emitting distinct echolocation clicks. They were hunting in a team.

Jude got to his feet, his chest sawing, heart clenching, perspiration streaming down his sides.

Parnell put down his bottle and grabbed Jude's arm. "Come with me, dude."

They hurried out of the pavilion. In the distance Jude saw the bats swarming down a path. He followed Parnell into a smaller tent and they secured the window flaps. There was a rustling sound, and two slippered feet jutted out from beneath a cot. "Get out of my tent," a disembodied British voice called. "I don't want to breathe your germs."

"Lighten up, Walpole," Parnell said.

A man with a round face pushed out from under the

cot. "Put on a surgical mask," Walpole said. His eyes widened when he saw Jude. "You, too. The box is on the table. You can't be too careful in this part of the bush. It's crawling with pathogens."

From outside, Jude heard more gunshots. A clattering noise went on and on, as if tin cans were rolling off the edge of a building.

Jude pointed vaguely at the window. "Those bats are huge."

"Like winged Doberman pinschers," Walpole said.

"Bigger than a Dobie," Parnell said.

From the *bai* came a raw scream.

Jude lowered his head. *I can't stay here*, he thought. *I've got to resign.*

"Yeah, try to resign," Parnell said. "That'll be fun to watch."

"No, it won't," Walpole said.

Jude looked up. Had they read his mind?

"We did," Walpole said, and his gaze sharpened. "Who is Meep?"

Jude hesitated. "A friend."

Walpole gave Parnell a long look.

"Don't panic," Parnell told Jude. "Walpole and I are the only two telepaths in the camp."

The gunfire ended. Parnell moved to the window and undid the covering, wincing at the sudden brightness. "The flying Dobies are gone."

He closed the flap and rubbed his eyes.

Jude started toward the door.

"Wait, dude. You'll need this," Parnell called. He held out a metallic blanket, like what they give runners after a marathon. Stay under the trees and run like hell. Maybe you won't burn."

"Thanks," Jude said, stretching the blanket over his head. When he got to his tent, Hamilton leaped off his cot.

"Whoa, Jude. Thank God you're not dead. It would be a shame to die on your first day in the bush."

Jude pulled off the blanket.

"You'd better hide that," Hamilton said. "Or Lenny and them will confiscate it."

"Why?"

"You still don't get it. If you've got UV gear, you can escape in daylight, while everybody is asleep."

Hamilton lifted his mattress from the cot and pointed to a silver wrap. It resembled a long, thick wad of tinfoil. "See? I got me one, too."

Jude turned to his cot and stuffed Parnell's blanket under the mattress. When he looked up, Hamilton was pacing the length of the tent.

"I hate to dump more crap on you, Jude. But there's a lot of talk around here. Once you sign up with Al-Dîn, they don't let you go. People are wanting to get the hell out. If we don't go soon, we'll die."

Jude nodded. "When do we leave?"

"I got a dig scheduled for tonight. When I get back, we'll put our heads together and come up with a plan."

From outside, the PA system crackled, and then Lenny's nasal voice blasted. "Briefing in the mess pavilion at eighteen hundred."

Insects boiled in the warm, dusky air as Jude and

Hamilton walked to the meeting. A few spotlights had been shattered, and glass littered the path.

"This camp is falling to pieces and Lenny knows it," Hamilton said.

"Or he doesn't care," Jude said.

They sat down at a table in the back of the pavilion. The other scientists were already seated, looking grim and hollow-eyed, as if they'd wandered into a funeral home. Jude didn't see Parnell or Walpole, but he wasn't surprised. When Lenny strode in, two men began whispering in French.

"You guys need to chill," Lenny said. He folded his arms and walked between the tables. "Let me explain what's going on. Then I'll try to answer your questions."

A dark-haired scientist stood up. He appeared to be in his midthirties, a wiry chap with elongated ears and a pixie face. "Why are the bats so large?" he asked.

"Survival of the fittest," Lenny said. "The bats gradually adapted to their environment. We found antelope and wildebeest bones in a cave—baby bones. They dated back four thousand years. The large bats were, and still are, supreme hunters. When they were still evolving, the smaller ones died off."

"Got an update on the death toll?" Hamilton said.

A blush spilled across Lenny's cheeks, bleeding into his port-wine stain. "If you don't let me finish talking, I'll add you to the list."

Hamilton's lips clamped shut. Jude inched down in his chair and forced himself to breathe slowly.

Lenny moved to the front of the pavilion. "We're in

an unmapped region of the Birougou," he said. "There's extreme biodiversity out here. The bacteria and viruses are just as unusual. The bats you saw this morning are unique. They carry an atypical DNA virus."

A man with auburn hair and a narrow fox-face raised his hand. "Have we been exposed to it?"

"No." Lenny grinned, showing his incisors. "No need to worry about this one. You're immune. Now. But three thousand years ago, you would have gotten infected. That's what happened to the Lolutu tribe who lived here a few thousand years ago. The Lolutu got infected with the virus—either they got bitten or they may have eaten the bats. The virus caused a change in the Lolutu's stem cells. A change that inhibited aging and boosted immunity. The Lolutu also lost the need to ingest food and developed a craving for blood."

Jude sat up a little straighter. Was Lenny saying that a virus had turned the Lolutu into vampires? Didn't he know that immortality wasn't a contagious virus?

Lenny paused dramatically. "The Lolutu were the first vampires."

"Bullshit," Hamilton said.

A man at Jude's table got to his feet. His small face was overpowered by a beard that grizzled out like a Brillo pad. "Vampirism is *not* a virus," he cried.

The other scientists sprang from their chairs and began shouting.

Lenny raised his hands. "Shut the fuck up so I can talk," he yelled. "Or the bats will be the least of your problems."

The group fell silent and returned to their seats.

"A few weeks ago we tested a bat," Lenny said. "It had high levels of monoclonal antibodies."

"Who cares?" The man with the pixie face shrugged.

"You should," Lenny said. "In our main lab, we injected vampire rats with monoclonal antibodies. This allowed the rats to endure sunlight for up to two hours. No burning. No blindness. No side effects."

Jude fixed his attention on Lenny, trying to look attentive, but perspiration rolled down his spine, dampening the back of his shirt. He remembered that long-ago day when Vivi was born and the doctors were fretting over her high monoclonal antibody levels. He pressed his fist against his churning stomach.

"The bats are dangerous," Lenny said. "But you guys are witnessing an epic moment in vampirism. We are hunting daylight. Al-Dîn will find a way for us to walk in the sun. But to do this, we need to collect—and test—some big motherfucking bats. We plan to bio-engineer their monoclonal antibodies and make a serum. A twelve-hour injectable drug. One that will block photosensitivity. It won't be a cure. But vampires can inject themselves as needed."

Lenny glanced around the room. "Any questions?"

No one responded.

"Meeting adjourned," Lenny said.

Hamilton touched Jude's shoulder. "Are you all right, buddy? You look sick."

"No, I'm fine."

"I got to get going," Hamilton said. "We're digging near the river tonight. I'd run away, but Tatiana is sending her Congo cyborgs."

It was full dark when Jude walked back to his tent. He couldn't explain why, but it felt bigger without Hamilton's effusive personality, filled with menacing shadows and echoes. But Jude needed solitude. He opened the cooler and pulled out a bottle of AB. He lay down on his cot, uncapped the bottle, and took a sip.

His daughter's blood had high levels of monoclonal antibodies. And so did the bats that Al-Dîn was studying. If these antibodies held the key to day-walking, and if this knowledge was made public, then his child would be hunted—and experimented on.

I've got to leave this camp, he thought. *I want to go home and protect my family.*

A rustling noise came from the flap, and Tatiana walked into the tent, holding a lantern. "Do you have time for a private briefing, Dr. Barrett? Or may I call you Jude?"

"Jude's fine." He put down his bottle and started to rise from the cot.

"No, you're fine. Stay there."

She set down the lantern and walked to his cot. Her gaze moved to Jude's desk and stopped on the photograph of Caro and Vivi. "Is that your wife?"

Jude nodded.

"And your child, too?"

"Yes."

"It's unusual for vampires to reproduce. How did you manage it?"

His pulse roared in his ears. He leaned forward and turned the picture away from Tatiana. "What's the story on the bats?"

"Don't worry about them," she said. "Lenny and I have everything under control."

"May I ask how?"

She perched on the edge of his cot, her gaze lingering on his face. "Sorry, Jude. I don't mean to stare. But your left iris is beautiful. All those brown specks in the blue. Are you just as unique as your eye color?"

"No."

"I think you are." She smiled, and her hand brushed over his trousers.

He shifted his leg away from her. "Can we get on with the briefing?"

"After *we* get it on." She crawled across the cot and wedged her hand against his crotch. "I'm attracted to you, Jude. Do you feel it, too?"

Yes, he felt it. But he didn't want to. His chest burned, as if a scorching wire were twisting through him. He pushed her away. "You need to leave. Now."

"What if I don't?"

"I'm married."

"So?" She rubbed the heel of her hand between his legs, moving back and forth, tugging his zipper a little lower.

"Don't." He scooted toward the edge of the cot and pulled up his zipper.

"Come on, Jude. It'll get your mind off your worries."

"I'm not worried."

"Right. Lighten up and have fun. Or you'll end up like Dr. Walpole. A raving lunatic."

"So, how often do the bats attack the camp?" Jude asked.

"Often. Sometimes they hit us in daylight."

Before he could respond, she lunged, pinning him against the mattress, stroking between his thighs, pushing against him with the flat of her hand.

"Your body wants me," she said.

"No." He tried to push her off, but she gripped him tighter.

Sensations rushed through his lower extremities, and he felt himself slide toward an edge, clear and flat as a sheet of glass. He sucked in air, and then his breath came out in a rush, blowing against her blond curls.

Stop. Her. Now. He grasped her hand and flung it away.

"What is your problem?" she said.

"I don't want this. I have a wife."

"She won't know." Tatiana reached for him.

He caught her wrist. "But *I* will."

She stared at him a long moment, then twisted away. "You'll be in Gabon for a month—with me. Remember, what happens in the rain forest, stays in the rain forest."

After she left, Jude reached into his backpack. He pulled out Caro's blue ribbon and touched it to his nose, breathing in her smell. Long before they were even born, their lives-to-be had intersected. His father, Sir John Fleming Dalgliesh Barrett, had been a prankster during his days at Eton, and his partner in crime had been Nigel Clifford, Caro's uncle. A stunt at St. George's Chapel had brought the Windsor guards rushing down, and the boys' fathers had been summoned from a cocktail party at the House of Lords.

Decades later, after Jude had begun studying the longevity gene, he'd corresponded with Nigel Clifford, and their letters had eventually led him to Caro—the old chap had been looking for a way to explain vampirism, and he'd brought Jude and Caro together.

He shut his eyes, remembering the first time he saw her. She was running out of her flat in London, her blond corkscrew curls flying around her. A jolt of sexual energy had almost knocked him to the pavement. He'd followed her to Heathrow Airport, blatantly ignoring the Barretts' family motto: "Be Skeptical."

Oh, what a mess he'd been in those days. Tidy and precise, his pencils lined up in a row. Shy and bumbling. More skilled at introducing a gene into bacteria than inviting a woman to the cinema. But he'd fallen headlong in love with Caro. He couldn't stop touching her, looking at her, smelling her. The scientific part of his brain had wondered if she'd emanated an addictive substance. Whatever it was, he wanted more.

From the beginning, they'd shared a strong, sensual connection, but they'd fit together in other ways. She'd been an historian, so they'd shared a love of academia, but unlike him, she wasn't pedantic. Her idea of a romantic date was an evening at the Bodleian Library. She was smart, funny, audacious, straightforward, and tender. She knew when to be ladylike and when to be risqué. Yet she could also be proper and bawdy all at once—that was thrilling. When they were together, Jude stood a little taller, feeling dashing and brave for the first time.

Just when the broken pieces inside him had begun to realign, he'd learned about her hybrid genes. He remembered how stunned he'd felt. Adrenaline had pumped through his veins, and a huge neon sign began flashing inside his head: *fight or flight*.

He'd picked flight. As he walked away from Caro that night, he decided to return to Dalgliesh, his family's home in York. His stepmother had turned it into a tourist attraction, and she always pointed out that the manor was built around a hawthorne tree. To this day it thrived in the cellar gift shop. That was when he knew that he couldn't leave Caro. If a tree could grow in the dark, then love was just as durable. Just as miraculous.

Jude awoke shortly before daylight, when Hamilton crept into their tent. Rain was hammering against the canvas roof. A few minutes later, Jude drifted back to sleep, and the next time he opened his eyes, it was still raining.

He rubbed his eyes and sat up. "What time is it?"

"A little after dusk," Hamilton said, tossing Jude a jacket with a hood. "Let's get something to eat."

Rain blew sideways, sweeping across the path, as Jude and Hamilton headed toward the mess pavilion. The air was overheated, thick and impenetrable. Jude pursed his lips with each breath, as if he were sucking oxygen through a wet carpet. As he moved down the path, he noticed that the spotlights had not been repaired and trash lay in heaps. Some tents had been flattened.

"What happened?" Jude said, tugging his hood over his head.

"They ran," Hamilton said. "A Swedish microbiologist and a primate expert."

"When?"

"You slept through the commotion," Hamilton said. "They got shot."

They stepped into the pavilion. Lenny stood up front with an armed Congolese soldier. "We're rationing the blood," he called. "You only get one pint a day. So make it last."

Tatiana walked up, her face streaked with water, her hair flat and dripping. "You guys need to come with me," she said, pointing at Jude and Hamilton.

"Where to?" Hamilton said.

"I've got some equipment at the old camp," she said, giving the men halogen lanterns. "I need you to help me bring it back."

She strode toward the *bai*, oblivious to the rain. A big-shouldered Congolese soldier walked behind her.

"Old camp?" Hamilton said, turning to Jude. "How many are there?"

"Maybe we should run for it now," Jude said.

"Bad idea." Hamilton ducked his head, and rain cascaded off his thick, springy hair. "She's packing a Glock. And her guard is armed. We could get killed."

They followed her across the wide clearing. Rain blew in visible sheets, the drops hitting Jude's arms like pebbles. They hiked into the foothills of the Chaillu Massif and climbed onto a rocky plateau. Tatiana's lantern moved ahead, a bright smudge in the downpour. She pointed to a dark cleft in the rocks. "There's a cave over there," she yelled. "Let's get out of the rain."

"Great," Hamilton muttered. "Caves and bats go together like cats and a shit box."

Tatiana grabbed a handful of vines and yanked them away from the cave's opening, then crouched down and slipped through the V-shaped boulders. The soldier nudged Jude and Hamilton through the opening, then pushed in behind them. Cool, mineral-smelling air wafted over Jude.

No guano, he thought. *Maybe no bats, either.*

Tatiana stood in a small chamber, her light flashing on the walls. They were smooth and pink, scaled with blue algae. From the darkness came the sound of rushing water.

Jude set down his halogen and pushed back his hood. Water pattered from his shirt, ticking against the ground. Hamilton and the soldier were soaked, too. Their clothes were streaked and dripping, giving off the smell of wet cotton.

Tatiana walked to the opening of the cave. She stared out into the rain, then glanced at her watch and sighed.

The Congolese soldier wandered toward the back of the chamber, his light shining on an underground stream. Jude picked up his lantern and walked to the edge of the water. Translucent fish huddled on the bottom, almost blending into the rocks. They were trout-sized, with spiny fins. The Congolese man dipped his hands into the water and splashed it over his face. The fish began to stir, swimming toward the man as he reached into the water again.

Jude set down his lantern and hunkered down. He threw a pebble into the water. It sank at an angle, pushed along by the current, then finally hit bottom. The stream was deeper than it looked, maybe fifteen feet.

The soldier bent closer to the surface and lowered his hand. A school of fish leaped up, their mouths glistening with teeth, and bit off his fingers. He screamed, his voice rising and falling, echoing in the chamber.

Jude grabbed the man's shoulders and tugged. Blood

jetted down into the water. More fish swam up, then leaped out of the stream, their jaws clicking. Three latched onto the soldier. He howled and began to flail, the fish dangling from his forearms, their bodies filling with color. One fish let go and snapped at Jude. He backed away. The soldier slipped out of his grasp and fell headfirst into the stream. The water churned, as if bullets were hitting the surface. More fish darted over and latched onto the man's body, pulling him down. A red flush spilled in the current, bits of flesh moving in eddies.

Hamilton ran over. "Jesus Christ. What the hell. Are they piranhas?"

The man burst out of the water, screaming.

"Help me get him," Jude yelled. He clamped down on the soldier's upper arm. Hamilton grabbed the back of the man's shirt. They dragged the man onto the rocky bank. The fish yanked to get him back.

"I got him," Hamilton said, tugging hard. Then, suddenly the tension was gone. The Texan stumbled back, holding an upper torso. He dropped it, then spun around and vomited.

The smell hit Jude, and his stomach twisted. He looked back at the stream. The soldier's hips and legs sank to the bottom.

"What's going on?" Tatiana called.

Hamilton wiped his mouth. "Man down," he yelled.

Jude watched the fish rush along the bottom, biting through the man's trousers, ripping into the soft tissue. As they fed, their scales turned a ruddy pink.

Tatiana walked up. "We'll recover the equipment later," she said. "Let's get back to camp."

"Your guard is dead," Hamilton said.

"I've hired more." She shrugged. "They'll be here in the morning. Now get moving."

"No, ma'am," Hamilton said. "I'm not leaving till I bury this man."

Tatiana kicked the torso into the water. Then she turned to Hamilton. "What man?"

"Why'd you do that?" he yelled. "You're sick."

She stepped closer. "What did you say?"

"I said you're a sick bitch." A pulse throbbed in Hamilton's neck. "You probably bit off your own umbilical cord."

Jude put one hand on Hamilton's arm. "Let it go," he said.

Hamilton pulled away. "I can't, buddy. I just can't."

Her face contorted. "Get your fat ass out of this cave," she yelled.

"No," Hamilton said.

Tatiana pulled out a Glock and fired. Hamilton's chin jerked up. Then he fell over backward with a thud. She turned. Jude's throat narrowed. He knew his life was ending, and his family would never know what happened.

I love you, Caro, he thought. *Love you, Meep.*

"Get it over with," he told Tatiana. "Go on. Shoot me."

"You're not getting off that easy," Tatiana said. "We might stay here and make a cozy home. I'll decorate. You can feed the fish. Or we go back to camp. Which shall it be? You pick."

The rain stopped while Jude and Tatiana were walking back to camp. Steam rose toward the black canopy, where no living creatures moved in the branches. A tight feeling expanded in Jude's chest, as if his lungs held too much air and he couldn't push it out. His arms hung limply at his sides, but the veins were distended with blood.

When they reached the camp, it was dark and deserted. The tents on the eastern side had been flattened. Jude went straight to his tent and peered out the window. A full moon hovered over the *bai*, where Tatiana was setting up the portable satcom, and the bright computer screen shone in her face.

Was the satcom working now? Jude wondered. Had it ever been broken?

Lenny paced in front of Tatiana, waving his arms. She shook her head and pointed toward the distant outline of the Chaillu Massif mountains. Lenny raised his fist in the air, his face contorted. Tatiana shoved him. He shoved her back.

Jude looked past them. The waterfall was a few kilometers beyond the *bai*. If he could reach the river, he would make it out of the Birougou. He turned away from the window and squatted next to the cooler.

Empty.

Okay, now what? he thought, and sat on his cot. He glanced at his travel clock. Four A.M. The sun would rise in one hour. He jammed his hands under his armpits. His body shook so hard, the cot squeaked beneath him. He didn't know what Tatiana would do to him. If he escaped, she would send the Congolese to hunt him down. But he couldn't leave while Tatiana was in the *bai*.

The low whine of a chain saw hummed in the air. Why were the Congolese felling a tree in the dark? He heard the crack of a tree, followed by an explosive *whomp*. Jude ran his hand over his face, brushing sweat off his forehead.

The chain saw kept going. Another tree crashed down. Jude's heart bumped against his ribs. He had two choices. *One.* He could stay, and only God knew what Tatiana had planned for him. *Two.* He could run now.

He didn't have time to reach the waterfall before daybreak. But he still had Parnell's UV gear. He lifted his mattress and pulled out the blanket. He turned it inside out and tied it around his waist. Then he slid Caro and Vivi's picture into his back pocket.

Where was his sunblock? He emptied his backpack on the floor. He lifted a tube of zinc oxide and shoved it into his front pocket. Then he walked out of the tent.

A Congolese soldier stepped in front of him. "Go back inside."

Behind him, Jude saw smoke rising from a bonfire. A new group of soldiers walked around the camp. They wore the beige uniforms of Malian mercenaries and carried Uzis.

"In the tent," the Congolese soldier said. He pointed his AK-47 at Jude's chest.

Jude stepped back.

Outside, he heard Tatiana greet the soldiers in Congolese. A moment later, she entered the tent. Too late, Jude remembered that the UV blanket was tied around his waist.

"I'm shutting the camp," she said.

"Why?"

"We have all the specimens we need. Besides, half of the team is gone."

Or dead, Jude thought. He searched her eyes for clues, but they held the flat vacuity of a mannequin.

"Where's Lenny?" he asked.

"Lenny who?" Her gaze moved from Jude's face to his waist. She lunged toward him, her face contorting, then jammed her knee into his groin. Pain and nausea twisted inside him. Jude bent over, mouth open, pulling in quick bursts of air. Water streamed out of his eyes. Her hands moved low. He thought she was going for his cock, but she pulled off his blanket. Then she lifted the zinc oxide tube out of his pocket.

"You won't be needing these items any more," she said. "Not where you are going."

Her boots clicked over the wooden floor. Over her shoulder she called, "I'll have the mercs bring you to my tent. Don't try anything stupid."

After she left, he pulled himself up and stumbled to Hamilton's cot. He reached under the mattress and yanked out the UV blanket. He stuffed it down the back of his trousers. Then he rummaged through the Texan's gear. He'd hoped to find a knife, but he saw only maps and ink pens. An aerosol can of deodorant rolled across the floor.

Jude snatched it. If he could get close enough to the bonfire, he could toss the can into the flames. The explosion would create a distraction, giving him time to run. He shoved the can into his pocket.

Two Malian mercenaries came into his tent and bumped their guns against the back of Jude's head. He fell down and hit his cheek on the side of the cot. The mercs lifted his arms and dragged him out of the tent. Heat slapped against the left side of his body, and he cracked open his eyelashes. Smoke billowed over the fire pit.

Gunfire spattered at the other end of the camp, and the Malians dumped Jude next to a tent. He lay still, his mouth pressed against the dirt, his heart plunking inside his chest.

Don't give up, he told himself. *Just don't. Give. Up.*

He heard the distant *tat-tat* of an AK-47. He lifted his head and wiped the blood off his face. Mercenaries ran down the path toward the mess pavilion, their legs cutting back and forth like scissors. They held torches, and the flames made a whooshing noise as they sped by.

A tall mercenary soldier dragged Lenny out of a tent and raised a machete.

"Please, I'll pay you," Lenny cried, blood streaming down the side of his face. "I'm rich. Name your price. Just don't hurt me."

The mercenary lifted the machete, and firelight ran down the metal. The blade fell in a merciless arc.

Jude looked away. In the distance, the tents were blazing, red sparks boiling up into the darkness. Now he understood what was really happening. Operation Daylight wasn't just being shut down, it was being erased.

He got to his feet, staggered to the fire, and pulled the aerosol can out of his pocket. He tossed the can into the fire and ran into the trees, racing toward a wedge of darkness, where the undergrowth was thicker. Blood ran into his eyes, and he scrubbed his palm over his face. He skidded down an embankment, his boots digging a trench through leaves.

Run, run, run.

He jumped over a fallen log and vaulted into the thick undergrowth, sticker vines hooking into his shirt, punching into his skin. Behind him he heard a concussive bang.

He glanced back. Five mercenaries were spreading out in the bush, moving fast. They wore night scopes and carried Uzis. Jude figured they'd be on top of him in seconds. He couldn't stay here. He looked to the right. The *bai* was empty. And the waterfall was on the other side. He needed to distract the soldiers again. He lifted a rotten log and heaved it to the right, down a slope. The log rumbled down, splitting and cracking.

Jude rushed in the opposite direction. When he reached the *bai*, he dropped to his hands and knees, then crawled through the weeds.

Go, go, go.

Halfway across the clearing, the weeds began shaking, and noise seemed to rise from the ground. He raised his head. Antelopes raced around him. Behind them, smoke drifted from the camp, into the *bai*, driving out the few animals that lived in this area.

Jude got up and sprinted into the forest. The air was starting to pale as dawn broke over the canopy, and his eyes burned. He heard the waterfalls roaring down into the narrow gorge. But to reach the falls, he had to cross a small clearing.

As he started toward it, gunfire erupted behind him. He darted a look. The mercenaries were a hundred yards away. If he hauled ass, he still had time to reach the waterfalls before sunrise. He got behind a thick mahogany tree and put on the UV blanket. Then he crouched low and moved toward the clearing.

At first, he didn't see the gorillas. Two adult males sat in the grass, grooming themselves. Behind them, the females chomped on branches, keeping a watchful eye on the babies. The silverback raised his head and sniffed. He got up, tilting his head.

Jude froze. He dropped to his knees and lowered his head. If he tried to run through the troop, the males would kill him. Through the corner of his eye, he saw a flurry of movement, and then the gorilla charged, swatting at everything in his path. There was a great creaking of bushes, then limbs hit the ground. The gorilla was so close, Jude smelled him. Musk and feces and urine. He expected the huge animal to jerk him up by one arm and throw him against a tree. One swipe of that paw, and Jude's eyeballs would have rolled out of his head.

The silverback lunged forward, grunting and calling to Jude in a territorial display. Through his eyelashes, he watched the sun climb over the trees. Mist hung in the air, sparkling in the light.

Bullets stitched across the field. The gorillas scattered into the trees. Jude got up and ran along the top edge of the falls. His blanket flew off and skated over the grass. His skin tightened and tingled, but he kept going. He could see water pouring down into the gorge.

When he reached the top of the falls, another gunshot cracked through the air. Something slammed painfully into his back, as if he'd been kicked. His legs went numb, and his knees collapsed. As he toppled forward, the world around him became unstuck. The sky whirled around him, and then the grass curved over his head. Another sweep of blue raced by. Everything moved in a circle. Sky, grass, sky. Then he was falling. The cold mist felt good on his face. So good.

The river took him with a wet slap, and he went under. He tried to kick his legs, but they wouldn't move. He held his breath as long as he could.

Caro, he thought. *I love you. I will always love you.*

PART THREE

TEN YEARS LATER

CHAPTER 6

Edward Keats

INNISFAIR HORSE STATION
HAHNDORF, SOUTH AUSTRALIA

The fate of the Barrett women weighed heavily on Edward Keats's mind as he led the gelding into the paddock. Caro and her thirteen-year-old daughter had spent the last ten summers vacationing at Innisfair, ever since her husband had gone missing in Africa. This past November, the ladies had arrived at the horse station, same as always, ready to enjoy the Australian summer. Now it was July first. Caro and Vivi were leaving this afternoon, ready to fly off to the Northern Hemisphere.

At least, Caro was ready. Keats winced as loud, angry voices hurtled from the stone manse. He steered the gelding around the paddock, the chilly wind snapping the edges of his nylon jacket. He'd never minded the cold, short days of winter.

But today felt different.

A blade-sharp wind scraped across the pasture, and dried leaves rose into eddies. The horses felt the strangeness, too. Ozzie tugged at the lead, jerking Keats's arm. The thoroughbred was a nine-year-old, a bit high-strung for a gelding, and he stamped his hoof against the ground, his eyes rolling back, showing white crescents.

"Steady, boy," Keats said.

"Mr. Keats!" called a high-pitched, girlish voice.

The old man turned. Vivi Barrett sprinted down the hill, arms pumping, her spiky, dark hair bouncing on her forehead. She raced through the meadow, then leaped to the black wooden fence and climbed onto the top rail.

"I wanted to say bye before we left," she said.

Keats smiled. Her accent was almost too American, as if she'd had elocution lessons.

"G'day, little miss," Keats said, then turned to the gelding. "Look who's here, Ozzie. It's Vivi."

He guided the horse to the fence, trying not to look surprised at the girl's appearance. A few days ago, she'd dyed her hair black and added pink highlights.

"Will you adopt me, Mr. Keats?" Vivi said, her blue eyes magnified by horn-rimmed eyeglasses. She didn't need them for reading—she was just being a teenager.

"Your mum would have a say about that." He smiled. "Don't you want to ride Ozzie one last time?"

"Can't. Mom has already packed my riding clothes." Vivi lowered her chin, and pink fluff dropped over her glasses. She hunched her shoulders and chipped at her black fingernail polish. Seconds later, the bright bits drifted to her black tartan skirt and stuck to her dark leotards.

Keats looked away. Wherever Vivi and her mum were going, it was the very last place this teenager wanted to be.

Another gust of wind hacked around Keats, and he faced the pasture. Off in the distance, five mares galloped, as if they'd been spooked. The hairs on Keats's arms stood up. Something was out there. And it was watching.

Keats had been raised on a horse station in the Adelaide Hills, just outside the quaint town of Hahndorf. But he hadn't been hired for his knowledge about thorough-breds. Mr. Raphael had hired Keats for his military back-ground: he'd served in South Vietnam, a hero in the First Australian Task Force, and he'd worked with British ground forces in the first Gulf War. Keats was also half-immortal and could read the mood of a horse. It was his only gift. He had worked at Innisfair for eleven years, and he was looking forward to the future. The only problem at the station was a few rabbits and their bloody holes.

Now, Ozzie's lips curled back, and he whinnied. Vivi reached out to stroke his mane, but the gelding pulled away.

"What's wrong with him?" she asked.

"He's just happy to see you," Keats said smoothly.

"No, he's freaked out." She frowned. "I know just how he feels. It's too bad I can't stay here. I'd feed him apples every day."

"You'll be back in November," Keats said.

"I shouldn't have to leave at all," she said.

Keats patted Ozzie's neck, wishing he could ease Vivi's

mind. In all the years the Barretts had come and gone, Keats had never seen her this upset. He thought it had something to do with her father—Dr. Barrett had just been declared legally dead, after being missing for donkey's years. Ever since the declaration, Vivi had rebelled. She'd quit riding Ozzie. She'd even refused to help Keats look for rabbit holes, and she'd been doing that since the very first summer she'd arrived at Innisfair, when she was a three-year-old child.

Now Vivi hung her head and sighed. "After we leave Innisfair, Mom and I are going to Italy for a few days. Isn't that pathetic?"

"Dreadful," Keats said. "Eat some pasta. Send a postcard."

"Okay, I will." Her lips moved into a trembly smile. She tucked her hair behind her ears, where three miniature razor-blade earrings dangled from each lobe.

Keats didn't want to be the one to tell her, but she'd never get them earrings through airport security in Adelaide.

A decade ago, when Mr. Raphael had brought the Barretts to Innisfair, Vivi had been a little girl, nothing but eyes and brown pigtails. She'd clung to her mum's hand. Caro had seemed ghostlike in a long black dress that hung on her frame. Mr. Raphael had explained the situation to Keats: Caro had just lost her husband; some kind of scientific expedition in Africa had gone terribly wrong.

Caro had been a jumpy little lady, always jolting when a door slammed. Once, she spilled her pocketbook, and two blue American passports had slid out. When Keats picked up the booklets, he noticed that the Barretts' photographs didn't match their names. She and the girl were traveling under aliases? What kind of trouble were they in? They weren't vampires, that was certain, but he suspected they might have some immortal blood.

Mr. Raphael never explained. He was a gentleman, and a vampire. He'd stuck to Caro and Vivi like an eyelash on a damp cheek. He'd spent that whole first summer at Innisfair, making a big production about the Christmas holidays, ordering lots of presents and pudding. Even the barn had been outlined in red lights that year.

Mr. Raphael was a big-hearted Italian chap, the most generous vampire Keats had ever met; but his little black dog, Arrapato, was an ankle biter. Both the beast and Mr. Raphael were smitten with Caro; she was crazy about the dog, but she'd treated Raphael cordially. Until this past Christmas. Keats had noticed how her eyes had lingered on Mr. Raphael a bit too long, and he'd looked at her the same way. It was almost as if they were talking, yet they hadn't moved their lips.

Keats thought they were in love. But they didn't know it.

Now Ozzie whinnied, a sound he reserved for his favorite humans. Keats looked toward the meadow. Caro was coming down the hill, walking in and out of dappled light.

Vivi looked, too. "Shit," she whispered. "I can't have a minute to myself."

As Caro moved toward the paddock, Keats wondered if she really was thirty-nine years old, or if her birth date was just as fake as her traveling name. She looked much younger, which made him think that she was a hybrid—Keats himself was eighty-seven but could pass for sixty-five.

Caro seemed determined to look older. Her drab sweaters were buttoned to her chin, and her dresses were shapeless and unstylish. She always had a long-suffering look on her face, putting him in mind of Grace Kelly in *The Country Girl*.

Today, she'd tied a brown sweater loosely over her shoulders. Her hair was pulled back with dozens of bobby pins, but no force on earth could tame those fractious curls, and the wind sent them flying around her like gold threads. Her beige pants hugged her curves, and the legs were neatly tucked into red leather boots. The bright footwear seemed odd, Keats thought, but a step in the right direction. At least she'd gotten rid of those scuffed black flatties.

"I've been looking for you two," Caro said, leaning against the fence.

Vivi didn't respond.

"G'day, ma'am." Keats smoothed his wrinkled hand down the horse's dark mane. "I'm trying to talk Little Miss into riding Ozzie."

"I can't," Vivi said. "I'm wearing a dress."

"Yes, but you've got on leotards," Caro pointed out. "Just hike up your kilt and ride."

"Mom!" Vivi scrunched up her face. "Besides, I'm wearing tennis shoes."

"Wear my boots," Caro said.

"Mom, I love you, but I don't love your footwear."

Now that the mother and daughter were side by side, Keats saw how different they were in looks and temperament. Caro was blond, tall, and willowy; Vivi was dark, short, and sturdy. Caro always hosted a Christmas party for the station hands; Vivi hid in her room. Caro wore little makeup, but her silver-blue eyes were thickly lashed; Vivi had drawn kohl around her dark blue eyes, and she was a dead ringer for a raccoon.

"If you aren't going to ride, you need to finish packing," Caro said.

"Maybe I'll stay at Innisfair." Vivi crossed her arms, and a dozen heart-shaped bracelets rattled.

"We'll return soon," Caro said.

"Not till November. That's forever and ever." Vivi let out a sob and sprang off the rail, hitting Keats's chest with such force, he couldn't catch his breath for a moment. He smoothed the back of that god-awful hair.

"You're a corker," he said. "Nothing but a corker."

CHAPTER 7

Caro

FLORENCE, ITALY

I walked down the Via dei Calzaiuoli, glancing over my shoulder every few seconds to make sure that Vivi was still there. It was a sunny morning in Florence, and the wide street was jammed with tourists. I stopped in front of the Duomo, smoothing the wrinkles in my black slacks.

"Forget it, Mom," Vivi said. "You're not dragging me in there."

My daughter was so proud that she'd been born in New York City, and she'd cultivated an American accent. However, she was dressed like a European Goth-girl—black capri jeans, a white ALICE DRINK ME T-shirt, and black Converse tennis shoes. A dotted hair band held back her pink bangs. She wasn't wearing the fake eyeglasses, but her makeup was dark and dramatic, the kind that makes people stare.

"You love the Duomo," I said.

"If you'd stop homeschooling me, I could learn about art the normal way. From textbooks and videos."

"But not in person," I said.

"Not now." She tugged my hand. "I'm starving. After we eat, help me find a postcard for Mr. Keats."

I glanced at my watch. "But it's only ten o'clock."

"My stomach is still on Australian time. I'm gonna faint."

She did look exhausted. Our layover in Dubai had been brutal, and I still felt disoriented. But Vivi didn't join in my little trick for jet lag: I always imagined the curve of the earth, the continents pasted onto the blue water, each hemisphere crisscrossed with time zones. I ignored the zones and divided my travels into the past, present, and future.

Right now, in Florence, it was a breezy, sunny morning. The past was somewhere far below—it was five thirty P.M. in Australia, and periwinkle dusk would be spilling over Innisfair. The future was somewhere above me. It was nine A.M. in Scotland, and a sheen of light would be spreading across the choppy waters of the Firth of Forth.

"Mom?"

Vivi's voice brought me back to the here and now.

"An early lunch sounds good," I said, then cast a long glance at the Duomo.

"You're the best," she said, then stood on her toes and pecked me on the cheek. The top of her head came up to my shoulders. I hugged her close, feeling her tiny bird bones, and felt a pang. I missed Jude so much. He could have explained why two relatively tall parents had produced a petite child. Apparently Vivi had inherited her bone structure from my father's side of the family. Philippe Grimaldi had been over six feet tall, but his mother had only been five-three.

Vivi and I walked in silence toward the Piazza della Signoria. The morning sun brightened the stone façade of the Palazzo Vecchio.

"So, where are we going after Florence?" Vivi asked. "To Venice?"

I hesitated. Raphael lived on Isla Carbonara, a speck of an island between Venice and Murano. After Jude had gone missing, Raphael had brought me to his villa. We'd been friends for the last fifteen years, but from the moment we'd met, we'd been able to converse telepathically. I couldn't do this with anyone else. Not Jude. Not Vivi. Not Uncle Nigel.

But I wasn't ready to see Raphael. A few months ago, I began having dreams about him, the kind that left my pulse thumping, my body slick with perspiration, my hips rising off the bed. Our relationship had always been warm but platonic. I wanted to give myself time to sort through these dreams. If I got near him right now, I wasn't sure what I'd do, and I didn't want to damage our friendship.

"No, we're not visiting Raphael," I said.

Vivi looked surprised. "What? We're not seeing the Prince of Darkness?"

"Raphael is your godfather. Don't call him that."

"Why did you pick a thousand-year-old vamp to be my godfather? Why not Uncle Nigel? He raised you. And don't say Uncle Nigel is too old. He will be seventy-two forever."

I didn't answer. My uncle was the sweetest, most loving man, but he could not stand discord. He hadn't always been a vampire, and he thought of his "condition" as macabre and inconvenient. He'd wanted to conceal it from Vivi until she was an adult, but I'd told her the truth. I'd told her everything, skimming over the barest details. Now I wondered if facts were just as damaging as lies.

I followed the smell of roasted lamb to the Antoco Faltone. A bald waiter with dark moles on his cheeks led us to a table and set down menus. I was in the mood for a truffle ravioli. Vivi wanted bread soup, zucchini flowers, risotto, and figs.

After we ordered, I straightened my spoon and knife.

"Mom, you're so OCD," Vivi said.

"I'm not." My fingers crept to my lap, and I aligned my napkin with a crease in my pants.

"Why does everything have to be perfectly straight?" she asked.

I'd explained many times, but she didn't understand. I'd lost control of my life, and arranging the utensils gave me a sense of security.

The waiter set down our food, his bald head dotted with perspiration. I repressed an urge to straighten the plates. I dug into the salad, but Vivi frowned at her soup.

The waiter's eyebrows shot up. "Is anything wrong?" he asked.

"Not with the food," she said, flashing a stare that could peel the skin from a tomato.

A blush crept up the waiter's face, and then he hurried to another table.

"Vivi, don't be bad-mannered because you're in a bad mood," I whispered.

"This isn't a mood, it's for real. You're making me spend the whole summer in Scotland."

"We've gone over this."

"You rented a castle!" She spat out the word as if it were an olive pit.

"Only for three months." I forked up a truffle.

"Do we *have* to go?" Vivi asked.

"Yes."

"Don't my feelings matter?"

"Of course. But I've already leased the castle. I've paid a hefty deposit, too. I can't throw away that money."

"You've got plenty of cash. Raphael helped you get rich on the stock market."

"We aren't rich."

"Huh. You've got enough money to buy Innisfair. If you don't, Raphael would probably give it to you."

"I don't know anything about running a thoroughbred farm."

"The Aussies call them stations, not farms."

"See?" I waved my fork. "I'm clueless."

"But we can learn. Keats will help us."

"I've always hoped that you and I could live at Dalgliesh one day."

"I'd rather eat fried grasshoppers."

"I thought you liked the castle." Every September,

when Dalgliesh was closed to tourists, we visited Lady Patricia. Vivi had played in the maze, explored the turrets, and walked the Scottish terriers. I'd thought the trips had gone well. Lady Patricia was seventy-nine years old. Technically, when her husband, Sir John Barrett, had died, Dalgliesh Castle had passed into Jude's hands, but Vivi wouldn't inherit the property until Jude died. Lady Patricia was afraid we might lose Dalgliesh, and she begged me to have Jude declared legally dead. I'd reluctantly agreed, and ever since, Vivi had been in a temper.

"Dalgliesh is okay," Vivi said. "But I don't want to live there." She blinked convulsively as if cinders had flown into her eyes.

The back of my neck tingled, the way it always did when she was concealing something. "What's really bothering you?"

A tear curved around her mouth and beaded on the edge of her lip. "Nothing."

I remembered that her idea of the perfect mother was Dame Helen Mirren. I straightened the olive oil cruet.

"Please stop doing that," she said, her eyes brimming. "I'm sorry, Mom. I didn't mean to snap at you. I'm just . . . I need air."

She threw down her napkin, pushed back her chair, and vaulted to her feet. The people at the next table gaped as she ran out of the restaurant. I left a pile of euros on the table and walked outside, my heart tripping against my breast bone. I wasn't sure where she had gone, but this lane went to the River Arno. I'd look there first. I loved this child beyond all else. Was I being too hard on her? Until now, she'd never cared where we lived. Usually we summered at one of Raphael's homes, but I'd leased the Scottish house, mainly because Manderford was located on the sunny East Lothian coast, a place noted for dry, radiant summers. I'd hoped that Scotland's long daylight hours would add a layer of protection from the Sinai Cabal, not that I'd heard from them in years. But I wasn't taking chances. I was also looking forward to mucking around on the beach with Vivi, exploring the museums in Edinburgh, and researching the history of the North Berwick witch trials—the region was infamous for sixteenth-century burnings. I wondered if any of the accused had been half-vampires like myself. Many hybrids had perished during the Inquisition.

I let out a sigh when I spotted Vivi beside the bridge. I remembered that long-ago night when Raphael had shown up at São Tomé. He'd led me out of the cottage, Vivi asleep on his shoulder. Now she stood just ahead of me, her pink hair stirring in the wind, but she still looked like my baby.

As I moved toward her, I took a breath and tried to channel Dame Helen. What came out was vintage momster: "Thank goodness you're all right."

Vivi's shoulders hunched. "It's daylight. All the Italian vampires are in their crypts."

"You're just tired. Let's go to the hotel." I put my arm around her.

She leaned away. "Why did you make my father officially dead? You know he's gone. Why did you need it on a piece of paper?"

So that was the real problem. We'd discussed the situation about Dalgliesh many times, but she was too caught up in her own misery to care about a pile of rocks. I knew how she felt. I'd spent so many years in mourning, I wasn't ready to move on. I wouldn't know how. What did legally dead mean, anyway? A document hadn't changed anything.

She narrowed her eyes. "I don't want to go to Scotland. There's nothing but heather and men in kilts. Maybe *that's* why we're going. So you can fall in love."

I wrapped my arms around my waist. An image from one of my dreams rose up. God, what was wrong with me? Actually, I had a theory. I was thirty-nine years old, on the cusp of my sexual peak, a dicey place for a hybrid, and my dreams were a manifestation of a hormonal storm. Yes, indeed. A summer away from Raphael would give distance from my prurient thoughts.

"The East Lothian coast has long, bright days," I said.

"Alaska is sunny this time of year."

"We'll go there someday."

She looked away. "No, we won't. We're gonna run forever. Because of that stupid prophecy, right?"

"I shouldn't have told you about that."

"No, I'm glad. Because at least I understand. And I've been thinking. Maybe you're scared of vampires the way you're scared of your silverware not being matched up. Don't make a face, Mom. Seriously, when has a mean vampire ever bothered us? See? You can't name a time. Maybe you're worried for no reason."

She had a point. No bald, bearded monks had shown up in a decade. Maybe they'd lost faith in the prophecy, or maybe they'd zeroed in on another hybrid.

"I like the idea of putting down roots," I said. However,

when it came to geography, I had to stop thinking of myself. Vivi was a teenager, not a little girl. From now on, I would ask her opinion before I made plans. "We'll find a place we both like," I added.

"That sounds good, Mom." All of her teenage bluster was gone. Her eyes shimmered, but the tears just stayed there and didn't run down her cheeks.

"Scotland isn't the only thing that's upsetting you," I said. "What's wrong, Meep?"

She wiped her eyes. "I had a dream about Mr. Keats last night. We were looking for rabbit holes. Not that I'm worried about him or anything. My brain is just telling me that we shouldn't have left Australia. Right, Mom?"

"Right." I hated lying, but I didn't think she was in the mood for a dissertation. Hybrid vampires have Freudian dreams like anyone else, but sometimes we see future events. Unfortunately the images are buried in symbols, and interpreting them is a highly individualized process. A dream about apples would make me think of temptation or Aphrodite's golden apples. Vivi might think of Snow White, a young girl who'd been victimized by adults. Or she could develop a craving for an apple tart.

She reached for my hand. "Can we get gelato?"

"Sure." I was still troubled about her dream, and I let my gaze linger on her face. Mothers aren't hardwired to see their child's chronological age. When I looked at Vivi, I didn't see a teenager with black hair and chunky pink bangs. I saw a toddler in my high heels and Jude's bowler hat, her diaper sagging past her knees. I saw a girl with shiny chestnut pigtails, tying her shoelaces for the first time. I saw a six-year-old flying ahead of me on a pink bicycle in Central Park.

If my mother had lived, she wouldn't see me as a grown woman. She'd see a curly-haired girl with gooseberry jam on her face; a kid who needed protection from wasps and rogue vampires.

Women learn how to be mothers from the people who raised them. My mother had sung a lullaby to me, and I'd sung it to Vivi, but I hadn't known when to stop. Some part of me was still chewing on those words.

> *Mother, may I go out to swim?*
> *Yes, my darling daughter.*
> *Hang your clothes on a hickory limb.*
> *And don't go near the Water.*

CHAPTER 8

Edward Keats

INNISFAIR HORSE STATION
HAHNDORF, SOUTH AUSTRALIA

An icy wind tugged at Keats's jacket as he opened the white mailbox. He pulled out a postcard and grinned. The glossy front showed a picture of the Tuscan hills; on the back, he recognized Vivi's back-slanted, minuscule handwriting. He hoped the little corker was all right. But he couldn't read her handwriting without his glasses, and he'd left them at his house. He tucked the card into his pocket, then climbed into his truck and drove toward the north pasture.

Every Wednesday after breakfast, he rode the fence line at Innisfair, looking for loose boards. A stallion paced restlessly in the tall, dry grass, his breath steaming in the morning air. Behind him, the land sloped upward to the red-roofed mansion, where yellow leaves skated over the lawn.

Keats sighed. Now that the Barretts were gone, the house looked sad and empty. Keats's small stone cottage sat below the main house at the bottom of the long driveway, but the cats on the front porch made it seem welcoming.

As he drove along the fence row, he saw a brown, motionless heap in the distance. A dead horse, most likely. A ball of tension gathered in Keats's chest. When he got closer to the animal, his palms slid over the steering wheel.

It was Ozzie. He'd been ripped from throat to belly.

Keats got out of the truck. The afternoon light fell at a slant, suffusing the field with gold. His heart thudded as he squatted beside the horse. Ozzie's eyes were glazed, his mane stiff with dried blood.

Keats shut the gelding's eyes, then dug his boot heels into the grass and pivoted, blinking down at the grass. A massive wound like this should have pooled, but the ground was dry, except for a heap of entrails.

He turned back to Ozzie, studying the gelding's legs. No bite marks. No broken bones. What had brought him down? Years ago on Fraser Island, a large pack of dingoes had killed a horse, but there had been a lot of blood then, and Keats couldn't remember the last time he'd seen a dingo at Innisfair.

He rocked on his haunches, the sun beating against the top of his head. The wind picked up and the leaves spun in eddies. Dark blue clouds roiled over the Adelaide

Hills. A storm was coming, and he needed to tend to Ozzie. Sighing heavily, Keats took out his cell phone and punched in numbers.

That evening, as rain sluiced down, he drove away from the barn. His headlights picked through the downpour, sweeping over his stone cottage. He shoved a bush hat onto his head, got out of the truck, and ran up to the veranda. Two striped barn cats always slept on the wooden swing, but the cushion was empty. He checked their kibble bowl. It hadn't been touched. He stared for a minute, his head lowered, water pouring off the brim of his hat.

He pulled off the hat, hung it on a nail, and walked into the cottage. In the kitchen, he tested his glucose. Three hundred twenty-six—way too high. He ate cheese and cold cuts, then walked toward the refrigerator to fetch his insulin. As he passed by the window, he saw a luminous glow. He pushed back the lace curtain. Through the rain-smeared glass, lights blazed from the manse. The house had been dark since the Barretts left. Caro had locked up, set the alarm, and put the key in his mailbox, same as always. She never varied her routine. Keats had the feeling that she was careful and precise all the time. But this year, she'd been upset about something. Maybe she'd overlooked a detail.

He leaned over the sink and pushed up the window, expecting to hear the burglar alarm. Nothing but the rain tapping in the trees. Then a figure passed by a window. He pulled in a breath, and his throat burned, as if he'd swallowed drain cleaner.

Trespassers.

Keats dialed the Hahndorf emergency number, but he knew it would take the police twenty minutes to arrive—longer if the road washed out. He hurried into the den, opened his gun cabinet, and grabbed a double-barreled shotgun. As he dropped a handful of shells into his pocket, he forced himself to breathe. He'd protected Mr. Raphael's estate for eleven years, and he planned to protect it for eleven more. Though his adversaries usually were rabbits, not thieves.

He decided not to drive, so he put on a black vinyl poncho and walked to the porch. He lifted his hat from the nail. The rain had slacked off, and fine white flecks were visible through the darkness, like bits of sawed bone. He strode up the hill, hanging back under the trees. Fog drifted past the house and moved toward a dark clump of evergreens.

These intruders were either dumb or desperate, he thought. He crouched next to the boxwood hedge and surveyed the courtyard. A black Toyota Camry sat in the driveway. In Vietnam, he'd been known as "Quiet Keats," and he could still move soundlessly. He edged forward, his boots moving silently over the gravel.

An Avis decal was pasted on the windshield, next to an Adelaide International Airport sticker. The visitor wasn't Mr. Raphael; he always arrived in a hired limo. Also, he would have notified Keats if he were coming. If Caro and Vivi had returned, they would have phoned, too. Maybe they'd tried; he'd been gone most of the day. He looked at the vehicle again. Had Vivi talked her mother into returning? But a Town Car always took the Barretts to and from the airport.

Better not to make assumptions, he thought. He eased around the side of the house. The back door stood ajar. He stepped into the kitchen and paused. Everything was tidy. No luggage in the hall. No umbrellas or galoshes. No grocery bags. The house was too quiet. If the Barretts were here, Vivi would be watching television and Caro would be cooking dinner.

Keats lifted his hat and set it on the counter. A scraping noise came from the study, as if a chair had been dragged over the floor. He made sure the gun's safety was off, then crept down the hall. His mouth went dry, a sign that his blood sugar was rising. He spun into the room, holding the shotgun in both hands.

A woman with short blond hair stood beside the bookcase. His gaze flicked over her. Pale skin. Late twenties. Shorter than him. Maybe five-six and 125 pounds. She turned, her eyes expressionless, as if she'd been caught folding the laundry, not breaking and entering.

He drew a bead on her. "Stop where you are or I'll put a hole through you."

Her blue eyes narrowed for an instant, and then she raised her hands in the air. The cuffs on her black leather jacket pulled up, showing her wrists.

"Please don't shoot." She spoke with a mild Eastern European accent, but on top of it was something plainer, as if she'd been born in Russia or Ukraine but had been educated in the United States, or had spent time there. Her right cheek twitched as if an ant were crawling toward her eye.

"Are you alone?" he asked.

"Why?" Her gaze sharpened, brazen and alert, like a

dingo watching sheep. She seemed to be waiting for his answer. Well, she wasn't getting one. Keeping his eyes on her, he moved one hand away from the gun, shut the door, locked it, and returned his hand to the gun.

The room was quiet, except for water dripping from his poncho. But he smelled her. She gave off the stink of old fruit, the kind where the flesh has turned soft and watery. A ketotic smell. Was she a vampire? Diabetic? On one of them fad diets?

"You're trespassing," he said.

"Wrong. I was invited." Her full lips curved into a smile.

"Step against the wall. Keep your hands in the air."

Her leather pants swished as she moved against the bookcase. Her hair was damp, curling around her ears. "Sir, please let me explain."

Keats's finger hovered over the trigger. "You've got thirty seconds."

"I apologize for this misunderstanding."

Right. A misunderstanding. Mr. Raphael had occasionally brought girlfriends to Innisfair, but this one wasn't his type. Maybe he'd dumped her. She looked like the kind who wouldn't go away without causing maximum damage.

"Twenty seconds," he said.

"I'm Tatiana Kaskov. Raphael said he'd made all the arrangements for my arrival."

Keats didn't comment. This felt all wrong. Mr. Raphael would have phoned.

"How did you get inside?" Keats asked. "How did you turn off the alarm?"

"Raphael gave me a key." Her eyes darted to the left.

She was a cool liar. He held the gun steady. "One more time. Why did you break in?"

"Is this how you treat all of Raphael's guests?"

"I'll call him right now." Keats moved to the desk, shifting the gun to one hand. He lifted the receiver and punched in 1 and 8. He heard a cracking noise and looked up.

Tatiana had moved to the other side of the desk, and she held a tangled cord. It took him a second to realize that she'd pulled the plug out of the jack.

He frowned. "Get back against the—"

She sprang at him, a blur of pale limbs and black leather—how could she move so fast? The receiver hit the desk. He barely had time to lift the shotgun and squeeze the trigger. The blast stabbed through his ear canals, pricking like needles, followed by a clanging noise. The stink of gunpowder climbed into his nose.

Tatiana lay on the ground, screaming and clutching her left leg. Blood splattered the wall behind her. She began to rock. Crimson threads streamed through a hole in the leather, just above her knee.

Keats's stomach muscles tensed. Damn, he'd shot a woman. But she'd rushed him. What kind of drug was she on? He broke open the barrel, smoke curling up. The empty casings clattered to the floor and rolled under the desk.

She got to her knees, grabbed at the curtain, and missed. Then she fell back down. Christ, she was tough. He reached in his pocket for more ammo, and Vivi's post-card glided to the floor.

Tatiana vaulted to her feet and lunged across the room.

She pulled the gun out of his hands and threw it against the bookcase. Her cold, damp fingers circled Keats's neck. She lifted him off the floor and grinned up at him, her lips moving like blood-fattened leeches.

"You're fucked," she said.

Keats's chest tightened. His lungs felt like dried gourds, seeds rattling against his ribs. He'd shot her. How was she standing? How had she lifted him?

She's a vampire, he thought.

He reached toward her, trying to grab her neck before he blacked out.

Her grip slackened, and he crashed to the floor. His mouth opened, and he sucked in air.

"Do you know that Raphael is a vampire." Tatiana leaned closer.

Keats tried to keep his face expressionless.

She smiled. "Guess what, old man? So am I."

Keats forced himself to look at her. "You're trash."

"No, I need blood." She pinched his cheek. "Your blood. But we'll party later. First, I will ask a few questions. Your answers will determine how you'll die."

So, that was how it would be. *Steady, old boy.* Fear wouldn't make him a better soldier.

"When did Caro and Vivienne leave Australia?" Tatiana asked.

"Why are you interested in them?" he said. Only one theory was plausible. Tatiana had been spurned by Mr. Raphael and assumed that he'd taken up with Caro.

"I'm asking the questions," Tatiana said. "When did they leave?"

He started to get up. She moved back to the desk, lifted

a bronze horse statue, and slammed it against Keats's knee. A cracking noise held in the air. Pain exploded in his whole leg, as if some part of the statue had moved inside him, galloping through his bones. He pursed his lips, trying to hold back the scream, but it burst through his teeth.

Tatiana smiled and tilted her head, as if listening to music.

The bitch was enjoying it.

"That's for shooting my fucking leg," she said. She reached inside her jacket and pulled out a narrow, curved knife. "When did they leave?"

Why did she care? What did she want from the Barretts? Whatever it was, he wouldn't give it to her. He licked his lips—they were so dry. But he was a soldier, and soldiers pushed on.

"A month ago." He paused and caught his breath. "Two months. I can't remember."

"I hate a liar." She raised the knife, and Keats saw a gold ring on her thumb. A man's ring? Something she'd stolen?

Everything seemed to move slowly. She dragged the blade over his hand. A streak of coldness passed through his flesh. His thumb was dangling by stringy red cords, and then they broke loose and the stump hit the floor, blood jetting onto the carpet.

Strangely, he didn't feel pain. Not yet. He knew soldiers who'd been tortured by the North Vietnamese regulars. Too much pain could turn into pleasure.

Tatiana picked up his detached thumb. She put the bloody end into her mouth and sucked, as if drawing meat from a crab's leg. She tossed the thumb over her shoulder. "Your blood is sweet. A delicacy. Can't wait to drain you."

"Rack off," he said.

"Sure, I'll leave. If you tell me what I want to know."

He still did not feel any pain. "A soldier never talks."

Tatiana tossed the knife to her other hand. "You're a soldier without a war. Next question. Where did Caro go?"

"Are you one of those vampires who can't read minds?"

Her eyes turned glossy and cold, like melted ice in the bottom of a cooler. "Do you know about Caro, old man? She's a half-vampire, and her daughter is a freak?"

"They're good people," he said, staring her down. Nothing could shake Keats's loyalty to Mr. Raphael or Caro. "And you're crack-a-fruity," he added.

Tatiana lowered the knife, and the cold metal scraped over his flesh, making quick, surgical cuts. Just enough for the blood to well up in the shallow creases.

"Next time it will be another finger," she said. "I love the smell of your blood."

Keats clenched his teeth. This was about pain. "Bring it on, you little cunt. Bite me. Shoot me. Cut off my legs. But we're finished."

"You'll talk when I start killing the horses."

Keats swallowed, and his throat made a dry click. She'd butchered Ozzie.

"One more time, old man. Where are Caro and Vivienne?"

"The space shuttle." He glanced past her, where the postcard lay on the floor.

Tatiana followed his gaze. She set the knife on the desk, then lifted the postcard off the floor. Her eyes switched back and forth, and then she looked down at Keats.

"Your eyes gave you away, soldier," she said. "Shall I read Vivienne's letter?"

Dear Mr. Keats,

You were right about Italy. It's not half bad. I'd rather stay in Florence than go to that crappy castle in Scotland, but my mom is making me. Please give Ozzie lots of apples. Remember to check your sugar! See you in November.

Love always,
Vivi

Tatiana shoved the postcard into her pocket. "A Scottish castle? How droll."

Tears ran down the sides of Keats's face. Fear rose up inside him, not for himself, but for the Barretts and for Innisfair. He felt streaks of white-hot pain rush through his knee and hand.

"Which part of Scotland?" Tatiana turned back to the desk and lifted her knife.

"Stuff it." He tried to ignore his cramping stomach, the sound of water rushing through his bowels. Sweat ran down the back of his neck.

Tatiana stepped on his wrist, pinning his arm against the floor. She pressed the tip of the blade into his forearm and dragged it over his flesh, moving in a figure-eight pattern. Blood welled up, obliterating the design, and streaked down the sides of his arm.

"Which city shall I try first?" Tatiana said. "Glasgow? Inverness? Edinburgh? Aberdeen?"

"Go to hell, you fucking rabbit."

"I'm actually doing a noble thing. Someone I work for is dying. He wants to feel the sun on his face before he leaves this world. Vivi's blood will make this possible." She looked up at the ceiling as she spoke, a half smile on her face, caught up in her own self-importance. Then, lowering her gaze, she removed the gold ring from her thumb and forced it onto his index finger.

He didn't want her jewelry touching his flesh, and he tried to pull away.

"This ring will torture Caro, just as I've tortured you." Tatiana leaned forward.

Keats felt the blade pass over his throat.

"Farewell, soldier," she said. "See you in hell."

CHAPTER 9

Vivi

MANDERFORD CASTLE
EAST LOTHIAN COAST, SCOTLAND

Vivi Barrett fought her way out of the nightmare, twisting from side to side in the four-poster bed. She kicked off the blanket and opened her eyes.

It was the same dream. She and Keats were riding around Innisfair, looking for rabbit holes. But this time he'd fallen into one, and she couldn't find him.

Breathe, breathe, breathe.

She sucked in air. Then she forced it out. She'd always had night terrors when she traveled, which was all the freaking time. It was jet lag, that was all. Keats was fine.

She pushed her bangs out of her eyes. How long had she slept? She squinted at the windows, where dingy light trickled onto a teal-and-red tartan carpet. Was it dusk, dawn, or a typical July day at Manderford Castle? If the

East Lothian coast was the brightest part of Scotland, she'd hate to see the rest of it.

Her hand fumbled on the bedside table. She lifted the travel clock. It was seven fifty-five P.M. In two hours the sun would set—if Scotland even had a sun. Vivi hadn't seen it. The curtains stirred and a damp breeze rushed in, carrying the harsh cry of seabirds. Their voices seemed to mock her.

Born weird, they cawed.

Well, she couldn't argue. Her stupid one-quarter vampire genes had given her keen hearing and smell, but that was it. She had the feeling her mom hadn't told her everything, as if Vivi could take only one-quarter of the truth. Oh, she knew about vampires and the hokey prophecy. But there had to be a worse secret. Like, maybe her mother was in a witness protection program. That would be really creepy.

She curled her toes, listening to the joints pop. One day she would find out her mother's secrets. A girl could hear juicy stuff if she kept her ears open and her mouth shut. Vivi had learned to be quiet and to notice details, to hear what people said beneath their words. Ever since she was little, she'd wrapped herself in silence, as if it were a crust, all crimped at the edges, her worries hidden like blackbirds in a pie, not that she'd eat a bird, and if anyone picked at her, Vivi would bite them with words, not teeth.

Just this morning, she'd sassed the housekeeper, Mrs. MacLeod. The old woman had a kind face, but she was bossy. She'd steered Vivi out the kitchen door, clucking to herself. "It's not natural to sleep this much. You need to get outside and breathe the sea air."

Vivi had stomped through the gray mist, past an herb garden, toward a path that led to the Firth of Forth. Even the sea had a stupid Scottish name. As she turned back to the house, she saw a stone wall. A wooden gate was in the center, big enough for a truck to drive through. Golf balls were scattered on Vivi's side of the wall. She threw them onto the fairway until she got bored.

Why had her mom rented a house next to a golf course? Would she insist that Vivi take lessons? She wasn't hitting a ball with a stick. She wanted to have girlfriends and go to parties and giggle.

Vivi had run home, straight to her room, but she'd dreamed about Keats again.

Now she pushed off the bed and looked toward the window. She heard a car rumble down the long gravel driveway, and she sat up. Actual visitors were coming? Maybe it was a golf cart. Or the Welcome to East Lothian committee, ladies with shortbread and itty bottles of scotch. A cute delivery boy would be too much to hope for. But anything was possible.

She scrambled off the bed, smoothing her bangs. She pulled on a pink leopard skirt and a black hoodie that was spattered with fake blood—KEEP CALM AND KILL ZOMBIES was printed across the front. She laced up her high-top sneakers and ran into the hall. A blue plaid carpet stretched toward a balcony, where suits of armor were lined up against the turret wall. The sound of the car was louder, and she paused by the arched window.

Quivering headlights sliced through the fog, and then a white, gangster-type limousine stopped in the court-yard. The driver got out, a stumpy man with ginger hair.

He was built like a beer keg. He opened the rear door, and a little black dog hopped onto the gravel. A tall man climbed out of the backseat, the wind stirring his chin-length blond hair.

Raphael and his dog were here? But they were vampires, and they never, ever got in daylight. Sometimes the freaks came out on rainy days. They were easy to spot because they wore reflective gear and zinc oxide. But Raphael wasn't a freak. He was totally awesome.

Vivi leaned closer to the window. Raphael's forehead gleamed with a thin white layer of sunblock. A tan duster coat fell to his ankles, the hem skimming above the walkway.

Vivi saw a flash of movement from the backseat of the limo. A long, shapely leg appeared, and then a stiletto heel clicked against the pavement. A blonde in a red dress rose from the car, tall and shapely as a Victoria's Secret model. She had wide-spaced brown eyes, high cheekbones, plump lips, and fluffy hair, which curled around her shoulders. Her creamy skin didn't have a drop of sunblock, which meant she wasn't immortal.

The blonde smiled down at Raphael. She was about two inches taller than him, and he was six-one. He had a thing for models, and models had a thing for him. Vivi felt a pang. Raphael had practically raised her, and she dearly loved him. But his women were a nuisance, focused on aerobic exercise and starvation. His last girlfriend had lived on Diet Coke and sunflower seeds. This blonde probably ate even less.

"You forgot somethin', Mr. Della Rocca," the driver called in a Cockney accent. He held out a green shopping bag.

"Thanks, Fielding." Raphael took the bag, then frowned at the dog. "Arrapato! Do not pee on Caro's bushes."

The blonde put her hand over her mouth and giggled.

Even her laugh is wacked, Vivi thought. Kind of metallic and tinkly, as if a hundred razor blades had fallen into a porcelain sink. If Raphael fell in love with that woman, Vivi would curl up and die.

She ran downstairs and skidded into the entrance vestibule, her shoes squeaking on the stone floor. It was a large room, round and castlelike, with a carved fireplace at one end. The flames brightened the walls, which were lined with armor, old shields, and antlers. A scuffed red plaid duffel bag sat in front of the door, her mom's in-case-they-needed-to-leave-in-a-hurry bag.

Vivi pushed it aside and flung open the heavy oak door. She looked up at Raphael. Even when he was holding still, he gave off energy and charisma, making Vivi think of a rock star with an electric guitar and ripped abs. But today his forehead was puckered, as if he were worried about something. Probably because every five-star hotel in Edinburgh was booked solid, and he didn't have a place to stash his ho in the daytime, so he'd brought her to Manderford Castle.

He smiled, showing white teeth with slightly prominent incisors. "Vivi, how nice to see you," he said brightly.

"Who let *you* out of the casket before sunset?" she said, repressing a grin.

"I heard that your mom rented this place," Raphael said, his voice smooth and silky as an Italian liqueur. "I had to see Casa TooMucha for myself."

Vivi laughed. Oh, gosh, he was handsome. If only he would get rid of the ho and start dating Momster. Then Vivi would have a dad.

His eyebrows went up, two dark slashes on his pale forehead. "Where's your mom?"

"In the attic, hanging from the rafters," Vivi said.

"I brought you a present," he said, handing Vivi the green bag. HARRODS was stamped in gold across the front. "A little something that reminded me of you."

"Thanks." A flutter moved through Vivi's chest as she lifted the bag to her nose. The paper smelled like him: cologne, ripe cherries, and pomegranates. She reached inside the bag and pulled out a box. It was too large for a pair of Sickgirl earrings and too small for a Frankenlover T-shirt. She tore off the lid.

Inside were a dozen marzipan pigs, pink and plump, lined up snout to tail. She imagined him walking through Harrods' Food Hall, looking for the most disgusting thing he could find.

The blonde leaned in for a closer look, her dark eyelashes fanning against her cheeks. "Oh, Raphael. How darlin'," she said.

Vivi blinked. She'd always had an ear for accents, but she couldn't place this one. Though if she had to guess, she'd say this bimbo came from the American South, way down deep, in a place that dripped with moonlight and water moccasins.

"Do you like your pigs?" Raphael said, holding back a grin.

"Love them. Thanks." Vivi set the box on a table, trying to decide if the gift was an insult. Or maybe he'd bought the first pink item he saw, knowing her fondness for the color.

"Pigs are a good-luck symbol," Raphael said.

"Can't have too much of that," she said.

He looked troubled for a moment. "May Gillian and I come in?"

So that was her name, huh? Vivi felt a surge of jealousy, and she shook her head. "Nope. Better not. I've got strep throat, and Mom's got a vomiting virus."

"I still need to see her." Raphael's eyes were the color of coffee beans, and they held an amused glint. She knew he wasn't buying her story.

He looked past her and quickly brushed his hair with his hands. A second later, footsteps pounded in the hall. Caro ran into the vestibule, her cheeks flushed, hair floating around her shoulders. A few strands stuck to her cheek, and she brushed them away. Her other hand smoothed the wrinkles in her lumpy gray plaid skirt. A hideous sweater hung past her hips, giving her a waifish look.

Arrapato ran to her, tags jingling, and she scooped him into her arms. She smiled at the blonde, and then her gaze moved to Raphael.

"It's so good to see you," she said. "It's been too long."

He stepped into the vestibule, the hem of his coat billowing. Without flashing his usual bordering-on-seductive smile, he took her hand. "Yes, Caro. It has."

"You were with us at Christmas," Vivi said.

They ignored her. Raphael leaned in toward Caro, the tips of his shoes pointing at her shoes. Then, still holding her hand, he turned back to the blonde. "This is Gillian Delacroix. She's from Baton Rouge, Louisiana."

"Nice to meet you, Gillian," Caro said warmly. "Come on in."

Raphael squeezed Caro's hand. "Can we speak privately?"

"Sure." She looked confused. "The library is just down the hall."

Vivi folded her arms. Why was Raphael really here? What would make him come out in daylight? And why was he trying to get away from the blonde? Usually his women were stuck to him like ticks. Probably they sucked his money, and he sucked their blood. Oh, why did she care? Why was she acting like a brat? She didn't mean to, but she was on edge because of jet lag and those nightmares.

Caro set Arrapato on the floor, then gave Vivi a pleading look. "Can you show Gillian around?"

"Show her yourself," Vivi said. *Crap, why had she said that?*

Gillian took a step forward, her gaze latched onto Raphael. "No, I . . . Can't I just go with y'all?"

"I won't be long," he said, regarding her with a benign expression, as if she were part of the décor. He turned back to Caro and laced his fingers through hers. They walked out of the vestibule, into the wide hall. It was lined with dark, oppressive woodwork and high plaster ceilings.

As far as Vivi knew, Raphael had never been to Manderford, but he seemed to know his way around. He led Caro into an oak study, one of the lovelier rooms in the castle, with bookcases, tall leaded glass windows, a crystal chandelier, and a crackling fireplace.

Arrapato stopped in the doorway, flashed a malicious glance at Gillian, then ran after his master. Raphael closed the door.

Gillian sighed, her breasts heaving beneath the silky red dress. "Didn't his mama teach him better manners?"

"Do you even know when his mom was born?" Vivi said.

Gillian dragged her gaze away from the door. "Say what?"

Vivi shrugged. "Forget it."

"Gosh, I've never been in a castle before."

"You're lucky."

"Yeah, right." Gillian smiled. "What's the story on Raphael and your mom?"

"They're old friends." Vivi stared at the library door, stifling an urge to press her ear against it. No, the dog would hear her and she'd get busted. But she wasn't going to babysit the girlfriend or give her the grand tour. Besides, she was starving.

"See you later," Vivi said, stepping backward.

"No, wait," Gillian called.

Vivi ran down the hall, past a room where deer heads hung on teal walls, through a billiard room that was all done up in green-and-red checks, and past a small staircase that was carpeted in brown plaid. This house had obviously been furnished by someone who was tartan crazy. And color-blind. Or maybe they'd thought the castle would attract a foreign renter if the décor hit on every Scottish cliché.

She turned into the kitchen. A huge china cupboard stood against one wall, the shelves crammed with mismatched plates and bowls. Mrs. MacLeod stood beside the gigantic Aga, where six pots bubbled merrily. Her cheeks were flushed, and perspiration dotted her broad nose. "I'm putting the finishing touches on your dinner." Mrs. MacLeod nodded, and her gray curls shook, each one large as a banger sausage. "I made lamb stew. Your mum says you like it with plenty of carrots and potatoes."

"Thanks." Vivi pressed one hand against her rumbling stomach.

Mrs. MacLeod stirred a pot. "I heard a car drive up. Does your mum have company?"

"Yes, ma'am."

"Shall I be setting extra dinner plates, then?"

"No, ma'am. I think they've already eaten."

Mrs. MacLeod looked disappointed. She turned back to the stove.

Vivi looked down at a pan of browned rolls, the tops glistening with melted butter. She glanced furtively at MacLeod. Most housekeepers didn't like you to eat before the meal, but these rolls smelled yeasty and buttery. Vivi shoved one into her jacket pocket and yawned. She needed caffeine. Anything to keep her from going to sleep and dreaming about rabbit holes. She'd be totally horrified if she had a nightmare while Raphael was here with his ho.

"Mrs. MacLeod, can you make a pot of coffee?" she said, her voice trailing into a yawn.

Mrs. MacLeod turned away from the stove. "We only have tea and milk."

"No Cokes or Red Bull?"

"What kind of bull?" Mrs. MacLeod asked.

"It's an energy drink." Vivi could almost taste the gingery, slightly bitter liquid. One can of Red Bull would keep her wired for hours, but jitters were better than bad dreams.

Mrs. MacLeod's head tipped back, curls trembling. She swiped her nose, leaving a comma of blood across her cheek. "You'll be needing that bull, won't you, little lady?"

"I'll be fine." Vivi frowned at MacLeod. The poor thing looked like she'd been in a fight. A bloody line curved out of both nostrils, but she didn't wipe it off this time. The ruffles on her apron trembled as she charged toward the back door, pausing to grab an enormous tapestry pocketbook from the counter. Then she walked outside.

Vivi ran after her. "Wait, where are you going?"

"To fetch you a bull, little lady," MacLeod said, her arms swinging.

Vivi glanced at the driveway. Raphael's driver sat in the front seat of the limo, his head barely visible above the steering wheel.

"Mrs. MacLeod, come back," Vivi called. "Your nose is bleeding."

But the woman was already climbing into a blue compact car. The door slammed on the hem of her apron. It dragged on the ground as she drove down the driveway What had made the old lady take off like that? And why was she bleeding?

Pain thumped in the backs of Vivi's eyes. She dragged

the roll from her pocket and bit off the end. The buttery taste filled her mouth. She walked back to the kitchen, stepping over dime-sized drops of blood, and shut off the stove. When she turned around, Gillian stood in the doorway, one leg bent at the knee.

"Want a roll?" Vivi asked.

"Thanks, but I'm watching my carbs." Gillian rubbed her bare arms. "It's gettin' chilly. Can I borrow a sweater?"

Vivi found MacLeod's beige raincoat in the closet, and she tossed it to Gillian.

"Thanks." Gillian draped the coat around her shoulders. "Is your mom a vampire, too?"

"No, are you a ho?"

"I'm a malpractice attorney."

"You could've fooled me. I thought you were an airhead."

"You're a rude little thing." Gillian pronounced *thing* with a hard *a*, making the word rhyme with *twang*.

Vivi grabbed another roll, shoved it in her pocket, and headed out the back door.

"Hey, don't run off again," Gillian called.

"So come with me," Vivi said, and walked into the yard, her tennis shoes squeaking over the damp grass. Cool, glazed air rushed past her face. She glanced over her shoulder.

Gillian was following her, backlit by the castle, its red sandstone walls jutting up, the crow-stepped gables and turrets casting long shadows. Smoke curled from the chimneys, each one stamping a black question mark against the fog.

Vivi had a few questions of her own. Why was Scotland so cold in July? Why had Raphael shown up before sunset? Why was he locked up in the library with her mom?

She stepped into the herb garden. It was rectangular, hemmed in with a boxwood hedge. Inside, gravel paths divided the rectangle into square beds, lavender and mint at one end, cooking herbs at the other.

Gillian leaned over, plucked a coriander sprig, and touched it to her nose. "This kinda smells like Raphael," she said.

"It's his new cologne," Vivi said, her voice hitched up into a yawn.

Gillian lowered the sprig. "How long have you known Raphael?"

"All my life."

"How old are you?"

"How old do I look?"

Gillian tilted her head. "Twelve?"

"Nope. Thirteen."

"Is your mom in some kind of trouble?"

Vivi cut her eyes at Gillian. "Why do you ask?"

"Because Raphael hired me to be a decoy."

"For what?"

"For your mom. I'm supposed to pretend to be her. I'll go off in one direction; your mom and Raphael will go in another. I thought maybe they were having an affair. And maybe your mom's husband is having her followed."

Vivi lifted the roll from her pocket and tossed it in the air. Either Gillian was lying or Raphael had gone mad. Because this woman was one hundred times prettier than her mom and lots taller.

"Decoy, huh?" Vivi said. "Sounds like a pickup line to me."

"It worked."

"Why would you want Raphael?"

Gillian's eyes widened. "Are you kidding? He's gorgeous. And he has such good taste. He walked into the Savoy the other night, and he was wearing the most divine Dolce and Gabbana suit. I swooned."

"Too bad he's a vampire," Vivi said.

"I like that part best. Vamps are fantastic lovers."

Vivi tilted her head, intrigued. She'd never heard an adult talk so openly. "How many have you dated?"

"A few. But I've never known any man like Raphael."

"He's okay, I guess."

"He won't tell me how old he is. Do you know?"

"I'm not sure. Maybe a thousand." Vivi shrugged. "Give or take a few centuries."

"How did he get so wealthy?"

"The Dutch Tulip Bubble."

Gillian looked confused. "The what?"

"Some kind of market crash in 1637," Vivi said. "The world went crazy for tulips. Bulbs sold for over a thousand dollars. Raphael got out before the bubble burst."

"You must be a smart girl if you know about financial bubbles. I bet you go to a fancy school, huh?"

Vivi hesitated. It was too gross to explain about her homeschooling. Maybe she ought to swerve the conversation away from herself. "My mom practically has a Ph.D. in history. She crams it down my throat."

"At least it's not algebra, right?" Gillian looked back at the castle. "You know anything else about Raphael?"

"Before he was a vampire, he was a monk."

"Now *that* is interesting. He doesn't act real monkly."

"It was a long time ago. He even went on a pilgrimage. Something about a homage to Saint James."

"It's *an* homage, not *a* homage," Gillian said.

"So you're a lawyer and the grammar police?"

"I taught English before I went to law school."

"Why do you talk like a swamp rat? Dropping your *g*'s. Pouring sugar on each word."

"Honey, it takes unimaginable skill to talk this way." Gillian sniffed the coriander. "So how did Raphael become a vampire?"

"It happened on his way back from Spain. He stopped in France. Got a job in Tours. My mom says he translated books. She says he knows all the dirt on the Vatican, but who cares?"

Vivi hesitated. Dammit, she'd almost told the real story—that her grandfather's voluptuous French cousins had bitten Raphael. Then Gillian would have put the rest of it together, that Vivi and her mom had some vampire blood. And that wasn't anybody's business.

Gillian sighed. "I've always liked older men."

"He likes anything with boobs."

"Then we'll get along perfectly." She smiled. "Can he read minds?"

"Sometimes. He can also adjust the volume on a stereo or a television set with his mind—even if he's in another room."

Gillian's smile broadened. "Cool."

"You're freaky."

"Honey, I'm from Louisiana. It's against the law to be

normal. But isn't it a little odd that you know so much about vampires?"

"Not really. I found out about them when I was nine. My mom and I were spending the Christmas holidays in Australia. Raphael and Arrapato came to visit. On Christmas morning, we sat in the dark living room—Mom always kept the curtains pulled tight. I couldn't see my presents, so I flung open the drapes."

Gillian made a face. "Yikes. What happened?"

"It wasn't pretty." Vivi lifted her eyebrows, remembering how light had blasted into the room. Arrapato had yelped, and smoke curled up from his fur. Raphael swooped down, his face red and blistered, and carried the dog out of the room.

"My mom explained that Raphael and Arrapato were vampires," Vivi said.

"And you believed her?"

"Eventually. At first, I thought she was crazy. If she'd said they were demons or hatchet murderers, I might have gone along with it. But vampires? And a vampire dog?"

"I thought the same thing when I saw Arrapato," Gillian said. "How could an Affenpinscher be a vampire? He has that precious, smooshed-in face."

Vivi leaned over and plucked a thyme sprig. It had taken her forever and ever to understand about the immortals. Her mom had seemed to know when to feed her more information. Raphael preferred type O blood, and he either drank it in a cup or injected it into his veins. Arrapato licked blood out of a bowl, but he was still a dog, and he would dance on his hind legs for a raw bone.

Gillian lifted her right foot. "He bit me the other

day. See those marks? I was afraid he'd turn me into a vamp. But Raphael said it wasn't that simple."

"Yeah, it's not three bites and you suddenly grow fangs. You have to get bit a lot. And drink vampire blood or get transfused with it."

Gillian crossed her eyes and laughed. "Ick."

Vivi repressed a grin. She'd never talked to a human about vampires, but it felt good. The wind picked up, tossing the herbs back and forth, and she smelled peppermint. But the fragrance wasn't coming from the garden. She also detected menthol. Not all vampires smelled alike, but all vampires carried an odor. Some gave off the tang of lemon oil, camphor, menthol, or fruity ketones. It was something in their sweat, and it made humans briefly relax.

She glanced at Gillian. "Do you smell that?"

"Smell what?"

"That minty-fruity odor."

"A little." Gillian's nostrils flared. "Why?"

"It's a vampire odor."

"You're a weird kid," Gillian said. "Cute, but weird."

"Whatever." Vivi glanced toward the golf course, and her scalp tingled. The fog was blowing out to sea, leaving behind the smell of vampires.

Lots and lots of vampires.

CHAPTER 10

Caro

MANDERFORD CASTLE LIBRARY

I sat on the edge of a green velvet chair, watching Raphael pace in front of the fireplace. Arrapato trotted behind him, his black tail whipping back and forth. Each time they passed by my chair, I smelled pomegranates and patchouli, coriander and cocoa. Leave it to a vampire—and his dog—to wear a cologne with a sense of history: Serge Lutens Borneo 1834. That was the year silk merchants added patchouli sprigs to their bales to keep moths away.

As a failed historian, I'm a font of useless trivia, all of it gleaned from textbooks. But Raphael has been a vampire since the eighth century, and his brain is filled with magnificent details, which is one reason I adore him. Best of all, he'd known my mother and father, and he was always remembering little stories.

He walked by my chair again, and I remembered the dream I'd had last night. I forced myself to think about something else. Why hadn't he invited his pretty girlfriend to join us? I'd never known him to be rude. He could be forgetful, like when he scheduled two dates on the same night, but he'd always handled these situations with finesse.

"What's up?" I asked. I tried to look into Raphael's mind. We could carry on whole conversations without saying a word—a fascinating way to communicate, even if it left me with a headache. Raphael's talents were stronger. He could look into my mind and pluck thoughts with the speed and efficiency of a neurosurgeon. When he didn't want me inside his head, he would block me. He was blocking now. It was a palpable thing, as if I'd bumped into a concrete wall.

He stopped in front of the fireplace and looked up at the portrait of a nineteenth-century woman. She appeared to stare back at him, an ethereal look on her plump face.

"I knew her," Raphael said.

Somehow I wasn't surprised. "Who was she?"

"Lady Margaret Manderford," he said, his voice ringing with music, like notes from a Puccini aria. "Her husband was a total bastard. And a golfing fanatic. Lady Margaret died of consumption."

Normally I would have had plenty of questions about Lady Margaret. When had she died? What was her relationship to Raphael? But something felt wrong about his visit. I'd known him for fifteen years, and yes, he often surprised me, but some aspects of his personality never changed. He hadn't shown up before dusk to give me a history lesson. He'd come to tell me something, and he was procrastinating.

"So did you just decide to fly to Scotland?" I asked.

"Fielding drove me. I was in London."

Raphael pulled a Kleenex from his pocket, scrubbed off the sunblock, and dropped the tissue onto the logs. Flames licked up, and light washed over his high, aristocratic cheekbones. He turned away from the fireplace and strode to a game table, giving off another wave of patchouli. As he rearranged the chess pieces, Arrapato sat at his feet. The dog sighed when Raphael started moving again.

"You're restless tonight," I said.

"Am I?" He stopped in front of a bowfront chest, where old tartan boxes were lined up in rows. I watched him move the boxes. He had lovely hands—long, tapered fingers, clipped nails, and sturdy wrists. He glanced up at the crystal chandelier.

"This room wasn't always a library," he said. "It used to be the dining room. I sat right over there."

He pointed toward the leaded glass windows, which overlooked the front lawn. "King George the Fourth sat at the other end of the table. He drank five glasses of wine and knighted everyone, including me."

"That's a lovely story," I said. "But I'd rather hear about this century. What brings you back to Scotland?"

"This room is too quiet," he said, and waved his hand. Music began playing from a stereo in the bookcase. I didn't quite understand his synchronization with electricity. It was mainly with televisions, computers, and stereos, but I liked it.

The Scottish Guitar Quartet began playing something

slow and moody. Arrapato seemed disturbed by the music. He got up, tags jingling, and trotted to the window. He stood on his hind legs and spread his paws on the glass.

Raphael knelt beside my chair and gathered my hands into his. "I have distressing news, *mia cara*."

A cold fist squeezed my heart, and I couldn't get my breath. Was Uncle Nigel hurt? He'd been on a dig in Machu Picchu, and I hadn't heard from him in weeks.

"Uncle Nigel is fine," Raphael said.

"You're reading my mind, but you won't let me in yours."

He leaned closer, pressing his chest against my knees. "I'm so sorry. But Keats is dead."

"What happened?" I blinked, and tears spilled down my cheeks. Mr. Keats was a hybrid, just like me, but he'd still developed maturity onset diabetes. The immortals weren't indestructible, and their physiology was unpredictable.

"Did he forget his insulin?" I asked.

"No." Raphael's voice cracked in the center of the word. In the fifteen years I'd known him, I'd never heard this much anguish in his voice. He kept smoothing his thumb over my hands, as if he were trying to push away my sadness.

A memory broke loose from the coldness in my chest, warm and shimmery, like a taste of sunlight. I saw Keats lift three-year-old Vivi onto a chestnut gelding. She'd rarely smiled in those days, but her mouth had opened wide, her face illuminated from within. Keats had brought my daughter back from despair.

"Was it an accident?" I asked, even though I thought

it unlikely. Mr. Keats had respected the immense power of a thousand-pound thoroughbred.

"Keats was murdered."

A booming sound filled my head, as if I had held a conch shell to my ear. *Oh, God. No.*

"I've talked to the detective superintendent," Raphael was saying. "There was no sign of forced entry. The security system was disabled."

"A burglar?" Innisfair didn't have an art collection, no wall safes crammed with money. Why would someone go to that trouble? What were they looking for?

Raphael's eyes glistened. He let go of my hands and cupped my face. "Keats was tortured. An infinity symbol was carved on his arm."

The room tilted, and I leaned back. Raphael's hands hung in the air, as if still holding my cheeks. I couldn't drag my gaze away from his wrist. His coat sleeve had pulled back, and I saw a black figure-eight tattoo on his forearm. All members of the Salucard Foundation bore this mark, including my late husband. The organization was nonviolent, dedicated to the preservation of the immortals' history and culture. I could not believe that the foundation would hire an assassin to murder anyone, much less Keats. But within the organization, smaller groups had formed, and some of these cabals had no moral boundaries. The Sinai Cabal hadn't bothered me in years, but time meant nothing to a vampire.

I swallowed, and my eyes met his. "You don't think that Salucard ordered the hit on Keats?"

"Absolutely not." Raphael lowered his hands and gripped the side of the chair.

"What about the Sinai monks? They've always been after Vivi."

"They would never put the infinity mark on a human."

"Who else would?"

"I don't know." He glanced away, and I knew he hadn't told me everything.

"Tell me the rest of it," I said.

"Forensics found two types of blood. Type A positive belonged to Keats. The other sample had no distinctive type—clearly a vampire."

I forced myself to take a breath. "Was Keats the target? Or you?"

"I haven't been to Innisfair since Christmas." He lowered his voice to a whisper, as if he couldn't bear to say the words. "You and Vivi had just left."

I started shaking. A strand of hair fell into my eyes, and he smoothed it back.

"I don't want to scare you, *mia cara*. But this vampire might have been looking for you or Vivi."

"A professional assassin would have known that we weren't in Australia."

"Right. Unless the assassin didn't know where you'd gone," Raphael said. "He might have thought that Keats knew."

I jumped when Arrapato barked. He dug his hind feet into the tartan carpet, then started kicking hard, as if he were marking his territory.

Raphael grabbed my hands again. "You and Vivi need to go into hiding. That's why I'm here. How soon can you pack?"

"I've got an emergency bag by the front door." I

paused, thinking of Vivi and her nightmares. "Maybe we should wait until we have more information about Keats."

"I'm not taking chances. You have to leave tonight."

"Vivi won't like it."

Raphael's gaze circled my face. "I'm sorry, *mia cara*."

I pressed my forehead against his shoulder. The wool felt slightly damp, but it gave off his reassuring smell. I heard Arrapato's low growl, followed by a creaking noise. It seemed to be coming from outside the library.

A rush of chilly air hit the back of my head, and I pulled away from Raphael. He looked past me, a startled expression on his face.

I wiped my eyes and turned. Vivi stood in the doorway. Raphael's girlfriend was right behind her. My, she was lovely. Her brown eyes were luminous, as if topaz light were shining behind them. She clutched a handful of herbs.

Raphael got to his feet. "Vivi, can you and Gillian please wait in the hall?"

Vivi ignored him. "Mom, I'm worried about Mrs. MacLeod. She should be back by now."

"Back from where?" I asked.

"Shopping," Vivi said.

"Again?" I felt confused. Mrs. MacLeod had gone to town this morning, and she'd returned an hour later, her car filled with groceries. She'd spent the rest of the day cooking. "When did she leave?"

Vivi shrugged. "Her nose was bleeding."

"Why didn't you tell me?"

She wouldn't look at me, so I knew something else was going on.

Arrapato growled under his breath. Then he began scratching the windows, his nails clicking over the glass. He looked back at Raphael and barked.

Gillian laughed. "He's a busy little thing. Can dogs have attention deficit disorder?"

Raphael hurried to the window, his coat rippling behind him. "Something is out there," he said.

I felt it, too. I got out of the chair and walked over to Raphael. He is five inches taller than me, and I had to tilt my head back to look into his eyes. He tapped the glass, directing my attention to the shadowy front yard.

Raphael's driver, Mr. Fielding, got out of the limo, pulling iPod wires from his ears. Behind him, the fog had cleared, and two lights burned at end of the driveway. I saw the outline of a blue Citroën.

"That's Mrs. MacLeod's car," I said.

Raphael kept staring out the window. "Why isn't it moving?"

I leaned closer, pressing my fingers against the diamond panes. In the driveway, dark shapes passed in front of Mrs. MacLeod's headlights, and a horn tooted.

Arrapato barked again, then butted my legs. I felt Raphael's cool hand grip my elbow, and a second later his voice streaked through my head.

Vampires.

Then, out loud, he said, "You have to leave. Now."

"No," Vivi cried. "We just got here."

Raphael steered me away from the window. As he passed by Vivi, he let go of me and grabbed her arm.

She wrenched away. "You're not the boss of me. Mom, tell him to back off. Or I'll—"

He hoisted Vivi over his shoulder, and hurried out of the room, Arrapato trotting at his heels. I ran into the hall. Raphael was straight ahead, his long legs moving in a blur.

"Hey!" Gillian cried. "What's going on?"

"Trouble," I called over my shoulder. I found my plaid bag in the vestibule, hooked the strap over my shoulder, and rushed into the nippy air. From the driveway, Mrs. MacLeod kept tooting her horn.

Mr. Fielding opened the limousine's rear passenger door, and Raphael put Vivi in the backseat. "What's going on?" she yelled, the cords standing out on her neck.

"Uninvited guests," Raphael said, then helped me into the backseat.

I looked up at the padded ceiling, where pinpoint lights raced around a tinted sunroof and moved to the rear window. I guided Vivi toward the L-shaped row of chocolate leather seats. "Sit down and put on your seat belt."

"No." She broke away, then ran up the narrow aisle, crawled through the open partition, and dove into the front seat.

"Vivi, get back here," I yelled.

"Fielding will take care of her," Raphael said.

I moved past a minibar, toward the back of the limo, and sank down in the plush seat. A loud pop came from the direction of Mrs. MacLeod's car, and then her horn blared without stopping. I glanced at Raphael. He was helping Gillian into a seat, unruffled and unhurried. She perched on the edge, tugging Mrs. MacLeod's raincoat around her.

"I hope those are deer hunters," she said.

Raphael climbed into the backseat, slammed the door, and sat down beside me. "Fielding, get us out of here," he called.

Fielding swiveled around and his broad face appeared in the partition. "There's a problem, sir. The driveway's blocked by vehicles. I counted three. Could be more."

"There's another way out," Vivi said, pointing toward the stone wall. "The golf course is right over there."

"Let's move," Raphael said.

The limo did a U-turn on the lawn, headlights wheeling over the trees, then sped toward the rock wall. Raphael pulled off his coat and tucked it around me. "You're shaking, *mia cara*."

"I'm okay." I tried to smile.

He patted my leg, then pushed away from the seat and knelt in front of the minibar.

"If you're mixing drinks, I'd love a vodka collins," Gillian said, her bottom lip shaking. I could tell that she was the sort of woman who used humor when she was frightened, but Raphael wasn't paying attention. He slid open drawers, dumping ammo into his pockets. Then he lifted a Colt .45.

Hugging the coat to my chest, I looked out the rear window. The glass had been tinted to repel UV light, but I saw figures moving in front of Mrs. MacLeod's headlights. Who was out there? The same vampires who'd killed Mr. Keats? Had they tracked us to Scotland?

Behind Mrs. MacLeod's car, four new lights blinked on. I turned to Raphael. "They're coming," I said.

"I'll be ready, *mia cara*."

The limo careened around the hedge maze. Headlight beams splashed over the rock wall, then picked out the wooden gate. Fielding stomped the gas pedal. The limo blasted forward. Wooden chunks from the gate flew over the windshield and drummed against the roof, and then pieces rattled down the trunk and clattered to the ground.

"Drive faster," Vivi yelled.

"You're busting me ears," Fielding said. "Put a bung in it."

I looked out the rear window again. Four lights trailed behind the limo. I wanted to warn Raphael, but when I turned around, my throat ached, as if I'd swallowed metal screws and washers.

His hands were steady as he loaded bullets into the .45. Behind him, the limo's high beams spilled bright cones through the grainy air. We sped past an Edwardian clubhouse, where men stood on the terrace, clutching whiskey glasses. Fielding turned toward a driving range, knocking over the distance markers, and cut back to the fairway. The sprinklers were on, and water pattered against the clipped grass.

I pulled Arrapato away from the window and held him against my chest. It had been decades since I'd been chased by vampires, but those events had toughened me in a way that I couldn't explain. I felt oddly calm. Then I glanced backward. The headlights veered apart, and muzzle flashes brightened the air around them. I heard bullets slicing around the limo, pinging against the rear fender.

Raphael opened the sunroof, and cold air blew into the car, snapping his shirt. He stood up through the sunroof and fired.

"Somebody tell me what's going on," Vivi yelled.

Raphael climbed back down into the car, the wind sweeping back his hair, and he launched himself on top of me and Arrapato, flattening us against the seat. His arm shot out, and he pulled Gillian toward us.

"Incoming!" Fielding cried. "Get down, Vivi."

A moment later, the limo shuddered, the way a jumbo jet will shake when it hits turbulence. Above us, the rear window exploded. Safety glass pattered on top of Raphael's shoulders. Icy air rushed into the limo, bits of glass clinking against the seats.

Raphael moved back. *"Mia cara?"*

"I'm fine." Arrapato's head popped up. Gillian sat up, too, picking stray bits of glass out of her hair.

I glanced frantically toward the front seat. "Vivi!"

"Mom?" She peered through the glass partition. Her tears had melted her kohl eyeliner, and black lines ran down her cheeks.

"Sir, we need more firepower," Fielding yelled. "It's under the floorboard."

Raphael put the safety on the .45 and handed it to me. He squatted in the center of the limo and peeled back the brown carpet. He lifted a box, flipped back the lid, and took out grenades. He pulled the pins with his teeth, released the levers, and vaulted toward the sunroof.

"Holy shit," Gillian cried, her eyes bulging.

Raphael dropped to the floor again. A boom knocked him against the minibar. Crystal goblets went flying. My ears were ringing so hard, I didn't hear the glass shatter. The air smelled like burned plastic. I raised myself up. Behind us, on the dark fairway, a car was on fire. There was another explosion, and flames surged up. The other car dropped back into the smoke.

In the front seat, Vivi's head popped up, and Fielding gently pushed it down.

"Should we go back for the other car, sir?" he called.

"No, that's what they hope we'll do." Raphael eased down on the seat beside me, one hand on the dog, the other on my knee. I sat still, conscious of the weight of his palm and the smoothness of his flesh. The air smelled like cologne, gunpowder, testosterone, and sex.

Raphael lifted his hand and let out a whoop.

They say that extreme danger can set off an endorphin rush. But I was feeling something stronger. A bolt of sexual awareness rushed through me, stronger than the wind that was flowing through the broken window. My heart started thumping. My breath came out in a rush. Every part of my body felt hot and cold and damp.

If the smoldering look on Gillian's face was any barometer, she was feeling the same way. She scooted in next to Raphael, pushing her breasts into his arm, and ran her tongue over her lips. She brushed one palm over the brown leather seat. "Gosh almighty, it's so soft and luscious," she said, squeezing the upholstery. "Like sitting on a chocolate pie."

"Where are you taking us, Raphael?" I asked.

He grinned, showing a flash of white teeth. "To see polar bears."

CHAPTER 11

Raphael

As the Learjet taxied down the runway, Raphael felt his pulse bumping against his temples. Not because of the car chase. Not because of the explosions. Not because of the mad dash to the Edinburgh airport. His heart was pounding because he was sitting between Gillian and Caro, and one of them was emanating a pheromone that pushed him beyond arousal.

Mio dio, he thought. The source of the hormonal storm was almost unbearable. He pretended to scroll through messages on his iPhone, but his senses were engaged. Using his peripheral vision, he studied Gillian's lovely face and body. Her Southern accent and manners were alluring, the ditzy attitude was annoying, but he suspected great depth behind this façade.

Was she giving off the pheromones? He dipped into her thoughts.

This decoy thing won't work. I know we negotiated a price and everything, but I'm not taking Raphael's money. I make two hundred K a year. I can buy my own Chanel bags, and I do. But you know what? I bet Raphael has never found a woman who isn't a gold digger. I'm not that way. And he's so damn good looking. I can just imagine his porcelain body on thousand-count Italian sheets. Once you sleep with one of them, that's it, you can't go back to human dick. That's why I'm here. Not to be a decoy. But because I can't get this vampire-lust shit out of my system. I want him. We could go into the lavatory now and join the mile-high club. But he's loop-de-loop about Caro. Wonder why? She's not beautiful. Maybe she almost has a Ph.D., but I haven't seen one drop of brilliance. Me, I've got a B.A. in English from LSU and a law degree from Tulane. If Raphael gives me trouble, I'll tie him up in litigation for years. Though I'd rather tie him up with scarves.

Raphael pulled out of her mind, trying not to smile. He lifted his iPhone and made a note to introduce Gillian to a charming vampire from Milan. Signore Lucio Savoldelli would appreciate her mind, as well as her beauty. Perhaps it would be mutual.

A shudder ran through the cabin as the jet picked up speed. He turned to Caro. She held Arrapato in her lap, telling him not to worry. Her cheeks were flushed, and she smelled as if she'd just stepped out of a pine forest. A curl fell across her cheek, and she smoothed it back.

A warm prickle ran down Raphael's spine. He tried to read her thoughts, but he couldn't. She sighed and buttoned up her cardigan. The wool outlined her breasts.

She scraped her teeth over her bottom lip. He became aware of a fullness in his groin, as if his trousers were too tight, and his zipper pressed painfully against him. He needed to conceal his hyperaroused state. Caro was sitting on his coat, so he looked around for a magazine or a blanket.

Nothing.

He reached for Arrapato, and the dog snapped at him.

"Lord have mercy," Gillian said breathlessly, glancing between his legs. "Somebody's packing a mighty big picnic basket."

He shifted away from her.

At the exact moment the jet angled off the runway, Caro looked up at Raphael and smiled. He smiled back. Why did it always feel so good to be around her? Maybe his brain had confused lust with chemical aftershocks. Danger possessed a confusing sexual element. After all, adrenaline had brought down dynasties and destroyed civilizations.

"A really big picnic," Gillian said, fanning herself.

CHAPTER 12

Vivi

As soon as the Learjet was in the sky, Vivi flung off her seat belt and marched up the aisle, where Raphael sat between her mom and Gillian.

"All right, somebody better tell me what's going on," Vivi said.

"We're flying to Norway," Raphael said, his eyes noncommittal.

"That's not what I meant." Vivi crossed her arms. "You threw grenades! You blew up a car."

He nodded, but didn't defend his crazy actions. Worse, her mom just sat there, petting the dog. The plane leveled, and Vivi almost lost her balance. She sat down hard in the seat across from her mom.

In the opposite row, Gillian leaned forward, pressing

her boobs against Raphael's arm. "Well, *I* thought it was exciting," she said. "Raphael, you were fantastic. You threw those grenades like the captain of a SWAT team."

Her gooey, sticky words dripped in the pressurized air. Vivi felt an urge to run to the lavatory and splash water on her face, but she forced herself to stay put. She glared at Raphael.

"Why did those men chase us?"

Her mom set the dog on Raphael's lap and unbuckled her seat belt. She got up and crouched in the aisle, looking at Vivi.

"We'll talk about this later, okay?"

"It's because of me." Vivi swallowed. "Because of that prophecy crap."

Her mom gave Raphael a helpless look, which made Vivi more upset. Like they knew something but were afraid to tell her. Maybe this wasn't about her. After all, they'd been perfectly safe for years and years. But the minute Raphael had shown up at Manderford, weird things began to happen.

"What is really going on?" Vivi asked Caro. "Is Mrs. MacLeod okay? Is someone chasing Raphael? Did he piss somebody off? Does he owe money to a casino?"

Caro shook her head. "Raphael hasn't done anything but try to help us."

"Liar," Vivi said. "Why did he show up in Scotland before sunset? Why were guns and bombs in his limo? Why did a jet just happen to be waiting at the Edinburgh airport? He knew something bad was going down, and he dragged us along."

Raphael glanced toward the front of the jet, where

Fielding sat on a beige leather sofa, hunched over a computer screen. "Our guests need refreshments," he called.

"Vivi, you need to calm down," Caro said. "And lower your voice."

"No. Ask Raphael why he hired Gillian to be your decoy." Vivi gave him a triumphant smile.

"No more talking, Vivi. I mean it." Caro spoke softly, but her face looked tired.

"I'll calm down if you do," Vivi said.

Caro got to her feet and sat down. A few minutes later, Fielding brought their drinks. A Sprite for Vivi and two frosty glasses with brown liquid for her mom and Gillian.

The blonde leaned across Raphael and held out her glass. "Give Vivi a sip of my old-fashioned. It'll calm her down."

Caro's eyebrows went up. "She's only thirteen."

"She's also having a panic attack," Gillian said. "I don't mean to traipse in your beeswax, but she needs bourbon. My mama used to give it to me when I was in diapers, and I turned out okay."

Yeah, right, Vivi thought, and put down her Sprite. She didn't want a drink; she wanted the truth. But she wouldn't get answers while they were on this stupid jet because her mom was secretive and freaky. She wouldn't say anything about the prophecy around Gillian, nor would she say anything mean about Raphael. He'd probably done something horrid, like bankrupted a small country. Or maybe he'd run off with someone's wife.

Gillian was still holding out her glass, red lipstick plastered on the rim; her arm was pressed firmly against Raphael's chest. "Raph, honey. Hand this to Vivi."

Raphael took the glass, ice tinkling, and gave Caro a questioning stare. She lifted one shoulder, not a full shrug, but the little half-gesture that people do when they've given up. Raphael leaned across the aisle and put the drink in Vivi's hands.

"Just one sip," he said.

Vivi turned the glass until she found a clear spot, then took a long swallow. It tasted sugary and tart, but on the way down, it burned like jalapeño jelly. Other than that, she didn't feel tipsy or happy or anything. She took another sip.

"Enough," Caro said.

Raphael looked amused, but he plucked the glass from Vivi's hand and gave it back to Gillian. Caro put down her drink and got up, then walked to the lavatory.

"Let her have another sip," Gillian told Raphael.

"I don't want it," Vivi said. "It tastes like mouthwash. And I don't feel a thing. So *there*."

"Maybe you've got a hollow leg," Gillian said, fishing a shriveled cherry out of her glass.

"I do not," Vivi snapped.

Gillian cut her gaze at Raphael. "Where did you learn to be a ninja vampire?"

"Ninja school," he said.

"Do you always carry explosives in your limo?" Gillian set down her glass.

He didn't answer. From the front of the jet, Fielding called, "At least he didn't bring the flamethrower."

Vivi's cheeks felt hot. She lifted her Sprite and slipped a piece of ice into her mouth. She wouldn't ever admit it, but Raphael had been awesome. He'd thrown that grenade like it was an avocado. She'd never seen anything blow up except on television. In real life, it was icky and cool, all at once. But loud. Her ears were still ringing.

She tapped the tips of her sneakers together, glancing at Gillian. Someday Vivi would wear a red dress, and her boobs would poof up like bread dough. She watched Gillian open a crimson leather pocketbook, pull out a mirrored compact, and finger her curls, humming to herself.

Vivi swallowed the ice, then shivered. "Why are you so calm?" she asked Gillian. "We almost got shot to death."

"Because it's over." Gillian rubbed a finger over her teeth.

"But it could happen again," Vivi said.

"Maybe. Maybe not." Gillian snapped her compact shut and dropped it in her purse. "Life is too itty-bitty to waste time on scary shit. You remember that, you hear?"

CHAPTER 13

Raphael

Halfway to the Arctic Circle, Raphael tracked the sensual smell to Caro. It moved out of her and burrowed under his skin. Or was he imagining it? He tried to look into her thoughts, but each time he tried, he felt a subtle resistance.

Was she blocking him? No, Caro wasn't into games. She was the most honest, decent woman he'd ever known. But there was something else. Something that kept pulling him in. The first time they'd met, he'd felt an elemental attraction to her, but what had she felt?

Nothing, that's what.

That was why he called her *mia cara*, because her name was too potent, and it left a blazing streak on his tongue.

She was so damn sexy. But she also had a tender, maternal side that touched him.

Last Christmas, he'd flown to Innisfair so Caro and Vivi wouldn't spend the holidays alone. Same as always, he'd brought too many gifts. They'd taken the foil-wrapped boxes to the hospital in Adelaide. He couldn't help but smile as he'd watched Caro on the children's ward, the kids' hands caught in her hair, pulling gold strands from her French twist. She'd held a bald toddler on her lap, and she'd looked up and caught Raphael smiling at her.

She'd smiled back. Nothing had passed between them, certainly not from her end. It was just a smile, a pretty one, flooded with peace, as if she'd finally found an unbroken place within herself.

Could she love anyone the way she loved Jude? he wondered. *Could she love me?*

She crossed her legs, and her tweed skirt made a whooshing sound, like a struck match. His pulse leaped up, drumming in his chest. He brushed his leg against hers, and the ice in her glass made a clinking noise. A flutter spiraled in his chest.

I am in trouble now, he thought.

Arrapato had been resting his nose under Caro's arm, but now he lifted his head and gave Raphael a warning growl. Caro stroked the dog's fur with her fingertips, then glanced at Raphael. "What?"

He leaned closer. *Are you all right*, mia cara?

Yes. We'll talk later, okay?

Caro glanced at Gillian, who was working on her

second old-fashioned, one high heel dangling from her toes.

No one can hear us, mia cara. *You and Vivi will be safe in Norway.*

Yes, but will you? How can you survive in twenty-four hours of nonstop sunlight?

I'll be fine. We've been there before, remember?

Caro touched his arm. *Sorry, I can't think straight. The last few hours have short-circuited my brain. Too much has happened. Keats, Mrs. MacLeod. Guns and bombs.*

I regret that, mia cara. *But they were shooting.*

No, no. I'm glad you fought back. But now that you've helped us, you'll be a target.

I don't care.

I do.

He searched behind her eyes, trying to sense any emotion behind her words. Something fluttered past him, as if an iridescent bird had sensed danger and soared away from it instinctively into a leafy tree.

She still had her hand on his arm. Her fingers felt so warm and alive. He quickly closed his thoughts, because she might panic if she saw too deeply into his mind. He'd been in love with her since the first time he saw her fifteen years ago. She'd walked into the library at Villa Primaverina, her hair flying around her shoulders. She was trailed by Jude, who hadn't seemed to notice he was in the presence of an angel.

But Raphael knew.

Caro was so much like her mother, and Raphael had never hidden his affection for Vivienne. Not that he'd ever kissed her, or been inappropriate in any way. But he'd adored both the mother and the daughter. Though that thought in itself was mildly unsettling. Yet there were times when Caro would look up and smile, and she looked like no one but herself. And he had to restrain his emotions because she loved Jude. Then Jude was gone, and the undertow of grief had swept in and sucked Caro down. Now, she'd had ten years to surface from the weight of that loss.

Last Christmas, he'd bought her an orange dress with a plunging neckline and an asymmetrical hemline. She always wore drab colors, and he'd thought the dress might be an instrument of change. She'd hugged him, but after the boxes and ribbons had been cleared, he'd never seen the dress again.

Raphael sighed. The territory of the heart had never been mapped; the terrain was uncharted, and yet it was quantifiable. Even in the eighth century, peasants and kings had understood that when life ended, love would continue.

Caro gave him a teasing smile. *Are you using me to make your girlfriend jealous?*

She's not my girlfriend.

Was Vivi right? Is Gillian a decoy?

Yes.

For what, exactly?

My plan was to send her to Villa Primaverina. I would take you and Vivi to the Svalbard Islands. I didn't think we'd be ambushed at your home. I made sure no one followed us. Fielding drove from London to Dunbar. I didn't dare file a flight plan.

Caro pressed her hand against her temple. *How did they find us?*

I can only assume that Keats was tortured and gave up the information.

But he didn't know where Vivi and I were. Caro shut her eyes. *Wait, Vivi sent him a postcard. She mailed it before I could see what she'd written. She thinks all vampires are like you and Uncle Nigel. She half believes the prophecy is something I made up. A way to control her. I can't make her understand.*

It's a form of self-protection, mia cara. *We don't know what she wrote in the postcard.* He pointed at her untouched drink. *May I have a sip?*

She held it out. As he reached for it, Arrapato leaped up and nipped the edge of his palm, dark eyes glowering.

"Bad Arrapato," Raphael whispered.

The dog showed his teeth, as if to say, *Next time I'll draw blood.*

CHAPTER 14

Caro

I leaned against Raphael's shoulder as the jet streaked over the dark, rumpled North Sea, toward the blinding glare of the Arctic Circle. He stayed with me as long as he could, then he and Arrapato moved to the back of the plane and climbed into a long, coffinlike metal box.

I shut my eyes and fell into a dream. The images were so graphic, I woke up, gasping. It was always the same dream. The moment I fell asleep, a dance would begin behind my eyes. Sensual music always played in the background, Ravel's *Bolero* and Nine Inch Nails' *Closer*, and Raphael would stare at me in a you're-more-than-a-friend kind of way. It was a courtship in dreams, with flirty, witty repartee, a slow dance of lovers moving closer and closer.

And in every dream, I saw a watery road to Villa Primaverina, where Raphael's villa rose out of the lagoon, the oyster-colored palace surrounded by gardens and Romanesque statues.

This is pathetic, I thought. *I'm pathetic.*

At one A.M., the jet touched down in Longyearbyen, a cold, grim village in the Svalbard Islands. Sunlight glinted on the rough, dark gray rocks that lined the runway. At the far end, an elk trotted down the pavement.

Five Norwegian men in puffer jackets loaded Raphael's box into the rear of a huge van. Fielding helped us into the backseat, which smelled like motor oil and gunpowder.

"Why is the sun shining at one o'clock in the morning?" Vivi asked, rubbing her eyes.

Gillian sat down beside her, tugging Mrs. MacLeod's raincoat around her. "Sugar, it's the polar day," she said. "That means the sun doesn't set."

"Not ever?" Vivi asked.

"It only lasts a few weeks," Gillian said.

The men climbed into the van, bringing with them a blast of cold air. We drove around the harbor, where ice floes bobbed in the dark blue water and snow-tipped mountains rose up into the clouds. Along the road, signs warned about polar bears. The town had one main street, and all around it, colorful houses fanned out like Christmas packages, each one wrapped in red, green, blue, yellow.

Vivi made a face when the van stopped in front of a red, three-story wooden house. The caretaker, Inge Utskjoer, met us at the front door. She pulled me into a hug, then turned to Vivi.

"My, you've grown," Inge said, smoothing a wrinkled

hand over her hair, tucking stray, white-blond hairs into a bun. She had pale blue eyes and a stubby nose.

"Hi," Vivi said, giving her a do-we-know-each-other look.

"You came here when you were a baby," Inge said. Behind her, the living room looked like an IKEA catalog—dark blue walls, natural pine chests, white bookcases, slipcovered chairs. Candles burned on a long dining table, plates and dishes lined up like soldiers.

Inge shooed us aside while the men carried Raphael's box through the door, Arrapato's angry, muffled barks drifting through the metal casing. The noise faded when the men turned into a narrow hallway.

"My sons will take good care of Mr. Raphael and Arrapato," Inge said, as if the arrival of a boxed vampire were a normal event.

Gillian and Fielding walked up. The man's eyebrows were level with her breasts. "Do you ever stop talking, darlin'?" he asked.

She patted the top of his head. "Go away, shorty."

"Maybe one of Inge's strapping sons can give you something to chew on," he said.

"I doubt it."

"Hey, Inge?" Fielding called. "Miss Delacroix wants to know if your sons are married or single."

Inge laughed and waved her hand, as if brushing away a mosquito.

Gillian bent over and brushed her lips against Fielding's ear. "If you don't show me some respect, I'll chop you into little pieces."

Inge hummed to herself as she poured blood into a

bowl for Arrapato. She chatted with Fielding, pointing out local delicacies on the buffet table: king crab, sushi, spring rolls, and fish sandwiches.

I sat next to Fielding, who was busily piling crab legs onto his plate. Vivi squeezed in beside me. "Mom, why does Raphael have a house where he can't go outside?"

"He bought it for us," I said.

Vivi gave me a long, level look. Then she picked up a fish sandwich.

Raphael walked in, his hair hanging in damp tangles, his cheeks uncharacteristically pale. Arrapato trotted behind him, looking just as disheveled.

Fielding's gaze swept over Raphael. "You don't look well, guv'nor."

Arrapato peed on Fielding's chair leg, and then the little dog stretched in front of the fireplace, his paws scratching against the rug, and heaved a contented sigh.

Inge bustled into the room, holding a basket of flatbread. "Such a shame about Mr. Keats," she said. "If you need a temporary caretaker, one of my sons can fill in."

Vivi sat up straight, her brow furrowed. "What's wrong with Keats?"

A hush fell over the table. Raphael looked at Inge and shook his head. She blushed and left the room.

"What's wrong with Keats?" Vivi asked again.

I tried to speak, but my throat felt raw, as if I'd swallowed a bone. Raphael turned to Vivi.

"Your mother was going to tell you later." He paused. "Mr. Keats passed away. I'm so sorry. I know you were fond of him."

A sheen came over Vivi's eyes. She balled up her fists and pushed them against her thighs. In a raspy voice, she said, "He *died*?"

Raphael nodded.

Vivi's mouth screwed into a bow. "But he was fine. What happened? Did he forget to test his sugar?"

Raphael was silent for a moment. "God called him home."

"That was mean of Him." Vivi's chin wove. She slid off her chair and ran up the stairs.

I pushed away from the table, intending to go after her. Gillian leaned across Vivi's empty chair and caught my arm.

"Let her work through this. She'll find you when she's ready."

"No, she needs me." I pulled away.

A pained look crossed Gillian's face. "I don't know what's going on, but I'm guessin' that it's pretty bad. Vivi isn't a baby. She's a teenager. You're mixing up her wants with yours."

I sat back in my chair and folded my arms. "You don't understand. Vivi has a skewed understanding of death. She's never lost anyone except her father. Not even a goldfish."

"All the more reason to let her be," Gillian said.

Fielding tossed a crab claw at her. "You're a nosey Parker, aren't you?"

"I just live to please," she said, flicking the claw onto his plate.

I helped Inge with the dishes, then went upstairs. I paused outside Vivi's door—everything was quiet. Too quiet. Maybe she'd fallen asleep. I tiptoed to my room and flopped onto the bed. Blackout curtains covered the windows, and lamplight fell over a blue rag rug, a pine desk, and a pine rocking chair where I'd once rocked Vivi.

Now, all these years later, I couldn't hold her in my lap, nor could I comfort her with words. She was going through a rough patch, as Uncle Nigel called it. Adolescence was particularly hard on hybrids, mainly because of hormones and developmental delays. And that was only the beginning of Vivi's problems.

Me, I'd been a flat-chested, moody teen, a girl who'd spent summers in Corfu or Bulgaria, or anyplace that beckoned archaeologists. I'd hunkered in squared-off pits, scraping a trowel over the dirt, longing for breasts and boyfriends, both of which had eluded me.

One year, I developed curves, and boys began to lurk around my uncle's stone house. But I couldn't seem to keep a guy. I'd blamed it on my uncle, because the moment I would bring a boy into the parlor, my uncle would drag out the vacuum cleaner, and the relentless hoovering made conversations impossible.

A few years later, I realized that I was deficient in some womanly way. I was straightforward with men, incapable of subtlety, and as a result, I said pretty much what was on my mind. Worse, I seemed to be frigid. When a guy kissed me, I felt self-conscious, as if I were in a restaurant, eating lamb stew with my fingers.

The guys always moved on, hooking up with girls who knew how to flirt and kiss. Sometimes a man would stick around—for a while. I was briefly engaged to a banker, but he failed to show up at the party my uncle had hosted for us at Danesfield House, an old country estate on the Thames. However, the fiancé had turned out to be an embezzler and a cheater. He'd missed the party because he'd run away with his secretary.

I'd gotten dumped so many times, I made a list of my fizzled relationships and called it *The Lost Boys*. Much later, I learned that my half-vampire genes were responsible—humans just didn't feel attracted to hybrids and vice versa. My own body chemistry hadn't fully awakened until years later, when I'd been bitten by a vampire, and a hormonal surge had left me with prodigious sexual longings.

I didn't know what would happen to Vivi when she matured. Like me, she was a late bloomer. She'd gotten her first period right before we'd left Australia, and I suspected that was the real reason she hadn't wanted to ride Ozzie.

How long could I protect my daughter from her own genes? I'd tried to be honest, but I'd doled out the truth in digestible chunks. She knew about vampires, hybrids, and the prophecy; eventually I'd have to tell her about the Lost Boys, and I had a feeling that this tidbit would upset her more than her possible role in a vampire apocalypse.

I dreamed that Vivi was a baby, and we were shopping in the open-air market at São Tomé. I set her down for a second to examine a melon, and when I looked for her, Vivi was gone.

I awoke with my hands knotted in the sheet and an unshakable sense of loss. I sat up, blinking at the window, where a white dazzle crept around the edges of the curtain and crept across the wall like fingers.

What time was it? The sky held the same luminous glow at three A.M. and three P.M. In all of this brightness, I'd lost perspective. Like a diver in deep blue water, I couldn't find the surface. I felt a suffocating pressure against my ribs, as if I were wearing a too-tight dress.

I got out of bed, but the dream about Vivi was still with me. I needed to make sure she was safe. I put on a robe, went down the hall, and cracked open her door.

Vivi sat up, the sheet falling across her Ninja Kitten sleeping shirt, the one I'd packed in our emergency bag. "Mom?"

"I didn't mean to wake you," I whispered. "Go back to sleep."

"Who can sleep in this weird light?" She patted the bed. "Come lay with me a while."

I eased onto the bed, and my body curved around hers. I steeled myself for questions about Keats, but she just lay there, breathing in and out.

"Mom, tell me about the desert. When you and Dad were hiding from the bad guys."

I pressed my cheek against the back of her head. "You know this story by heart."

"Yeah, but tell me again."

"Your father and I rode camels through the Wadi el-Deir," I said. "We could only travel at night—"

"Because my dad was a brand-new vampire and the sun would fry him, right?"

"True." I smiled. "Raphael caught up with us in the

desert. He took us into a cave that had drawings on the wall."

"Tell me about them."

"They looked like mermaids. When your dad and I held up our lanterns, the mermaids seemed to swim across the rocks."

Vivi knew the rest of it. The drawings in another chamber had depicted a prophecy of the immortals. The same images were repeated all over the world, in catacombs, caves, and a church on top of Mt. Sinai. The apocalyptic drawings were always the same: humans, skeletons, and a caged baby.

I waited for her to ask about the images and how they were mixed up in the so-called prophecy. Instead, she snuggled closer. "Tell me about your wedding."

"Raphael took me and your daddy to Monaco. I bought him a wedding ring and had it engraved, *To J love the Lass*."

"Why did he call you *the lass*?"

She knew the answer, but I pretended that she didn't. "He grew up in Yorkshire. It's an endearment."

My voice sounded steady, almost serene. I never thought I could talk about Jude without choking up, but here I was, telling Vivi about my runaway veil. Her eyelids dropped lower and lower. She pushed her face into the pillow and sighed.

"Mom, what did he call me?"

"Meep."

A smile flitted across her lips. Jude would have been so proud of Vivi. Talking about him tonight had made me feel peaceful.

After she fell asleep, I wandered down to the living room. Raphael stood next to the fireplace, staring into the glowing red coals. He'd changed into beige twill shorts, a blue oxford cloth shirt, and loafers without socks. His summer-in-the-Hamptons look, I privately called it.

He glanced up. "Couldn't sleep?"

"No." I tried to look into his mind, but I slammed against something hard and impenetrable. What was he hiding?

"Maybe a nightcap will help." He moved to the bar and lifted a bottle of sweet Italian liqueur he'd brought from the jet. He poured it into a tall narrow glass and added ice cubes.

Just the way you like it, mia cara.

"Raphael, if you keep slinging thoughts in my direction, I'll get a headache." And it was true. I could take only so much telepathy before my brain fought back. I carried my glass to an overstuffed sofa and sat down. I kicked off my flats. I took a sip, and ice clinked against the glass.

Raphael carried the bottle to the sofa and sat down beside me. "Did you check on Vivi?"

I nodded. "She's asleep."

"I didn't tell Inge about Mr. Keats's death. She's a hybrid—and telepathic. I can only assume that she picked the information out of my head."

"Or mine."

Still gripping the bottle, he leaned back. "Let's come back here in October. It's cold and dark, but Vivi will enjoy the aurora borealis."

I looked into my glass. In October, Longyearbyen

would be dark twenty-four hours a day. The polar night brought all kinds of tourists—including vampires. "Will it be safe?"

"We shouldn't abandon all hope, *mia cara*."

"Don't you worry." I took a sip of liqueur. "I'm an optimist even when hope is gone. I really believed that Jude would come home."

"I know. Me, too."

I took another sip. "Who sent those vampires to Scotland?"

"I don't know."

"But I've got to find out. It comforts me to know the enemy. And I want to believe that Salucard is the enemy."

"They're an old, honorable organization." He wedged the bottle between his thighs. "They've tried to supervise the cabals. When one becomes too powerful—or radical—Salucard banishes them. But the cabals do not disband. They grow."

"Whatever happened to the Egyptian cabal that initiated Jude?"

"They still belong to Salucard. The monks protect some of the immortals' artifacts."

"You and I stole an important one," I said, thinking of *Historia Immortalis*, an eighth-century illustrated manuscript that depicted the history of the immortal race. Years ago, Raphael and I had taken a large chunk of the book from the monks, and then he'd helped Jude and me escape from the monastery. Now, Salucard had the artifact.

"We're definitely not the Sinai Cabal's favorite people," Raphael said, squeezing my hand. "But they wouldn't send assassins to Manderford Castle. A more dangerous cabal must be responsible."

"Do you have a list of suspects?"

"I'm working on it."

"Until then, we'll keep running." I sighed. "I hope this group didn't track our flight to Longyearbyen."

"No vampire will come here."

"You did."

"An old friend works at the Svalbard Airport. He's monitoring all flight plans to Longyearbyen. Another friend is watching the port. Inge's sons are armed. They're taking turns watching the house."

"I'm still worried."

He leaned his shoulder against mine. "Lay down your fear for one night, *mia cara*."

"I can't choose how I feel."

"Yes, you can. You always have a choice."

"Then I'm choosing fear. It makes me alert."

He set the bottle on a table, then turned back to me. "You look tired. Try to sleep. I'll keep watch."

But I wanted to stay awake. I finished my drink, put down the glass, and tucked my arm behind my head. Raphael's eyes followed my hand. His gaze was almost palpable. Maybe it was the alcohol or maybe it was a vampire trick, but I hoped he would keep on looking.

As his patchouli-and-pomegranate smell wafted between us, the trembly place in my chest broke open like a goose egg, and a peaceable feeling ran inside me. He began kneading my shoulders just the way I liked. I tipped back my head and smiled.

He smiled back. "What?" he asked.

I shrugged. I didn't understand what I was feeling, but it seemed like old fashioned lust. I hadn't been with a man in a decade, and if I didn't move this second, I was going to kiss him and ruin everything.

I stood, and the room began to spin. The air stirred, and Raphael was suddenly beside me, holding my elbows. My arms felt boneless and I sagged against his chest.

"I've got you," Raphael said, and his hand dropped to my waist.

His voice rang through my head like music, and I felt dizzy. Maybe I was jet-lagged, because I couldn't be drunk this fast, not after one glass.

"You're not drunk, *mia cara*," he asked. "You're exhausted."

"It's not polite to read my thoughts, Raphael."

"*Mi scusi*. I lose my manners when I'm around you." He stared at me so long, I thought he might kiss me. *Please God, let him do it.*

"I'll help you to your room," he said.

"I'm not sure that's necessary," I said, but he was already leading me up the stairs, into my room. I pushed a thought in his direction.

I don't want to be alone. Stay with me awhile.

He led me to the bed and pulled back the covers. I locked my arms around his neck. Deep inside me, a sane, sober voice said, *This is a mistake, the kind that changes a good thing into a bad thing.* What was I thinking? People were all around. My daughter. Fielding, Gillian, Inge.

But I wanted Raphael. I pulled him closer and tilted my head at an angle. He'd kissed me only once, and that had been fifteen years ago. But I still remembered it. That kiss had made me climax, but now I believed that it had also planted an idea, one that had finally worked its way to the light, a trembling sprig that would fold back on itself if the wind blew too hard.

"Everything is different now, *mia cara*," he said.

That was just what I was afraid of, but before I had time to think about it, his lips met mine, and his tongue moved through my teeth. It was different from that long-ago kiss, and it pulled me into a sunlit place. He tasted of vanilla and ripe cherries and something earthy that made me instantly aroused. I sensed that he was holding back, and that excited me.

Then his whole body tensed, and for a second I thought he might push me away. His arms trembled as if he were holding something inside him, something I wanted. I slipped my tongue deeper into his mouth, and he groaned. His hand cupped my breast, and I arched against him, a pulse ticking at the base of my throat and in my wrists.

Still kissing, we fell back on the bed, and the mattress creaked beneath us. I slid my foot behind his knee, urging him closer. A low sound started in his throat when I lifted my hips. I brushed against his zipper and felt a hard bulge.

Oh, my. I hadn't expected that. I put a little more movement behind the kiss. He was breathing faster and faster. His hand dropped to my knee. I shivered when the flat of his palm slid up my thigh.

I'd never known such need. He settled his full weight on me. His thighs pushed against mine, his knees nudging my legs apart a little at a time.

"Wait, wait," I said. If he moved one inch, if he even breathed on me, I would plunge right over the edge.

"We've waited too long," he said in my ear. Then my panties were gone and he was guiding himself inside me. He was big, just as I'd expected. My breath caught. He smelled so good. Felt so good.

"Raphael," I whispered.

"I've wanted you so long," he said.

Was this true? His voice sent tingles along my spine, and I arched my back, urging him to move deeper. He still had a way to go, but I could feel my orgasm building, as if I were walking on top of a bridge, teetering back and forth, about to topple.

Just as I started to fall, a whining started up at the bedroom door, followed by furious scratching. Then Arrapato began to howl. Raphael pulled away. Before I could sit up, he was out the door and gone.

Saved by the dog, I thought.

I sat up, brushing my hair out of my eyes. Raphael and I had made love only halfway, so maybe our friendship was only half ruined. I could blame it on the liqueur, but I'd be lying. My body still wanted Raphael, but my mind said, *You can't ever do this again*. Besides, some part of me still felt loyal to Jude. I'd always thought of myself as Penelope—but without suitors. Still, I'd been waiting for something.

When I finally went to sleep, I dreamed about the night my husband had left the island, when he'd been headed to the Gabon rain forest. We'd stood in the airport, holding each other. Saying good-bye was even harder than I'd imagined. My throat tightened, as if I'd swallowed a stone, and I couldn't speak above a whisper. I said all of the right words and yet I left out the most important ones.

As he walked onto the small runway, the wind caught his shirt, and it filled with air, snapping around him. I ran to him and caught his elbow. I could barely choke out the words. "Be careful."

"I'll be back in a month," he said.

He kissed me. I thought of my nightmares, the toothed fish and flying shapes, and the stone in my throat grew into an avocado pit. Some part of me must have known what would happen. Why had I let him go?

Now Jude's face was all around me. His smile, white and radiant, slightly amused. I could see him climbing out of the old claw-foot tub, his arms loaded with books.

I awoke in the shadowy bedroom, my hair webbed across my mouth, my heart thrashing. I turned, half expecting to find Jude beside me. My hand skimmed across the sheet and kept going.

CHAPTER 15

Caro

———

LONGYEARBYEN, NORWAY
SVALBARD ISLANDS

Sunlight glanced off the rooftops as Vivi and I walked
toward the Kaffee House, the world's most northern coffee shop. She hadn't mentioned Keats or Scotland—in
fact, she seemed phlegmatic. Inge's middle son, Henrik,
trailed behind us, a high-powered rifle propped on his
shoulder. No one in town seemed to notice, not even the
chief of police, who smiled at Henrik and said, "*God
morgen.*"

It was indeed a good morning. It was a bit chilly,
thirty-four degrees, but we'd made it through the night,
and nothing terrible had happened. Then I remembered
what Raphael and I had almost done.

Vivi pushed ahead of me, weaving between people in
fleece hats and ski jackets. It was Sunday, and the main

street was jammed with locals and tourists. Here on the Arctic frontier, it was easy to spot the residents because they carried guns. The Svalbardians were so rugged, they'd numbered their streets rather than giving them cutesy names.

I walked past a store that rented guns to tourists—it was illegal to walk beyond the town's well-marked safety zones unless you had a firearm. You never knew when you might run into a polar bear. Like I needed more fangs in my life.

Daylight gleamed on Vivi's razor-blade earrings as she ran up the steps to the café. She stepped past a sign that read LEAVE YOUR GUN OUTSIDE. She opened the café's door, and a bell rang above her head.

I was right behind her. The air smelled of cinnamon buns and coffee. I walked across the narrow room, toward red padded booths that ran along the windows. A counter stood on the back wall, and a family with stair-step blond boys had claimed the stools.

I sat down across from Vivi. Just outside the window, Henrik stood with his rifle, glancing down the street, his breath frosting the air. I unzipped a pale blue jacket that I'd borrowed from Inge. A waitress with a chipped tooth brought water and menus. Vivi and I ordered lattes and *krumkakes*. Then something crashed behind us, followed by a high-pitched cry.

The waitress hurried over to the family, and stepped over a puddle of hot chocolate and broken crockery. The mother was soothing one of the boys, wiping his hands with a napkin.

Vivi watched them a moment, and her lip jutted out

so far, a crow could have used it for a perch. She turned away, earrings clicking violently.

I slid my hand across the table and touched her hand. "Talk to me, Meep."

"About what? Fjords? Glaciers?" She pulled away. "But you know what? At least no one in this town pretends to be normal."

The waitress returned with our lattes and pastry. After she left, Vivi glared at me. "What kind of trouble is Raphael in?"

"He isn't." I glanced out the window. Gillian walked down the street in a puffer jacket that was identical to mine.

"Mom, look at me. Why are you defending Raphael?"

I dragged my gaze away from Gillian. "He hasn't done anything wrong. He's done everything right."

"Oh, that's a good answer, Mom." She leaned across the table. "Is he mind-controlling you?"

"Don't be silly." I felt queasy, and I pushed my mug aside.

"Whatever." Vivi slumped down in her seat and tugged at her pink bangs. I studied her face. It was bland as a cabbage, but what was hidden behind those layers?

"Are you still having bad dreams?" I asked.

"Nope." She took a sip of her latte.

"Do you want to talk about anything?"

She shook her head, then pointed at my mug. "Your latte is getting cold."

"I don't want it. I'm feeling—" I broke off as a blinding pain gathered behind my eyes.

She held up one hand. "Mom, I know you're trying to

help. But I'm not ready to talk. Okay? So just drink your latte."

No, I didn't want it. I was sick to my stomach. I gave Vivi a helpless look. Her face had turned purple, as if she were holding her breath. I saw my hand lift the mug and bring it to my mouth. I drank fast, as if I were swallowing a dirty river, nothing but silt and sour heat rushing to my belly. Finally the mug was empty. As I lowered it, a red drop slashed across the white rim. I reached up, patted my mouth, and my fingers skidded.

"Mom? You okay?"

I held out my hand. Blood.

Vivi started to whimper. She pulled napkins from the metal dispenser, then leaned across the table and pushed the thick wad into my hand. I pressed the tissues to my nose. In seconds, the paper felt soggy, and I heard something patter against the table. I pinched my nostrils and tipped back my head.

"Get ice," I said in a clogged voice.

The Norwegian family began to whisper, and it was the strangest thing: Until now, I'd known only a few words of this language—*hallo, takk, God morgen*—but I suddenly understood what the mother was saying.

Don't stare at the lady, Gunnar, she was saying. *Yes, I know she's bleeding. Turn around and finish your chocolate.*

A few seconds later, I couldn't understand her. I felt something wet and warm hit the back of my hand and curve around my wrist. I pressed the tissue under my nostrils. The cushion in my booth hissed as Vivi squeezed in next to me. She pressed a bag of ice against the bridge of my nose.

"Here's fresh napkins, too," she said, her voice shaking. "Mom, I'm so sorry,"

Why was she sorry? It wasn't her fault. I swallowed, and my ears popped. I pressed the new tissues under my nose. The waitress came back and dragged a sponge over the table, leaving a beaded crimson swirl on the Formica.

"Are you all right, miss?" she asked.

I nodded, dimly aware that Vivi kept dipping a napkin in water, scrubbing the front of my jacket. A gust of floral perfume swept over the booth, then Gillian sat down across from me, her face pinched and white. "Honey, are you okay? Should I find a doctor?"

"It's just a nosebleed," Vivi said.

Gillian blinked at the bloody napkins. "It looks like a slaughterhouse."

I dabbed my nose. "It's stopped," I said. "Let's go home."

Halfway to the red house, Vivi burst into gulping sobs. Gillian draped an arm around her. "Your mama is fine."

"No," Vivi said. "I wanted her to stop talking. I wanted her to drink her latte. I wanted it so bad. Then she started bleeding."

"You didn't cause it," Gillian said, pulling her closer.

"But Mrs. MacLeod's nose bled, too."

"Honey, that's why God made noses."

Their voices seemed to come from the bottom of a glacier. Behind me, I heard Henrik's boots crunching on the frozen gravel. I remembered how sick I'd felt in the café, and how much I hadn't wanted to drink that latte. And yet, at the same time, I'd felt compelled to lift the mug. My mind and body had been disconnected.

I took a step, and the sky tilted. The sun flipped upside-down. Before I hit the ground, Henrik took my elbows.

"*Takk*," I said.

"You're welcome," he said in English.

Vivi broke away from us and ran inside the house. Gillian helped me into the dark foyer and pulled off my stained jacket.

"Lord, it's gloomy in here," she said, groping for the coatrack.

I could see more than I wanted. Dark splotches covered the front of my sweater, as if someone had flung a glass of burgundy at me. Vivi wasn't in the room, but her coat hung on the rack. Probably she'd gone to her room.

As I walked toward the stairs, I heard the jingle of Arrapato's tags, and then Raphael got up from the sofa. His eyes widened when he saw my sweater. "What happened?"

"Nosebleed," Gillian said. "Somehow Vivi got it into her head that she caused it. But it's just the cold air. And all that traveling Caro's been doing. Airplanes are notorious for drying out the sinuses."

Raphael's forehead wrinkled. "Would you mind if I talked to Caro alone?"

"Yes, I *do* mind," she said. "I've been shot at, chased by assassins, and brought to a wasteland. I'm freezing my butt off, *and* I broke a fingernail."

"I'm sorry you're unhappy, Gillian. But I still need to talk to Caro." He took my hand. "Let's go to my room."

The kitchen door opened, and Fielding's head popped out. "Come here, Gillian. I made you a little something."

Her gaze passed over him. "How little?"

"It's hard to explain." He winked.

"Just a second, shorty." She turned to Raphael and wagged her finger in the air. "I'm not finished with you, mister. Lay one hand on Caro, and I'll whip your ass."

After Gillian walked to the kitchen, Raphael's mouth quirked up at the corner, and the other edge slanted down, his signature I've-got-a-secret look.

I didn't protest when he led me to his room. It was just like mine—white walls, window covered with blackout draperies, knotty pine furniture. Before he shut the door, Arrapato shot through and stared boldly up at his master.

"*Testa di merda*," Raphael told the dog, and then both of them walked to the bathroom. A moment later I heard water running.

I stood next to the bed, trying to ignore the tightness in my chest. A coppery tang rose up from my hands and sweater. Red crescents were packed beneath my fingernails. I wanted to plunge into a soapy tub, but I felt sure that Raphael wanted to talk about last night.

He came out of the bathroom holding a damp washcloth. He rubbed it gingerly over my upper lip. In seconds I was all caught up in his smell and the pressure of his fingertips beneath the rough, damp cloth. I gulped down a breath.

"Hold still, *mia cara*. I won't bite."

"A pity. One little nip, and you'd be flat on your back." I snapped my fingers. "You'll be gasping for air. It took Jude a long time to build resistence to my poisons."

"I'm not worried."

I put my hand on his cheek. His nostrils flared, and I

knew he could smell my blood. "This is serious," I said, but I wasn't referring to my tainted antigens. "I'm sorry about last night. I wish I could blame alcohol, but I can't."

"Mia cara—"

I lowered my hand. "We can't let that happen again, Raphael."

"I didn't bring you to my room to seduce you, *mia cara*. I didn't want Gillian to hear what I'm about to say."

"We could've talked telepathically."

"You've just had a nosebleed. Do you want a headache, too?" He put the washcloth in my hands. "Tell me what happened."

I started with the latte and ended with the ice pack. When I finished, he said, "It's not the cold air. Vivi might have caused it."

I just stared. "How?"

"Hemakinesis."

"What?"

"A telekinetic ability. It's linked with Induction."

"What's that? I'm confused." I sat down on the bed.

"Your grandfather could bend thoughts—that's Induction. And sometimes he made people bleed—hemakinesis. These talents are rare. Without them he wouldn't have survived the Albigensian Crusade."

Raphael was referring to my father's father, Etienne Grimaldi of Limoux, France. Their castle was one of the few that hadn't been sacked during the crusade. Most of the clan, including my grandfather, had died later, during the Inquisition. They'd also had precognitive dreams.

I rubbed the washcloth over my fingers. "You're wrong.

Vivi isn't telepathic. She can't read minds. Wouldn't she need to hear a thought before she could bend it?"

"This isn't about telepathy. It's another type of energy, and it's about control. Her will becomes her victim's will."

I quit scrubbing my hands and looked up. "Victim? You're scaring me."

"You need to be scared."

"Of my own child?"

His gaze dropped to the front of my sweater, then moved up to my face. "She would never hurt you intentionally. But Induction and hemakinesis are weapons."

"You're saying she inherited this from me?"

"You're a Grimaldi."

"I can't bend thoughts. I've never been able to read anyone's thoughts but yours. And I can't make people bleed."

"Vampire genetics isn't my forte."

But Jude had understood it. I squeezed the washcloth. It felt just as cold as the air between me and Raphael. "Why would Vivi suddenly develop this . . . what's it called?"

"Induction." He paused. "She's almost fourteen. Her body is starting to produce hormones."

I frowned. He was talking about her cycle. I didn't know about hormone production in humans, but I knew how it worked in hybrids.

"Don't look so worried, *mia cara*. I know a psychiatrist who can help her."

My stomach did a little flip. "Vivi needs a shrink?"

"Dr. Sabine d'Aigreville is an expert in vampire telepathy and telekinesis. She lives in Paris. If Vivi is an Inducer,

Sabine can help her develop and master these raw abilities."

"Is this why Keats was killed? Because someone thinks Vivi has a peculiar talent?"

"You're her mother and *you* didn't know." A muscle worked in his cheek, and he looked away.

"You're holding back," I said.

He sighed. "I don't want to add to your worries. But I spoke with the detective who's handling the murder investigation at Innisfair. Keats's hands were mutilated, except for one finger. On that finger was a gold ring. The police assumed it was his wedding band."

"I never saw Mr. Keats wear a ring. He wouldn't let Vivi wear jewelry when she went riding. He said it was just one more thing to get snagged in a bridle or reins."

"It wasn't his ring, *mia cara*." Raphael paused. "It was Jude's."

Something fell inside my chest. I dropped to my knees, and the washcloth hit the floor. "It was on his finger when he went to Gabon. It was too tight. He never took it off."

"The inscription says *To J love the Lass*."

"You're telling me the ring made it out of the rain forest, and *he* didn't?"

Raphael looked away.

I clawed the neck of my sweater. It felt too tight. I couldn't breathe. What were the odds that Jude's wedding band would turn up ten years later on the hand of a murder victim? Was the killer taunting me, hoping I'd think Jude had suffered? Or had Jude lost the ring in the bush?

Raphael turned back to me. "Are you sure he was wearing it, *mia cara*?"

"Yes." I swallowed. "I guess it's possible that someone found his body and took the ring. Maybe they sold it."

"How would a random buyer make the connection that *J* stands for Jude? Or that you are the Lass?"

"I don't know. Maybe the ring was sold again and again. Someone figured it out. Someone who'd known Jude."

I looked up into Raphael's eyes, trying to feel his thoughts. Pain sliced through the left side of my chest. "You believe that someone on the expedition team stole the ring? And that same person killed Keats?"

Raphael was blocking me, but the sudden flash in his eyes told me that I'd guessed his thoughts. "Or maybe Jude is still alive," he said.

"Come on, Raphael. You don't believe that. If Jude had survived, he would have found a way back to me and Vivi."

"We need to know if he was wearing his ring the day he disappeared."

"How?"

Raphael hunkered beside me and took my hand. "The moment I found out about Keats, I called my friend in Interpol. He's been researching the team members on Jude's expedition."

"But all of them died." I remembered how I'd badgered the Al-Dîn Corporation after Jude went missing. They'd insisted the team had perished in a fire. I hadn't believed them, and I'd hired an American firm to look into it. Raphael had contacted Interpol. They'd all reached the same conclusion: No one on that expedition had survived.

"A British virologist made it out of Gabon. Dr. Emmett Walpole."

"And it took Interpol ten years to figure this out?"

"Apparently Walpole dropped off the grid. He's been moving around. Now he's living in Zermatt."

"I don't see how Interpol found him."

"Two months ago he flew into Berlin. He acted paranoid. Bought a one-way ticket. A custom's agent questioned the authenticity of the passport. The authorities let him go, but he ended up on an Interpol Red Notice. His passport cleared Zürich a few weeks ago. From there, he was simple to trace."

"Has he been traveling under his real name all this time?"

"I don't know. But I'm going to find out."

I had to concentrate on what Raphael was really saying. Was he leaving Longyearbyen? Was he going to fly to Switzerland and talk to this virologist? Zermatt seemed like an unlikely place for a vampire. They didn't like high altitudes.

"I'm going tomorrow," Raphael said.

He'd heard my thoughts? I tugged my hand out of his grasp.

"Can't you phone this man? Or e-mail?"

"He might run."

"Why? Because of the passport incident?"

"Or maybe he saw something in Gabon that he wasn't meant to see."

I exhaled. "Will you be safe?"

"Zermatt is a good place to hide from vampires."

"And a bad place to be trapped," I said. "They don't

allow cars. You can't drive away if things get hairy. You'll have to take the train."

"I've been to Zermatt many times." He smiled. "You and Vivi need to come with me."

"But we're safe in Longyearbyen."

"Inge takes Coumadin. She could hemorrhage if Vivi tried to Induce her."

"That's a big leap, Raphael. We don't know for sure if she has this. . . skill. Maybe my nose bled because I've been on too many airplanes."

"That's not why."

"You don't know. You're not a doctor."

His hand grazed the side of my face. "I'm not taking chances."

I leaned back. "What happens when we leave this island? Whoever is chasing us will know the second your jet leaves."

"We're not flying. I chartered a boat to Amsterdam."

"You're speaking as if this is a fait accompli."

"Our new passports will arrive this afternoon," he said.

"That was fast. Hope they're not flagged."

"Inge's sons know the right people."

"And so do you." I paused. "What happens after you talk to Dr. Walpole?"

"We'll go to Paris. Sabine can help Vivi."

"And you trust this doctor?"

"Yes."

"What about Gillian? Is she coming, too?"

He nodded. "We'll need a decoy when we leave Zermatt. She can go to Villa Primaverina, and we'll go to Paris."

"Why can't we go to Paris first?"

"Dr. Walpole moves around. I don't want to lose this chance to see him."

"If Vivi's going with us, she'll need to tone down her hair."

A floorboard creaked in the hall. The bedroom door swung open, and Vivi glared at me. "Good luck with that, Momster."

———

Gillian walked to town and returned with hair dye and bland clothing. She lured Vivi into the kitchen, then made a big show of kicking me out. Gillian and I had planned the makeover ahead of time. I knew Vivi wouldn't let me tamper with her style, but she might listen to Gillian.

An hour later, I heard a scream. Vivi ran into the living room, tears beaded in her eyelashes. Her hair had been dyed auburn, and Gillian had given her a short, androgynous trim.

"I could pass for a boy," Vivi wailed. The razor-blade earrings had been replaced with discreet pearl studs, one in each lobe. She wore jeans and a gray flannel hoodie.

"You look adorable," I said. And she did, even if she seemed much younger than thirteen.

Gillian came out of the kitchen. "Relax, your hair will grow."

Vivi wheeled around. "Give me the scissors. Let's see how you like a crew cut."

"Lose the attitude," Gillian said.

"Attitude is all I've got."

As Gillian left the room, I put my hands on Vivi's shoulders. "Will you please calm down? We need to pull together as a family. When this is over, you can dye your hair green, and I won't say a word."

"You really think this trouble will end? Because I don't." Her face crumpled. "This is Raphael's fault. He's in some kind of mess. He's put us in danger, and it's not fair!"

"It's the other way around, Vivi. We've put *him* in danger."

Her chin trembled. "It's because of me, isn't it? Because I've got that thing inside me. That Induction thing."

A humming sound began in my ears. "Who told you about Induction?"

"I heard you talking to the Prince of Darkness." She wiped her eyes. "I know what I am. A freak."

"You are not. You're smart and brave and beautiful."

"If you believe that, you're whacked."

"Gillian's right. You need an attitude adjustment."

"That won't help. I've got a nest of vampires in my family tree."

"So do I."

"But you don't give people hematomas."

"You can learn how to control it."

"What if I can't?"

"You will. And you know why? Because you're like your father." Tears pricked my eyes, but I kept going. "When Jude was a young man—a human—he was doing research that almost got him killed. Vampires cut the tendons in his heels and set his lab on fire."

She swallowed, then wiped her eyes.

"Your dad lost everything," I said. "He was forced to leave his home and his family. He taught himself to walk again. Then he met me. And we made you."

"Big mistake." Her eyes filled again.

I took her face in my hands. "You have the strength of the Barretts inside you. It's greater than the messed-up genes you inherited from me. You will get through this, because you are Jude's daughter. He loved you. And he would have been so proud."

"Oh, Mom." She pushed her face against my neck. "I'm sorry. I don't mean to be a brat. I'm just scared."

"I know, Meep." I pulled her close, but I couldn't shake the feeling that she was moving away from me, and no force on this earth could make it stop.

CHAPTER 16

AL-DÎN COMPOUND
SUTHERLAND, SOUTH AFRICA
JULY 8

Half a world away, in a windowless compound, a six-hundred-year-old vampire contemplated his mortality. Mustafa Al-Dîn leaned back in the leather infusion chair, taking care not to dislodge the intravenous tubing in his right arm. Stem cell leukemia had made him vulnerable to the faintest of light, and a red glow illuminated the treatment room, blurring the tiled walls.

A sable ferret climbed onto the chair, its nails scratching over the leather, and it perched on Mustafa's leg. The vampire laughed, then reached in his pocket, pulled out a plastic bag, and removed a glistening cube of raw meat.

"Bram, come closer," Mustafa said.

The ferret's long body seemed to glide over Mustafa's

silk pajamas, and then the animal tilted his head and bit into the meat.

"I wasn't always like this," Mustafa told the ferret. "Once, I dined with Sultan Mehmed II. I commanded the *sipahis*. Do you know what an honor that was—to lead an entire cavalry division? To be a hero in the Ottoman army?"

The ferret crept closer. Mustafa pulled another chunk from the bag. He smiled as Bram sank his fangs into the meat.

"Oh, you should have been there the day I rode out on my white stallion," Mustafa said. "I crossed the Danube to kill the infidels. I was feared by thousands. Now I am dying."

The door opened, and Tatiana Kaskov stepped into the treatment room, leaning on a cane. She wore camouflage shorts, and a bulky bandage covered part of her thigh. Her gaze went to the intravenous machine. "How are you feeling?"

"Stronger. But you're limping." He fed another piece of meat to Bram, then cut his gaze back to Tatiana. "What happened to your leg?"

She sank down in a chair. "A crazy Australian shot me a few days ago."

"Be more careful," Mustafa said.

"I won't let it happen again." She reached out to pet Bram, and the ferret snapped, barely missing her thumb.

"Have you found the girl?" Mustafa asked.

"We almost had her in Scotland. She and her mother have dropped off the grid."

"Any leads?"

"Not yet."

"Keep looking." Mustafa scratched the ferret's chin. "Bram and I want to feel the sun on our faces before we die."

"I've found a lab that's selling black market equipment," Tatiana said. "They might have hybrids. We can breed our own quarter vampires."

"That will take months. But go anyway."

She got to her feet, leaning on the cane. "I'll call when I get to Romania."

"Romania?" Mustafa cried, and Bram slunk back.

"That's where the lab is."

"No." Mustafa shook his head. "I want nothing to do with the Romanians."

"Why not?"

"I don't want to talk about it."

"No problem. I'll redouble my efforts to find the Barrett girl."

A man with grizzled hair strode into the room, his lab coat whiffling around his ankles. He wore blue scrub pants and paper booties covered his shoes. A white badge was clipped to his coat pocket. DR. J. HAZAN was printed in black letters. He carried a thick medical chart.

"I'm feeling stronger today," Mustafa said. "The chemotherapy must be working."

Dr. Hazan's topaz eyes moved from Mustafa to Tatiana, then down to the ferret. "I wish I had better news," he said, opening a metal chart. "Your white blood cell count is a hundred and ten thousand."

"Could it be a mistake?" Mustafa asked.

Hazan tilted his head from side to side, as if considering

the matter. "The machine might not be calibrated prop-erly. I will check and run another test. But these values are too high. It looks like the methotrexate isn't working."

"Use another drug," Mustafa said.

"It's not that simple. Your cancer cells have become resistant."

"Try something else," Mustafa said. "I need more time."

Hazan faced Tatiana. "What about that doctor you brought from Beijing? Why hasn't he made progress with Mustafa's gene therapy?"

"He is working diligently," Tatiana said.

"No, he isn't," Hazan said. "Yang isn't pulling his weight. He doesn't seem knowledgeable about gene therapy."

"He's an expert," Tatiana said.

Hazan closed the chart. "He's a troublemaker."

"I don't like your attitude," she said.

He smirked. She lunged across the room and grabbed Hazan's throat. The chart fell from his hand and clattered to the floor. He began wheezing. The ferret dove up Mus-tafa's pant leg, and the bulge moved to his knee.

"Enough, Tatiana," he said. "You're scaring Bram."

She let go of Hazan and pushed him against the wall. He rubbed his throat.

Mustafa's gaze flicked over Tatiana. "Bring Dr. Yang to me."

"Right away." She gave Hazan a venomous stare, then hobbled out of the room, her cane thumping on the tile.

After the door closed, Hazan stepped away from the

wall. "You need to rein her in," he said, his voice tight. "She's out of control."

"Her emotions are strong when it comes to me," Mustafa said. "I turned her into a vampire."

"You?" Hazan blinked. "But when? You've been ill for so long."

"Right after the Soviet Union collapsed. She needed something new to believe in."

"She is Russian?" Hazan's eyebrows went up. "Her accent isn't Eastern European."

"That is intentional. She is a talented linguist. Her father wanted her to dance in the Moscow Ballet. He was a physician like you. A doting father. But he died when she was young. Her mother was a bitter woman. She squashed Tatiana's dream."

"How did she get from ballet lessons to the Al-Dîn compound?"

"She worked in East Berlin for the KGB. Then the Wall fell, and she went to the United States. After Gorbachev stepped down, she came to Istanbul. We met. And for a while, there was no East or West. Only me. And her. She is dear to me. Do not provoke her again."

"No, sir." Hazan swallowed.

Mustafa gently pulled the quivering ferret out of his pajama leg. "You have scared Bram. Leave us alone."

Dr. Hazan averted his gaze and slipped out of the room, his lab coat sweeping behind him. After the door clicked shut, Mustafa gave the ferret a piece of meat. The door opened again, and Bram dove under Mustafa's arm.

Tatiana led Dr. Yang into the room. Two Turkish guards walked in behind them, carrying AK-47s.

"Come closer, doctor," Mustafa said.

Yang took a mincing step forward. He was a middle-aged Chinese man, and pockmarks covered his face. His white lab coat was neatly buttoned, showing the top edge of a blue scrub shirt. He brushed his dark, straight bangs off his wide forehead.

"Dr. Yang, how long have you been a guest in my compound?" Mustafa said.

A flicker appeared in Yang's eyes. "Nine months, sir."

Mustafa frowned. He hated the Eastern mindset, but he understood it. Yang's goal would be to "save face" at all costs. His dignity and pride would be more important than the truth.

"Is my treatment ready?" Mustafa asked.

"Not yet," Yang said.

"Another delay?" Mustafa said.

"I am having trouble programming your T cells. The mice are not responding to the treatment."

"You said this in January. And you said it again three months later. Now it is July, and nothing has changed."

"I'm culturing more T cells. They will be ready in a few weeks."

"But I might not be here to listen to your excuses." Mustafa glanced at Tatiana. "How much has this project cost so far?"

She walked toward Yang, pulling out her smartphone. A few moments later, she said, "Almost three hundred thousand dollars."

"Such a waste," Mustafa said.

Yang's gaze moved from Tatiana to Mustafa. "I did not know money was an issue."

"No, but time is. And I do not like to fund bad investments." Mustafa waved at Tatiana. "Is he the best you could find?"

"The very best," she replied.

Yang clenched his hands. "I was one of Beijing's leading pioneers in gene therapy. I have published dozens of papers. I have a Ph.D. and an M.D. I *am* the best."

"You were," Mustafa said. "Hubris has been your undoing."

"Please, I need a few more weeks," Yang said, his voice rising.

"Tatiana, find me another geneticist," Mustafa said.

"But he's close to a breakthrough," she said.

"I am." Yang gave Mustafa a pleading look. "Sir, may we speak alone?"

Tatiana grabbed Yang's arm. "Mustafa needs to rest."

Yang's gaze was latched onto Mustafa. "You don't understand what's going on."

Mustafa signaled his guards. "Tatiana, please help the guards escort Dr. Yang to the animal laboratory. Lock him in the bat chamber."

"No, *no*." Yang dropped to his knees. "I can tell you things."

"If he speaks again, shall I cut out his tongue?" Tatiana asked.

"Slowly," Mustafa said.

The guards hoisted Yang to his feet and dragged him

out of the room, his legs kicking, his screams punching through the crimson air. Tatiana followed them. The yelling ended after the door clicked shut.

Mustafa leaned back in his chair, enjoying the sudden quiet. He lifted Bram and smiled. "You are a prince among ferrets," he told him. "Act like one."

PART FOUR

HEART-SHAPED
WORLD

CHAPTER 17

Caro

ZERMATT, SWITZERLAND

Vivi and I walked out of the Zermatt railway station, flanked by Gillian and Fielding. Four new bodyguards pressed in around us, men with shaved heads and sunglasses.

Vivi tugged my sleeve. "Will we be safe here?"

"Vamps don't like Zermatt. The high altitude bothers them."

"What about Raphael and Arrapato? Will they get sick?"

"We'll know tonight."

A red horse-drawn carriage waited outside the station. *Seiler Hotel Mont Cervin* was painted in gold above the door. The driver held up a card that read, Della Rocca.

"We're the Della Rocca party," I said. I gave him my plaid bag, grateful that Raphael had arranged this ride.

"Mom, I don't know about this," Vivi said, her face pinched and wary.

"It's all right, Meep," I said in a soothing tone. "Zermatt doesn't allow motorized vehicles. The driver works at the Mont Cervin. That's where we're staying, okay?"

"Okay."

Gillian set down two Louis Vuitton bags, then looped her arm around Vivi. "Isn't this the darlingest carriage you ever saw? Aren't we lucky?"

"I guess," Vivi said.

A minute later the four of us were seated, and the carriage was moving toward the sunny main street, the guards hurrying behind us. I looked out my window at the crowded Bahnhofstrasse. Hotels and restaurants lined the street, their balconies overflowing with flowers, and flags stirred in the crisp morning breeze. Snow-tipped mountains rose up into a pale blue sky. Ahead of us, a group of tourists spread apart and an electric taxi glided forward, emitting a faint hum.

"Oh, the air smells so clean." Gillian folded her hands. "This is a storybook town."

Fielding reached across the seat and tweaked her ear. "With a happy ending, I hope."

"Honey, if you don't stop pestering me, I'll have no choice but to tar and feather you."

"Good luck finding tar," Fielding said.

"Pancake syrup will work just fine."

The carriage slowed as goats trotted down the middle of the street, their bells tinkling, the wind ruffling their black-and-white fur. Vivi's face split into a grin as she leaned against the window. I caught myself smiling, too.

We checked into the Mont Cervin Palace.

Our suite had a view of the Matterhorn. The porter set Raphael's luggage in one bedroom, my plaid bag in another.

Vivi ran her hand through her hair, making it stick up in tufts, then flopped down on the sofa. "I guess we can't go outside, huh? Look around? Grab some fondue."

"Maybe later."

"Like when I'm fifty years old."

For a moment I saw myself through her eyes—my arms always open, ready to catch her before she tripped. I loved this child so much, I'd sucked the life right out of her.

I moved to the window and opened the yellow curtains. I stood in a puddle of light facing the Matterhorn.

"Here we are in another cold place," Vivi said.

A rap at the door made me turn around. "It's just us," Gillian called.

Vivi leaped off the sofa and let them in. Gillian had changed into a chocolate cashmere sweater dress that darkened her eyes. On her feet were cream stilettos. She was loaded down with shopping bags. A rough, red spot covered her chin, and she covered it with her hand when she saw me gawking.

Fielding walked in behind her, smelling of soap and toothpaste, his cheeks flushed. He wore a purple velour jogging suit and tennis shoes. He stopped beside Vivi. They were exactly the same height.

"I saw a game room at the end of the hall," he said, pointing over his shoulder. "Let's check it out."

"I'm so over games," Vivi said.

"You've never played air hockey?"

"Get real. Momster won't let me go anywhere with you."

Gillian edged closer to me. "It'll be all right."

I felt dizzy, as if I were at the top of a Ferris wheel, and Gillian was beside me, rocking the seat. But I knew my daughter would be secure with Fielding.

Everyone was staring at me, so I walked to the door and opened it. "Have fun," I said, forcing myself to smile.

"For real?" Vivi blinked.

Fielding steered her into the hall. "Let's go before she changes her mind."

Gillian shut the door. "I know what you're thinking," she said. "That I slept with Fielding. Well, I did. And let me just say, he knows how to play my xylophone. But we'll talk about men later. We've got to get cracking. We don't have much time."

"For what?"

"You need to teach me how to be you. See, I'm leaving for Italy day after tomorrow. And I'll be posing as you. Just to throw off those vampires." She opened one of her shopping bags, lifted out a U.S. passport, and flipped it open. "I'm you."

Caroline Barrett was printed beneath Gillian's smiling picture. She ran her finger over the laminated photo. "I wonder how much this fake passport cost Raphael?" she said. "It looks real. It's got a hologram and everything."

I looked up. "How much will it cost *you*? Gillian, you can't be my decoy."

"Why the hell not?"

"Do you have any idea what's going on?"

"Yeah, Fielding told me." She waved her hand. "I know

about Keats, your husband's ring, the prophecy. But I just
don't believe that Vivi is a thirteen-year-old harbinger of
death."

"What if she is? Would you still travel to Venice with
this passport?" I tapped the document.

"Hell, yes."

"Please don't. I've got a bad feeling."

"Caro, I haven't known you long, but you strike me
as the type who always has bad feelings. You're confusing
pessimism with voodoo mysticism. Nothing bad will happen. I'm going to Italy, and that's that. If I were scared—
or if I just didn't want to do it—I wouldn't be here."

"That's just it. Why are you putting yourself at risk?"

She slipped the passport into the bag. "I'm not doing
this on a whim. Sure, at first I was trying to get cozy with
Raphael. But he's not into me. Besides, I feel really sorry
for Vivi."

I stiffened. "What do you mean?"

"No offense, but I had nice parents and a bad childhood. The kids at school bullied me. That's what happens
when a girl is different. I was leggy and matured early. I
lived in a world of swamp rats. I'm talking about little
old girls with stubby legs who wept if they grew taller
than five-three. Where I grew up, petiteness was a
religion."

She paused, took a breath, and continued. "I'm drifting off the point here, but you need to understand why
I'm doing what I'm doing. The decoy thing. See, my
daddy was a repo man. Nobody ever tried to kill us, but
we weren't beloved. We were ostracized. Why, you would
have thought my daddy was the executioner at Angola."

I watched her face, trying to concentrate. She talked so fast, I had trouble keeping up.

"Your daughter is isolated," she said. "If I can help Raphael catch the rat bastards who want to hurt y'all, then Vivi can be a regular kid. And you can get on with your life."

"These people are worse than rat bastards, Gillian. They have no moral boundaries."

"You're not lookin' ahead. In a few years Vivi will be looking at boys—maybe she already is. She needs normalcy."

"And you're probably thinking you can make a difference. But this can't be fixed."

"I have to try. Look, I'll be honest. I'm not doing this totally for Vivi. There's a hurt child inside of me, and I'm trying to fix her. Every time I help someone else, I kinda help me. So don't try to talk me out of it." She slapped my leg. "Before we get to work on my new look, we need to go over one more little thing."

I was instantly wary. "How little?"

"He's six foot one. Blond. Dark eyes. And his first name starts with an *R*."

"What about him?" I crossed my arms.

"Raphael is in love with you."

"No, he isn't."

"I've seen how he looks at you."

I felt the heat rise to my face.

"See?" She pointed. "You're blushing. Honey, that man is all under your skin. Don't be a fool. Let him love you."

"I can't talk about this right now."

"When would be a good time? You've been a widow how long? I bet you've got cobwebs up inside you." She put her arms around me. "I know you lost the love of your life, but you've got to let him go."

My face tightened. "Jude's wedding ring was found on the hand of a man who'd been tortured and murdered."

"I was shocked when Fielding told me. I'm so sorry."

"Then you know why I'm not concerned about cobwebs."

"If you don't move on with your life, Vivi can't move on with hers. What's gonna happen when she's eighteen? She'll replace those razor-blade earrings with something really bad, like the unholy trio—sex, drugs, and alcohol. Aren't you worried about that?"

"I just want to keep her alive. That's why I'm concentrating all of my energy on her."

"Honey, that's the problem. You're concentrating too darn much. Fielding says you've always focused on her. Oh, don't get all huffy on me. No one's saying you're a bad mom. You were *too* good. So good, you haven't noticed that she's almost fourteen. The rules have changed. What you see as loving attention, Vivi sees as suffocation."

Tears gathered behind my eyelids. Some part of me knew that Gillian was right, but I wasn't ready to concede.

"You're saying I'm worse than a momster. I'm an anaconda."

"An anamomda?" Gillian said helpfully.

"If Jude were here, he'd know what to do with Vivi."

I could see him so clearly, the man he would have been. He would be sitting at a desk, books and scientific journals stacked around him, and he would toss Vivi the keys to his car. He'd say, *Drive carefully, Meep. And if the police stop you, run like bloody hell.*

Gillian shook her head. "Your husband isn't here. And Raphael doesn't strike me as the kind of man who'll sit on ice while you get your priorities in order. I've seen how he operates. When he gets it in his head to travel somewhere, he makes a few phone calls and takes off."

I smiled. "True."

"But you're slow and methodical. You think you'll fly apart at the seams if you fall in love with a reckless man. But he's exactly what you need."

"The timing couldn't be worse."

"Uh-huh. Like I said, when will be a good time?"

"When people aren't dying."

Gillian waved her hand. "If your problems went away, you'd think of a hundred more. And you want to know why? Because your heart was broken, and it hurt so goddamn bad. You'll never open yourself to that kind of pain."

I stared, awestruck. She stared back, her brown eyes gleaming with intelligence, as if she'd seen through my bullshit. "Are you sure you're not psychic?" I asked.

She smiled. "A good lawyer understands human nature. I learned everything I know from Granny Delacroix. She used to say that you can't control love any more than you can control a hen that's laying an egg. It happens when it's ready, not when you're ready." She lifted a bag. "Enough girl talk. Help me get ready for my trip."

CHAPTER 18

Raphael

MATTERHORN GOTTHARD RAILWAY
TÄSCH, SWITZERLAND

An hour after sunset, Raphael carried his dog onto the red train that led to Zermatt. He walked past a group of Asian tourists, found an empty seat in the rear compartment, and lifted Arrapato onto his lap. Both of them stared out the window, watching the tracks fall off into darkness.

Raphael had never been to Switzerland in daylight, but he smelled the coldness blowing off the mountains. He'd chosen a circuitous route from Amsterdam, changing vehicles every two hundred kilometers, but he felt as if he'd forgotten something.

Arrapato looked up at him, ears trembling, and Raphael knew the dog wanted to bite him. "You've never been like this," he said.

Arrapato looked away in disgust.

"I should have named you Diabolique," Raphael whispered. "You scratched that bedroom door on purpose. You didn't want me to make love to Caro."

The dog glanced back and tilted his head.

"Just say it, Arrapato. You think I'm bad for her."

The dog scraped his paw over his muzzle. Raphael imagined dozens of canine thoughts spinning up, curled like a watch spring.

"You think I'm a ladies' man, don't you?"

Arrapato gave him a contemptuous look.

Raphael shrugged. A vampire could be defined as blood and bone and testosterone—and stem cells. The term *man-whore* could apply to many. But not him. Not anymore. "I've reformed. You know this, Arrapato."

Not that it mattered. He and Caro hadn't spent more than two seconds alone since that sunny night in Longyearbyen, when he'd told her about Jude's ring. He'd wanted to give her time to absorb the news, and to give himself a chance to control his emotions. He remembered how she'd stared up at him, her lips stained with her own blood, pewter lights shining through the blue in her eyes. An ache had spread through his loins. He'd wanted to climb on top of her, moving one inch at a time, sinking his weight on her thighs and breasts, feeling her warmth float away from her skin like sunlight on a peach.

She'd closed her mind before he could see how she'd really felt. Or maybe she'd felt nothing.

He bent closer to the dog. "I'm going to tell Caro how I feel. That I love her."

Arrapato snorted, as if to say, *I double-dog dare you.*

CHAPTER 19

Caro

MONT CERVIN PALACE
ZERMATT, SWITZERLAND

I'd calmed down by the time Arrapato and Raphael arrived that evening. Then Gillian and Fielding worked me over. They wanted to take Vivi shopping. "I've got it worked out," Gillian said. "We'll dress up like tourists and blend in." She opened a bag, pulling out fanny packs, baseball caps, and baggy fleece shirts printed with the Swiss flag.

I finally relented.

Vivi couldn't stop grinning. She flung her arms around me. "Later, Mom."

Gillian punched my shoulder. "See? Wasn't that easy?"

Raphael and I went downstairs to the restaurant. The dinner hour was winding down in the Grill le Cervin. We had the place to ourselves, except for three middle-aged women who were eating dessert.

A waiter led us over a red Persian rug, past empty tables where beige napkins were fanned out like starfish. An open grill stood at one end of the room, giving off the smell of charbroiled fish and beef. After we were seated, I kept rearranging the salt and pepper shakers.

"I feel safe in Zermatt," I said, then shifted my fork an inch to the left.

"That makes one of us."

I lifted the pepper shaker. "Will Vivi be all right with Gillian and Fielding?"

"Yes," he said, watching my hands.

I put down the shaker.

A waiter in a crisp white shirt and a black vest took our orders—rare chateaubriand for Raphael, cress soup and grilled prawns for me.

Raphael leaned back in his chair. "We should come back at Christmas. The porter told me that lights are strung on the balconies and in the trees."

I pushed my water glass directly over the tip of my knife. "I'm sure it's lovely."

"So are you." He rose from his chair, leaned across the table, and kissed me. I was so surprised, I pursed my lips, as if I were about to take a breath before plunging into icy blue water. His tongue gently stroked mine. I was dimly aware of the amused murmurs from the middle-aged women. Then I felt him pull me into a dark place. His pulse was all around me, like a strummed violin. A shiver raced between my legs.

Oh, no, I thought. *Not here.*

Before I climaxed, Raphael broke the kiss and sat down. He smoothed his hand over the front of his shirt;

I could feel the middle-aged ladies watching. I breathed in and out. I was caught somewhere between extreme arousal and anger. I rearranged my spoon and knife.

Then I felt him inside my head. Mia cara, *look at me.*

Dammit, why did you do that?

You know. Because of what happened in Longyearbyen. I can't stop thinking about it. I can smell you on my hands. Your smell is inside me. I'm crazed. I thought . . . I thought if we were in a public place, I would keep my hands to myself.

I lifted my chin, narrowing my eyes for an instant. *But you didn't.*

Are you attracted to me at all, mia cara?

You're giving me a headache. Does the gift shop sell aspirin?

He made a sweeping gesture with his hand. *I'll buy you a gift shop. I'll buy you an aspirin factory.*

We stared at each other. His lips twitched at the edges, as if he were trying not to smile. I couldn't hold my mouth still, either. We burst into laughter.

His hand slid across the table, and he touched my fingers. *Let's go upstairs,* mia cara. *Let's start over again.*

It was tempting. I couldn't remember a time I'd been completely alone with Raphael, because we were always surrounded by chauffeurs, butlers, and guards. And Vivi had always been with us. When she was younger, she'd crawled all over us, begging to be tickled or tossed in the air.

I shook my head.

He sat straight up, and I heard my ears pop; I knew he'd gotten out of my mind. Thank God. I lifted my wineglass and took a long drink.

The waiter brought my soup. I arranged my napkin in my lap, taking my time, brushing my fingers over the rough linen, knowing that Raphael was watching. I wanted to do something naughty, but I looked Amish in my black sweater set. So I undid the top four buttons on my cardigan, then leaned over my soup bowl, giving him a full view of my cleavage.

Raphael's eyebrow went up, and then he smiled.

I finished my wine and ordered another glass. I am not much of a drinker, and I could almost hear the alcohol fizzing inside my bloodstream. I wanted to see if I could tempt Raphael to lose his composure, the way he'd almost made me lose mine. So I slipped off my right shoe. The tablecloth wasn't long enough for my nefarious plan, but what the hell. I lifted my spoon and dipped it into the soup. At the same time, I brushed my toes over Raphael's leg.

He drew in a breath.

I slid my foot under his pants leg and drew a squiggly line on his ankle.

"You are wicked," he said.

"And depraved," I said, then slid the spoon into my mouth.

He dabbed a napkin on his upper lip. "I can't believe you're doing this."

"You started it." Actually, I was a little surprised at myself. I'd never acted inappropriately in a restaurant or any public place; I mean, really. Look at all the trouble I was in. It had to be the wine, right? Yes, definitely. It wasn't because of my dirty dreams or the memory of that night in Longyearbyen.

I glanced around the restaurant. The middle-aged

women had gone, and a busboy was piling dishes into a plastic tub. I raised the spoon and slowly licked off a thin layer of soup.

Raphael lowered his napkin. "We're supposed to do a blitz attack on Dr. Walpole tonight. Now, I don't think I'll be able to go."

I withdrew my foot. Raphael looked disappointed. I dipped my spoon into the bowl again, then drew lazy circles in the broth. Then I lifted the spoon and slowly fit it into my mouth. Then I repeated the process.

"Oh, this is so good," I whispered.

"Caro." His voice held a desperate edge.

"Yes, darling?" I said sweetly. I lifted my foot, slid it between his thighs, and pressed my sole against his crotch. I felt something hard and thick.

He blinked.

"There's something sensual about soup," I said.

"I wouldn't have guessed."

"There's an art to eating soup. You have to thrust the spoon into the broth, pushing it all the way into the bowl. Like this." I demonstrated. "See? You put it in and pull it out."

The whole time I'd talked, I was kneading his crotch with my toes.

He exhaled so hard, ripples moved across the surface of the soup. Two spots of color bloomed in his cheeks, and a pulse throbbed in his neck.

"Your heart is beating so fast," I said.

"Make it beat faster." He slipped his hands under the table and grabbed my ankle. He pulled my foot against him. His lips parted, and a little burst of air came out.

I lowered my spoon, watching his face.

"*Mia cara*, please. I'm begging you. Let's go upstairs."

"Raphael, do you want to take me to bed?" I whispered, trying to look innocent.

"Yes."

"Do you want to make love to me?"

"God, *yes*. Caro, please. I can't wait . . . another . . . second."

The waiter returned and set down a sizzling platter of buttered prawns. I repressed a smile. Oh, I was going to have fun with the textures and layers of these crustaceans.

The waiter put down Raphael's plate. "Will there be anything else?" he asked.

"No, thank you," Raphael said, keeping his hands under the tablecloth. He didn't speak until the waiter left.

"We should stop," he said.

"You're holding my foot. I'm not holding yours."

His pupils dilated. I knew he was trying to look into my mind.

Okay, this could be entertaining. I took a huge gulp of wine and set down my glass. Then I picked up my fork and scraped it over the prawns. When he slipped into my head, I was ready.

Raphael, I want to feel you inside me. I want you to enter my deepest places. I want to taste you—

I forgot what I was thinking when he wrapped his hand around my foot and began moving his thumb in a circle. He lifted his other hand to his mouth and wet his fingers.

"What are you doing?" I asked.

"You'll see." He lowered his hand and ran his fingers between my toes.

I barely had time to gasp before the orgasm roared through me. I felt like I'd been hit by a wave, sucked down by a current, water rushing over my thighs and hips and breasts, all of my secret places. Oh, it felt so . . .

Another wave pulled me under. My pulse crashed in my ears. I gasped. My fork clattered against the table. When it was over, I couldn't get my breath. Perspiration skidded down my neck.

He was smiling. I'd underestimated him; I'd thought that I could reduce him to a quivering puddle. And just *look* what happened. "You ought to be ashamed," I said.

"Yes, but I'm not." He winked.

When we walked into our suite, Vivi had not yet returned. The rooms were dark and empty. Arrapato's tags rattled as he trotted around us in tight circles, a blue squeak toy gripped in his jaws. As I switched on lamps, I found a note from Vivi. She'd returned to our room and couldn't find me. She was having dinner with Gillian and Fielding, and the guards were still with them.

I remembered the joy on her face when she'd seen the goats. It didn't take much to make her happy. She needed more of those moments.

"What happened to you in the restaurant?" Raphael said. "Were you toying with me? Or were you attracted?"

"Both."

"Mia cara." He pulled me into his arms. I leaned against him, brushing my head against his chin. A hot rush moved through me, like a flame burning holes in

paper. A small vestige of sanity took hold. *Don't do it, Caro*, I warned myself. *He's not good for me. I'm not good for him. Besides, if Vivi walked in, how would I explain?*

He leaned in to kiss me, and I stepped back. "Just don't. Please."

"We can get another suite." He eased forward.

"While you're at it, get me another life. One without murderers or prophecies."

He lifted my hair, bunching it around my chin. "Let me take you away from all that. Just for one night."

Only one? That was the real problem. His fingers threaded in my hair, grazing across my cheek. I could barely draw in a breath. Some part of me knew how it would feel to make love with Raphael, because of that night in Longyearbyen. But my dreams had been explicit and colorful, large and fraught with meaning, like one of my favorite paintings in the Louvre, Veronese's *Wedding at Cana*. Instead of water into wine, the transformation would be widow into wanton woman.

"That's a lot of words starting with *W, mia cara*," Raphael said.

"You just can't stop reading my mind," I said, straightening his lapel. "Let me spare you the trouble. I'm thinking about more *W* words. *Wail. Withered. Wallis Warfield Simpson Windsor.*"

"I love your mind." He moved closer. "I've been dreaming about you. Vivid dreams. Every night. Something is changing between us. Can't you feel it?"

Yes, I felt it.

"You're dreaming about me, too," he said. I moved back, tilting my head. He'd really been dreaming about me? Just thinking about that made me tingle. I wanted to finish what we'd started, but not until we were completely alone. I needed to cool the air between us and focus his attention elsewhere.

"I thought of another *W* word," I said. "*Walpole*. Let's find him."

CHAPTER 20

Caro

Raphael tucked Arrapato under his jacket, and we walked out of the hotel, into the cool night air, past cafés and shops that blazed with light. Dr. Walpole lived just beyond St. Mauritius Church on Kirchstrasse, so we headed in that direction, trailed by our guard. He was a stocky man, each shoulder the size of a country ham.

As I moved down the crowded Bahnhofstrasse, my plaid bag thumped against my hips. I rarely left it because it contained the things that I needed to control my uncontrollable life. Illegal passports, breath spray, hairpins, pocket calendar, euros.

Then I thought about Vivi. This small separation felt like a huge step. An optimistic one.

Raphael brushed up against me, gripping Arrapato. "It's chilly tonight. Are you warm?"

I wasn't sure if he was talking to me or the dog. I slid my hand into the pocket of a white down jacket. I'd changed into tight jeans, and I'd tucked the legs into my red boots. Gillian would approve of this outfit. Just thinking about her made me worry. She was taking a huge risk. Even if vampires didn't attack her, she could be jailed and deported for using an illegal passport.

"Gillian is an attorney," Raphael said. "She knows the law. And she wants to help us."

I glanced up at him.

"I know you're frightened for her. But you cannot control everything and everyone."

"And you're a master at sweet-talk."

He handed Arrapato to the bodyguard, then led me around the back of St. Mauritius Church, toward a black iron fence, and we turned into the Mountaineers' Cemetery. Flowers lay beneath many of the headstones, and candles flickered in the distance.

I glanced at my watch. The second hand had stopped. I tapped the dial, and the hand swept around once and stopped again.

"Look at these inscriptions, *mia cara*."

I lifted a strand of hair out of my eyes. This was just like Raphael to deviate from a planned excursion and go on a nighttime cemetery tour. I paused beside a weathered slab. Arthur Emory had died in 1963, while climbing the Weisshorn. Next to him, A.K. Wilson, age twenty-six, had perished on the Riffelhorn in 1865. I walked past a stone that read, *Be Not Afraid*.

My vision blurred. I felt disoriented, as if I'd stepped into a place where time malfunctioned. I wiped my eyes as I walked past a tall gray stone. A red pickax was propped against it, next to a bouquet of white edelweiss blossoms. The epitaph read, *"I Chose to Climb."*

"We all have choices," Raphael said.

"And every choice has a risk," I said. "I'm not ready to—"

He silenced me with a kiss. I felt pieces of myself scatter into the chilly night air. The front of my jacket made a whispery sound as I pressed against him. Then he drew back.

"I love you, *mia cara*. But I cannot compete with a ghost."

I flinched. *Be not afraid.*

"I've known you fifteen years," he said. "You and Jude were together five. Give me one night, Caro. Just one. If I don't please you—"

His voice rang through me, a holy sound like church bells. I shook my head. "Pleasure isn't the issue. It never was."

"I want to feel you," he said. "I want two people in the bed. You and me. Tell me that you want this, too."

My knees began shaking. "We're in a graveyard," I whispered. "Have a little respect."

"Can you vanquish your ghosts for one night?"

"Not until we talk to Dr. Walpole," I said.

We walked out of the cemetery. Raphael retrieved Arrapato from the guard and took my hand. We turned into a stucco-and-timber apartment building. The lobby was furnished with brown nubby sofas, a dusty potted plant, and three security cameras. The air was cold and smelled medicinal. We walked up the stairs to the second floor and walked along a blue-carpeted hall, the guard lagging behind, checking out the security cameras that angled down from the ceiling.

I turned my face away. Raphael stopped in front of a blue door. Off to the side were a blank nameplate and an electronic keypad. Black masking tape covered the doorbell. He tucked Arrapato under his jacket, ignoring the ferocious growls, then knocked.

Behind us, I heard a rustling noise—the sound a pit viper might make if it crawled over a silk blanket. Then I heard a strangled gasp and shoes stamping the carpet.

I turned.

A guy in a hazmat suit held a pistol to our guard's head. "Hands in the air," he told us. His voice was muted by a Plexiglas helmet, but I detected a British accent. He was tall and rangy, and a black patch covered one eye. The other one bulged like a hard-boiled egg. His free arm snaked under the guard's chin.

"Get your hands up. Hurry. Or I'll cap him."

The guard lifted his hands. I raised mine, too. Raphael was holding Arrapato, so he could lift only one arm.

"I said both hands, you bloody idiots," the guy in the hazmat suit yelled. A circle of mist spread inside the Plexi-mask and disappeared. He pushed the gun a little harder against the guard's temple.

"Raphael can't raise his other hand," I said. "He's holding a dog. Don't shoot him."

Arrapato chose that moment to poke his head out of Raphael's coat, his pale pink tongue lolling out the side of his mouth.

"I'm going to put my dog on the floor," Raphael said. "I will move slowly."

"No!" the man yelled. "It might have germs."

I kept holding my hands in the air, ignoring my tingling fingertips. I was pretty sure we'd found Dr. Walpole. At first, the black patch over his left eye had confused me. Vampires have acute vision, and I'd never seen one wear a patch.

"Please let go of my friend," I said, nodding at the guard. "You're choking him. He's having trouble breathing."

"Why does your friend have a gun? He's a guard, isn't he?" Walpole's good eye wobbled. "Who the bloody hell are you people?"

"I'm Raphael Della Rocca, and this is my friend Caro. We're looking for Dr. Emmett Walpole."

"Never heard of him," Walpole said. "But if I had, why are you looking for him?"

"I need to talk to him," Raphael said.

"Why?"

"It's private," Raphael said.

I recognized something of myself in Dr. Walpole. He was an example of a man who'd taken caution too far.

He tilted his head, his nostrils twitching, and another burst of condensation hit the glass. "Are you people vampires?"

"I'm a hybrid," I said quickly. "But the dog is a vampire."

The doctor looked at Raphael. "What about you, Romeo?"

"You know what I am," Raphael said.

Walpole turned to the guard. "What's the name of your employer?"

"Mr. Della Rocca," the guard said in a strangled voice.

"Why did he hire you?"

"To protect the lady and her daughter." The guard winced.

Walpole took the guard's gun. "Get on the floor. Spread eagle. But don't touch your nose to the carpet."

The guard put his hands on his head and lowered himself to the ground. Walpole walked toward me and Raphael. "Get on the floor."

"No," Raphael said. "We're not here to harm you."

"How can I be sure? Do either of you have any diseases?"

Raphael and I shook our heads.

I felt Walpole probe the edges of my mind the way a moth flutters around a lampshade. I forced my thoughts to go still, and the fluttering receded. He turned to Raphael. "What about the dog?"

"He's never sick."

"Does it have fleas or mites?"

"No. They can't stand the taste of a vampire's blood. You should know that."

Walpole's jaw moved, as if he were chewing on this information. "Are you sure you haven't been exposed to a viral illness?"

Raphael nodded. "My immune system is strong. So is Caro's."

Walpole pulled a plastic bag out of his pocket. Inside were plastic handcuffs. He handed it to me. "Tie up your guard."

I set my plaid travel bag on the floor, then shuffled forward. The guard was holding his face off the carpet, just as he'd been instructed. I looped the ties around his wrists, then moved cautiously back to Raphael. He put his arm around me.

Walpole gave me the once-over. "Well, well. What have we here? A blond Dorothy Gale." He gestured at my red boots. "You know, the girl from *The Wizard of Oz*. And you've even brought Toto and the wizard. Lovely!"

I tried to keep my face still and emotionless. Vampirism had a tendency to magnify human quirks, but Walpole was full-bore paranoid. What had broken his mind? Something he'd seen in the jungle? Or had he been psychotic before the expedition?

"A vampire with a dog can't be all bad," Walpole said. "I'll let you come inside. But only for a minute."

Keeping his good eye on us, he walked to the door. Then he faced the security box, blocking our view of the keypad. A series of beeps stabbed up into the air. I heard a click, and the door whooshed open.

"Take off your boots, Dorothy," he said. "You, too, Mr. Vampire. The plaid bag stays out here, too."

Raphael kicked off his loafers, then held my elbow while I struggled to kick off my boots. Walpole led us into his apartment, past a table that was sheathed in plastic. Photos sat on top, each frame encased in a plastic bag. I glimpsed a smiling, middle-aged woman in a tweedy jacket, and two spotted dogs sat at her feet. Except for the table, the room had no other furniture. The white walls and ceiling gave off a clean, astringent smell with a trace of camphor. I smelled something else, too, dirt and darkness, making me think that I'd fallen into a rabbit hole.

Walpole sprayed Raphael and me with something that smelled faintly of chlorine bleach. He set the guns on the table, pulled off his helmet, and scraped his gloved hands through his hair. Sweaty, taffy-colored strands jutted up in all directions. Then he picked up his pistol. If he'd held a torch rather than a gun, he would have been a dead ringer for the Statue of Liberty.

Raphael nodded at the gun. "Caro and I aren't armed. If you don't put away those weapons, we're leaving."

Walpole continued to hold the gun. "Is that a threat?"

"No, but you could accidentally shoot someone I love," Raphael said.

When Walpole didn't lower the gun, Raphael touched the back of my hand. "We're wasting our time, Caro. Let's go."

As he led me to the front door, my shoulders tightened. I didn't like turning my back on Walpole.

"You're wrong," the doctor called. "I would never shoot anyone in the back."

I bit my lip. So much for blocking my thoughts. What else had he picked up? I turned. He set the gun on the table and held up his hands, fingers splayed.

I stepped toward him. "It's good to meet you, Walpole."

He moved back. His eye went to the gun, then flicked back to me. "Did the Al-Dîn Corp send you?"

I shook my head. "No."

"How can I be sure?"

"I don't care if you're sure," I said.

Raphael put a warning hand on my elbow.

Walpole tilted his head. "You're really not here to kill me?"

"My husband went on an expedition to Gabon ten years ago, and he didn't come home." I watched his face. How was his paranoid brain processing this information?

"What does that have to do with me?" he asked.

"You were on that expedition. My husband's name was Jude Barrett. I need to know what happened to him."

"Why should I tell you?" Walpole said. "Because you want to put your husband's *ghost* to rest?"

Raphael squeezed my hand, and then his voice sliced through my head. *Quick, close your thoughts.*

Something seemed to uncoil from Walpole's eye, a force that reached inside me and tugged, as if a rubber stopper had been pulled from a drain. I felt a heaviness move inside me, the weight of water as it spiraled down a pipe. Then I felt the twisty thing leave.

Walpole's good eye cut to Raphael. "Oh, I see. She won't consummate the relationship. Which shouldn't be confused with consommé. Though the truth is slippery as soup on a spoon." He turned back to me and grinned, showing crooked white teeth. "Isn't it, missy miss?"

My cheeks burned. Walpole's gaze sharpened. "What's his name again?" he asked.

"Jude Barrett."

Walpole's eye circled my face. "Was he a big chap? A biochemist? Early thirties? British, wasn't he?

I nodded.

"I see." His eyelid twitched, giving his face a lunatic sharpness. "What's your question?"

"Was my husband wearing his wedding ring?"

Walpole gave me a pitiable look. "Why do you ask? Because you think he and Tatiana were snogging?"

"Are we talking about the same Dr. Barrett? Who is Tatiana?"

"The team leader," Walpole said. "Russian. Quite pretty. Crawling with STDs, I'm sure. I stayed away from her. But the other chaps didn't."

"So, do you remember if Dr. Barrett wore his wedding band?" I asked.

"Actually, I do. He was in my tent one day, and I saw it on his finger." Walpole's eye narrowed. "Anything else?"

"Just one," Raphael said. "What happened on that expedition? How did you escape?"

"That's two questions," Walpole said.

"Here's a third," Raphael said. "Was Jude wearing his ring when trouble started at the camp?"

"How would I know? Every day was troubled. Why all this fuss over a ring? And please don't tell me it's a family heirloom."

"You're right," Raphael said. "It's about more than a ring. I'm in love with Caro, but our relationship is going nowhere. She needs closure. We'd appreciate anything you can tell us about Jude."

I tried to find an empty space in my thoughts, but it was damned hard.

Walpole rubbed his temple, as if the gentle movement helped loosen the memories. "I've got to be honest . . ." He paused and looked down at his gloved hands.

I felt so disappointed. Usually a liar will preface a sentence with *To be honest*, but I tried to keep an open mind. Maybe Walpole would tell the truth.

"I only saw Dr. Barrett once," he said, averting his gaze. "I don't know what happened after the mercenaries arrived."

"Mercenaries?" I said.

"You didn't know?" Walpole gave me a pitiable look.

"Initially I was told that the team had gone missing," I said. "Then I found out about the fire. The camp was burned, wasn't it?"

"I suppose all of that's true—technically." Walpole sniggered. "I can't give you a time frame. It was so long ago. Early one morning, just before dawn, I heard gunfire. I got up and looked out my flap. Mercenaries were all over. I didn't want those ugly men to touch me. So I cut a slit in the back of my tent and ran into the trees."

"So you didn't see what happened to Jude?" Raphael asked.

"How could I?" Walpole's eyelid moved up, as if it had been stitched tightly to his brow. "The mercenaries had lit a huge fire. Smoke was everywhere. Men were screaming. I ran. I kept going until I reached the waterfalls. Then I got caught piggy-in-the-middle by daylight. That's how I lost my eye. I hid behind the falls, but the water didn't quite cover me."

"Why were the mercenaries at the camp?" Raphael asked. "To guard the scientists?"

"No, we had Congolese guards. They were killed, too."

"Too?" I cried.

Arrapato began to whimper, and Raphael stroked his head.

Walpole's eye moved to the dog, then up to Raphael. "I went back to the camp after sunset. The bodies had been piled up like cordwood. Nick Parnell was poking around the camp—he'd escaped, too. He told me that the mercenaries had killed everyone. I hope they ripped Tatiana apart."

The level of anger in his voice surprised me. "Excuse me?"

"I hated her," Walpole said. "We all hated her. She took a fancy to your husband."

What was he implying? I struggled to keep my face slack.

"Tatiana went into his tent several times," Walpole said.

"How do you know?" I narrowed my eyes. "A few minutes ago, you claimed that you saw Jude once."

"His tent was near mine. I saw Tatiana go in and out. When she went into a man's tent, it wasn't to discuss business. Like I said, everyone slept with her. Except me."

I swallowed. I just couldn't believe it. Jude hadn't been the type to womanize. Our vows had been a sacrament.

"Don't mourn him," Walpole said. "Build a life with Toto and the Wizard. By the way, don't bother to look me up again. I'll be gone by this time tomorrow."

Raphael sighed. "What happened after you got out of the jungle? Did you contact Al-Dîn? Did you tell them what happened?"

"No." Walpole ran his hand through his hair.

"Why not?" Raphael looked puzzled. "Are you telling us everything?"

"Yes."

"Why have you been in hiding for the past decade?" Raphael said.

"Why are you turning this interview into an interrogation?" Walpole snapped. "But you seem like a decent chap, so I'll explain. I don't like to stay long in one place—too many germs."

"You're a vampire," Raphael said. "You have a superior immune system. Why would you worry?"

"Germ warfare," he said. "The Chinese are involved. I'm serious. Bird flu is coming. H5N1 will recombine. When it's airborne, look out; vampires are going down."

CHAPTER 21

Vivi

The next morning Vivi stood in front of the Alpine Center with Gillian and Fielding, watching the glacier goats trot down the main street. Tourists were lined up on both sides of the street, aiming their cameras at the herd.

Vivi reached out and her hand skimmed over a goat. It seemed as if she'd left Australia a thousand years ago, but it had been only eleven days. She'd never been this happy, and she was starting to think about the future. One day she would live in Zermatt, and she'd get a pet goat. She'd learn how to hang glide and ski. She might even climb the Matterhorn.

Gillian took Vivi's hand. "Let's walk around." Fielding and two bodyguards scurried behind them. They rode the train to the Matterhorn, past the glaciers, and returned to town late that afternoon. They stopped in a jewelry store, and Gillian bought herself a diamond horse-shoe ring. It fit perfectly on her pinkie finger. Vivi was hungry, so they went into the Portofino Grill and stepped around an old boat, where the *antipasti* was set out, and moved into the crowded blue dining room.

After Vivi was seated, she looked up at Gillian. "Did my mom have a nervous breakdown? Because she never lets me do stuff like this."

"Your mom is fine," Gillian said, lifting her menu. "Don't question every little thing she does."

"Why not?" Vivi asked. "She questions me."

"Enjoy the moment," Gillian said.

"Because it'll pass?"

"Sugar, everything passes."

Vivi's hand stole across the table, and she touched Gillian's new ring. "I wish you weren't leaving tomorrow."

"I'll be at Raphael's villa if you need me. You know the phone number?"

"Mom does."

"I've never been to Italy," Gillian said. "Think I'll like it?"

"Raphael lives on an island. It's close to Murano. The décor is red, white, and black."

"Sounds pretty," Gillian said, then looked down at her ring. "I think our luck is fixing to change."

Hours later, Vivi walked into the hotel suite, loaded with packages. The room was dark, the curtains pulled tightly over the sunny windows, hiding the view.

"Hey, Meep," Caro said, coming out of her bedroom.

"Look what Gillian and I bought," Vivi said.

She followed her mom into the bedroom and dumped the bags on the bed. Caro began folding the white blouses and beige denims.

"Gillian told me to buy neutrals," Vivi said.

"I love what you picked out," Caro said.

Vivi sat on the bed, watching her mom work on each garment, flattening the edges with her palms. "Gillian says we're leaving Zermatt," she said. "She's going to Italy."

"She'll love it, won't she?" Caro lifted a striped tan blazer.

Vivi folded her arms. "Where is Raphael taking us now?"

"Paris." Caro set the blazer on the bed and reached for an ecru sleeveless top.

"Can't I go to Villa Primaverina with Gillian?"

"We've got an appointment with Dr. d'Aigreville in Paris."

"We? When did you and Raphael become a *we*?"

"We're not."

"You said it again." Vivi sighed. She knew she was acting bratty, but she couldn't stop. That little taste of freedom had changed her. She felt older. Tougher. And she owed it all to Gillian.

Caro set the shirt on a tall pile of clothes. "You knew about Paris."

"But I never agreed to see this doctor. You're doing stuff without asking me."

"It's a one-hour appointment, not brain surgery," Caro said. "Raphael and I will be there."

"Why do I need to see a doctor? You don't know for sure if I gave you a nosebleed." Vivi shoved the pile of clothes, and they slid across the bed into a messy heap. "You can't make me go."

Caro looked as if she'd just walked into a house with a lit cigarette and realized too late that she smelled gas.

Raphael walked into the bedroom, wearing faded jeans and a Nine Inch Nails T-shirt. "What's going on? I could hear you two yelling in the hall."

Vivi looked at him from under her eyebrows. "Maybe you shouldn't stay in the same suite with us."

"Don't be rude," Caro said.

Vivi felt anger boiling up inside her. If she'd put eggs under her arms, they would have been hard-cooked in thirty seconds. "I'm tired of being jacked around."

"Your mother and I are trying to help you," Raphael said.

"It doesn't feel like help. Every time I start to like a place, I have to move. Now you're sending Gillian away."

"Don't be so self-centered," Raphael said. "Not everything is about you. Gillian wants to leave."

"Go away, Raphael. I want to talk to my mom."

He walked to the bed and helped Caro refold the clothes.

Vivi clamped her lips together. Oh, she wanted to hurt someone. She wanted Raphael to check into another hotel. And she wanted her mom to stop folding those freaking clothes. She heard a roar inside her head.

A red ribbon uncurled from Raphael's ear. A crimson drop splashed onto the shoulder of his T-shirt. Another thread ran over his chin and disappeared under his jaw. He swiped his neck and blinked at his fingers. He sat down hard on the edge of the bed, and another pile of clothes toppled over.

Vivi's throat felt thick and scratchy, as if she'd eaten a spoonful of termites. Raphael kept staring at his fingers. They were bloody. Caro's mom ran to the bathroom and came back with a damp washrag. She dabbed at Raphael's ear. "Am I in trouble?" Vivi's eyes filled.

"No," her mom and Raphael said at the same time.

"I'm so sorry. I didn't mean to hurt you." Vivi felt sick to her stomach.

"I know," Raphael said.

"I guess I do need to see that doctor, huh?" Vivi said.

———

Two nights later, Vivi was huddled in the back of a Mercedes sedan, watching the A-6 highway race behind them like dirty water. Raphael sat next to Caro, talking about the catacombs and sewers in Paris's underground like he was some kind of tour guide.

Vivi's throat tightened, and she slumped down in the seat. Getting to Paris hadn't been easy. They'd been on the road for forty-eight hours, mainly because Raphael had changed vehicles and drivers multiple times.

She sat up straight when she saw the Eiffel Tower. When she was little, she'd thought that Paris was two cities—the Left Bank and the Right Bank. A few years ago, she and her mom had stayed in an apartment on Boulevard Saint-Germain. Vivi's bedroom had faced the tower, and she'd kept her window open all the time, listening to the street noise, watching students rushing to the Sorbonne. One day she would buy flowers from one of those carts, and she'd pop into a café and air-kiss a gorgeous guy.

The Mercedes crossed the Pont Neuf Bridge and drove up Rue du Louvre, past the north wing of the museum and the post office. Traffic in Paris always made Vivi light-headed. The whole city had a strange beat, slow yet jittery, like molasses poured onto a frayed electrical cord.

When the car turned onto Place des Victoires, Vivi sat up straight and looked at the storefronts that lined the square. A monument of King Louis XIV on horseback stood in the center of the roundabout. The Mercedes drove around it, shot down a narrow street, and stopped in front of Raphael's townhouse. Men with earphones spread out on the sidewalk, edging toward the car.

The driver rushed to open a side door. Vivi stepped out into the night air and squinted up at the house. It looked like a miniature Louvre, the same limestone façade, lacy iron balconies, and a blue mansard roof with dormer windows.

The security men formed a wall around Raphael as he led Caro and Vivi through a blue paneled door, into a private courtyard where potted lemon trees sent a delicious fragrance through the night air. A gargoyle rainspout ran down the wall, its mouth poised over a limestone basin.

"So when will I see the doctor and get my head shrunk?" Vivi asked.

"Later tonight," Raphael said.

Vivi followed her mom into a wide entry hall where a staircase rose up to a shadowy landing. "Maybe we shouldn't stay here," she said, her voice echoing.

Caro turned. "Why not?"

"Raphael lives on a busy street," Vivi said. "People will see us coming and going. What if those goons are still chasing us?"

"Don't worry," Raphael said. "My company sometimes rents this house to musicians and actors. People are always in and out. No one will pay attention to us. Especially if we wear disguises. We—"

"Which actors have stayed here?" Vivi asked.

"Oh, Shakespearean types." Raphael smiled. "Are you ladies hungry?"

"Starved," Caro said.

Raphael walked toward a black door at the end of the hall. "Chez Georges is just around the corner."

"Don't we need reservations?" Caro asked.

"You worry about the wrong things, *mia cara*." Raphael opened a closet, pulled out a blond wig, and handed it to Vivi. She wished she hadn't left her fake eyeglasses in Scotland. They would have looked good with this wig.

"Where did you get this?" she said. "Did you shave Lady Gaga's head?"

"It's your disguise," Raphael said.

She put on the wig and lifted a curl. "Can I have different one?"

"You look cute," he said, then handed Caro an ash-blond wig. The stiff curls fell over her shoulders like uncooked spaghetti. Thick, boxy bangs skimmed her eyebrows.

"This is stupid." Vivi straightened her wig. "If it's not safe to walk around in Paris in regular clothes, why don't you just order pizza?"

Arrapato barked, then spun around. "You can come, too," Raphael said, fitting the dog into a Sherpa bag. The dog pushed his nose against the mesh door and whimpered.

"Yes, I know," Raphael said.

"Do you understand what he's saying?" Vivi asked.

"No, but he understands my tone of voice, and my tone says, *Don't draw attention to yourself—or us*." Raphael put on thick, horn-rimmed glasses and a dark wig. He handed the Sherpa to Vivi. "Pretend like he's your dog."

"I wish he were mine." Vivi hooked the strap over her shoulder and sighed.

Two baldheaded guards in khaki shorts and polo shirts followed them out the back door, down a narrow street. Vivi had never been to Chez Georges, and she wasn't sure she liked it. Inside, the dining room was narrow as a shoe box, jammed with tables, the walls lined with gold mirrors. However, the food smelled great. Her stomach rumbled as she breathed in great drifts of garlic, butter, and browning bread.

Raphael greeted the maître d' in French. The man looked confused for a moment, peering over the rim of his reading glasses. Then his small dark eyes blinked open wide, and he smiled. He seated the trio in a corner and handed out menus with a flourish.

The moment Vivi got settled, the back of her neck tingled, as if spiders were edging down her collar. She glanced at the next table, where an older woman was staring at Raphael. She was so short the table came up to her chest. Her straight copper hair was cut just below her ears, and her bangs looked as if they'd been trimmed with a Weed Eater. Her dark eyes held a fierce gleam. In her arms was an orange cat, and it peered at Vivi, too.

"*Que voulez-vous?*" Vivi heard someone say.

A waitress in a black-and-white uniform loomed over the table. Her face was flat as a pie pan, almost too large for her body. Vivi's mom ordered escargot and foie gras; Vivi couldn't decide between scallops and steak au poivre.

"Bring her both," Raphael said. "I'll have steak, too—rare—and a soup bone for my dog."

"Excellent, *monsieur*," the waitress said.

A few minutes later the maître d' walked up with a soup bowl, a bloody bone jutting up. "*Pour le chien*," he said, slipping the bowl into Arrapato's Sherpa.

Vivi glanced at the next table. The copper-haired woman held a cigarette, her eyes narrowed. Vivi felt as if she were a selection on the dessert cart.

"Mom, that dwarf keeps looking at me," she said.

Raphael and Caro glanced up. The copper-haired woman was talking to her cat, holding its broad, flat face in her stubby hands.

"What dwarf?" Raphael asked.

"How many do you see in this restaurant?" Vivi said. "She's right over there. And she was watching me."

Caro straightened the salt and pepper shakers and made no comment. Raphael took a sip of water, something Vivi had never seen him do. The waitress brought bread, melted goat cheese salads, and little tureens filled with pâté. As she left, Vivi cut her gaze back to the cat woman.

The table was empty. Smoke curled up from an ashtray.

At ten P.M., Vivi climbed into the back of a stretch Hummer with Caro and Raphael. All three of them still wore their disguises, though Vivi longed to pull off her wig. She spelled out dirty words in the air with a curl as the vehicle sped down the Champs Élysées.

Paris was going to be horrid, Vivi thought. She'd never seen Raphael act this paranoid. And he'd totally stolen Gillian's idea about disguises. Maybe Dr. d'Aigreville would give him Xanax.

The Hummer turned onto a tree-lined avenue and stopped in front of an apartment building that resembled a white wedding cake. A Mercedes pulled in behind the Hummer, and two security guards got out. Caro and Raphael tucked Arrapato into the Sherpa, and then guards led them into the building. A doorman made them wait in the creamy marble lobby while he called Dr. d'Aigreville's penthouse. Finally the man directed them to a creaky, old elevator that had mirrors and an old-fashioned iron grille that pulled shut. It was horrible.

Dr. d'Aigreville waited just inside a tall black door.

This was the woman Vivi had seen at Chez Georges. The same short copper hair and chopped-off bangs. Her eyes were level with Vivi's. The woman tore her gaze away and embraced Raphael. They air-kissed each other's cheeks.

"*Hé! Mon ami*," Dr. d'Aigreville said. "*Tu m'as manqué? Comment vas-tu?*"

Raphael smiled. "*Je vais bien, merci. Et toi?*"

"*Bien.*"

Raphael started to make the introductions, but Vivi

cut him off, glaring at the doctor. "I saw you at Chez Georges. You had a cat."

"And you were with a vampire *dog*," Dr. d'Aigreville said in a gravelly, tobacco-stained voice.

"Are you a vampire like Raphael?" Vivi asked.

"No, I'm like you and your mother." The doctor paused. "A hybrid."

She showed them into her living room, her stubby reflection moving over the glossy parquet floor. The walls were white, with ornate plaster trim. Two sleek, modern sofas faced a marble fireplace mantel. All of that was white, too. On the opposite wall, five doors opened onto a terrace, and a breeze stirred the white silk draperies. Beyond the terrace, the city spread out. Cars and motorcycles moved around the brightly lit Arc de Triomphe.

The view was totally awesome, Vivi thought, but the traffic noises hurt her ears.

Dr. d'Aigreville and Caro went onto the terrace and shut the door. Raphael set the wiggling Sherpa on the floor. "Arrapato smells Marie-Therese," he said.

"Who?" Vivi asked.

"Sabine's cat."

Vivi stepped closer to a baby grand piano, where a mewling sound was coming from under the bench. The orange cat gazed up at her with furious copper eyes. Damp white beads clung to its whiskers, as if it had just finished lapping milk. The cat gave her a look that seemed to say, *We're going to own your ass.*

"Raphael, I don't trust the doctor," Vivi said. "What if she pushes my mom off the balcony?"

"She won't."

"Why did they go outside to talk?"

"I don't know."

"Can't you listen in?"

"No."

Vivi chewed her thumbnail. "How long will they be out there?"

"As long as it takes," Raphael said.

CHAPTER 22

Caro

CHAMPS ÉLYSÉES
PARIS, FRANCE

I walked to the balcony rail and stared down at the night-time view of Paris, watching car lights sweep around the Arc de Triomphe. Even though it was after ten P.M., tourists wandered down the sidewalks.

The psychiatrist walked up beside me, the wind stirring her little-girl bangs. The top of her head was even with my breasts, and her hair shone like copper wires. A small white scar ran under the bangs.

"You have a lovely view, Dr. d'Aigreville," I said.

She smiled. "Call me Sabine."

"I saw you at Chez Georges. Are you a regular patron?" I paused. "Or were you stalking my daughter?"

"Both. I wanted to observe Vivi in the wild, so to speak," Sabine said. "I arranged it with Raphael—please don't be angry. I asked him not to tell you. He resisted. But he finally agreed."

I felt a pinch of irritation. "Did you learn anything useful?"

"Vivi is an Inducer."

I spread my hands on the balcony rail, feeling the rough, cold limestone. "What does this mean?"

"Your daughter can influence another person's thoughts through neurokinesis."

"How? She can't read thoughts."

"No. Not now, anyway. Who knows what will happen—hybrids mature slowly. But I digress. Right now, Vivi cannot read thoughts, but she can impose her will upon another person. She's also hemakinetic."

I knew what this word meant—Vivi could make people bleed. But I didn't understand how it worked. "Can you elaborate?"

"Hemakinesis is the control of blood. It's closely aligned with the skill of Induction." Sabine crossed her fingers. "When Vivi feels passionate about an issue, her thoughts can influence another person's thoughts. Meanwhile, Vivi is having a physiological reaction. Her pulse and respiration increase. Her body hums with adrenaline. To prevent harming you or others through an accidental hemakinesis, Vivi must learn to control herself. One example: She must master the depth and rapidity of her breaths. Right now, she can't. And her energy spills everywhere, without direction. Like water bursting through cracks in a dam. When those cracks get bigger, and they will, she could cause you to have a cerebral hemorrhage."

My eyes burned as I looked toward the Champs Élysées. I cupped my hand over my mouth.

"I've given you a simple explanation," Sabine said.

Of course. What else? I lowered my hand and curled my fingers into a knot. "Is this why we've been hunted? Because my daughter can make people bleed?"

"It's possible. But doubtful. Raphael believes that your child is being pursued by prophecy fanatics. They are not motivated by money. You cannot reason with them. They will not stop until they have Vivi." Sabine touched my arm. "I can teach her how to defend herself."

"What if these vampires are hemakinetic, too? How can Vivi defend herself?"

"Vampires have limited psi abilities," Sabine said. "Some are telepathic. Some aren't. I'm sure you're familiar with Raphael's talents?"

I nodded.

"His telepathy is slightly above average, but his audiokinesis is rare." Sabine paused. "It's different with hybrids."

"I'm not sure what you mean."

"It would take too long to explain hybrid genetics. We can be extraordinarily kinetic."

"I'm not."

"You will be. Eventually. As I said, hybrids are late bloomers." She gave me a shrewd look. "I don't mean to boast, but I am an expert on this subject. One very famous quarter vampire could project illusions—Alexander the Great. He used projection as a military weapon."

Under normal conditions, I would have quizzed her about Alexander, but I was too numb to speak.

Sabine leaned against the rail. It came up to her chest. "How old is Vivi?"

"Thirteen. She'll be fourteen in August."

"This is the optimal time to begin her training. If Vivi is being pursued by assassins, she will need to protect herself—and you."

"How?"

"As I've already said, she must learn how to use hemakinesis as a weapon. For example, in the future, let's say that five murderers—human or vampire—break into your home. Vivi will be able to disable them all."

My mind was still caught on the word *weapon*.

"I will also show her how to focus and distribute her energy. In other words, she'll learn how to improve her aim. She will hit the target and won't injure you or Raphael."

A target? I lifted my hands from the railing and tugged my sweater sleeves over my fingers.

"After Vivi learns how to control her powers, she won't be vulnerable to anyone. Vampires may always hunt her, but if they do, God help them. They'll do so at their own peril."

"And you'll be teaching her?"

"Yes."

"But you're a psychiatrist. I assumed that you would make a diagnosis and refer us to someone else."

"To whom? I'm an Inducer, and I'm hemakinetic. I'm damn good at both. Would you like me to demonstrate?"

"No." I pushed up my sleeves. If only I had flatware to straighten. Or a pepper shaker. Sabine was watching me, so I tucked my fists under my arms. "How long will the training last?"

"Two months, maybe three. I know that sounds protracted, but just think how long it takes to learn a foreign language."

"I'm not sure we can stay in Paris that long. Especially if we're visiting you every day. Someone might notice."

"Vivi will live with me for the duration of her training."

A burning pain spread around my breastbone, as if I'd swallowed hot coffee. I turned away from the view. "Please don't take this the wrong way. But I barely know you. We met fifteen minutes ago."

"I understand your concerns."

I heard a scritching noise and looked at the terrace door. The orange cat was raking her claws over the glass. Sabine gave the animal an adoring look. "I'll be with you in a moment, Marie-Therese," she told the cat.

Normally I trusted people who talked to animals, but I honestly didn't know what to think about Sabine. And I couldn't be too careful with my child.

"Vivi has never been away from me," I said. "Not even one night."

Sabine placed a stumpy hand against her chest. "I could never leave Marie-Therese with a stranger."

Was she telling the truth? Or patronizing me? "I'm sorry we wasted your time," I said.

"I'm not worried about my time," she said. "I'm worried that Vivi won't harness her powers."

"She won't hurt me."

"She already has."

"I'm not scared. Vivi is coming home with me, and that's the end of it." I started walking toward the door.

"No, it's not the end," she said.

I heard a grinding noise, the kind an old car makes when a dog races across the road and the driver stomps the brake. I felt the tug of gravity, and my chin tipped back. Suddenly I was looking up at the night sky.

"Please listen to me, Caro," Sabine said.

Inside my head, a thought took shape and hardened. The truth lay inside me, the truth of me and Vivi, everything we were and everything we would become. But my logic was skewed and selfish. I was protecting my child for the wrong reasons. If she had diabetes, would I refuse to give her insulin because the needle might cause too much pain? No, of course not. If I delayed Vivi's treatment, I was thinking of myself, not her.

The gravity retreated, and my head snapped back. *She's Inducing me.*

Sabine's gaze met mine, and it seemed to move through me, as if she'd looked all the way to my childhood, back to the night I'd hidden behind the waterfall.

"Your mother protected you," she said. "Now you must protect Vivi."

"Don't you dare look in my thoughts," I whispered.

"I understand why you don't like me. I'm brash and pushy. I say the wrong thing at the wrong time. But I am the only person who can help your daughter—without betraying her. My blood is the same as yours."

"You may be a hybrid, but we're not alike."

"Your father was Philippe Grimaldi. My mother was his cousin—Aimée d'Aigreville. She and her sister Esmé turned Raphael into a vampire."

"That happened in the eighth century. Aimée couldn't possibly be your mother."

"She was."

I studied Sabine's face. Her complexion was smooth. A few wrinkles fanned away from her eyes. Small lines were etched on her upper lip. I'd assumed that she was in her early fifties. "Just how old are you?"

"I was born in 1928." She smiled. "You'll age slowly and gracefully, too. So will Vivi. I know what it means to be caught between two worlds, human and vampire. We don't fit into either place. Maybe you've made peace with this sense of dislocation. But Vivi hasn't If she doesn't learn the parameters of Induction, she will put herself and others at risk."

"Your scare tactics aren't working."

"One day Vivi might walk into a coffee shop and order a latte," Sabine said. "The waitress could be having a horrible day. Let's say that she brings Vivi a double espresso. If Vivi complains, the waitress might smart off. Maybe Vivi's had a worse day. Or the waitress reminds her of the girl who stole her boyfriend. So Vivi blasts her—*Bring me a latte*—and the waitress starts to bleed. After a series of these incidents, whoever is tracking Vivi will be able to pinpoint her location. She'll attract others, too. People who will wish to exploit her."

My throat felt raw, and it hurt to breathe. "But you said Vivi was a weapon. She could kill the trackers."

"Not unless she knows how." Sabine paused. "There's more, and you're not going to like it. Vivi must learn how to resist the allure of Induction. The more one uses it, the more one enjoys it. It can become a harmful coping mechanism, a way to blow off anger. She might become dangerous. And that will attract dangerous people."

"I understand what you're saying, Sabine. But I'm not leaving my daughter with you. You are welcome to live with us. We're always moving around, but—"

"No."

"I'm sorry. She can't stay here."

"Oh, yes I can," Vivi said from the doorway.

I turned. She was holding the cat.

Sabine's eyes flicked from Vivi to Marie-Therese.

Vivi walked up to me, the wind lifting her fake curls. "Mom, it's okay. Let the doctor help me. I won't mind being here."

I shook my head.

"I'm scared to be around you and Raphael. Just go home and let me get better. It'll be like summer camp. I always wanted to go, and you wouldn't let me. Please, Mom. I made you and Raphael bleed—and I wasn't even really mad."

"We don't know anything about this doctor," I whispered.

"Raphael can vouch for me," Sabine said.

"He can also vouch for supermodels," I said.

Sabine smiled. "You'll have trouble finding a woman he can't endorse."

"Look, Mom," Vivi said. "I'm the one with Induction. I get to make the decision. You've got to trust the doctor."

"It's too soon."

"I've got an idea. What if you exchange prisoners?"

Vivi put the cat in my arms. "Sabine keeps me. And you keep Marie-Therese."

———

When Raphael and I left Sabine's apartment, the stretch Hummer was gone, replaced by a white BMW with tinted windows. Instead of returning to Place des Victoires, we turned into an underground parking garage. It was a well-lit space, full of echoes. I got out of the BMW, carrying the Sherpa, and moved toward a navy blue Mercedes, wincing each time Arrapato barked.

Minutes later, we were safely inside the house. Raphael walked ahead with the cat. I followed him to the kitchen. It was a large room with white cabinets, black granite counters, and stainless appliances.

"You look exhausted, *mia cara*." Raphael put Marie-Therese on the counter.

"I am." I unzipped the Sherpa, and Arrapato gazed up at the cat, a growl caught in his throat.

Raphael opened the refrigerator door, and light spilled across his face. He lifted a jar of cream, poured a dab into a bowl, and set it in front of the cat. She tiptoed across the counter, her reflection gliding in the black granite. Arrapato dropped into a play bow, front paws on the floor, tail in the air. The cat ignored him and placidly lapped cream.

"Can Sabine really help Vivi?" I asked.

"Yes. That's why I brought her to Paris."

"Is Sabine capable of taking care of a teenager?"

"She's a professional." He lifted Marie-Therese into his arms and led me to the ground-floor salon. Arrapato shot ahead of us, ears perked, tail whipping back and forth. The cat sprang out of Raphael's arm and leaped onto the ice-blue curtains.

"Oh, go ahead, kitty. Rip them to pieces," he told the cat, then sank down on a Louis XIV sofa that matched the draperies. I walked over to Marie-Therese, gently extracted her claws from the silk, and set her on a gilt table. Arrapato parked himself beneath it and whined. I stared down at him. "Will you hurt her?"

"He'd drain that cat in two minutes." Raphael snapped his fingers.

"We'd better keep them apart." I sat down beside him and cupped my hands around my elbows. "The last time I visited you, this room was mint green. Now it's blue. It's pretty."

He pressed two fingers against his temple. "An unfortunate accident."

The edge in his voice caught my attention. "What kind? Water damage?"

He snorted. "I wish."

"What happened?"

"I hired an interior designer. She did what she wanted." Two red patches appeared on his cheeks. "With the design, I mean."

"Oh." As I stared at him, I caught the tail end of his thought, *Merda*.

His mouth drew into a tight line. After a moment, he said, "Would you like a drink?"

"It won't help." I knew he was leading me away from the rest of his thoughts—probably his disagreeable affair with the interior designer—but I was too heartsick over

Vivi to care. My hands fell away from my elbows, and I slumped against the sofa.

"Don't be pessimistic, *mia cara*."

"I just left my daughter with a half vampire."

"Sabine has a medical degree from Harvard."

"Why does that feel like a non sequitur?"

He took my hand and rubbed the back of my knuckles. "How can I make you feel better?"

"You can't." Not with words, anyway.

"Let me try. History always relaxes you. Open your mind."

"Okay." I shut my eyes and leaned my head against the back of the sofa. The room fell away, and images from Raphael's mind whirled around me. The bleak *tramontana* wind, scraping over the Italian Alps. Holy water poured over a sleeping infant's forehead. A dark rush of espresso into a white cup. Marzipan lambs at Easter, nestled in a straw basket. A dark-eyed monk cutting his hair on Maundy Thursday, blond strands falling to a stone floor. I saw lavender light pouring onto the Tuscan hills. I smelled ripe grapes and coriander and damp earth. I heard a coin fall into an Etruscan well. Before it hit the bottom, I was calm. I thanked Raphael, then Marie-Therese and I went to my bedroom.

CHAPTER 23

Vivi

Vivi stood next to the living room window, watching traffic move down the Champs Élysées, headlights sweeping around the Arc de Triomphe. This night had lasted forever and ever. And she was beginning to regret her decision to stay in this penthouse. It was too white. She turned back to the doctor, who sat placidly in a white chair. "Why were you at Chez Georges tonight?"

"It was part of the examination. I cleared it with Raphael, of course."

Traitor. Vivi could feel her apple dessert creeping up the back of her throat. "So you Nancy Drewed me?"

"I'm sorry if I offended you."

"I'll get over it." Vivi sighed. "Are you angry because I gave your cat to Mom?"

"No, I thought it was clever."

Vivi smiled. "What should I call you? Doctor? Teacher?"

"Sabine is fine. Would you like a cup of hot chocolate before we begin the test?"

"How many are there?"

"Tonight? Just one," Sabine said. "You look thirsty."

A cup of hot cocoa did sound nice. Vivi nodded. "Yeah, okay."

"The kitchen is just beyond those doors." Sabine pointed to the other end of the room.

Vivi took a step, then turned. "Aren't you coming, too?"

"No." Sabine looked amused. "Why?"

"I don't know how to make cocoa."

"Did I say *you* had to make it?" She made a shooing motion with her hand. "Lesson one. Don't be too quick to make assumptions."

Vivi chewed her lip. Could Sabine whip up food in her mind? For real? Vivi had to see this. She walked into a bone-white kitchen. Mismatched dishes, also white, were crammed into a rack. A tall, raw-boned woman with muddy eyes stood next to the stove, stirring a copper pot. Her skin was the color of melted Godiva chocolate. She wore an orange cotton dress, and a crucifix dangled from a gold necklace. She looked at Vivi and snickered.

"You're drink is almost ready, Heidi."

"Heidi had short brown hair." Vivi yanked off the wig and fluffed her bangs.

The woman's gaze swept over her. "You ain't gone make me bleed, are you?"

"No."

"I'll whip your ass if you do." The woman tipped the copper pan over a mug. A few dark drops hit the counter, and she wiped it up with her finger. "What you looking at, Heidi?"

Was something wrong with that lady's hearing? "My name is Vivi."

"I know who you are." The woman set the mug in front of Vivi. "Not that you asked, but my name is Lena."

Vivi reached for the mug and took a sip. "It's good."

"I learned how to cook when I was just yay big. I grew up in Memphis. Big ole family. My grandmama owned a café. First thing she taught me was how to make cocoa."

"Are you a vampire?" Vivi asked.

"No." Lena snorted. "Are you?"

"One-quarter," Vivi said, watching the woman's face.

Lena laughed. Her voice was throaty, strung up with barbed wire, the way Maleficent might have laughed when she'd plotted to kill Sleeping Beauty.

"What's so funny?" Vivi asked, starting to get peeved.

"Laughing is better than crying, ain't it?" Lena grinned, showing a gap between her front teeth. "What you keep staring at, girl?"

"I'm a very observant person." Vivi took another sip, and the warm chocolate tumbled through her chest. She lowered the mug. "Why is Sabine's house so white?"

"Dr. Sabine would say that she likes the color. But if you ask me, she feels dirty."

"She's afraid of germs? Or is she a neat freak?"

"Naw, not that kind of dirty. She thinks her blood is tainted. See, her mother was a vampire. She married another vampire, that d'Orsay scoundrel. They belonged to the Occitaine Cabal. Big shots. Her daddy still lives in that mansion near Saint Germain des Prés."

"Wait, I thought Sabine was a half vampire."

"She is. Her mama went and had a love snarl with a human. Got herself knocked up with Dr. Sabine. It caused a shitstorm in the d'Orsay household."

Vivi blinked and sat up a little straighter.

"What's wrong now, Heidi? Ain't you never heard cussing?"

"Sure. But I'm confused. I thought Sabine's last name was d'Aigreville."

"It is. Mr. d'Orsay is Sabine's legal dad. He treated his wife poorly. Mrs. d'Orsay's maiden name was d'Aigreville." Lena walked back to the stove, grabbed the copper pot, and set it in the sink. "After Dr. Sabine was born, Mr. d'Orsay wouldn't give the child his name. She took her mama's. That's why the doctor call herelf d'Aigreville. Poor girl got banished from Paris when she was six weeks old. She was sent to the d'Orsay house in Aix-en-Provence. Her family forgot she existed."

"Wow, that's cold."

"Ice cold. Dr. Sabine grew up with cats and nannies. She don't have nothing to do with the d'Orsays. She wanted to, but they'd cast her out."

"Why didn't her mama keep her?"

"She died."

"But how? I thought you said Mrs. d'Orsay was a vampire. They don't up and die."

"They say she cut her wrists and bled to death. But personally, I think Mr. d'Orsay had his wife put down. Just like she was a dog."

"Seriously? He snuffed her?"

"I don't know for sure. I'm just guessing." Lena opened the cabinet and took out the copper polish. "If you ask me, Dr. Sabine was lucky. She gets along just fine without them Occitaine assholes. She took after her human daddy. She's kind and smart like him. He's a doctor, and she was determined to make him proud. She went to medical school in America. Did training in England and Lord knows where else. A rich vampire paid for everything—I ain't saying who."

"Raphael?"

"Maybe." Lena smiled. "Finish your chocolate. Dr. Sabine's waiting for you in the library. First door on the right."

Vivi drank the rest of the cocoa and wiped her mouth. Why had Lena told her these private things? Was she a gossip? Or had she been instructed to brief Vivi? To distract her so Sabine could eavesdrop on Vivi's real thoughts?

She stared down into her mug, willing her mind to be just as empty, then looked up. "Can Sabine help me?"

"Sure." Lena nodded. "But you asking the wrong question. Ask yourself if *you* can help you."

Vivi wandered to the library. The white shelves were lined with books, each one wrapped in thick, creamy paper and tied with twine, as if colorful jackets needed to be hidden.

Sabine sat behind a carved desk, writing in a notebook. She glanced up, and her reading glasses skated to the end of her nose. "I'll be with you in a moment, Vivi."

"Take your time." Vivi looked up at a picture of a

tumble-down castle. It sat on a hill, the French Alps rising in the distance. It reminded her of something, but she couldn't say what.

Sabine rose from her chair and walked around the desk. "That's an etching of Château of Peyrepertuse."

"I bet it was pretty at one time. How did it get ruined?"

"It sits on a craggy hill. Time and wind whittled it. *Peyrepertuse* means 'pointy hill,' by the way." Sabine tilted her head. "You and your mother have been on the run for a while, haven't you?"

"All my life."

"Tell me about your education. How many schools have you attended?"

Vivi shrugged. "My mom homeschools me. See, I went to a school in Australia, but it didn't work out."

Sabine didn't look surprised. "Why not?"

"I got picked on. A guy kicked my shins. I shoved him. Blood squirted out of his mouth. I didn't think I pushed him that hard." She shrugged again. "Maybe I Induced him."

"Is that the first time you suspected you could do this?"

"No. I didn't figure it out until I was in Norway. See, people have always bled around me. I figured it was their problem. But it felt different when my mom's nose started to gush in that coffee shop."

"Why was it different?" Sabine asked. "Was it your mother's first nosebleed?"

"No." Vivi swallowed. "Something felt different inside me. I felt this whoosh behind my nose, like I was getting ready to blow out a humongous sneeze. Mom's head snapped back, like she'd felt it, too. When I saw the blood,

I was so freaked. I knew I'd done it. I don't know how I knew."

"How did you feel when you made Raphael's ear bleed?"

"I just wanted him to leave me alone. I was mad. But I didn't want to sneeze. I'm sorry I hurt him. He's like a dad to me."

Sabine began to walk in a circle around Vivi.

"What?" Vivi asked, turning with her.

"You're hungry, aren't you?" Sabine asked.

"No, I'm—" Vivi hesitated. Well, maybe she could eat a chocolate croissant. "I guess."

Sabine grinned, showing a row of small, crooked teeth.

"What's so funny?" Vivi asked.

"You'll see."

Sabine was still smiling when Lena walked into the room, holding a white tray. She set it on a table in front of the sofa. "Eat up, girl. And don't you leave no crumbs."

Vivi stared at the tray. Two croissants oozed dark chocolate onto a white plate. There was also a glass of milk.

Sabine glanced up at Lena. "Are you bleeding from any orifice?"

"Like hell." Lena snorted.

Vivi folded her arms. She studied Lena's nose and ears but didn't see any blood. She had the feeling she'd missed a private joke between the women.

"It's not a joke," Sabine said.

Vivi frowned. "Did you read my freaking mind?"

"Yes. I also Induced you to want a croissant. Then I Induced Lena to bring it."

Vivi thought about that a minute. "Is that how I made my mom drink the latte?"

Sabine nodded. "Did you injure anyone else in the café?"

"No." Vivi tilted her head. "Why didn't you make Lena bleed?"

"She's got good aim," Lena said, and glided out of the room.

Vivi ate both croissants, pausing to take gulps of milk. She'd never felt this hungry.

Sabine crooked a finger at Vivi's half-finished glass of milk. "Are you finished?"

"Yeah. You want a swig?"

"No. I hate milk. And I especially hate to drink from someone else's glass."

Vivi nodded. But she wasn't sure why Sabine was telling her about food quirks. Was she expected to reciprocate? She was just about to tell Sabine how much she hated haggis, when the doctor leaned forward.

"Vivi, I want you to Induce me to drink your milk."

"Now? But you just said you hated milk. And you hate to drink after others."

Sabine flipped her hand, as if dismissing Vivi's words. "Induce me."

"I'm not sure I can."

"What were you thinking right before your mother's nose bled?"

Vivi put her hands in her lap and tapped her fingers together. "I didn't want to talk to her. And she was talking too much. I wanted her to drink her latte because it would keep her mouth busy. I was angry because I hated

Norway. And I was angry at Raphael, too. Then Mom picked up her cup and drank. Blood gushed all over the place."

"All right," Sabine said. "I want you to feel angry at me."

"But I'm not."

"Did you know that you'll have to spend several months with me?"

"Yeah. So?"

"You can't see your mother at all."

"For real?" Vivi swallowed, and her throat clicked.

"Yes. And you won't be eating croissants all day long. You'll be working hard." Sabine clapped her hands. "Go on. Get angry. Force me to drink your milk."

"Why can't I see my mom?"

"Because I'm a mean lady. Because I won't let you. I won't let you go anywhere."

Vivi took a breath. She imagined living in this noisy penthouse, cooped up with Lena and Sabine. No croissants. The Induction lessons would be like algebra, but worse. She imagined Sabine picking up the milk, taking a long swallow, lowering the empty glass, a white ring around her mouth. She wanted Sabine to drink that crappy French milk and suffer.

Vivi pushed out a thought. *Pick up the glass. Drink my milk. Drink every drop.*

Sabine released an exasperated sigh. "Try harder."

Drink my damn milk.

"If that's all you've got, you can go home in the morning," Sabine said. "You aren't an Inducer. You can't hurt anyone."

"But I did."

"You're a dilettante."

Vivi felt pressure behind her nose, then her pulse whooshed between her ears. Every pore in her being wanted Sabine to quit talking. To fill her mouth with milk.

DRINK MY MILK, SABINE!

The doctor crossed her arms, and her smile widened. "Sorry, you'll have to do better."

"I'm exhausted. Let me take a break," Vivi said. A headache flickered behind her eyes.

Sabine started to say something, and then her brow tightened and a thin red line snaked out of her right nostril.

Vivi sat back, breathing hard. *Did I do that?*

Sabine patted her lip, then lowered her hand. A red sheen covered her fingertips. Another, thicker thread curved around the doctor's lips like a clown's mask. It ran under her chin, down her neck, and vanished under her collar.

Vivi's hand trembled as she held out her napkin. "Here you go."

Sabine tipped her head back and pinched the napkin around her nose.

"Did I cause that?" Vivi asked.

Sabine nodded.

"But you didn't drink the milk."

"I wanted to." Sabine's voice was muffled by the napkin. "But I knew you were Inducing me. My training kept me from lifting the glass."

"How can my thoughts do *this*?" Vivi looked at the spattered blood on Sabine's blouse. She felt nauseated.

Sabine lowered the napkin. "Induction and hemakinesis are psi talents. You were trying to bend my thoughts to your will. I bent back. That created resistance. Adrenaline was released into my bloodstream. My blood pressure began to rise. My heart pumped faster. Your hemakinesis affected my vascular system—dilating the arteries and vessels. Luckily, only a capillary burst, and my nose bled."

"Oh," Vivi said, but she didn't understand.

"We'll get into the physiology of Induction later, after I've taught you how to control your raw talent."

"What do you mean, raw?" Vivi pushed down an image of an uncooked roast sitting in white butcher paper, the purple blood seeping around it.

"Your talent is unfocused. I will help you control it. When we're through, you will be able to influence the thoughts of one person, or a whole group of people."

"And I won't hurt them?"

"Not unless you want to. Even then, the damage will depend on a person's individual physiology. Someone with high blood pressure might bleed a lot. A person who takes blood thinners could hemorrhage. So could a menstruating woman. The amount of blood depends on how hard they fight back with their minds. How much resistance they exert. You see, resistance is a subconscious reaction. Strong-willed individuals will be harder to dominate. But you'll be able to do it."

"So no one is safe from me?"

"I'm safe. You can't hurt me."

"What about Lena?"

"She'll stay out of your way during the lessons," Sabine said. "Do you have any questions about psychokinesis?"

"I don't even know what that means."

"*Kinesis* refers to movement. *Psycho* is the mind. The realm of thought. When these two things come together, movement occurs in the mind."

"I know about telepathy. Raphael can read minds. Can all vampires do that?"

"No. I'd say twenty-five percent can read minds."

"Do all hybrids and vampires have kinetic talents?"

"Only a few vampires—Raphael is one. But most hybrids have some type of kinetic talent."

"My mom doesn't."

"She's slightly telepathic. As for the kinesis, she probably has a touch of something. She just doesn't know it. Or she hasn't developed it. Some hybrids are audiokinetic. That means they can mimic sounds—a barking dog, a cat. Chronokinesis is the ability to alter the perception of time."

Vivi stared at her empty plate. Just talking about her mom made her homesick. Her stomach felt swollen, as if she'd eaten wet newspaper. Then she looked up at Sabine.

"Before I Induced you, you said I couldn't see my mom. Were you trying to make me mad? Or were you telling the truth?"

"It's the truth. I'm sorry."

"Then we've got a problem. When I agreed to live with you, I thought I'd see my mom. I really need to be with her. She's on her own. All she has is me."

"Your mother isn't alone. She's with Raphael, and he will protect her. But it's up to you, Vivi."

"Your apartment is too noisy."

"We don't have to stay here. I have a home in Valbonne."

"Where?"

"It's near Grasse—that's a charming town. Not far from the Côte d'Azur. I know a marvelous bakery. We can eat fresh baguettes every day."

"You'd leave Paris without your cat? Maybe we can stop by Raphael's and get her."

"I have an idea Marie-Therese will be here in the morning. And so will your mother."

"How do you know? Did you read her mind?"

"No, no. Marie-Therese will drive your mother insane with yowling." Sabine dropped the bloody napkin on the tray. "You can say good-bye to Caro before we leave the city—just don't tell her where we're going."

"Why not?"

"Telepathic vampires are drawn to Paris. If your mother knows where we're going, that information could be snatched out of her thoughts."

"Why would a random vampire look into my mom's mind?"

"Caro is beautiful."

"True. But what would this vampire do with Mom's thoughts? He wouldn't call up the bad guys and tell them where I'm staying."

"Probably not. But let's look at a hypothetical situation. Let's say this random, telepathic vampire is having financial problems. He looks into your mother's head because she's pretty, and he sees that a girl named Vivi Barrett is an Inducer. Maybe the vampire takes a deeper look and sees the rest of it. Then he sees where you will be going. This vampire might try to sell this information."

"Raphael doesn't know who's looking for us. How could the vampire find out?"

"Not all immortals are like Raphael. He is honest. He adores you and your mother. And he isn't selling information." Sabine folded her hands. "I don't want to take chances with your safety."

"Can you let Raphael know where I'll be? His mind is stronger than Mom's."

Sabine hesitated, then nodded.

"Fresh baguettes sound nice." A smile tugged at the corners of Vivi's mouth. "When can we leave?"

CHAPTER 24

Caro

PLACE DES VICTOIRES
PARIS, FRANCE

A noise awoke me a little before dawn. I raised my head from the pillow and glanced around the bedroom. Gray light spilled through the tall windows, brightening the parquet floor. I tilted my head and listened.

Silence.

I pressed my cheek into the pillow. Just when I started to drift back to sleep, I heard a ripping sound. I opened my eyes. Marie-Therese sat on the chaise longue, her front paws moving over the silk as if she were playing a piano. As her claws pricked the fabric, the echo held in the darkness, loud as a jackhammer, and I began to regret the catnapping.

"You miss Sabine," I whispered.

At the sound of her mistress's name, the cat leaped off

the chaise and dove behind the curtain. A murderous wail rose up. I felt sorry for the cat, but I needed a few more hours' sleep or my head would be fuzzy.

The cat let out another high-pitched yowl.

Fine, I'd sleep in the ice-blue parlor. I grabbed my pillow, padded to the door, and opened it. Two gift-wrapped boxes fell into my room. I lifted the card and blinked at Raphael's ornate handwriting.

Mia Cara,

A little something to make your sadness fly away.

Love,
R

I smiled. Nothing made him happier than buying presents, but every time he gave me an expensive gift, I was reminded of the impermanence of wealth. I still remembered how Jude and I had watched our savings dwindle. But surely this wouldn't happen to Raphael. He had lived long enough to benefit from financial bubbles. He'd even helped me make smart investments.

I heard a brittle meow, and then the cat ran over to the boxes and gave me a look that said, *His investments are fine, but you are an ungrateful snot.*

"Oh, all right," I told the cat. I opened the first box and lifted a darling white cotton dress that was printed with crimson sparrows. Red Christian Louboutin pumps were nestled in the smaller box. I got dressed, trying to ignore the flutter in my chest. The hem of the dress brushed against my knees. The heels fit perfectly, and even though I always wore flats, I rather liked these.

At seven A.M., I decided to return Marie-Therese. Sabine was probably qualified to take care of my child, but I couldn't take care of a feline. Neither Raphael nor I could guarantee the cat's safety. Even if Arrapato didn't attack her, this house had dozens of hidden nooks and crannies that led heaven knew where, and Marie-Therese might get lost.

I tucked her in my arms, went downstairs, and rang up the limo driver. Two security men led me outside to a car I hadn't seen before, a black Jaguar with tinted windows. The tallest security man climbed in next to the driver, a grandfatherly fellow with tufts of silver hair jutting out of his ears. I gave him Sabine's address.

Fifteen minutes later, after switching cars near the Jean Sans-Peur Tower, I was sitting in the doctor's white kitchen, dropping sugar cubes into my coffee. On the opposite end of the room, morning sunlight poured through the arched windows. A two-note police siren bleated in the distance, briefly stamping out traffic noises from the Champs Élysées.

"I knew you'd come back," Sabine said. She bustled around in a white quilted robe, her slippers scuffing over the tile floor, the cat weaving joyfully between her legs, as if they'd been separated for years rather than hours.

"Because you read my mind?" I said. "But how could you know what I was going to do before I myself knew?"

"I know my cat. She's driven off dozens of pet sitters with her screeches. Lena says it sounds like a pig being barbecued alive. Lena's my chef."

My gaze moved to Sabine's counters, where crocks and olive oil jars were crammed on a wooden tray. A garlic braid hung beside the stove, with pods missing here and there. A bright red Provençal dish cloth lay beside the sink. The colorful objects made me feel better until I glanced at a sunny hallway, where suitcases were lined up.

"You're not leaving, are you?" I asked.

Sabine followed my gaze. "Yes."

I rested my palms on my lap. "Were you going to tell me?"

"No."

Unbelievable. The gall of this woman. "Where are you taking my daughter?"

"I'd rather not say." She moved away from the counter and shut the door.

"I need phone numbers and an address."

She poured a cup of coffee and carried it to the table, her slippers brushing over the floor. She pulled out a chair but didn't sit down.

"Do you want this information locked inside your head?" she asked. "Any vampire could pluck them. Without meaning to, you could put Vivi at risk."

"She's my daughter."

"I understand your fears. I've got them, too. My penthouse is relatively safe, but it's noisy. Vivi herself expressed concern about the traffic. The first part of her training is critical. If she masters the early lessons, the rest will move faster. Isn't this what you want?"

I rubbed my hands on my dress, leaving damp streaks on the fabric. "Yes."

"We'll return to Paris at the end of August. Then you can visit."

I stared into my coffee. A decade's worth of fear and uncertainty churned inside me. I resisted an urge to straighten my spoon. If I took Vivi to Raphael's house, I would agonize about her out-of-control talent, yet the thought of being away from my only child was unbearable. Did I really have a choice?

Sabine sat down across from me. "Yes, you do."

I lifted my coffee cup, then put it down. "Please don't read my mind. And I'd prefer if you stayed in Paris. Just in case there's an emergency—at your end or mine. We need to be in contact."

Marie-Therese leaped onto the table and began licking her paw. Sabine took off her glasses and polished the lenses with a napkin. Her movements were calm and deliberate, almost identical to the cat's.

"Caro, have you ever spent any time around artists?"

"No."

"A painter believes his time must be guarded," Sabine said. "They put up walls. God help the fool who tries to break through. If you try, the painter becomes disoriented. He loses focus. Whatever force was guiding the artist's hand is gone. And it may never return."

I waited for her to continue, but I could already see where this lecture was headed.

Sabine put her glasses back on. "Vivi needs an artist's discipline and focus. Her training will move faster if she isn't distracted by her emotions. Each time she sees you, she will get homesick. And the process will take longer."

I stared at the table. My spoon was crooked. And the

tongs in the sugar bowl jutted out at a weird angle. Everything on Sabine's table was bunched together and messy. What did she know about mothers and daughters?

"Maybe she'll be homesick anyway," I said.

"It will be worse if you're nearby." Sabine poured cream into her coffee. "Tell me about your parents. Was your mother a vampire?"

I watched her spoon move in circles. If she was really a member of the Grimaldi clan, she already knew what had happened to my family. Why would she ask a hurtful question? Did she think I was mentally fragile? That I couldn't talk about my family without crying?

"Mother was human. Dad was a vampire. Philippe Grimaldi. Your mother's cousin."

"Your parents died when you were a little girl, didn't they?"

"Vampires murdered them. Do you know the rest of the story?"

"I want to hear it from you," she said.

I spoke in a calm, clear voice. When I finished, I opened my hand and pointed to a half-moon scar on my palm. Some part of me could still feel the shape of the doorknob and the rush of heat.

Sabine took a long drink of coffee. "How old was Vivi when her father went missing?"

"Three."

"Does she remember him?"

I shook my head. Then I felt a sudden urge to talk about Jude. "Vivi looks just like him. A female version."

"He must have been handsome."

"Yes. He was." I could see him so clearly, the way he'd

turn and smile, his chin dimpling, his T-shirt stretched over his wide shoulders.

"Your daughter might resemble her father physically.But she's assimilated your personality traits. Both of you are guarded. Cautious. You've erected so many walls."

"Caution is a survival trait."

"It won't allow you to enjoy that beautiful frock." Sabine waved her hand at my dress. "Is it a Carolina Herrera? Love the sparrows. A bird in flight means that troubles are leaving. A real sparrow is brown, of course. I'm sure that Ms. Herrera didn't intend for the color red to symbolize anything. Certainly not the blood ties between a bird and her offspring. By the way, a sparrow is an excellent mother. Just as you've been to Vivi."

I sat up a little straighter. The compliment caught me by surprise. *Was* it a compliment? "Thank you," I said. "I think."

"One thing worries me," Sabine said. "You don't have an identity, other than being an orphan, a widow, and a mother."

A fluttering noise filled my head, as if all those sparrows had ripped away from my dress and were soaring into the air. "I came here to return your cat," I said. "Not to get a personality analysis."

"Well, I'm giving you one anyway. You've lost your parents and your husband, but you've allowed those tragedies to define you. Now you're losing your child. Never mind that it's temporary. You feel nothing but loss. You can't feel joy when Raphael gives you a present."

"I did, too."

"You're a frugal soul, whether from necessity or choice. And his extravagance always bothers you. Perhaps it makes you feel miserly."

Sabine had spoken barely above a whisper, but her words sliced across the table. I hadn't been thinking about Raphael. How had she known about the dress? Had she dug into my subconscious thoughts? I had a sudden image of Sabine holding long, sharp tweezers, digging through the moldy parts of my brain.

"How do you know that he gave me this dress?"

"I read his mind last night. He'd ordered the dress from his iPhone—he e-mailed Ms. Herrera herself. Raphael knew the dress wouldn't make you happy, but that's all he knew to do."

"You don't know anything," I said.

"I know too much. Raphael has been my friend for thirty years. He has a big heart and a vast disposable income. I wouldn't be a physician if he hadn't financed my education. But like any man, he has flaws. I've never known a time when a beautiful woman hasn't been hanging on his arm. Never the same one, of course. Not that serial dating is wrong, unless you happen to be on the wrong side of the relationship. Taming him would be a Sisyphean task."

She'd hit a tender place, one I didn't like to examine too closely. Like Uncle Nigel always said, vampires and fidelity go together like tiramisu and turnips.

"You're meddling," I said.

"I'm offering insight."

"I don't want your help. If you keep going, I won't let you help Vivi, either."

She lifted an eyebrow. "Do you have any idea why he has invested so heavily in real estate? And in this economy?"

"That's his business."

"In all the years I've known him, he's owned two homes, one in Australia and one in Italy. Then about ten years ago, he started buying houses and resorts all over the world. Now I know why. He bought them so you and Vivi would have safe places to stay. Have you ever wondered why he went to all this trouble?"

Trouble. That word summed up my fears. I didn't want to be an encumbrance. He'd felt obligated to help me. Maybe because he'd known my parents, and he was Vivi's godfather.

"I'm not sure what you're getting at." I drank the rest of my coffee.

"Haven't you wondered why he keeps putting himself at risk? He could have dinner with a different Chanel model every night. But he's chosen to escort you two all over the world. He took you to Longyearbyen—during the polar day."

"I didn't ask him to do that."

"Are you being deliberately obtuse? I saw how he watched you last night. He's in love with you."

I set down the empty cup a little too hard, then bent over to see if I'd cracked the saucer.

"Caro, you're falling in love with him."

"What does this have to do with Vivi? Are you trying to distract me? To make me look inward?"

"A little introspection wouldn't hurt. Caution has

become your default reaction to everything. It's out of control, just like Vivi's Induction."

"You're as much fun as a lobotomy."

"Prudence won't keep anyone safe. It's better to be emotionally flexible. Knowing when to run and when to be still. And when to take a risk."

"I've lived on the edge so long, I can't afford to be careless."

Sabine reached across the table, lifted my hands, and spread them apart. "Your left hand represents caution. Your right signifies recklessness. Two extremes. With a huge spectrum in between."

She paused, as if waiting for me to comment. When I didn't, she slid my left hand an inch closer to the right. "Move a few degrees away from caution and you arrive at watchfulness. The middle of the spectrum is perspicacity."

I exhaled. "How can I get there?"

"You've already started."

"I hope you're right." I glanced toward the closed door. Just beyond that lay the suitcases. "Vivi's clothes are at Raphael's."

"You knew you were coming here. Why didn't you bring them?"

"I was focused on the cat."

"No, no. You came here to make an exchange—Marie-Therese for Vivi."

I could feel her peeking into my deepest thoughts. I blocked her. "She needs clothes, Sabine."

"You're still trying to take control," she said. "This

afternoon Lena is going shopping at Moschino Teen. Vivi gave her a list—she loves pink the way I love white. I'll make sure she doesn't wear anything that will draw attention. And don't try to pay me."

I lifted my cup and started to take a sip, when I realized it was empty.

"I need more coffee, too." Sabine pushed away from the table. She went to the counter and lifted the pot. "You might want to take a cleansing breath. Vivi is awake. She will be down here any second."

Sabine was a witch. She knew everything.

She'd just finished refilling our cups when footsteps pounded in the hallway. Vivi swung into the kitchen, one hand caught on the door frame. She wore a white cotton nightgown that I'd never seen before. Her mouth opened wide when she caught sight of me.

"Mom!"

My heart stuttered as I looked into my daughter's eyes. So much like Jude's, the same deep blue, with defiant brown specks in her left iris.

"Sabine told me you'd be here today," she said.

"I returned Marie-Therese."

"Awesome." Vivi swirled into the room, the gown flowing around her ankles. She gave me a peck on the cheek, then plopped down into an empty chair.

Sabine lifted the pot. "Would you like coffee or juice?"

"Juice, please," Vivi said.

Sabine opened the refrigerator and lifted a carton. I glanced back at Vivi. She looked rested and happy.

"Everything will be fine," Sabine said. She placed a tall

glass of juice in front of Vivi. Then she left the room, Marie-Therese trotting behind her.

Vivi took a sip of juice. "Is that a new dress?"

I nodded.

"It's pretty. And it totally shows off your boobs."

I put my elbow on the table and leaned toward her. "Where is Sabine taking you?"

"It's a secret. The next time you see me, I'll be cured. You and Raphael won't have to worry."

"I'm not worried. I have faith in you."

"Then don't look so freaked out. Sabine knows what she's doing."

"Super."

"Oh, Mom. Nobody but dweebs and noobs say *super*."

"I've always been dweeby."

She sprang out of her chair and dove at me. "I'm gonna miss you."

I pulled her close, smoothing her hair and breathing in the smells of herbal shampoo and soap, along with a deeper fragrance that was uniquely Vivi—milk and buttered rice. "I love you beyond all else, Meep."

"Forevs," she whispered.

On the way to the front door, she pulled me into a creamy library and stopped in front of a framed etching. "I hate to say this, Mom. But you remind me of this picture."

"How am I like a ruined château?"

"Well, the walls are standing, but the best parts are gone."

"That's not so." I pulled her into my arms. "You're the best part of me."

As I walked out of Sabine's building, I noticed that the black Jaguar had been replaced with a silver Audi. I climbed into the backseat and wrapped my arms around my waist. Morning sunlight streamed into the car as it rushed down Avenue George V, toward Pont de l'Alma, then angled into a parking garage on Quai Branley. I sat there a moment, blinking in the dim light. I'd completely lost track of time. On the Jaguar's dashboard, the digital display read: JULY 14.

Raphael had shown up in Scotland eight days ago—or was I mistaken? Maybe it was seven or nine days ago. The whole month of July was a blur. I had no idea where we would be eight days from now.

Sabine's words floated up: *He's in love with you.* But was he really?

You're falling in love with him? God help me if that was true.

I moved to the new car, a brown Mercedes. As I sank into the leather seat, I felt weighted down by Sabine's words. Each one churned in my stomach, as if I'd been force-fed my least favorite foods: sushi, liver, anchovies. I didn't want to admit it, but I saw the point of that indigestible meal.

Maybe I was a little too guarded, but I wasn't sure I could change. After Vivi was born, my focus had been her safety. As a result, my life and Jude's had narrowed to pinpoints—Vivi's world was even smaller. If I could make the clocks spin backward, if I could return to the moment she was born, I would make the same choices. And I always would. Just thinking about this made my throat constrict, and I could barely pull in a breath. How I loved her.

The Mercedes headed back across the Seine and threaded its way through the twisting, medieval streets to Saint-Honoré. I looked out the window. The store-fronts were filled with dazzling colors. Pedestrians walked by Christian Lacroix, Hermes, and Dolce & Gabbana. Tourists were laughing and taking pictures.

As we got closer to Place des Victoires, the driver and the guard discussed the best strategy to escort me from the vehicle to the house. The guard was a beefy man, and his knit shirt could barely contain his muscles. He looked strong enough to yank the Prada store out of the cement. All of Raphael's security men looked the same—no distinguishing marks, no jewelry, no unusual features. They dressed casually, no bright colors or designer labels. Indistinguishability was part of the strategy.

The guard handed me a red wig, sunglasses, and a full-length white shawl. I put them on. How long could I keep running? At which point do you crash and burn? How much was this plan costing Raphael?

Stop it, Caro. You're not his financial planner. Do not question his tactics.

The Mercedes stopped in front of the blue-paneled doors, and I was swept into the sunny courtyard. The majordomo met me at the front door. Monsieur La Rochenoire's narrow face was dominated by dark, wooly brows, and as he looked at me, they moved violently, like caterpillars doing pushups. A long chef's apron covered the front of his white dress shirt and dark trousers.

"Monsieur Della Rocca is in the third-floor lounge,"

he said in a thick French accent. "He would like to see you."

"Now?" I was surprised. Raphael spent the daylight hours alone. That was when he infused himself with blood.

"Yes, *madame*," La Rochenoire said.

I gave him the wig, and he held it aloft, as if it were a biohazard, then dropped it in a closet. Before he'd signed on with Raphael, La Rochenoire had managed the households of diplomats and, more recently, the president of France. He was also a skilled chef. As he led me up the marble staircase, his apron gave off the aromas of thyme and fresh-baked bread.

Smells that never failed to make me ravenous. But as I followed him to the third floor, my appetite dimmed, as if Sabine's indigestible words were still roiling inside me. At the end of the arched hall, I heard clicking dog tags, and a second later, Arrapato stood in a doorway, his tongue caught between his teeth. I lifted him into my arms, and he greeted me with a cold, slobbery kiss.

"I'm in here," Raphael called.

I carried Arrapato into the shadowy room, and La Rochenoire closed the door behind me with a soft click. All six balcony doors were covered with arched wooden panels, and each one was painted with a trompe l'oeil sky. I stopped by a table and turned on a lamp.

Raphael was sitting on a black leather sofa. His white, blousy shirt was open at the neck, the cuffs unbuttoned. He wore tattered jeans, and his bare feet were propped on an ottoman. He put down a leather book.

"I've been worried about you," he said. His gaze swept

over the sparrow dress, not in a lascivious way. He seemed relieved to see me. I didn't see a trace of the man who'd reduced me to a quivering nub in Zermatt. He was making it easy for me, and I liked that. I liked it a lot.

I sat down beside him. "Thanks for the dress. It's lovely."

"Sei bella." He patted Arrapato's head and didn't ask where I'd been. That was another thing I adored about him—he never pried. Of course, maybe he'd already read my mind, but I didn't think so. He'd had centuries to figure out the feminine brain.

"I went to Sabine's," I said.

He glanced up from the dog, regarding me with an amused expression. In the faint light, his eyes were the color of dark brown sugar. "I hope the cat went, too, because I can't find her," he said. "And Arrapato looks guilty."

The dog's tail beat against the cushion. "Marie-Therese is fine. But Sabine is leaving Paris—with my child. She wouldn't tell me where she's going. Neither would Vivi."

"Paris attracts telepathic vampires. That makes it a telepathic city. Sabine doesn't want to put you or Vivi at risk."

"I can shield my thoughts."

"Of course you can." He put his arm around me, and I leaned against his billowy shirt. A hug was just what I needed. I breathed in his reassuring smell, pomegranates and patchouli and rain-drenched earth. I got lost for a minute in the softness of his shirt and the firm skin beneath it.

He moved a little closer, and his hair swung down. I fought the urge to tuck the lock behind his ear.

There was a rap at the door. Raphael and I moved apart. "Yes?" he called.

"*Alimentation pour madame, monsieur*," La Rochenoire called.

"*Oui, entrez, s'il vous plait*," Raphael said.

The door creaked open, and the majordomo stepped into the room, carrying a glass of lemonade on a silver tray. His apron was gone, and he'd put on the tailored black jacket that he always wore. As he lowered the tray, lavender sprigs bobbed against the rim of the glass. I thanked him and lifted the glass.

"I haven't had lavender lemonade since I was a child," I said.

La Rochenoire looked pleased, then turned to Raphael. "Rain is on the way, sir. Scattered showers tomorrow evening, followed by a few overcast days. Shall I arrange for more security?"

Raphael nodded, looking vaguely troubled.

Vampire weather, I thought.

La Rochenoire left the room. I lifted the glass. It was packed with shaved ice, and each sip tasted sugary and tart. Raphael was smiling.

As I lowered my glass, Sabine's words came back to me again, and I was afraid Raphael would read my thoughts. "How did you meet Sabine?"

"At a soiree. She'd crashed the party to see Monsieur d'Orsay. She pleaded with him to accept her as his daughter. He threw a cup of blood in her face. The edge of the cup hit her forehead."

I thought of the white scar that curved under her bangs.

"Everyone in his crowd laughed," Raphael said. "She walked out onto the rooftop terrace, blood dripping down her face. It was windy that night, and cold. Sabine was crying so hard, her nose was running. She straddled the rail, and I was afraid she'd jump. I told her that I knew where to find her biological father. She climbed off the rail."

"Who was he?"

"A Canadian physician. But he'd moved to Paris. Dr. Hoffman was barely five feet tall. Stocky, dark eyes, auburn hair. A male version of Sabine. He was an internist at the American Hospital. But the Occitaine Cabal made sure he was dismissed. For a while, he worked as a gardener in Neuilly-sur-Seine. He encouraged Sabine to become a physician. But he could not afford to send her to school."

So that was why Raphael had financed her education. I lifted the glass and took a sip, breathing in the lavender smell. "Is he still alive?"

"Oh, yes. Sabine and I helped him set up a practice in Zürich."

I was starting to understand why Sabine was so fond of Raphael and why she'd cleared her schedule to work with Vivi. I traced my finger around the rim of the glass, then moved the lavender stem up and down in the glass. It was an unconscious gesture—at least I think it was. But then I saw Raphael's gaze follow my hand. It was shameful how much that excited me.

I crossed my legs. But the friction only caused more stimulation.

"You seem restless," he said.

"Do I? Maybe I should go jogging."

"Swimming is more private."

His pool was in the cellar. The last time I'd seen it, spiders were running up the walls, and the water smelled like brimstone. "You want me to swim in the birthplace of evil?"

"You're thinking of the old pool," he said. "I renovated the cellar last fall."

"A renovation wouldn't help," I said, trying not to smile. "But an A-bomb might."

"Go ahead and laugh. It's going to be in *Architectural Digest* this fall."

"A demonic cellar? That'll be a first. Who was the designer? The one who messed up your drawing room?"

"No, a brilliant architect. Come on, I'll show you."

And just like that, I was having fun again and feeling guilty about it. I put down my glass, and we walked into the hall, past a hand-painted mural that depicted scenes from a vineyard.

"I have a new elevator, too," he said.

He clicked the center panel and a door swung open. We stepped into a tiny car. Raphael looked around for Arrapato. The dog sat in the hall, glaring at us, his head resting on his paws.

"See?" I said. "The dog knows we're going to a bad place."

"Just wait," Raphael said as the elevator whirred downward. "You'll take back all of your cruel words."

The door opened, and a fresh smell washed into the car. Music drifted from speakers in the ceiling, and Cary Brothers began to sing "Take Your Time." The cellar of the damned had been banished. Clay pots bursted with ferns and vines. Three teak chaise longues were lined up in front of an angular pool, which shimmered with a pristine radiance.

At the far end of the cellar, another mural showed an Italian garden. A tiled bar held stemware and liquor bottles. On the counter was a huge brandy snifter filled with matchbooks from nightclubs. Next to the bar was a thick walnut door that stood open, showing a narrow stairwell.

"Where does that lead?" I asked.

"The courtyard."

"And you just leave it open?"

"There's a door at the top of the stairs. It stays bolted. Hold on, let me check." He dashed up the stairs. I moved to the bar and lifted a matchbook from the snifter. Le Truskel on Rue Fey Deau, an after-midnight club. I dropped it.

He returned. "It's locked."

His hand closed around mine, and he guided me around the pool to the mural. "During the renovation, my architect found an old smuggler's tunnel. It was used by the French Resistance."

I glanced around, looking for a door. "Where is it?"

"Hidden." He gestured at the mural. It covered the entire back wall—cypress and linden trees, benches, pergolas, rose beds, and fountains. I studied each image, looking for the outline of a door, anything with straight lines.

My gaze returned to the cypress trees. I ran the flat of my hand over the wall, feeling the rough paint. Then my fingers bumped over a rigid edge. I pushed against it. A door swung away from the mural. Standing behind it was a metal door with an electronic keypad.

Raphael punched in the code, 2276. The door grated open, swinging on its hinges, and cool, sour-smelling air drifted out. Rough limestone steps plunged into darkness. Way off in the distance, I heard dripping water. I opened the door wider, and light from the cellar shone on the old stone-and-mortar walls.

"Where does it lead?" I asked.

"To a bigger door," he said. "Much thicker than this one."

"What's beyond that?"

"The sewer." He gazed off into the darkness.

"You haven't gone exploring yet?"

"No."

"Let's go sometime."

"Really? You'd tramp through a smelly labyrinth?"

"Why not?"

"It's a date," he said.

A *Les Misérables* date, I reminded myself. We'd need hard hats, flashlights, nose plugs, and tall rubber boots.

While Raphael put the mural back together, I walked around the pool. The water lapped against the smooth turquoise tiles that lined the perimeter. I tucked my hair behind my ears, but it wouldn't stay. The humidity was causing curls to spring free all over my head. I glanced over my shoulder.

Raphael was smiling. "You walk with a dancer's awareness," he said. "Alert and poised. Shoulders back. Head up. Floaty steps."

"Funny you should say that. When I was six years old,

I got kicked out of ballet class. The instructor said I had flat feet."

"They're not flat now." He walked toward me, glancing from my ankles to my face. A dazzle moved through me. I had a couple of options. I could get in the elevator or I could do something reckless. I mean, why not? So what if we make love? I didn't need to turn it into something it wasn't. A dweeb could be cool, right?

I kicked off my shoes and dipped my right foot into the warm, silky water. This was about as wild as I could get. If only I were bold enough to strip down to my bra and panties, but Raphael had always seen me fully clothed, except for that one tiny moment in Norway, and the bedroom had been dark. I hadn't seen much of him, either.

He edged in beside me. His pupils dilated, obscuring the dark irises. A pulse leaped in his neck. "Are you going in?"

"I don't have a swimsuit."

"Coward."

If I didn't do something, and soon, he was going to kiss me and I wouldn't stop him. The music changed, and I recognized the melancholy opening notes to "Be Here Now," a poignant ballad about lovers and their unstable inner walls.

I thought of the sparrow dress that Raphael had given me. Now his stereo—which he was controlling with his mind—was playing symbolic music. What was he trying to tell me?

His hand grazed mine. His skin felt cool and slightly rough. Water pattered to the stones as I lifted my foot from the water. Steam drifted from the surface, glided under the hem of my dress, and brushed across my thighs.

"Don't think too much, *mia cara*."

Who could think? I couldn't catch my breath. All I had to do was put on my shoes, and he'd smile and make a joke, putting us both at ease. He was so good at changing a debauched situation into a pleasing one.

I stepped back, and his hand fell away. I wiggled my damp feet into the pumps, and then his hand caught my cheek. My nipples tingled, and I leaned into his hand. He looked into my eyes, then lowered his head until his lips were almost touching mine. I slid my hands along the back of his neck, knotting my fingers in his hair, and gently tugged his face closer to mine.

"You're still thinking," he said.

"Not that much." But he was right. My mind was on premeditated orgasms.

His hands tightened around my waist, and he lifted me off the floor. I felt a rush of cool air on my feet as my shoes slid off and clattered against the floor.

"*La sua bellezza porta via il mio fiato*," he said.

It took a few seconds for my brain to translate: *Your beauty takes my breath away.*

He was such a good liar. He moved me higher, and my toes brushed over his shins, scraping over the rough khakis. I felt a massive hardness behind his zipper. I locked my ankles around his waist, and pleasure unfurled deep inside me.

My face was just a little above his, and I leaned down to kiss him. He tasted like grape juice, the kind that's served at communion, just a dribble in a tiny glass, never enough to fill you. One of his hands moved to my face. The other slid down to my bottom. I was dimly aware that the music had changed, something a mermaid might listen to, all wordless and watery. He slid the tip of his thumb into my mouth, and I gently sucked the plump mound until his breath came in short gasps.

Inside me, a wave rose to a peak, quivering, then crashed through me so fast I barely had time to catch my breath before the next swell moved in. His lips felt cool against my neck. My head tipped back, and I shuddered against him.

Raphael's iPhone rang. He ignored it and kept kissing my throat. The phone stopped trilling abruptly, and the phone in the elevator buzzed. He went on kissing me, moving his lips up and down my neck.

I put a little more energy behind the kiss, and he moaned.

His cell phone went off again. Arrapato's muffled barks echoed from the elevator shaft. I dragged my lips away from his.

"Raphael, something's wrong."

"No." His lips went back to my neck.

But I was distracted by the ringing, and I eased away.

Raphael groaned. He set me down and pulled the phone from his trouser pocket. In the seconds before he raised it to his ear, I heard La Rochenoire's excited voice, but I couldn't make out the words.

Raphael's eyebrows slammed together. He abruptly turned. "What does she want?" he said. From behind he looked tall and chiseled, and I had no trouble imagining him naked.

"Yes, yes. I'm on my way," he said, and dropped the phone into his pocket. His hand caught my arm. "I won't be long."

He was leaving me in the cellar? Renovated or not, I wasn't staying here.

"I'll come with you." I started to follow, but the terror on his face stopped me.

I drew back. "What's wrong? Has something happened to Vivi?"

"No, no. Just a household disturbance. Please wait for me."

He'd spoken with a light tone, but he'd looked at the elevator, as if he were impatient to rush upstairs.

He hadn't been gone three minutes when I heard shouting—a woman was cursing in French. "Fucking incubus," she yelled, her voice soaring down the elevator shaft. It seemed to be coming from the first-floor drawing room.

Raphael's told the woman to leave—loudly. There was a crash, and I heard weeping. Okay, it didn't take telepathy to figure this out. One of Raphael's girlfriends had found out he was in town.

I stepped into the elevator. Before I reached the first floor, I heard Arrapato's yelp, followed by a scrabbling noise. The elevator door slid open, and I walked into the hall, hurrying to the ice-blue drawing room.

The heavy doors stood ajar, as if someone had shoved them. I peeked inside. The room was empty. The air smelled odd and sulfuric, as if a match had been snuffed out. The windows were shuttered except the one in the middle; the wooden panel gaped open crookedly. Had it been wrenched from the frame?

A wedge of sunlight glimmered on the floor, where a copper bowl lay upside down, dozens of antique keys spilled around it. I knelt beside the bowl, lifted a dark bronze, baroque key, and studied the fleur-de-lis on its bow. When I'd been an undergraduate at King's College, I'd studied etymology; the Old English word for *key* basically meant a solution. A tool to unlock hidden places. Uncle Nigel used to say that if you owned a key, you owned something you didn't want to lose.

I heard a noise from the doorway and looked up. Monsieur La Rochenoire stood just outside the room, his face bland and unreadable. "Dinner will be served at six in the dining room," he said. "Unless you'd like a tray sent to your room."

The key made a decisive clink when I set it in the bowl. "I'm not hungry."

"As you wish, *madame*."

"Where's Raphael?"

"I do not know."

I hadn't expected him to lie. I pushed the bowl aside and glanced at the gilt mantel clock. A quarter after two. Raphael couldn't leave the house until dark. I turned back to La Rochenoire. "But he's home?"

His face still held no expression. Then one wooly eyebrow began to twitch.

I got to my feet. "I heard shouting."

La Rochenoire tucked his hands behind his back. "If you change your mind about dinner, let me know."

After he left, a deep weariness pushed in around me. I couldn't stop yawning—a sure sign of anxiety. It was still daylight, but I went up to my room and slumped onto the bed. Now I understood why I'd kept my distance from Raphael all these years. I was the opposite of cool. I couldn't settle for casual sex, although *casual* was the wrong word, because sex with a vampire wasn't laid-back, though it involved getting laid. Over and over. It was addictive. Once you'd had sex with one of *them*, you had no desire to be with a human.

This reaction has a physiological basis. Vampires are built for predation, and all good predators know how to attract whatever they want. When vampires become aroused, they exude some type of chemical that causes euphoria in the victim, along with temporary numbness— luckily, I was immune to the latter symptom.

But I wasn't immune to the next phase: an exaggerated sexual response. A male vamp doesn't experience a refractory period after orgasm. He can literally make love for days. Or he can send his partner into a climactic frenzy with the barest touch. When Jude had kissed me, sometimes I climaxed. And I'd already witnessed what Raphael could do.

As for Raphael . . . well, I couldn't stop thinking about what had happened by the pool. Then I heard Arrapato's muffled barks, and I knew that they were in this house.

CHAPTER 25

Caro

PLACE DES VICTOIRES
PARIS, FRANCE

I slept through supper, breakfast, and lunch. I awoke at four P.M., and when I finally got moving, I found a note wedged under my door.

Mia cara,

Please join me at 7 P.M. for a picnic in the courtyard.

R

I turned over the note to see if he'd written on the back, but it was blank. That was all? No explanation about the screaming woman? I carried the note to the window and pushed back the curtain. The afternoon sky was packed with gray clouds, and I remembered Monsieur La Rochenoire's weather prediction. Rain was headed to Paris. Before I shut the curtain, a golden shaft of light cut through the dirty clouds and brightened the slate rooftops across the street. Somehow that made me feel better.

A maid with curly gray hair brought a tea tray and set it on the table. Sugary beignets sat on a paper doily, next to pots of butter and gooseberry jam. Steam drifted from the teapot's curved spout.

"Where's Monsieur Della Rocca?" I asked.

"Upstairs, *madame*," she said. "He and the little dog were injured yesterday."

I felt all the blood leave my head. The room swirled, and I sat down on the chaise longue. "Are they all right?"

"*Oui, madame*. A small injury."

"What kind?"

"You must ask Monsieur La Rochenoire." She backed out of the room, her forehead puckered. "If you need anything, ring the kitchen on the house phone."

I poured a cup of tea and sat back down on the chaise longue. Had the screaming woman punched Raphael in the eye? No, the maid had said that Arrapato had been injured. What could have happened to them? I remembered the broken window panel and the scorched smell. They'd been sunburned?

He's well enough to host a picnic, I reminded myself.

I'd almost slept with him—again. I shouldn't be thinking about Raphael. I should be thinking about my daughter. Was she still in Paris? Or had Sabine taken her away? Maybe when Vivi returned, we could go shopping like a regular mother and daughter. I had such fond memories of the time that Uncle Nigel and I had gone to the Marché aux Puces de Saint-Ouen. If you pumped a flea market with steroids and added a dash of caffeine you'd get the Marché aux Puces.

Vivi would love the flea market. I'd buy her earrings, bracelets, vintage dresses, anything she wanted. And we'd come home on the Metro like normal people.

I took a sip of tea, and as the warmth moved through me, I thought of Jude. When we'd gone into hiding, I had believed the danger would eventually end. Perhaps my parents had thought the same thing when they'd moved to Tennessee. Their narrow, carefully constructed world hadn't saved them. But like Jude always said, if they'd lived in the open, they would have died sooner.

Jude and I had made the same choices that my parents had made, except we'd kept moving. We'd been convinced that my parents had died because they'd stayed too long in one place. But now, I realized that Jude and I had overlooked a critical point. My parents knew who'd been chasing them, and why. I couldn't put a face or name to the threat.

Who were the players? What did they want? To kill my daughter or put her in a cage? Who'd slaughtered Keats and put my husband's ring on his finger? Who'd sent assassins to Scotland?

I'd had a decade to think about evil, but now it seemed as if fear was my biggest enemy. Fear is portable. It fits into the tiniest suitcase and speaks all languages. It can reduce your life to the width of a pin head. Maybe it was better to spend one morning at the flea market, with your senses fully engaged, than to spend a hundred years in a fortress.

———

Just before seven, I got dressed. I found a white, ankle-length tank dress in my plaid bag. I put it on, then slid my feet into purple flip-flops. I wasn't sure what to expect at the picnic, but I hoped my clothes would telegraph my intentions: *I'm not sprucing myself up for you. I'm a slob who doesn't even paint her toenails.*

As an afterthought, I tied back my hair with a thin black ribbon. Then I grabbed a white sweater and buttoned it up to my neck. I walked down to the first floor. The courtyard was just off the blue drawing room. Lamps burned softly on the tables, warming the icy color scheme. The panel on the French doors had been repaired, and one stood open, letting a breeze stir the curtains. I stepped outside, my flip-flops ticking over the pavé stones. Lavender and rosemary grew in pots, and their pungent scents blotted out the gritty exhaust fumes that clung to Place des Victoires.

"Mia cara." Raphael stood near the fountain, smiling in a way that made my pulse whoosh in my ears. His navy twill shorts hit just below his knees, showing athletic calves. The wind kicked up the edges of his white shirt. His hair had been freshly shampooed and hung just below his chin. A red flush spread across his cheeks, as if he'd just returned from a day at Cannes.

Arrapato shot across the courtyard, his singed fur sticking up. I bent down to pet him, and I felt a knotty patch. "What happened?"

I was looking at the dog, but from the corner of my eye, I saw Raphael shift his feet.

"The burns are almost gone," he said.

I nodded. Vampires healed rapidly thanks to an abundance of stem cells—a crucial component in immortality.

"The blue-obsessed designer broke into my house," he said. "La Rochenoire found her in my bedroom. She was throwing lamps and vases. By the time I arrived, she was trashing the drawing room." His gaze drifted toward the French door. "She opened one of the wooden panels. The sun burned me and Arrapato."

"Oh." I was starting to see more than I was prepared to handle. I'd never been in Raphael's room. "Where were your security people?"

"She conned her way inside. They even helped her carry in something. I haven't found it yet."

"When you do, make sure it's not ticking."

"I broke up with her a year ago."

I paused, thinking. "How'd she know you're in Paris?"

"Her friend saw me at Chez Georges."

"But you wore a disguise that night."

"I can't explain it."

"Maybe you need a better wig." I smiled. "And meaner security guards."

He pushed his hand through his hair. "If someone recognized me, they might have noticed you and Vivi. I've been complacent. Maybe arrogant. I thought the disguises and cars would be sufficient."

"You're not arrogant, Raphael."

"Do you want to know why I broke up with the designer?"

"No." And I didn't. This surprised me, because two minutes earlier, Raphael's hyperactive love life had been very much on my mind. I couldn't think of anything that would have brought me to this calm place—unless Sabine had Induced me to be tranquil.

But the weather was looking a little wicked. Clouds bunched over the courtyard, blotting out the stars. Arrapato sensed it, too. He wriggled away from me and trotted across toward the house. He peed on the blue draperies. I was glad.

Raphael smiled. "You're an unusual woman."

"A barrel of laughs."

He put his hand on my elbow. "The picnic is just around the corner."

A yellow paisley cloth had been laid over a bed of clipped thyme. Votive candles flickered in between pots of lemon balm and peppermint. I sat down on the cloth, stirring up a fresh, green smell. Raphael had gone to a lot of trouble, and I was touched.

He sat across from me and opened a basket. He pulled out clear plastic boxes, the lids stamped with the name of a pricey food emporium. Quiche, Camembert, baguettes, strawberries, foie gras, *tarte au citron*. A bottle of Sauvignon Chinon.

"It looks delicious." I pulled off a piece of Camembert and slid it between my lips. He tipped the wine bottle over my glass, and I smelled violets and raspberries. As I took a sip, I couldn't remember my senses ever having been this alive, caught up in the fruity taste of the wine, the smell of Raphael's cologne, the wind stirring the lavender, the fragrant herbs beneath the paisley cloth.

"You look beautiful, Caro," he whispered, then lifted a strawberry.

I released a breath. From the moment we'd met, he'd called me *mia cara*. Rarely did he say *Caro* or *Caroline*. When I was a girl, the other kids had referred to me as *Karo syrup* and *Cairo*, but on Raphael's tongue, each letter of my name seemed to rise into the air, elegant and curled as calligraphy.

He bit into the strawberry and rubbed the moist fleshy side over his lips. Then he pressed the berry just below my ear. I felt a droplet slide down my neck and slip beneath my sweater.

I shivered.

He ate the berry, which shocked me, then undid the top button on my sweater and blew on my neck. I began tingling all over. Why did that feel so good?

"More?" he said.

I nodded.

He progressed to the next button, and I felt a rush of cool air. He kept going, as if he were pulling a ribbon from a gift box. Then the sweater was off, and my breasts were rising and falling beneath my thin cotton dress.

He leaned into me, holding my gaze. "I want you, Caro."

"I want you, too."

"Are you sure?" he whispered. "Because if you aren't, I'll wait."

I was sure about many things. I was sure that we were going to make love, and it might change me, change us, change everything we thought we knew. He had been my friend and protector, but I was ready to take him into the deepest part of me.

"Yes, I'm sure."

He grazed his teeth over my lips, and I tasted the sweetness of the berry. His head moved down the front of my dress, his breath cool and fruity, blowing against the cotton.

"You're shaking, *mia cara*."

"Mmm-hmm."

He fit himself on top of me, his twill shorts scratching my skin. He slid his right hand beneath the small of my back. His tongue moved past my lips, just the right balance of tension and softness. His other hand brushed under my dress, skimming between my legs, tracing the lace edge of my thong. I arched against him when his finger moved under the lace and dipped inside me. I wound my arm around his neck. He tugged at the lace garment, urging it down over one hip then the other, down my thighs and then it was gone.

"You smell like sunlight," he said, pushing his knees between my legs, gently nudging them apart. His head moved under the dress, and his tongue found me. A delicate dance began, and each stroke made my thoughts dissolve. He pulled up my dress, bunching it around my waist. My hips rose from the blanket, and the tiny spasms became larger, each one frilled with pleasure.

A long while later, his head moved up and then his eyes were level with mine, and an immense hardness pressed against me. Over his head, the sky flickered, bleaching white for a few seconds, and then I heard thunder. He moved his hand between my legs again, and I shuddered. A raindrop hit my shoulder; another tapped against the back of my hand. Then a light ticking rain began to fall.

The wind whipped his hair, blond strands darkening by the rain. He pressed his full weight on me, and I sank down into the thyme. Rain picked around us, plunging against the stones like rice poured into a bowl. A candle hissed. In seconds his cotton shirt was stuck to his skin like wet tissue paper.

He kissed the side of my mouth, delicate and tickly as a butterfly wing. My hand moved to his zipper, and I caught the metal tab and moved it down. I helped him take off his shorts, then opened my legs wider.

He entered me a little at a time, moving gently. I was damp and ready, and I squirmed against him, a siren, singing to him with my body, luring him into softness.

Rain swept around us, hammering into the stones.

His teeth pressed against my neck.

"No," I said.

"Why not?"

"I'll explain later." I slid my foot behind his calf, then lifted my hips off the blanket. He was only halfway inside, and I moved beneath him. Keep going, I thought. Just a little deeper. A little. He embedded himself with one deep thrust.

I could feel him moving inside me. I climaxed instantly. My hands skidded over his back. He was holding me so tight, his heartbeat seemed to pass through me.

"Am I hurting you?" he whispered.

"No, no, no."

He kissed me again, and I tasted the rain on his mouth.

I came again. I cried out, trembling. He swelled inside me, and I tilted my hips, urging him deeper. He put my fingers in his mouth, then moved my hand between our damp stomachs and moved lower, to the exact place where we were joined. The rain seemed to be falling inside me, right there, where he was moving.

"*Ti amo, mia cara*. I have always loved you."

My thoughts scattered as he plunged deeper and deeper.

"And I always will, Caro." His breath hit my cheek, and his thighs tensed. I tried to slow down, but it was too late. He drove into me one more time, and his face tightened, his dark brows slanted together. An earthy wetness filled me, and I was swept into a cataclysmic place where time had come unhinged. Past, present, and future coiled around me in overlapping circles, pulling me into the hidden place where pleasure is born.

I was still trying to catch my breath when he lifted me off the damp paisley cloth, into his arms. He'd gotten dressed—when had I missed that? I felt a little dizzy as he carried me into the house, my wet hair swinging against my shoulders.

Halfway up the stairs he put me down and pressed me against the wall. His lips came down on mine, his hand cupping the back of my head, the other cradling my bottom. I ran my palm over the front of his zipper. He was already thick and hard. I gave him a teasing smile and moved my hand to his shoulder.

He put it back.

I tugged at his zipper and reached inside the gap. "You should have warned me, Raphael."

He kissed me again.

I pulled my lips away. "Take me to your bed."

He swept me into his arms and carried me up the stairs, to the third floor. He turned into a long, narrow room. Our lips met again as he set me down. Still holding him, I leaned back, and my gaze went straight up to a painted ceiling, clouds and fat cherubs. Then I looked down. A king-sized bed was on the right side of the room, with a poofy, bronze silk comforter folded back. Beyond, two balcony doors were covered with light-blocking shutters.

Raphael looked back at the door, where Arrapato stood, one paw raised. "Are you in or out?" he asked the dog.

Arrapato trotted across the floor, leaped into his own bed, and attacked a plastic mouse toy. As violent squeaks rose up, Raphael began peeling off my wet clothes. Music started to play, and the last part of "Exogenesis Symphony" began to pick up speed.

"Is this your room?" I asked, looking around for the angry decorator's touch—shattered lamps and slashed chairs. But everything was tidy.

"Yes."

My dress hit the floor with a wet slap. Then his shirt and shorts dropped. He put his arms around me. The box springs shuddered when we fell sideways onto the bed.

"We'll go slower this time," he said.

I awoke in tangled sheets, still flushed from all of the lovemaking. The bedroom was very dark, and I could hear rain tapping behind the shuttered window. Raphael lay on his back, one hand flung over his head. I had never seen him asleep, and he looked vulnerable and enticing, all at once.

If I fell in love with him—and I was already halfway there—I would have to let go of my prudent nature and open myself to the unknown. I would need to trust him, and in some ways, trust is harder than love. The unknowable future makes everyone vulnerable, but if I kept protecting myself, I would never be truly alive.

Also, I had to pee. Truly.

I slid off the bed and walked to the bathroom. It had been renovated, too. The ceiling was more than twenty feet high. The fixtures were modern—raised glass sinks, nickel faucets, and dark, clean-edged cabinets. On the left side of the room, a steel staircase led to a mezzanine with an iron catwalk. Behind the catwalk, on the wall, was a huge black-and-white photograph of a woman.

A glamour portrait? I thought and stepped closer. The woman was in her twenties, with wide eyes, shoulder-length hair, and high cheekbones.

Okay, fine. Raphael was a bachelor. He'd never hidden his girlfriends, but they'd never lasted more than a few weeks, as if expiration dates had been stamped onto their rear ends.

I walked to the sink and splashed water on my face. My hair had dried in Medusa-like curls. Charming. I stepped back and gazed up at the mezzanine. The woman's smile seemed to say, *I'll get you my pretty, and your little dog, too.*

Who was she? The blue-loving interior designer? Someone else? My vote went to the designer. Earlier tonight

Raphael had mentioned that she'd brought something into the house. Was this it, this photograph? That would explain why she'd needed the security team to bring it inside.

Only one person could answer this question, and he was asleep.

I heard a jangling noise and looked down. Arrapato bumped his cold nose against my leg. I bent over and scratched his ear. "Oh, the stories you could tell. Right, little man?"

His tail beat against my leg.

I felt breathless as I walked back into the dark bedroom. It smelled of sex and ketones. I slipped under the covers and pressed my cheek against the pillow. Arrapato plopped down on the floor and watched me with his shiny black eyes.

Never in my life had I felt jealous, but I wanted to squirt shaving cream all over that damn photograph. I shut my eyes, trying to sort through my feelings. A woman's photograph couldn't change my growing feelings for Raphael. Not unless I wanted them to change.

But I couldn't ignore the physics of a relationship. When two people sleep together, that closeness can create more closeness—or distance. Of course, it depends on the people. Maybe distance doesn't matter if you're cool and cosmopolitan. If you can look at sex as a pleasurable activity, and you don't get all needy, or try to pretend you're not needy.

But I wasn't cool. I was out of practice. It had been a while since I had dated, and the rules had changed.

It's worse if you're a hybrid. We're biologically weird,

and at some point it becomes impossible to hide that weirdness. There's some type of biochemical, almost like a pheromone, that oozes from our pores and attracts and spurns humans—sometimes at the same time. But vampires are drawn to people like me. Unfortunately, my antigens will make them run to the nearest emergency room.

Raphael stirred beside me. He slid his arm around my waist and pulled me against him. His lips stopped on my neck. "Anything wrong, *mia cara*?"

"You remember that thing you mentioned? The item your designer friend brought? Well, I think it's in your bathroom."

The bedsprings creaked as he rose from the mattress, and then his footsteps brushed over the rug. A few moments later, I heard him climb the metal stairs. He returned, carrying the large frame in one hand, as if it weighed no more than a paper clip. He opened the panel to the balcony and pushed open the door. Rain sprayed across the photo as he heaved it over the balcony. There was a pause, and then I heard a muffled clatter on the pavement.

He got back in bed and cupped his hands on my face. "I only want to be with you."

"It's okay, Raphael. Really. Don't worry."

"I want you to understand. Sex was always uncomplicated and entertaining. I gave women flowers and my time and my body. But not my soul. Never my soul. If I give it to you, I can't take it back."

A long while later, I fell asleep and dreamed about Raphael tossing that picture. I woke up and tried to sort through the meaning in the dream. Raphael's gesture seemed pretty damn symbolic. He was throwing away his old life. But I couldn't shake the feeling that something evil was creeping around the edges of this house, probing for crevices and secret corridors, its treacherous fingers digging through the walls and catching us unaware.

CHAPTER 26

Caro

The next afternoon, the rain stopped falling, and a gassy green haze washed over Place des Victoires. As I stood next to the kitchen window, I felt as if I were staring through a glass of absinthe.

I rubbed my forehead. So much had happened since Vivi and I had left Australia. I'd assumed that July would pass quickly and uneventfully. True, I was telepathic, but I would never earn a living as a fortune-teller.

Arrapato whined from the dark hallway. I closed the wooden shutter, blotting out the strange light, and the dog trotted into the room, gripping a scrolled paper in his mouth. He dropped it at my feet. I scratched his ear, then lifted the paper.

Come to the library. I love you and miss you.

R

I couldn't help but smile. I'd been gone twenty minutes—a girl has to eat carbohydrates. At least, this girl did. The hem of my blue dress whirled around my ankles as I followed Arrapato up to the third-story library.

Raphael sat on the sofa. He'd showered, and his damp hair hung in blond panels around his chin. He wore a Coldplay T-shirt and gray sweatpants. As I walked by him, he drew me into his lap. He lifted my hair and wound it around his neck.

"I could find my way out of a labyrinth if you were with me," he said.

My hips shifted over his thighs, and I felt him grow beneath me. Gently tugging my hair, he leaned back onto the sofa, pulling me on top of him.

"You're insatiable," I said.

"You're a hybrid. That's why you can keep up with me." His fingers caught the hem of my dress.

"What if someone walks in?" I asked.

Raphael glanced at the floor, where Arrapato glowered at him. "Guard the door, please."

The dog snorted and turned away. A minute later I heard his toenails snick over the wood floor. The next thing I knew, my underwear was gone and so were Raphael's sweatpants. He caught my face in his hands.

"No woman has ever made me this happy," he said.

"Not in a thousand years?" I ran my finger over his bottom lip.

"I've been waiting a long time to feel this way. I didn't think I would." Keeping his gaze on me, he nipped my finger, then let go. "I feel like I'm eighteen years old and I've just discovered sex."

"Mmm-hmm." I ran my finger over his bottom teeth. "You can't bite me."

He drew back. "Not ever?"

"I could make you ill." I paused. "Unless you took a Benadryl tablet."

"I'll find some later." He made a playful lunge for my neck.

"No." I explained about the antigens and antibodies. I even threw in a mini lecture about vampiric neurotoxins.

While I talked, he moved his hand under my dress.

"You have to take antihistamines at least fifteen minutes before you bite me," I said.

"I'll order some immediately." He grinned. "But until the medicine arrives, you can bite me, right?"

Afterward, we lay on the sofa. He traced his thumb along my cheekbone. I rested my hand on his chest, feeling his heart vibrate beneath my palm.

Raphael sighed, and I glanced up. Tiny scabs were forming at the base of his throat, where I'd nipped him.

"What's wrong?" I asked.

"I'm really sorry about that photo. I only dated her a week."

"It's not a problem."

"But the woman who put it there might be one," he

said. "She'll talk. Loudly and often. The wrong people might find out I'm in Paris. Then you will be at risk."

"Maybe we should leave," I said. "Let's go to New York."

"Maybe," he said.

Vivi and I had spent one summer at Raphael's condo in the Chelsea Mercantile Building. We'd bought groceries at Whole Foods, and every Saturday we'd walked to Barnes and Noble, where Vivi would gather an armful of children's books. That was the year that Raphael flew to New York and helped me celebrate her fifth birthday. We'd taken her to Alice's Tea Cup, then we took a carriage ride in Central Park.

"Manhattan might be the last great place to get lost," I said.

"True," Raphael said. One side of his mouth frowned; the other quirked up.

"You've got that look again," I said.

"What look?"

"The one you get when you want to tell me something, but you're not quite ready."

"We might be leaving Paris, after all." Raphael squeezed my hand. "Do you remember when Walpole mentioned the other survivor? I've located him. Dr. Nick Parnell made it out of the rain forest. He might know something."

My head filled with a rushing noise. "Where is he?"

"Marrakech."

"You're flying down there?"

"Yes."

"Why?"

"To see how his version fits with Walpole's account."

"You don't think he told us everything?"

He shrugged. "Discrepancies are just as important as consistencies."

"Why would Walpole lie?"

"I didn't say he lied. I think he omitted details."

"Like what? He told us that Jude was wearing his ring."

"There's more."

"How can you be sure?"

"I've got a feeling. Not prescience, but something else. It's like when the barometric pressure falls, and the east wind smells of ozone. You know bad weather is coming. Sometimes I feel a shift deep inside me. When it happens, I trust it."

"When are you leaving?"

"I'm not sure. Will you come with me?" He leaned back, watching me. His eyes were as brown as brown can get. I thought of leather, shaved chocolate, roasted espresso beans, rain pattering onto grape vines. River water rushing over umber stones. The dark, burnished gravity of this man pulled me in.

I am in love. After all this empty time, I am in love. And I am coming alive.

PART FIVE

BLOODSTREAM

CHAPTER 27

Gillian

VENICE, ITALY

The train pulled into Venice at sunset. Gillian had thought the city would remind her of New Orleans in its pre-Katrina days, another flat, marshy landscape that had been gussied up with ornate buildings, but she'd been wrong.

As she walked away from the station, she decided that Venice was more than a charming city, it was the pulsing heart of beauty itself. Plum-colored clouds drifted over the Italianate palaces and arched bridge, the images quivering in the water, as if a whole other city lay at the bottom of the lagoon.

I love this place so damn much, I might move here, she thought. She had traveled from Switzerland to Italy as Caroline Barrett, and no one had questioned her. She hadn't seen any vampires, either. And she'd been looking.

Tomorrow morning, a boat would meet her at the quay and take her to Villa Primaverina.

As she walked by the Grand Canal, a *vaporetto* sliced through the water, leaving a foamy wake. *What a lovely name for a water taxi*, she thought. The sun was going down, staining the water blood red. That was pretty, too. She angled toward Piazza San Marco, and the breeze stirred her sedate beige dress. She was afraid her Caro-like wig would fly off, so she tugged at the curls. When she passed by the arcades, two young men said, "*Bella, bella.*"

They were cute, not vampy in the least, but she kept walking. She'd never been this happy, even though she missed Fielding. Lord almighty, he was a fine man. Not a vamp, but damn close. He'd gone back to London—just until those badass vampires were caught. Then he would fly to Italy.

I'm in love, she thought. And the guy didn't even have fangs. She couldn't wait to start having ginger-haired babies. She'd send Christmas cards to every bitch in Louisiana, a super nice photo-card of her, Fielding, and the kids.

A bell tinkled over her head when she stepped into a gift shop. She bought blue Murano glass earrings for Caro, a pink T-shirt for Vivi, an I HEART VENICE key chain for Fielding, a jeweled collar for Arrapato, and green marbled writing paper for Raphael.

When she came out of the store, the alley was dark. She eased around a group of tourists and moved down a fragrant, medieval street. It was narrow, lined with boutiques and cafés. She heard footsteps behind her, and for some reason they sounded menacing. She turned.

A pretty woman with short blond hair strode into a gift shop. She wore a gorgeous outfit—leather and silk.

Gillian felt something stiff and warm brush against her leg. She glanced down. It was a little old cat. Cross-eyed and scrawny. Gillian hunkered down and petted its fur.

"You look half starved," she said, stroking the cat's forehead. Poor thing looked like it hadn't eaten in days. "Stay right here, and I'll bring you some food, okay?"

She walked into a *trattoria*. Platters were lined up on a buffet table. She took a plate and spooned up anything that looked catworthy—sardines, anchovies, broiled crabs. The restaurant wasn't crowded, but she couldn't find a waiter. She sat down at a table and pulled out her Italian phrasebook. How could she say *I need a doggie bag*?

A shadow fell across the table. Gillian looked up. A short-haired blonde held a plate and a glass of wine. A huge shopping bag dangled from her wrist. It was the woman Gillian had seen earlier. Damn, she knew how to rock an outfit: tight leather leggings and a cute white blouse with itty black bows down the front.

"May I join you?" the blonde asked. Her eyes were the prettiest shade of blue, and they gazed longingly at the empty chair.

Gillian hesitated and looked past the woman. Empty tables were scattered everywhere. Well, some people didn't like to eat alone. And this woman didn't look like trash or anything. She was wearing close to three thousand dollars in clothing, not including tax. A few weeks ago, Gillian had tried on a pair of those exact same leather leggings at Harrods, $835 a pair. And the blouse was a

Nanette Lepore. Three hundred forty-eight bucks. On the woman's feet were black Christian Louboutin pumps, and they had black spikes jutting out everywhere like a porcupine. $1,495. Not that Gillian was counting.

"Be my guest," Gillian said, sweeping her hand at the chair.

The blonde sat down, giving off a sweet herbal smell and something earthier, like copper and salt water. "You have a unique accent," the woman told Gillian. "What country are you from?"

Gillian almost said *Louisiana*, but she caught herself. Wait, was she still posing as Caro? Or could she be herself? Better to act coy. "Can't you guess?" she asked.

"That wasn't my question." The blonde smiled, but it didn't quite reach her eyes.

An electrified knot tightened at the base of Gillian's spine, a feeling she used to get when she lived in New Orleans and walked home from the law library and heard footsteps behind her. A tight coil of energy would ball up in her spine, and then she'd run. She felt like running now, but that was silly. Wasn't it?

Gillian twisted her pinkie ring around and around on her finger, light spinning from the diamonds.

"I like your ring," the blonde said.

"Thanks."

The blonde was staring, as if she were waiting for Gillian to continue. A waiter passed by and Gillian waved. "Sir, I need a doggie bag."

He nodded and veered toward the kitchen door. The blonde leaned closer. "You have a dog?"

"Lord, no. I saw a skinny cat in the alley. She looked

like she could use a meal." A bead of perspiration slid down Gillian's back. "I saw you earlier. You went into a shop. Did you find anything pretty?"

The blonde opened a bag and pulled out a large copper pan. It had a brass handle and a thick bottom. "I paid too much. But I like it."

"You must be a chef," Gillian said.

The blonde's mouth flickered at the edges, and then she slid the pan into the bag. She looked up as the waiter returned with a to-go box. "Please bring my friend a glass of wine," she said.

"No, no." Gillian waved her hand. "I was just leaving."

The blonde spoke to the waiter in Italian, then turned to Gillian. "I'm Tatiana. What's your name?"

"Oh, I answer to just about anything." Gillian laughed. "Tall girl. Blondie."

Tatiana lifted her glass. "Are you traveling alone?"

Gillian hesitated. "Not really."

"Either you are or you aren't."

"My husband is waiting for me at the hotel," Gillian said.

"Husband?" Tatiana looked amused.

The waiter passed by the table and set a wineglass at Gillian's elbow. She ignored it and began scraping the anchovies and sardines into the take-out box. She didn't know how much the food would cost, so she put a handful of euros on the table.

"Hope you enjoy Venice," she told Tatiana.

"I will."

Gillian left the restaurant. The alley had cleared out,

and the cat sat on his haunches, licking its paw. "Kitty?" Gillian said. "Here's your supper."

The cat bolted down a narrow opening between two buildings. Gillian walked to the edge. It was too dark to see anything, and it smelled like garbage. A raspy meow cut through the shadows.

Gillian took a mincing step forward. "Come on, kitty."

Behind her, a woman said, "Caro?"

Gillian turned. A copper pot slammed into her temple. The wig flew off her head, and she staggered backward. *What the hell.* The side of her head began to throb. Something wet ran down the side of her face.

"Hey, why did you do that?" Gillian yelled. "Who the hell are—"

The pot struck the side of her head again, and a ringing pain filled her ears. She dropped the to-go box. Another blow clipped her on the chin. She fell to her knees, and the gritty cobblestones cut into her flesh. Blood streamed out of her mouth. Her hand shook as she dragged it over her face, passing through a sticky wetness. She lowered her hand. A dark stain covered her palm.

Tatiana stood over her. "Who are you?" she said.

"Fuck you," Gillian spat with a mouthful of blood.

Tatiana swung the pan again. Pain exploded in Gillian's forehead, and she moaned.

"Check her purse for ID," Tatiana told someone.

A man stepped out of the shadows. "Passport says Caroline Barrett," he said.

Gillian felt fingernails dig through her hair, biting into her scalp. She screamed as her neck bowed.

"Shut up," the man said, and pushed the barrel of a gun between her teeth.

She stopped yelling. Pain moved inside her skull like scalding-hot gumbo poured into a bowl, but she forced herself to be calm. If she showed fear, it would just excite them.

Think like a public defender. These reprobates wouldn't shoot her in an alley. No way. Too many tourists. They'd take her money and go. That was all they wanted. But Lord almighty, she was hurt bad. She needed to call an ambulance.

"Where's Vivienne Barrett?" Tatiana said.

Gillian's teeth clicked against the metal. This wasn't a robbery. She was going to die. Her bladder let go, and a cramp twisted in her bowels. A garbled sound came out of her throat.

"Take the gun out of her mouth," Tatiana said.

The barrel scraped against Gillian's teeth, and the man stepped back.

"Tell the truth, and I will not kill you," Tatiana said.

"Caro is in Paris," Gillian said. "She's with a vampire. Raphael Della Rocca."

"What about the girl?" Tatiana asked.

"She's with them."

"That's all you know?"

"Yes."

"Excellent." Tatiana lifted Gillian's hand, pulled off the diamond pinkie ring, and slid it on her own finger. She smiled as she jammed the wig onto Gillian's head. "Take her inside," she told the man. "Then, take your time."

Another man stepped forward, holding a grinning Venetian mask in his hands. He put it over Gillian's face. The men grabbed her arms and yanked her off the pavement.

"You promised you wouldn't hurt me," she said, her voice muffled. Her knees buckled, and the men jerked her upright. Through the holes in the mask, she saw them lead her past an open door that smelled of fish. High above her, someone played a piano.

"Where are y-you taking me?" she asked.

The man on her left brushed his mouth against her ear, his breath stinking of overripe fruit. "To hell."

CHAPTER 28

Caro

PLACE DES VICTOIRES
PARIS, FRANCE

It was the blue hour, *l'heure bleue*, that brief time when the sun slips below the horizon and the air is stained with cobalt light. I put on a periwinkle cotton dress and little flat shoes and pinned my hair into a bun. Then I left a note on the desk for Raphael:

> *Gone swimming. Will you join me? P.S. No swimsuit, please.*
>
> *XXOO*

I took the elevator to the cellar, then walked to the shallow end of the pool. I kicked off my shoes and looked down at the steamy water. Life would be almost perfect if

I could put every evil vampire on the space shuttle. I missed Vivi so much. But I had to trust Sabine. She would take care of my daughter.

Raphael and I were leaving for Morocco tomorrow, but I wasn't sure what we'd find. I'd tried not to obsess about Jude's ring. I didn't know when it had been removed from his hand, but I felt sure it had involved torture. Whoever had placed it on Keats's finger had meant for the pain to continue—from my end. But I wasn't going to allow it. If you let fear enter your mind, it destroys hope and creates a third entity, a dark sludge that pushes through the bloodstream, tainting every thought until you're afraid all the time.

I stared at the pool, trying to remember how it had looked before the renovation. In those days, it had been a swamp, and I'd been afraid to get near it. Now it was a pristine blue bowl. Clean water lapped at the tile edges. If a hellhole could be transformed into an oasis, then anything was possible. All my life I'd believed that goodness would triumph over malice. But I couldn't change evil. I could only refuse to let it change me.

Raphael joined me a few minutes later. He walked up, his chest rising and falling under his shirt.

"You're really going in without a swimsuit?" he asked.

"Have I ever lied to you?" I took off my dress, and it skated over the limestone floor. Next, I dropped my lace thong on the stone floor, and then I stepped down into the water and swam to the deep end. I looked back, treading the silky water, my fingers spread slightly apart.

Raphael hadn't moved.

"Come on in," I said.

"You know I hate to swim."

"You had the River Styx in your cellar, and you turned it into a spa. But you still won't swim?"

"No." He smiled.

"This is a pool paradox," I called. I floated on my back, and my hair fanned out around me, tickling my shoulders. I was barely moving, but the water held me up. I felt just as weightless inside. Right now, I wasn't worried or trying to control the future. Dangerous people were somewhere in this world, but they weren't coming after us today.

Raphael pulled off his shoes, and they clattered onto the stones. His shirt fluttered over his head like a white bird and landed on a chaise longue. He unzipped his jeans. His boxer shorts were red, printed with Eiffel Towers. Everything dropped into a messy pile.

Behind him, light streaked across the walls. "Come to me, Raphael."

He dove into the water and swam along the bottom, his legs white and chiseled, his arms moving in great arcs. He surfaced and slicked back his hair.

I swam closer and closer until we were almost touching. His hands caught my waist and moved lower, tracing my hips. "We'll be in Morocco tomorrow night," he said. "I've leased a *riad* in the medina."

"What's the vampire culture like in Marrakech?"

"It's harder to recognize the immortals. Some wear djellabas. Some don't."

I dropped my hand through the water and found him. As he moved nearer, my hand slid all the way down his length.

His breath dented the water. "You are a temptress, *mia cara*."

"I'm just a girl in a pool."

"A girl who makes me so happy." He reached for my hands and brought them to his lips.

"I hope I always do."

He kissed my knuckles. "Let me turn you into a vampire."

"My blood could hurt you. You have to build antibodies."

"But *my* blood won't hurt you. You're immune to the neurotoxin. I can transfuse you. Very simple. No bite marks on your beautiful skin."

"Stop." I put my fingers over his mouth. "I can't think about becoming immortal until Vivi is older."

He lowered my hand. "I will help you take care of Vivi. I don't want to lose either of you."

"Let's don't think about sad things," I said.

He kissed me hard, until something began to build around us, like musical instruments in an orchestra pit, tuning and tweaking. I gripped him tighter, and the music broke loose inside me.

CHAPTER 29

Tatiana

PLACE DES VICTOIRES
PARIS, FRANCE

Smoke curled from Tatiana Kaskov's cigar as she sat in the passenger seat of the Hummer.

"Drive around the Place des Victoires once more, Maury," she said.

"Sure thing," Maury Sullivan said in a Boston-cream-pie-accent. He was Al-Dîn's chief security officer, a human from Massachusetts, a disgrace to all New Englanders, in Tatiana's opinion.

The night sky stretched above the limestone buildings that lined the square. She squinted at the luminous store-fronts, then glanced along the sidewalks. A few tourists milled around.

"Make sure you don't leave any witnesses," Tatiana said.

"That will be a problem." He lifted one hand from the wheel and rearranged the thin, reddish hairs on top of his head.

"Take care of it."

"Are you kidding?" Maury said. "This is Paris. Your plan stinks. There's an easier way to do a takedown."

"Just do it." Tatiana kept her face still, trying to hide her distaste for this man.

"It's going to cost more. You only gave me twenty-four hours to assemble my team," he said. His lips looked as if they'd been flattened by a rolling pin, and the tips of his ears were fluted like pie dough. He smoothed his hand down the front of a two-thousand-dollar gray silk suit, his fingers splayed over a striped lavender tie. His sleeve pulled back, and Tatiana saw his Rolex.

Pretentious asshole.

Maury guided the Hummer around the square again, the dark sky racing over the buildings. "This location blows," he said. "See how the roads fan away from the square, cars moving in all directions? This means people. Potential witnesses."

Tatiana ignored him and studied Della Rocca's house—four stories, balconies, blue mansard roof. The windows on the third floor glowed like honeyed lozenges. Scattered lights were visible on the other floors. The manse nearly took up one block, wedged between two narrow roads, where businesses and apartment buildings were lined up. Her gaze moved away from Della Rocca's house to the six-story apartment building across the street. She glanced up at the blue-tiled roof. "I don't see your team," she told Maury.

"They're in place," he said. "They'll use gas-propelled grappling hooks and rappel down to Della Rocca's balconies. They'll shoot out the glass and   "

"I know what they'll do," she snapped.

"But we'll only be rappelling to the south-side balconies. If I'd had more time, I could have put a team on the roof of the other apartment building. Then we could've hit the north end of the house and sandwiched Della Rocca." Maury lifted both hands from the steering wheel, smashed them together, then dropped one wrist over the wheel. "It would have been fast. Over in minutes."

Tatiana shook her head. "You've had plenty of time. You're not taking down an embassy. You're going after a thirteen-year-old girl."

"Give me another day, and I can put those teams in place."

"This is going down tonight."

"Sheesh." He angled the Hummer down a side street, turned into a shadowy parking lot, did a U-turn, and headed back toward Della Rocca's mansion. A black Rolls-Royce pulled up to the curb. A blue wooden gate opened, showing a glimpse of Della Rocca's courtyard. Two bald-headed guys stepped out and walked toward the Rolls.

"I've got a bad feeling," Maury said. He lifted a hand from the steering wheel again and smoothed his tie, adjusting the gold clip that held it in place. "Even with suppressors, it's going to be loud. We're gonna attract a crowd."

"Then create a distraction," she said.

"That's been covered. We've got a bomb threat at the Ritz."

She snorted. "That's the best you came up with?"

"What, you want a car bomb outside the Louvre? A sniper at the tower?"

"Why not?" She shrugged.

"I want my men to get in and out of Della Rocca's before the police arrive."

"Like I care about that."

Maury's eyes hardened. "Me and the guys, we've worked together a long time. They're ex-Blackwater. Tough. Smart. Loyal."

Tatiana crossed her legs, and her green dress slithered up her thigh. She stared down at the diamond horseshoe ring on her pinkie finger. Light from the dashboard hit the platinum band, showing a tiny streak of blood. She licked it off, then turned to Maury.

"Your guys are human," she said. "Replace them."

"I can't find another crew like this one."

She glanced at her watch. "What about Della Rocca's security team? They're all over the damn place. Will they be a problem?"

"My ground crew will take care of them. Once we're inside, we'll disable the alarm. But it's a huge house—it's got, what? Fifteen bedrooms? Two kitchens? A cellar?" Maury shook his head. "Places like this always have hidey-holes. I can't guarantee that we'll even find Della Rocca."

"Just get the girl," Tatiana said.

"If she's there. Surveillance hasn't seen her."

"She better be. Because I know where you live. You just bought a house on Beacon Hill. Your wife drives a green Mercedes convertible. Her name is Sharon, right? She dyed your fucking poodles to match the car. She likes to shop."

Maury gripped the steering wheel, his knuckles jutting up. "Leave Sharon out of it. You got a problem, deal with me."

"So now you're giving the orders?" Tatiana folded her arms, feeling the hard outline of the Glock beneath her jacket. In her mind's eye, she saw herself lifting the gun, squeezing the trigger, watching Maury's head sling back, his brain pan emptying onto the windshield. The smell of cordite rushing into her nose. But she had to keep this bastard alive until she'd delivered the girl to Mustafa. And until she, Tatiana, had worked out a deal with the old Turk.

"Look, you gave me twenty-four hours," Maury said.

"Say that one more time, and I'll shoot off your balls."

"I don't have to take your abuse. This isn't how Al-Dîn operates."

"I've been running the corporation for years. Mustafa is too ill." Tatiana paused. "I *am* Al-Dîn."

CHAPTER 30

Caro

PLACE DES VICTOIRES
PARIS, FRANCE

It was midnight. All of the clocks in Raphael's manse chimed twelve times as I walked to the third-story library. I wished I could make those clocks run backward. I'd fallen headlong into an emotional and physical affair with my best friend, and I had only one regret: that we'd lost so much time. But I had only myself to blame.

When I stepped into the room, Arrapato ran over to greet me. Raphael sat on the desk, shuffling through papers. Monsieur La Rochenoire stood off to the side, talking on his cell phone, his eyebrows moving like caterpillars. Behind him, the balcony door panels stood open. Through the glass, a bruised sky stretched over Place des Victoires.

"Caro." Raphael walked over to me and kissed my

hand. "We'll leave as soon as the limo arrives." He gave me the new passports. "We're traveling as Jean-Aubry Gaultier and Louise Gaultier."

"Merci." So we were posing as husband and wife? I unzipped my plaid bag, removed the false bottom, and stashed the passports.

He squeezed my shoulder. "I don't want to frighten you, but Gillian is missing."

Missing. The word cut through me like a blade. I looked up into Raphael's eyes.

"She never checked into her hotel. She wasn't at the quay this morning. Maybe she got on the wrong train." He hugged me closer. "I've got a team working on it."

La Rochenoire lowered his cell phone. "The driver won't answer his phone. And the guards won't pick up, either."

Arrapato darted away from me and began pacing in front of the balcony doors, as if he knew we were leaving him with La Rochenoire. I moved out of Raphael's arms, bent over, and lifted the dog into my arms.

A thump hit the outside wall. From the ceiling, prisms on the chandelier tinkled. Arrapato let out a honking, gooselike bark.

"Something hit the house," I said.

Arrapato stared at the east windows. I looked, too. Just beyond the glass, I saw ropes. It looked as if empty clotheslines had been strung between Raphael's balcony and the building across the street.

I pointed. "Raphael, why are ropes tied to your balcony railing?"

He crossed the room in two long strides. A muscle

flexed in his smooth jaw. "Caro, take Arrapato to the cellar. Hide in the tunnel."

I lifted my bag with my free hand and hooked the strap over my shoulder. A shattering noise came from downstairs, as if all the windows had been knocked out.

Raphael ran to the other end of the library and pushed against a wooden panel. It swung open. He handed a pump shotgun to La Rochenoire. Then he lifted a sawed-off shotgun and filled his pockets with ammo. He took out a box of tear gas canisters.

"Caro, please go."

I looked past him. A man in black tactical gear was flying through the night air, attached to the rope, moving straight toward Raphael's balcony. In one gloved hand he held a semiautomatic that was fitted with a suppressor. He wore a helmet with a night vision scope.

"Raphael, La Rochenoire," I cried. "Get down!"

I dropped behind the sofa, clutching Arrapato. I heard a pop. The glass in the French door exploded. Then I heard a thud on the balcony. I heard the sound of boots crunching over shards. A banging noise rose up, as if the man were kicking out the rest of the glass.

Raphael and La Rochenoire opened fire. I peered around the edge of the sofa. The man had kicked the doors open, but he'd dropped to a crouch. His vest was peppered with holes. A bullet pinged off his helmet. Buckshot hit his knees and thighs, gouging the wall behind him. Red patches spread across the bottom of his uniform.

"Shit," he said. "Goddamn."

An American? I thought. Was he a vampire?

He lifted his gun, and a red laser danced over the sofa and ran across the paneled wall.

I squatted, my heartbeat whooshing in my ears.

Raphael scuttled over to me. "Are you all right?"

I nodded. His hands were steady as he reloaded the gun. He got up, fired, dropped back down. I heard the man crash into a table, and then his gun discharged. The south windows exploded. I rose up again. The man was on the floor, trying to get to his knees. La Rochenoire yanked off the man's helmet, shot him in the eye, and kicked him to the floor.

I looked toward the balcony. A second man was rappelling from the next-door rooftop, his body moving in an arc toward our balcony.

Then the lights inside the house went off.

Go to the cellar. Now. Raphael took my arm and pulled me into the hall. From downstairs, we heard shouts. He let go of me, walked to the staircase, and threw a tear gas canister. Then he rushed back.

He briefly shut his eyes, massaging his temples, and the lights blinked on. I knew he'd done it. He pointed at the hidden elevator door. *When you get there, punch the red emergency stop button. Then go to the mural. Enter the code. It's the numerical equivalent of your name: 2276.*

How will you and La Rochenoire get to the cellar?

The stairway.

But it's in the courtyard. Those soldiers are down there.

I'll be fine, mia cara. *Send me a strong thought when you're safe. Then wait for me.*

I nodded.

I'll find you. I love you. He kissed me, then hurried back toward the library.

I ran down the hall, my bag slamming into my hip. I opened the panel and got inside the elevator. My arms shook so hard, Arrapato began to whimper. As the car passed the first floor, I heard screams and muffled claps. This was an orchestrated attack—but by whom?

I was breathing through my mouth by the time I reached the cellar. As I punched the red emergency button, I heard gunfire echo from the shaft. Arrapato was wiggling—he despised the cellar. I looked toward the mural. It would be dark in that tunnel. I lunged to the bar, grabbed several packets of matches from the brandy snifter, and ran around the pool. When I got to the mural, I opened the panel. Noises boomed from the elevator shaft. I heard shouting. A concussive rumble sent water surging out of the pool.

I faced the metal door. My hand hovered over the electronic lock, and my vision blurred. Raphael had chosen my name for the security code. On a numeric keypad, *C* and *A* would be 22; *R* would be 7. *O* would be 6.

I wiped my eyes, then punched in 2276. The door dragged open, and cold air hit my face. Arrapato dug his nails into my arm, his eyes bugged. I moved to the top step, and my plaid bag brushed against the walls. I slung the bag to the ground, then reached back and shut the mural door. I shifted Arrapato to my left arm and lit a match. The flame shot up. I closed the metal door behind me and edged down the uneven steps.

"Steady, Arrapato," I said, my voice flying up into the

dark. I held up the match. A circle of light throbbed against the stone walls. The rest of the tunnel dropped off into stygian darkness. I didn't hear anything behind me. What if Raphael didn't make it?

The match burned out, singeing my fingers. I lit another one and walked to the end of the tunnel. The flame reflected on a metal door; it had an electric keypad, too. Just beyond it, I heard the distant rumble of the Metro.

Raphael, I'm safe.

While I waited for him to answer, my legs wobbled. I held the match above my head and knelt on the packed dirt floor. I couldn't go through that door without Raphael. Why wasn't he using his telepathy?

Arrapato squirmed out of my arm and shot into the dark, racing toward the cellar door.

"Come back," I yelled, and the match snuffed out. I heard a snort, then the clink of tags. A cold tongue brushed against my hand. I groped for the dog's head and felt an ear.

"Arrapato, you knew those soldiers were there, didn't you?"

He licked my right hand and started on the left. I thought of Raphael and La Rochenoire, and a ripping sensation tore through my chest. It hurt to breathe. I had trusted the Fates to leave me and Raphael alone. I had said I was falling in love with him, but that wasn't true. I was *in* love.

Why hadn't I told him the truth? I'd never cared this deeply for any man, except Jude. I was grateful for the time I'd spent with my husband, and I would do everything within my power to protect our child. But when I'd lost Jude, I'd lost myself. I hadn't wanted to feel anything. I was like a patient who was convalescing from a near-fatal illness and could not stand to hear loud noises or see bright colors. I'd required a bland, pablumesque existence.

Now, I wanted to wear a red dress and high heels. I wanted to listen to hip-hop music. I wanted to eat tangy food, so hot that it left a curl of smoke on my tongue. I couldn't lose Raphael.

Where are you?

A tear slid down my cheek. "Please God, I won't ask you for another thing. But let him come back to me. Don't take him away."

Arrapato seemed to think I was talking to him, and he barked. Then he bit the hem of my dress and shook it. At the end of the tunnel, near the cellar door, I heard a click. The panel opened, and a wedge of light spilled down the rock steps. The smell of chlorine rushed through the darkness, mixing with the stink of gunpowder and blood. A tall shadow filled the doorway. I tried to grab Arrapato, but he was too fast.

A flashlight zigzagged over the wall. *"Mia cara?"*

I had never loved the sound of a voice more than this one.

"Over here," I said.

I got to my feet. A light wobbled toward me. Raphael raced down the corridor and swept me into his arms. "Caro."

I pushed my face into his neck and hugged him as hard

as I could. *Thank you, God. Thank you. I will love this man as long as I'm breathing.*

"Monsieur La Rochenoire was right behind me," Raphael said.

Relief swept through me. I pulled back, and my hand skidded over something wet. He winced. I tugged the flashlight out of his hand and aimed the beam at his arm. His right sleeve was drenched in blood.

"You've been shot." I felt dizzy, as if I were the one who'd been hit.

"It's nothing," he said. "But my house is on fire."

La Rochenoire stepped into the corridor, panting hard. "I secured the staircase door, sir. But I heard them climbing down the elevator shaft. They'll be in the cellar any minute."

He fastened the doors to the cellar and hurried over to us. He held the flashlight while Raphael punched in the code. The steel door opened, and we stepped through. The other side of the door had a clever limestone façade. Raphael closed it, and the panel blended seamlessly into the wall.

"Let's move," he said, and took my elbow. I heard rushing water, and a foul smell rushed up my nose. This was the second layer of Paris, one that attracted punks and tourists.

La Rochenoire's flashlight swept over a curved, concrete ceiling. Metal stairs stood at one end, and sewage moved down a concrete channel. A metal sign next to the stairs read RUE DES PETITES PÈRES. The tunnels were named, each one running beneath a street that bore the same name.

Arrapato sneezed. I put my sweater around him.

La Rochenoire started to walk toward the staircase, but Raphael pulled him back.

"Too close. And we don't know how many hired goons are out there," Raphael said.

"What if they come into the sewer?" La Rochenoire asked.

"Let them," Raphael said, pulling me along.

"Wait. Let me check your arm," I said, aiming the flashlight on his sleeve.

"The bullet creased me. It's nothing."

He was right. His shirt was damp, the color of burgundy wine, but the wound had stopped bleeding. It was about three inches long, the width of red yarn, and a scab was trying to form.

"Let's keep moving," he said. "We need to get you away from the Place des Victoires."

We turned down a narrow passageway, past an open concrete trench where muddy liquid rushed by, giving off a methane stench. The walls were damp and glistening. Raphael's flashlight swept over a rat. It scuttled into a crevice.

Les egouts de Paris. I almost expected to see the ghost of Jean Valjean.

We followed Rue des Petits Champs for a long time, water pattering over our heads, our shoes wet and squishy. Above us, pipes gurgled. Finally we made our way past Rue Saint-Honoré. I needed to catch my breath, so we sat down on a metal staircase, beneath a sign for Rue de Louvre. I handed Arrapato to La Rochenoire, then put down my plaid bag and rolled up Raphael's sleeve. The wound had scabbed.

La Rochenoire squatted beside us, petting the dog. Raphael caught his gaze.

"When we get out of Paris, will you take Arrapato to Villa Primaverina?"

The majordomo gave the dog a doubtful stare. "Yes, *monsieur.*"

"Both of you will be safe there," Raphael said.

"What about Madame Barrett?" La Rochenoire asked.

"She's going with me."

La Rochenoire's bottom lip began shaking. "These assassins garroted the limousine driver and the guards," he said, his voice shaking with rage. "I think they killed the servants. What was the purpose of this attack?"

"They were looking for Vivi and Caro," Raphael said.

"Bâtards." La Rochenoire spat on the ground. "They sounded American. And they wore bulletproof vests. Tactical gear. Were they human?"

"Mostly. They were special ops," Raphael said. "A few were vampires."

We emerged from the sewer near the Louvre. We caught a taxi near the Pont Neuf. The driver went six yards, then slammed on the brakes and ordered us to get out. We crossed the Seine, ignoring curious stares of tourists, and walked toward the Latin Quarter. I'd packed clothing for Raphael and myself in the plaid bag, so I had an outfit for La Rochenoire.

We ducked into a sushi bar. I handed clothes to the men. I tucked Arrapato into my bag and stepped into the restroom. I didn't have a wig, I smelled like the bowels of Paris, and our security team had been slaughtered, but I refused to lose hope.

I emerged ten minutes later in jeans and a hooded long-sleeved T-shirt. Arrapato's fur was damp, smelling of industrial soap. The men waited by the door in clean shirts and trousers. I looped my arm through Raphael's, and we walked out into the night.

CHAPTER 31

Vivi

ST. PAUL DE VENCE, FRANCE

The noon sun pushed against the top of Vivi's head like a fist. Sabine had picked the hottest day in July to take a road trip, but she didn't seem to mind the heat. She breezed through the gates of St. Paul de Vence and walked up a cobbled path, into the walled village.

Vivi rushed behind her, panting. The Rue Grande was jammed with tourists, so they turned down a narrow alley. Boutiques and studios stretched out on both sides, and in the distance, the sun brightened a row of tall sand-colored buildings, their pale blue shutters propped open, potted ferns on the windowsills.

A tall man stepped out of a black door, trailed by a Yorkie. "*Allez, allez*," he told the dog. Both of them hurried down the alley.

"People actually live here?" Vivi said.

Sabine glanced over her shoulder. "A lucky few."

They turned into a fruit store and bought pears, then headed up a steep lane. Vivi lifted her straw hat and pushed back her bangs. She was tired and sticky-hot. How could a woman Sabine's age have so much energy?

"Where are we going?" she called.

The doctor angled toward another lane, her copper hair shining. "To the du Puy Plateau," she said. "A delightful cemetery."

Vivi's mouth went dry. She didn't want to see a graveyard.

"You'll love the view," Sabine said.

Vivi was a sweaty mess by the time they'd climbed the steps to the cemetery. It was long and narrow, hemmed in by a wall. Inside, monuments were crammed into rows. The wind tugged at Vivi's hat, and she grabbed the brim. She moved closer to the wall, looking down at hills and valleys and rooftops. A slash of blue water shimmered in the distance.

"Is that the Mediterranean?" she asked.

Sabine nodded. "Lovely, isn't it?"

"Oh, yes." Vivi's thoughts soared. A pulse ticked in her ears. She had never felt this euphoric. Holding on to her hat, she moved in a circle, looking at the living people who milled down the paths.

"This way," Sabine said, walking down the first row of graves, past a cypress tree. She stopped next to a flat, white tomb, where stones were scattered across the top. "Marc Chagall is buried here."

She bent over, lifted a pebble from the path, and set it on the tomb. "He was a famous artist."

Vivi put a brown stone next to Sabine's.

"St. Paul de Vence was a fortress," Sabine said.

"I like it," Vivi said. Maybe one day she would live here. She'd have a Yorkie, too. Her mom could visit all the time. Caro would love St. Paul de Vence, with its clear, dazzling light.

Mom, I miss you like crazy, she thought. *But I'm glad to be with Sabine and Lena*. Vivi felt her mouth curve into a huge smile. She was enjoying her Induction lessons, but she preferred the day trips to Nice and Cannes. Grasse was pretty cool, too. Sabine and Lena had taken her to three perfumeries, and they'd bought jasmine soap.

The wind felt cool on her face as she followed Sabine around the cemetery. She wondered what Lena was cooking for supper. Vivi shut her eyes and pictured Sabine's house. It was nestled in the hills, and a long, curvy road stretched out to Valbonne.

"Okay, I've seen the graveyard," she told Sabine. "Let's get something to eat."

Sabine lifted the pears from the paper bag. They ate in silence, watching the tourists take pictures of each other. Vivi angled the hat over her face, then stepped behind a cypress tree. She held still, trying to make herself small and inconspicuous.

"You needn't be scared all the time," Sabine said, then bit into her pear.

Vivi's chest puffed out. She wasn't scared, just super cautious.

Another group of tourists walked up the path. A teen-age guy lagged behind a middle-aged couple, obviously his parents, their stiff blue jeans making swishing noises. Fanny packs were slung over their hips, and matching I HEART PARIS caps were perched jauntily on their heads.

The woman turned and waved at the boy. "Elijah, get up here and take me and your daddy's picture."

Elijah looked down at his feet and shrugged. His hair was dyed green, stiffened by gel, and his bangs rose straight up. It looked as if broccoli were growing from the top of his skull. He wore sunglasses, shorts, and a Gym Class Heroes T-shirt.

Sabine touched Vivi's arm. "I wonder if Elijah's eyes are blue, brown, or green."

"Who cares?" Vivi said.

"I pick brown," Sabine said. "Now, Induce him to take off his sunglasses."

Vivi frowned. "No. I might hurt him."

"You've aced your lessons," Sabine said. "You're ready for a live subject."

"You mean victim." Vivi put her half-eaten pear into the paper bag. "I won't do it."

"I'll buy you a whole baguette."

"I'll buy my own."

"You can Induce him, Vivi."

"You're whacked."

"Fine. Have it your way. I will Induce the young man to walk over here and flirt with you."

"He's not even my type. Besides, I'm not ready to Induce a real person."

"I'll be the judge of your readiness."

"This is wrong on all kinds of levels. Even if I don't hurt him, it's still wrong."

"It's wrong for executioners to hunt you."

Vivi winced. "Different kind of wrong, and you know it."

"You'll have to eventually test your abilities on a human."

"That guy might not even be human. He could be a hybrid."

"With those parents?" Sabine shook her head. "I don't think so. And before you ask how I know, I looked into their thoughts. Elijah is miserable. He's sixteen years old and touring France with his parents. They treat him like a five-year-old."

"Duh, wonder how that feels. Maybe you should Induce them to lighten up."

"No, I'll Induce *you* to Induce *him*." Sabine looked at her watch. "You've got one minute to decide."

"You're a psychic-criminal," Vivi said, then she glanced toward the tourists. The mother stood beside Elijah.

"Be careful," the mom was saying. "You don't want to fall and get a boo-boo."

"Whatever." Elijah shrugged.

"Forty-five seconds," Sabine said.

"You're a control freak," Vivi said. "A dangerous one. I hope you don't make Elijah bleed. I hope you know how to do CPR."

"Forty seconds."

"Quit pressuring me. I need longer than forty seconds. What if he's a hemophiliac?"

"Thirty-four seconds."

"Okay, okay. I'll do it." Vivi stared at Elijah. Oh, she hated this. The wind rushed around her, and she took a big gulp of air. Then she concentrated on the guy's sunglasses. A humming noise began inside her head, as if a tuning fork were quivering between her ears.

Take off your sunglasses, Elijah.

She held her breath, fully expecting his head to explode.

"Breathe, Vivi," Sabine said.

Elijah took off his sunglasses.

"Keep breathing," Sabine said.

Vivi's chest rose and fell as she looked at Elijah. No blood. At least, not yet. She tried not to smile, but her lips twitched upward.

"Elijah has lovely brown eyes," Sabine said.

"I'm still waiting for the hemorrhage." Vivi's gaze shifted to his parents. They looked perfectly fine. The mother kept motioning for Elijah to join them by the wall.

Sabine grinned. "You get an A-plus. Are you starting to see how Induction works?"

"I was totally focused on Elijah. And I felt something vibrate inside my head."

"Good." Sabine nodded.

"In my mind, I told him to remove his sunglasses, and at the same time, I grunted a little. Just like you said to do. Like I was holding back a burp."

"Perfect. Always address the subject by his or her name, if you know it. And remember to breathe."

"Why can't I hold my breath?"

"It causes the energy to build. You would have

over-Induced him. And he would have bled." Sabine smiled. "I didn't think your training would move this swiftly. You'll be finished by the end of summer."

"That'll make my mom happy."

Sabine dropped the remains of her pear into the bag, then smiled at Vivi. "Let's find you a baguette."

CHAPTER 32

Caro

MARRAKECH, MOROCCO

Night air blew around Raphael and me as we walked through the crowded streets of Marrakech. We passed through the medina, where Berber storytellers' voices mingled with the snake charmer's music, and then we turned down a narrow alley. Two Moorish guards followed at a distance.

We stopped in front of Riad le Pavilion. It was an eighteenth-century house, the color of burnt cinnamon. A brass knocker dominated a carved wooden door. I touched it.

"How unusual," I said. "Why is the knocker shaped like a human palm?"

"It's a Hamsa," Raphael said. "A symbol that spurns the evil eye."

"We'll need it."

Our Berber houseman carried the luggage into a second-story bedroom. After he left, Raphael and I fell onto the mattress, then pulled off our clothes and drew the gauzy mosquito netting around us.

Two nights later, we'd barely moved, except to wander through the Djemaa el-Fna Square. Although many blond-haired couples were wandering in the medina, Raphael hadn't wanted to draw attention our way, so we'd worn traditional Moroccan attire, tucking our hair under the hoods.

The warm evening breeze stirred the hems of our black djellabas as we passed through open-air food stalls, where steam wafted up into the darkness. We worked our way through the souks, the colors fanned out like spilled crayons, the aisles rimmed with silk slippers, brass bells, baskets, rugs, and silver teapots.

By the third evening, I'd almost forgotten why we'd come to Morocco. The 112-degree heat had made me drowsy. That night, Raphael and I lay in bed, the mosquito netting stirring around us, tepid air skimming over our sweaty limbs. Through the shuttered window, I heard the final call to prayer.

"That's the *Isha*," Raphael said. "The twilight prayer."

The tinny voice spiraled from the minaret at the Koutoubia Mosque, a shimmering, ethereal sound, intricate as the threads in a silk slipper. I rested my cheek on Raphael's shoulder, and my hand drifted along his arm. His bullet wound had faded to a pink line.

He lifted my hair. "I'm trying not to read your mind," he said. "But you seem pensive."

"I was just thinking about *Brideshead Revisited*," I said. "Didn't Sebastian Flyte come to Marrakech?"

"And to Fez." Raphael wove a strand of my hair around his wrist.

The call to prayer ended, and I heard the snake charmer's music uncoil from the medina. I slid my fingers up to Raphael's neck and brushed over the stubble, past his chin, and traced the outline of his mouth.

He kissed my fingertips. "I love you, *mia cara*."

I turned up my face, remembering the night I'd waited in the cellar passage. I still hadn't pinned the *L*-word on him. Why was I afraid?

"I love you, too," I said.

"You mean, you're falling *in* love with me," he said.

"I'm already there, Raphael."

The sheets rustled, and then he pulled me on top of him. He stared into my eyes. "Say it again, *mia cara*."

"I'm in love with you, Raphael Della Rocca. I am so in love with you."

I leaned in to kiss him, and he caught my face in his hands. "I can't lose you. Ever."

"You won't."

"You're not immortal."

"No." I frowned. I thought we'd settled this—for now, anyway. I rolled off him and moved to my side of the bed.

"But you want to be with me forever, don't you?" he asked, pulling me against him.

"It doesn't matter what I want. I saw what Jude went through after he'd been transformed. He had stomach pains, headaches, nausea." I paused. "You and I are on the move. I don't know where we'll be in a week. And I've got to think of Vivi."

"But when you are ready—and I hope you will be someday—it doesn't have to be a difficult process. I talked to Dr. Nazzareno. You can receive immortal blood through an IV infusion."

How long had he been thinking about this? Before or after we'd made love? Dr. Nazzareno lived in Venice. When had Raphael talked to him? And why hadn't he mentioned it sooner?

I pulled away from him and lay on my side. As I traced my finger over a wrinkle in the sheet, I glanced at him. "When did you talk to Dr. Nazzareno?"

"I called him before we left Paris." He turned on his side and inched closer to me. "Please don't be angry."

"I'm not. But immortality is a dead issue, so to speak."

"I'm pushing you too hard, aren't I?"

"A little."

"I don't mean to. And I would never do anything to endanger my godchild." He sighed. "I can't stop thinking about the time we have left. I want to live with you for a thousand years."

I ran my fingers over his lips, brushing against his teeth. They were white and radiant, with slightly prominent incisors. Sometimes when we made love, I would become so aroused, I bit him—not hard, of course, just a nibble. But I hadn't allowed him to bite me. I was too frightened of the biochemical backlash. If only we'd thought to bring antihistamines; then he could give me a little nick, and I would give him one—at the same time.

To a vampire, the mutual exchange of blood was equivalent to simultaneous orgasms. But my blood would make him ill. Besides, where could we find Benadryl in Marrakech?

"Un momento." He scooted out from under me and dropped his arm over the side of the bed. I heard him fumbling in his leather travel bag, and then he brought up a small square box. "I brought an EpiPen, too," he said.

I tried to hide my surprise. "You're just full of secrets," I said.

I imagined his teeth on my neck, and something streaked through my belly.

He shook the box. "Are you ready for a field trial?"

I nodded. "Just don't bite too hard, okay?"

"Never." He opened the box, ripped open a bubble pack, and swallowed two pink pills. Then he lifted my arm and glanced at my watch. "Fifteen minutes," he said. "Might as well be fifteen thousand."

I put my arms around his neck and drew his mouth toward mine. Our lips touched and his tongue moved in lazy circles, searching and probing. I sucked the tip, and a low moan started in his throat.

I slid my hand away from his neck and touched his throat, feeling the soft vibrations move against my palm. I breathed faster and faster. His hand covered mine, and he guided it lower, down his chest, through the springy, blond hairs, across his flat belly, to the silky curls between his thighs.

Still kissing me, he placed my hand against him. The girth of this man never failed to surprise me. When I curled my fingers around him, they were separated by a wide gap. His hand dropped away, and a moment later, it pressed firmly into my buttocks.

My fingers were still caught between us. I squeezed him. He stopped kissing me and released a breath. I slid my hand over his firm plushness, and with each stroke, he swelled.

"*Innamorata di te*," he whispered.

His teeth grazed over my bottom lip. I felt a tug deep inside me, and a tiny, half orgasm rippled through my belly. He lowered his head to my breast and ran his tongue around the beaded tip of my nipple. A pulse began to thump between my legs.

"How many more minutes?" I said, my voice echoing in his mouth.

"Patience, *mia cara*." He pulled away from me, then moved lower in the bed. His knees dented the mattress. He leaned forward, slid his hand under my calf, and raised it from the sheet. He kissed my instep and moved up to my ankle. As he kissed it, fluttery sensations darted to every part of my body.

My leg began to tremble when his mouth grazed down the inside of my knee. He licked my flesh, then blew on the wet streak. A burst of coldness make me tremble. His thumb and index finger came together and he traced his nails over my skin, as if he were writing a secret message.

"Slowly, *mia cara*," he said, gently lowering my leg. He reached for the other one and ran his teeth over the backs of my toes. I arched my back.

"I want you now," I said in a shaking voice.

"And what do you want, *mia cara*?" His tongue skated over my shinbone, and then he reversed the direction.

"I want you to bite me." I shivered again.

"We must move slowly," he said. "Give the medicine time to work."

"Okay," I whispered. "Okay."

He kissed my fingers, nibbling the tips. Little pulses surged inside me, then gathered strength, pounding between my legs.

"It's almost time," he said.

"Thank God."

He moved on top of me, and I sank into the mattress. I was conscious of the pressure of his knees as they nudged my thighs apart, first one, then the other. He slipped his hand between us and found me.

"You are so ready, *mia cara*." He kissed the side of my mouth.

I sighed, moving my hips in a circle, urging him to move closer. But a vampire's sense of time is different. He slid his full length inside me, then pulled out halfway.

"Deeper," I whispered.

Again, he sheathed himself and began to thrust. Each stroke made me gasp. Still pumping, he flattened his hands against the mattress and rose up. Tiny drops of perspiration fell against my breasts. I lifted my hips, meeting him again and again. I wanted to feel his teeth against my neck; I wanted him to taste every part of me.

"Mia cara." He stopped moving and held my gaze. "Are you ready?"

Oh, yes. I am ready. I was breathing so hard, it took me a second to answer. I cupped my hands under my breasts. "Do it."

He lowered his mouth to a spot just below my

collarbone and pressed his teeth against my flesh. His incisors sank down, and he began to suck. An icy sensation moved through my chest. Raphael drank, pulling harder, and my climax began to build. It seemed as if hundreds of bells were ringing, moving in wider and wider arcs, the clappers rocking back and forth, louder and louder, faster and faster, into a hammered sound.

When it was over, he blotted the sheet against the marks, and a tiny red carnation bloomed on the linen. He held pressure.

"Are you all right, *mia cara*?"

I couldn't answer. I lay there, panting. He'd taken only a little bite, but every pore on my body felt alive. Between breaths, I said, "It was like bells. Cathedral bells. Now, we do it together." I pushed him against the mattress, then lowered myself onto his chest and put him inside me. He groaned, caught my waist, tugged me closer. My teeth broke the skin on his shoulder. The taste of salt and iron filled my mouth, and as I began to drink, orgasms rang through me again and again.

Raphael pushed his face agaist my neck, and his teeth pricked the flesh below my ear. He swallowed, his throat clicking, his hips thrusting against mine. The sensations grew stronger, the way music builds, rushing to the place where we were merged. He lifted his mouth from my neck. "You're making me come," he said.

"Don't stop."

He put his mouth back on my neck. And then we were in the music together, a holy, incandescent sound that moved between us, something beyond the physical, a fitting together of our minds. Pleasure spun around us like music. It felt as if we'd stepped into a Puccini aria, the notes spiraling up, then plunging down, weaving around us, until we were part of the air.

I had made love before. I had loved before. But not ever this way.

———

Later that evening, we decided to make an unsolicited visit to Dr. Nick Parnell's *riad*. Raphael and I slipped on djellabas and pulled up the hoods. It was a bit warm for a pashmina scarf, but I added one anyway, tucking it around my neck, hoping it would hide the bite marks.

Raphael gave me a long, searching look. "Parnell is a skilled telepath. You must guard your thoughts around him. Do not think about Vivi."

I nodded. I'd read the Interpol intelligence report, but I still had a few questions about this man. Twelve years ago, Dr. Parnell had been a popular lecturer on the academic circuit after he'd discovered a new and interesting insect in Cameroon. He'd gone to work for the Al-Dîn Corporation. After the expedition went awry, Parnell had dropped off the grid. It was easy to understand why. He was involved with international drugs and arms trafficking. After the coup in Guinea-Bissau, he had double-crossed a heroin kingpin.

His girlfriend was a minor celebrity: Addison Yarborough was Zeke the Freak's daughter. Zeke was a burned out American rock star. Sex and drugs had left him addlepated, yet he'd managed to father nine children, all by gorgeous women. When I was a young girl, I'd gone to a concert in London. The Freak attracted a large Goth fan base, mainly because his funeral dirge music was laced with images of blood, fangs, and death. His performances were theatrical—open caskets, black capes, white Kabuki makeup, and vats of dry ice.

"Wasn't Addison's mother a gorgeous Chanel model?" I asked.

Raphael nodded. "She was the Freak's third wife."

"If Dr. Parnell is trying to keep a low profile, he's chosen the wrong girlfriend," I said. "She prefers to be addressed as 'Herself.' With a capital H. She was in a movie a few years ago, and on the press junket, she complained to an *E!* reporter that acting was too hard, not that she was against hardness, but she didn't want it to be career-related." I lifted my finger and added, "A direct quote from Herself."

Raphael laughed.

I'd seen Addison's photos in gossip magazines. She was emaciated and popeyed. Her black waist-length hair had chunky white stripes, as if a penguin had been her stylist.

"How did Dr. Parnell and Addison hook up?" I asked.

"Maybe he was one of the Freak's groupies." Raphael shrugged. "Or maybe Addison is a vampire groupie."

Raphael and I walked across the brightly lit medina, then cut through the souks, our beefy Moorish guards following at a discreet distance. We passed by spice shops where burlap bags were lined up in a row, displaying vibrant mounds of paprika, cayenne, turmeric, ginger, saffron, cinnamon.

Straight ahead, a crowd had gathered in a tiled pavilion, watching a feral cat. The animal was gray and bony, and it stood absolutely still, as if it had been pasted onto the cobblestones. Then I saw why—it was stalking a baby pigeon, which perched on the ledge of a low, multicolored wall. The baby had apparently fledged prematurely, and now the frantic mother swooped above it.

The cat moved an inch and froze, except for the tip of its tail, which jutted upward like a crooked finger. Then it sprang toward the wall, skidded onto the ledge, and collided with the fledgling. Feathers churned in the air as the cat and bird slipped off the ledge and fell over the side. There was a thump.

"Don't look, *mia cara*," Raphael said.

But I couldn't turn away. The fledgling soared up, fluttering in a zigzag above the ledge. The cat hurled itself into the air, a streak of gray fur, and bit into the bird's neck. With a triumphant flick of the tail, the feline raced along the ledge and jumped down into an alley behind the souks, the mother pigeon straggling behind.

I couldn't stop thinking about the cat as Raphael and me turned down a twisty alley. Dr. Parnell lived four minutes away from Djemaa el-Fna Square in a seventeenth-century *riad*. As we stepped closer, the thick, rose-pink walls gave off the smells of age and decay.

Raphael banged on the door. It creaked open, and a man in a red fez appeared, a shotgun slung over his shoulder. A scar ran down the left side of his face, sliced through his eyebrow and curved down his cheek. Raphael spoke to him in Arabic, then crushed money into his hand.

The man showed us into the *riad*. Inside, the décor was pink and black—the walls, furniture, and artwork. I heard laughter from a dim part of the courtyard: a masculine boom and a girlish giggle. We stepped around a rose-tiled fountain and a banana tree that was strung with white lights. Smoke drifted through the air, stinking of marijuana. A bar stood at the other end of the courtyard, and gnats circled a bowl of limes. A half-empty gin bottle stood next to a smudged glass.

Dr. Nick Parnell sat at a table, holding a naked brunette woman on his lap. Teacups were scattered on the table, which was spattered with blood. When Parnell saw Raphael and me bearing down on him, he sprang to his feet, his genitals outlined beneath his tight pants.

The woman slid to the floor and her brown eyes widened. She sat there a moment flipping back her dark hair; dozens of bruises were stamped on her neck. Was this Parnell's new girlfriend? What had happened to Addison Yarborough?

"Can I help you?" Parnell asked. He was a tall, hard-muscled man, trapped forever in his late twenties. He possessed the terrible beauty of a predator, reminding me of the cat I'd seen earlier. His bleached-blond hair fell to his shoulders, and his roots looked as if they'd been rubbed with a charcoal stick. His hazel eyes narrowed as he peered at the guard. Parnell shouted something in Arabic. The guard dropped back into an arched doorway.

Parnell turned back to Raphael and me. "Okay, you've got two seconds to explain who the hell you are."

I put one hand on my waist, whether to comfort or steady myself, I couldn't say. "I'm Jude Barrett's widow."

Parnell's gaze swept over me. "Who?"

As I explained about the Gabon expedition, his eyes hardened. He snapped his fingers. The brunette got to her feet and ran across the courtyard, her bare feet slapping on the tile. She darted through the archway, where

Addison Yarborough now stood, gripping a martini glass. She'd inherited her father's teardrop nose, along with her mother's famous legs. The black-and-white striped hair streamed past her shoulders.

She saw me gawping and stepped back into the shadows.

I glanced at Parnell. His downward-turned mouth indicated that he hated unannounced guests.

"How did you find me, pretty lady?" he asked.

Raphael took my hand. "*I* did."

"Why?" Parnell asked.

"We have questions about Dr. Barrett's last days on the Gabon expedition," Raphael said.

One corner of Parnell's mouth kicked up into a sardonic smile. "Are you two an item?"

I didn't answer, and he gave me a penetrating stare, as if he were trying to scour my mind for details. I focused on Jude's face—the wind stirring his brown ponytail, his blue eyes crinkling at the edges, dark stubble running down his jaw.

"What do you want to know?" Parnell asked.

"Tell me about the mercenaries," I said.

Parnell sat down in a metal chair and put one hand on top of his head. "Whew, that was a long time ago, dudes." He looked up at the banana tree. "Let's see, I'm trying to think. We were camped near a *bai*. I was in my tent when the gunfire started. I got out and ran into the bush."

"Did you see Jude Barrett?" I asked.

"Nope. I didn't see him or anyone, sorry. If I had, I wouldn't have tried to help them. I'm not the heroic type. Is that what you wanted to hear?"

He spoke with a brash eloquence, making me wonder what kind of life he'd had before he'd become a vampire. Maybe he'd owned a Mercedes convertible and driven it with the top down across the Golden Gate Bridge, his hand on a woman's knee, a Coldplay song blasting from the radio.

"What else do you remember?" I asked.

"The mercs spoke Bambara."

"They were from Mali?" I repressed a shudder. Gaddafi had found his murderers in the Mali military.

Parnell shrugged. "They wore Malian army uniforms."

"Who hired them?" Raphael asked.

"I didn't ask." Parnell's lips crumpled into a bitter smile. "I meant to, but they were too busy cutting off heads and setting fires."

"How do you know?" Raphael said. "I thought you ran away."

"I saw enough."

I began trembling, and Raphael put his arm around me.

"You guys make a cute couple." Parnell smiled, looking from me to Raphael. I heard distant sound from the square, the hum of a motorbike and jangling music.

Parnell lifted a teacup and winked at Raphael. "You should try this—gin, mint tea, and blood. A heady mix. In fact, you should feed mint to the pretty lady. Her blood will taste sweet."

"Was my husband wearing his wedding ring?" I asked.

Parnell shrugged. "Like that would have made a difference."

"About what?" I asked.

"Are you sure you want to know, pretty lady? Can you handle the truth?"

I nodded.

"That's what all women say—they can handle it. But they can't." He looked into his teacup. "Tatiana had the hots for Jude."

I just stared.

"You know how it is." He lifted one shoulder. "Vampires in a rain forest. Things heat up. Everyone fucked Tatiana. Even me."

"She was your lover?" I asked.

"You know, that word baffles me. What does 'lovers' mean, exactly? Tatiana had a need and I had a need, and we took care of it. Not very loving."

Raphael stared at him a long time. "Why were you in Gabon?"

"The money. Why else?" Parnell laughed. "The Al-Dîn Corp was looking for the Lolutu tribe. Day-walking vampires. Supposedly the original immortals. Extinct, of course. They lived in Birougou's caves. Hunted in daylight. Kidnapped women from other pygmy tribes and used them in blood rituals. The Bakas say the Lolutu could assume animal form. Crocodiles, fish, bats."

"How did you get out of the bush?" Raphael asked.

"Walked." He turned to me. "Listen, I hate to be rude, but Addison and I have plans. Addy? Can you escort the lovebirds to the door?"

Parnell gave me a swift, sudden look. My scalp tingled, and I felt pressure behind my eyes. He was trying to read my mind. I willed my thoughts to go clear. But what had he seen?

Addison stepped through the archway, her striped hair draped over one shoulder. She wore a short black dress that showed off her legs. She gave Raphael a side-eye glance. He put his hand on my waist.

"Lovely evening, isn't it?" she said. She led us through a long, narrow room where the man in the fez sat on a pink sofa with the naked woman, passing a bong. I tried not to look, but I was thinking, *Drugs and prostitutes in an Islamic country?* I didn't know why I was surprised, but I was.

As Raphael and I stepped out of the rose-tinged *riad*, Addison called, "Where are you staying?"

"Not far," Raphael said.

"Far is a place? Maybe I'll visit." She gave him a smoldering glance, then slammed the door.

CHAPTER 33

Caro

RIAD LE PAVILION
MARRAKECH, MOROCCO

The next evening at dusk, Addison Yarborough showed up at our *riad*. She stepped past the Berber manservant and scanned the courtyard.

"Wow, I love your *riad*," she said. "It's much more chic than ours."

"Come in," I said, even though she was already standing in the hall. She hadn't worn a djellaba, and the hem of her sleeveless pink dress hit just above her knees. A white scarf was tied around her neck, and it streamed down her shoulders and blended into the striped hair. A fuchsia hibiscus was pinned behind her left ear, and her large eyes were lined with kohl, putting me in mind of Vivi.

"So." Addison smiled. "Can we talk? It's important."

I led her to the rooftop terrace, past a splash pool, toward a wooden sectional sofa. The sky had turned purple except for a low-lying red haze that slashed over the Atlas Mountains. Lights were coming on in Djemaa el-Fna, and I heard street music.

Addison sat down in the middle of the sofa and put a straw Kate Spade bag on the white cushion. She opened it, and I saw dozens of pill bottles and little bags that looked suspiciously like cocaine. She took out a blue pill and swallowed it, then cast a furtive glance over her shoulder, toward the stairway. I knew she was looking for Raphael.

"It was hot today, wasn't it?" she said, closing her purse.

"Yes," I said. "But it's cooling off." The temperature had reached 102 degrees at noon, but now the heat was starting to dissipate. A tepid breeze carried the smells of couscous and fresh oranges.

She played with a thick silver bracelet, moving it up and down her wrist, over a knob of bone. She glanced at the door again. "Where is Raphael? Or is it still too bright for him?"

I didn't answer, because I'd heard a question within a question. I couldn't read her thoughts, but I sensed that she was curious about my relationship with Raphael.

She pulled off her silver bracelet and moved it to her other wrist. "How long will you and Raphael be in Marrakech?"

"I'm not sure."

"Have you been to the souks?" She flicked her gaze back at the door.

"Several times."

"I hope you got good prices." She turned back, and her eyes met mine. Her pupils were the size of black pepper pods, circled by enormous blue irises. "Negotiating requires an attitude," she added. "Grit plus caveat emptor."

While she chatted about the seamy side of Morocco, I watched the sky darken. Stars winked over the mountains. The Berber manservant brought mint tea in a silver pot and two blue glasses. He set down a platter of melon slices and cheese, the items wrapped in palm leaves.

Addison gave me a pleading look. "I really need to see Raphael."

I signaled the Berber man. "Please ask Monsieur Della Rocca to join us," I said in French.

"Yes, *madame*." He lowered his head and moved toward the door.

After he left, Addison's lips drew into a bow, wet and pink.

"Nicky is gone," she said, biting down on the word *gone*. "He left last night."

I took a sip of tea, trying to hide my surprise. A distressing coolness plowed through my chest. "When is he coming back?"

"Who knows? Maybe never. He bought a one-way ticket to London." Her eyes looked shiny, as if she were holding back tears. "I'll probably never find another vampire."

I heard footsteps on the stairs, and Raphael walked

through the door, the breeze stirring his hair. He wore a white crewneck T-shirt, and the thin cotton showed the outline of his biceps. One hand was tucked casually into the pocket of his blue shorts, pulling the fabric across his crotch. The muscles flexed in his thighs and calves as he walked toward the sofa. I remembered how, barely an hour ago, I'd tucked my bare foot around that calf.

The coldness in my chest scattered, and I smiled up at him.

He sat down beside me, his weight denting the cushion. He'd just showered and shaved, and I breathed in his smell. He reached for my hand, locked his fingers through mine, and pulled me into a kiss. His lips felt plush and soft. I had a sudden image of Villa Primaverina at high tide, green waves crashing against the seawall in the same rhythm of lovemaking.

I'd forgotten about Addison until she cleared her throat. Raphael kept kissing me, and I leaned back, my lips barely an inch from his. "We have a guest. Addison says Dr. Parnell left Marrakech."

Raphael's fingers tightened around mine, and then he glanced at Addison.

She sighed and crossed her legs, pulling the dress over her knees. "You spooked him. Both of you."

"Is that why you're here?" Raphael said. "To complain?"

"I came to tell you why he left."

Raphael gave her a long, analytical look. Any second now he'd dissect her thoughts and memories, and she'd end up with a headache.

She rubbed her temple. "Please don't do that. Nicky

used to give me migraines. His mind is like an elevator door. It opens and closes. And when it's open, he sees everything people don't want him to see. When you were at my *riad*, he saw something in your head or Caro's. And he left *me*."

Raphael's jaw tightened.

Addison unwrapped the white scarf and pointed to old bruises on her throat. "Nicky and I did a lot of coke. And when he's wired, he talks. He forgets that he's telling the same story. But I know it's a true story because the details never change."

"Details about what?" Raphael asked.

"The Al-Dîn Corp. A long time ago they hired him to study bugs in Gabon. Nicky said it was the kind of job you couldn't leave. Like that Eagles song, 'Hotel California.' When you signed up with Al-Dîn, they owned you. They owned Nicky. He couldn't leave. He'd been in Gabon a long time before Caro's husband arrived."

I tried to keep my face expressionless. Where was Addison going with this story? Was she even telling the truth? "I don't understand."

"You will." She smiled tolerantly. "Your husband replaced a biochemist who'd gotten killed by bats. Dr. O'Donnell. Nicky said the bats lifted the guy off the ground. They flew off with him."

I studied Addison's face. It showed no trace of guile. But her pinpoint pupils, twitchy gestures, and rapid speech indicated that she was wired. Maybe she'd been high when Parnell had told her about the expedition, and she'd fabricated her own version.

Apparently Raphael was thinking the same thing. "Bats can't lift a man," he said.

"They were huge," Addison said. "And they carried viruses. The CEO of Al-Dîn went on the expedition with Nicky, and he—"

Raphael leaned forward. "Who?"

"Mustafa Al-Dîn," Addison said. "He's a Turkish vampire. He shot one of the bats. Then he had his picture taken with the corpse—he and a Baka guide held it up. The damn bat was crawling with Marburg Virus. Mustafa got sick and had to be transported out of the jungle."

"You sound like you know this man," Raphael said.

"No." She shook her head. "Nicky told me about him."

Raphael gave her a dubious glance. "Only a small percentage of vampires come down with hemorrhagic fevers."

Addison shrugged. "I don't know how viruses work in the undead. I just know that Mustafa recovered. But his immune system went haywire. He ended up with stem cell leukemia. He left Gabon. And he put his lover in charge of the expedition. Some bitch named Tatiana. I know what she and Nicky did. Not that I'm jealous or anything."

Raphael waved his hand impatiently. "What about the bats?"

She took a sip of tea before she spoke. "Tatiana decided to catch one. She put a team together. Then she made Nicky and some other guys go into a cave. They were supposed to get a baby bat."

"Did they?" Raphael asked.

"Not on that jaunt. Things got too hairy. People died.

Al-Dîn began looking for more scientists." Addison's eyes flicked over to me. "Your husband replaced Dr. O'Donnell."

Pressure was gathering behind my eyes. I did not want to hear the rest of her story. Was it phony? If not, had she embellished Parnell's tales? St. Augustine had written that the truth could sound like a lie, and a lie could seem truthful. It depended on the speaker's verbal skill.

Raphael tugged his earlobe, as if he didn't trust what he was hearing.

She smirked. "You guys think I'm a loon. I'm just trying to help."

Raphael and I looked at each other. *She's crazy, mia cara.* He turned back to Addison, "Did Parnell tell you what happened to Jude?"

She nodded. "When the mercenaries came, Nicky said there was a lot of confusion. He took advantage of it and ran like hell to a clearing. But daylight was coming, so he went back into the forest and climbed a tree and hid in an old gorilla nest. It was shady under the canopy, but he covered himself with branches and fronds to block the UV light. Then he heard gunfire. He looked down and saw Jude running toward a waterfall. The mercenaries were right behind him. They shot Jude in the back, and he went over the falls. Nicky said it was a three-hundred-foot drop."

I felt dizzy. I leaned back against the sofa and forced myself to breathe.

Addison tilted her head, watching me, her gaze iniquitous. "Nicky said the soldiers climbed down the falls. He lost sight of them. But he thought they were searching the river. Nicky heard more gunfire. And then everything was quiet."

I couldn't absorb her words. I felt distraught, as if I'd been watching an air show and a plane had slammed into a mountain.

Raphael put his arm around me.

"I'm sorry," Addison said, her lips twisting, as if she were holding back a smile.

I narrowed my eyes. She wasn't sorry, not one bit. She'd come here to wound me, and to also signal her availability to Raphael.

She lifted her pocketbook and stood. "Now you know how your husband died. But you've told me nothing. I still don't know why Nicky ran away from me. I don't know what he saw inside your head. But it must have been bad."

"He saw nothing," Raphael said.

"You better hope he didn't." She winked. "If you get bored with the grieving widow, give me a call."

CHAPTER 34

Nick Parnell

Human odors engulfed Nick Parnell as he walked in Heathrow Airport, past the food court in Terminal Three. His pulse quickened as he breathed in cologne, pizza, tobacco, burned coffee, and blood. Straight ahead, a long line twisted away from the British Airways help desk. As he passed by, he caught the tang of acetone and overripe fruit.

The odor of human ketoacidosis, he thought. And of hidrosis—a vampire's sweat.

Nick's tailbone prickled as if he'd sat on an anthill. He darted into an alcove and studied the passengers. A teenage boy with a mohawk. A mother soothing her ginger-haired infant. A long-legged brunette reading *Vogue*.

Where was Tatiana?

Two days ago, he'd called Al-Dîn Corp's main office in Cape Town, South Africa, and he'd reached a bull-headed receptionist. "Let's cut through the shit," he'd finally said. "Find Tatiana Kaskov. Tell her that Dr. Nick Parnell has information about Jude Barrett's kid. Got a pen? Here's my phone number."

Tatiana had called an hour later. Nick had cut a deal: For one million euros, he'd tell her where to find Vivienne Barrett.

"Meet me at Heathrow," he'd said. "Terminal Three. The Caviar House Seafood Bar—not the oyster bar."

It was a foolproof plan. She couldn't kill him in an airport. Every part of her body would be scanned, right? She couldn't bring a weapon past security. Besides, witnesses and cameras were all over Heathrow. He'd thought she would try to negotiate a lower price, but she'd agreed.

Nick walked to the Caviar House, but Tatiana wasn't there. Next, he checked the monitor. No arrivals or departures from Cape Town. Something was wrong. Had she set him up? Probably.

He bought tickets to Bangkok, Stockholm, Chicago, and New York, all of them departing at various times. It had been a pain, too—it seemed as if every tourist in the world had converged in London. But Heathrow was always like this in late July. At least he'd gotten tickets. Now, if Tatiana showed up with thugs, Nick could get on a plane.

He walked back to the Caviar House. Still no Tatiana. His shoes clicked over the floor as he hurried down the corridor. As he passed by a guy who wore black leather pants, Nick smelled beer, sweat, and urine.

The guy sniggered. "What are you looking at?"

Hey, asshole, he wanted to tell the boy. *I've been a vampire for fifty years. Long before your whore mother pushed you out of her cunt.*

The guy's laughter followed Nick down the hall. He wasted time in the boutiques. He pulled out Addison's Visa and bought jeans, Gucci loafers, and a white Dior dress shirt. He stuffed the bags under his arm and headed to the No. 1 Lounge. Soon, he'd need blood. If Tatiana didn't show up, he'd have to go into downtown London.

When he stepped into the lounge, his tailbone started burning again. He heard piped-in music, something Celtic. The smell of sausages and onion soup rushed up his nose. A group of Asian businessmen walked by, carrying laptops. Through a gap in the crowd, he saw Tatiana. She sat at a table, backlit by dark windows. Her hair looked blonder than he remembered. A glass of white wine sat at her elbow. She reached past it and tapped a thin cigar into an ashtray. The strap of her summery yellow dress fell over her shoulder.

Tatiana wearing a dress? Maybe it wasn't her.

Her disinterested gaze scraped over him, then flicked away. She lifted the cigar and took a puff. Nicky saw a tattoo on her wrist.

It's her. The realization crashed into his head with the force of a North Sea breaker. Cold pressure rushed around him in all directions. She lifted her cigar, as if saluting him, but her eyes held a savage gleam. A sick feeling curled in his belly.

Let's get this over with, he thought.

He turned down a hall, toward the restroom. He'd just opened the door when Tatiana cut in front of him. The cigar was gone, and she held an empty wineglass. A travel bag was slung over her shoulder.

He forced himself to smile. Damn, he shouldn't have come to the lounge. It had real glass and real pottery plates. "You look great," he said.

"You look like crap." Her other hand shot out and gripped his elbow. She towed him into the bathroom and shoved him against the wall. With one smooth motion, she slammed the door and wrenched the knob.

Great, he thought. *Now I'm trapped with this crazy bitch.*

She kicked him in the groin. A sob burst through his teeth, and he bent over double. Pain ran through him like spilled acid. Through a haze, he saw her sling her travel bag on the lavatory counter. Then she smashed the wineglass against the sink.

He felt a rush of air, and then she was holding the pointy end of the glass against his neck. His heart pumped hard. What did she plan to do? Scar his face? Blind him? He'd like to see her try.

"I thought we had a deal," he said.

"Don't scream or I'll puncture your carotid," she said. "Your blood pressure will drop, and you'll fall to the ground. You'll watch me cut out your heart. And I won't be gentle."

"Go ahead," Nick said through gritted teeth. "Slice me up. You'll be drenched in my blood. You won't make it out of the lounge."

"Don't worry. I've got clothes in my luggage. Move, Nick." Pushing the glass against his neck, she guided him toward a stall. "Get inside."

"No."

"I didn't hear your answer." She pushed the glass into his neck.

He felt a sting, and then a cold tickle ran down his throat. "For God's sake, Tatiana, can't we get a beer and discuss this?"

"I prefer the stall." She shoved him inside, toward the toilet. "Turn around slowly," she said.

He shuffled his feet in a circle, feeling the shard graze his neck. Then he was looking directly into her eyes.

"You've got holes in your plan," he said. "Same as always. You can't read my mind. If you kill me, how will you find Vivienne Barrett?"

"We can make this hard or simple," Tatiana said. "Which shall it be?"

"Simple."

She laughed. "I wish you could see the look on your face. I could set it to music. "Jim Morrison's 'The End' with a little Cradle of Filth."

At the other end of the restroom, the doorknob rattled, and someone began to knock.

Without looking away from Nick, Tatiana yelled, "Come back later. I'm vomiting. One of those twenty-four-hour viruses."

The doorknob went still.

Tatiana's face held no expression. "Answer my question and maybe you will not die in a restroom stall. Maybe you'll make your connecting flight. I'm afraid you've missed the last call for New York. But the Copenhagen flight is on time."

The backs of his eyes burned. Dammit, he wouldn't cry. Not in front of her.

"Where is Vivienne?" she asked.

"I'm not telling."

"We had a deal."

"Yeah. For a million euros, not a piece of glass in my neck."

She twisted the shard a little deeper.

He winced. "Put down the damn glass and we'll talk."

The inside of his shirt felt cool and wet. How badly had she cut him? The lounge was packed with businessmen, and they'd been drinking. Any second now, someone else would get a full bladder and knock at the door.

Tatiana's faint smile seemed to hold back a manic energy. "For all I know, you've set me up," she told him.

"I haven't. I swear it." Perspiration slid down Nick's forehead. "Put down your weapon. We'll renegotiate. I'll take less money. But I get to walk. It'll be win-win for us both."

But Nick was starting to understand how quickly his plan had reversed. She wouldn't let him go. She never left witnesses.

Her breath hit his face, stinking of camphor and cigar smoke. "You brought me here for nothing," she said. "Do you think I'm stupid?"

"No, I—"

"You don't know where Vivienne is, do you?"

"Yes."

"How did you find out?"

"Della Rocca brought Caro to my *riad*."

Tatiana stared at him a long moment, and her pupils dilated. "How did they get out of Paris?"

"I don't know anything about Paris. I was wired the night they showed up."

"Was Vivienne with them?"

"Maybe. Maybe not."

"Where is Della Rocca now?"

"Marrakech."

"And?"

"I'm not saying another word."

Tatiana dragged the glass along Nick's neck. "If I miss my flight, I'll really be pissed."

Terror sliced through him. He didn't want to die today. He wasn't ready.

"Good-bye, Nick," she said.

"Wait, stop." He panted. "If I tell you where to find Vivienne, will you let me go?"

"Yes."

He drew in a breath, held it, let it out in a rush. "Vivienne isn't with Caro."

"Liar. She'd never go anywhere without that child."

"I read Della Rocca's mind. He knows where the kid is. He kept the information from Caro."

"Why?"

"I don't know."

"Where is the girl?"

"Back off and I'll tell you," Nick said.

Tatiana stepped back, holding the wineglass. A drop of blood fell off the sharp edge and hit the floor.

Nick put his hand over his neck. Blood seeped through his fingers. He edged backward, toward the toilet. His plan was to hop on the seat and vault over the metal stall.

"You're too close," he said. "Move away."

Tatiana eased back. "Quit fucking with me, Nick."

"She's with someone named Sabine. They're in

Provence. I couldn't see the name of the town. I couldn't stay in Della Rocca's head for more than a few seconds. He really loves that Barrett chick."

"Love is nothing," Tatiana said.

"You're going to kill them both, aren't you? Never mind. I don't want to know." He glanced at the toilet seat, then bent his knees, preparing to jump.

Tatiana lunged forward and slashed his carotid. Arterial blood jetted across her face like cherry-colored paint. Another spurt hit the stall and ran down. Nick dropped to the floor, clutching his throat.

Tatiana moved above him. "You didn't *really* think I'd let you walk out of here."

A gurgling sound came out of his throat. He watched her rip open his shirt, listened to his buttons ping on the tile. A cool draft stirred over his chest. He heard music playing somewhere, so he couldn't be dying.

"Poor Nick," Tatiana said. "When adrenaline hits, you're all flight, no fight. If you'd stayed in Marrakech, I wouldn't know anything. And you'd still have a beating heart."

She placed the jagged edge of the glass just beneath his ribcage, then she made an incision. Her hand thrust deep inside him, groping and digging.

He felt a tug. A burst of pain. The whole world turned red, and somewhere music was playing.

CHAPTER 35

Caro

VILLA PRIMAVERINA, ISLA CARBONARA
VENICE, ITALY

I watched the lights from St. Mark's Square spread out as the helicopter angled toward Raphael's private island, where Villa Primaverina cast a glow on the dark waters of Laguna Veneta.

Security boats patrolled the island, and their lights bobbed in the waves, brightening the floats and buoys that created an obstacle course around Isla Carbonara. A floating sign warned trespassers of Arrapato's ferocity: PROPRIETA PRIVATA GUARDI DA DEI CANI.

The helicopter began to descend, the blades stirring the olive grove, blowing leaves toward the four-story Italianate house.

Raphael's manservant, Beppe, waited by the helicopter pad, holding Arrapato in his arms. Beppe was part Italian and part Swiss, a bald, big-shouldered man of an indeterminate age—and completely human. His chin was long and knobby like a bell pepper. He always wore a white dinner jacket with gold buttons.

"Caro, you've been gone too long," he said, kissing my cheek.

"I've missed you, Beppe," I said, reaching up to hug him.

Arrapato began to howl, then leaped into Raphael's arms. The dog's tongue shot out and he licked every inch of Raphael's face. After a few moments, Arrapato realized I was there, and he gave me a melty, apologetic stare. But he would not let Raphael set him down.

We found Monsieur La Rochenoire in the kitchen with Beppe's wife. Maria was a professional chef—Raphael still loved to smell food. She got huffy when La Rochenoire put on an apron.

"Where's the butter?" he asked, peering into a stainless-steel refrigerator.

Maria gave him the stink-eye. "Olive oil is on the counter. Sauté the porcini in oil."

"Oil?" He spat out the word.

"If you want butter," Maria said, "buy a dairy farm in Normandy."

As the argument escalated, Raphael and I slipped out of the kitchen, leaving the cooks to debate the finer points of French versus Italian cuisine. Me, I would eat anything as long as it didn't involve fish eyes or sheep entrails.

"Let's walk into the garden," Raphael said.

"If we're going to do more than walk, you might want to take your Benadryl," I said.

"Good idea." He pulled a box our of his pocket and swallowed two pink tablets. On our way out the terrace door, he lifted a silk quilt from the back of a sofa and took my hand.

Arrapato ran ahead of us, loping through the shadows. The constellations curved over Isla Carbonara while Raphael and I spread the quilt on the lawn. We sat down and he draped his arm around me.

Arrapato glanced back, as if making sure we were still there, and then he raced around the garden, peeing on the bushes and kicking up tufts of grass.

"I'm trying not to look into your mind," Raphael said, smiling down at me. "But you're so quiet."

"I was just remembering the first time I came to the villa," I said. "It was almost fifteen years ago. Right around Christmas. You bought me a red Chanel dress, and you hired a makeup artist and a hairdresser—just for drinks on the terrace."

Those days seemed distant, like pieces of a torn dream, but I remembered that night so clearly. Jude had come with me to the villa. He'd been human, filled with angst. He probably wouldn't have come if a trio of homicidal vampires hadn't tracked us across Venice. I'd worn crazy disguises then, too.

The more things changed, the more they stayed the same. I don't know who said that, but it's true.

"I remember every moment of that night," Raphael said. "I kissed you. A bit heavy-handed, I admit. You were outraged and told me to never do that again."

"I was in shock. You were also dipping in and out of

my thoughts. I heard you say, 'You could love me, *mia cara.*' And at that moment, I thought I could. Then you made me climax."

"That was rude." He traced his finger along my arm. "I was so attracted to you. But you loved Jude."

"Do you remember what you said after that kiss?"

"You told me that you couldn't be with anyone but him."

"And you said I would change my mind. That I might fall for you. And you promised great sex."

He lifted an eyebrow. "Did I lie?"

"No."

"Good."

"You said you would wait for me. I thought you were a playboy, someone who didn't understand love. I was so wrong." I watched his finger slide along my arm. "After Jude died, why didn't you tell me how you felt?"

"Because our first kiss had ended in disaster." Raphael smiled wryly, then he gazed toward the lagoon and didn't speak for a long moment. "I was happy to be near you. It was enough."

My chin was shaking so hard, I couldn't answer. The Inverna began to blow, sifting through the olive trees, stirring Raphael's hair. I caught a strand and tucked it behind his ear.

He put his head in my lap. He cupped his hand around my cheek. "Come live with me and be my wife."

I leaned over him, and my hair fell around us in a veil. "I'd love to."

"Do you want a long engagement?" he asked.

"Not too long."

His hand dropped to my neck. "A church wedding or something small? Maybe in the garden?"

I breathed in the smell of lemon verbena. "The garden."

"What about next week?" I heard a smile in his voice.

"That's too soon." I smiled. "I want Vivi to be our flower girl."

"We can have two weddings. One next week, in the garden, and a second wedding after Vivi returns."

"Do you need two ceremonies to feel married?" I teased.

"No, but what if we make a baby tonight?"

I shut my eyes, remembering when Vivi was little. I'd put her plump toes against my lips and I'd give them air kisses. She'd always smelled of talcum and milk. I'd always wanted more children. I still did. My eyes blinked open. Wouldn't it be selfish of me to bring another hybrid child into the world? Assassins would have two targets.

"I heard that, *mia cara*," he said. "You know what Mark Twain said. 'If you have one egg in a basket, watch that basket.'"

"I've been watching Vivi's basket for a while," I said.

He let that pass. "Our child would have three-quarter vampire genes," he said.

"Hypothetical child," I said.

"You grew up without siblings. Vivi needs a sister or a brother. They can protect each other, if anything should happen to us. They won't be alone. And I want to have a child with your eyes."

"You've forgotten one salient point," I said. "It isn't easy for hybrids and vampires to make babies."

"Then we will need to practice," he said, rising from my lap. He pulled me into his arms and carried me into the gazebo and set me down next to a Grecian column. Arrapato sped around us and leaped onto the rattan sofa, then stretched out full-length. He flashed a triumphant stare, as if to say, I've thwarted you again.

Raphael took off his trousers. His gaze never left my face as he slipped his hands under my dress, tugged off my panties, and picked me up. I locked my ankles around his waist and his hardness pressed between my legs.

"We haven't made love standing up in at least two days," I said.

"Three days," he said, bracing his shoulders against a column. "You smell so good. Like sun-drenched olive trees and lemon verbena."

I smiled and put my arms around his neck. His chest leaned against mine, and I felt his heart booming, his whiskers scraping on my cheek, his breath ruffling in my hair, the pressure of his hands on my backside. I reached between us, and slipped my hand through the gap in his boxer shorts. My fingers brushed down his erection, caressing his smooth flesh, then I moved up and smeared the damp bead on his tip.

His breath was coming in short puffs, and so was mine. "Raphael, I want you. I've never wanted anyone this much."

"I want you more."

My teeth nipped the swell of his bottom lip, and I sucked it. He kissed me, and a current raced from my throat to my fingertips. Tiny veins of rapture seemed to enter my bloodstream, and I climaxed. Then he was inside me, his buttocks thudding against the column, pushing deeper into me. Another orgasm broke loose, and I skimmed my teeth over his neck and pinched the flesh. I bit down.

He groaned, and his mouth dropped to my throat. I felt the prick of his incisors, and my hand tightened on the back of his neck. As we tasted each other, a pulse started to beat between my thighs. He kissed my mouth, and I tasted blood. A convulsive force moved low inside me, sweeping through me. He kept thrusting, saying my name, and I climaxed again. His breathing became erratic, and as he spilled into me, I imagined a dome of water rising out of the Adriatic Sea, tipped with white foam, and pouring onto the shore.

All sound left the world: the wind stopped blowing in the olive trees, the waves froze against the sea wall, water quit pattering in the fountain. Then the noises rushed back at once and I was coming again and he was coming, and it was all starting over.

———

Later, we walked back to the villa, still flushed and breathless. Beppe and La Rochenoire were in the game room, watching Sky News on the widescreen TV. Arrapato leaped between them and tucked his nose under the Frenchman's arm.

The television screen showed a picture of Nick Parnell. It was an old photograph—his hair was shorter, and he had a mustache. The image changed to a stock photo of Heathrow Airport.

"Last night, a passenger discovered the body of Dr. Nicholas Parnell in the restroom of a lounge at Heathrow," the announcer was saying. "Police have not ruled out a ritualistic murder at this time."

"Ritualistic?" I said.

Light from the television played over Beppe's glossy head. "The victim's heart was removed," he said.

Raphael looked stunned. "The news reported this?"

"No," Beppe said. "It's all over the Internet. A Guinea-Bissau drug lord ordered the hit."

The hairs on my arms lifted, and I sat down hard on a love seat. Raphael strode toward me, his eyes rounded. I couldn't shake the feeling that time had reversed, and he was moving away from me, walking backward across the lawn, his legs scissoring through the shadowy garden, moving back into the gazebo, stepping through a tear in the fabric of the night, into a realm without clocks. And I could not follow him, no matter how hard I tried.

CHAPTER 36

Vivi

VALBONNE, FRANCE

Sabine's house was perched on a hill, next to a vineyard, and down in the valley, the lights of Valbonne were starting to shine. The sun had just gone down, but Vivi wasn't ready to go inside. She sat in the grass, watching Marie-Therese chase a purple butterfly. Its wings were the exact color of the lavender clouds that wafted across the sky.

In just a few days it would be August, her last month in Provence. Then she would return to Sabine's penthouse. She sighed, picturing the noisy, all-white rooms. But at least she'd get to see her mom.

"Come help me set the table, child," Lena called from the pergola.

Vivi turned. Lena stood by the old wooden table, arranging dishes and flatware. She'd made escargot

risotto, fava beans, marinated olives, tiny radish sandwiches, and a salad with red and yellow cherry tomatoes.

"Be right there," Vivi called. She got up, dusted grass
off her shorts, and ran to the pergola. Marie-Therese raced
ahead of her and leaped onto a wooden sideboard, watching Vivi grab a pile of napkins.

Lena set down a plate and glanced toward the stone
house, where lamps were glowing in the windows. "I'll
whip Sabine's ass if she lets her food get cold again."

"I heard that," Sabine said, walking into the pergola.
She set down a basket that was crammed with small
baguettes, then turned to the sideboard and scratched
Marie-Therese's ear. The cat began to purr.

Vivi placed a napkin beside each plate. She and Sabine
had spent the whole morning in Grasse, strolling past the
pale tangerine-colored houses and poking around the
Cathedral Notre-Dame-de-Puy. They ended up in a
crowded square where people were walking their dogs.
Vivi sat on a bench, Inducing a group of middle-aged
tourists to stay away from the pastry shop. Sabine had
given her an A-plus.

"You have saved these people from ingesting too many
calories," Sabine had told her.

Now, Sabine pulled out a chair and sat down. "Tomorrow we're going to the Fête du Jasmin."

"What's that?" Vivi asked.

"A festival." Sabine winked at Lena. "You should come
with us."

"Only if you go to the fruit market," Lena said. She
sat down and shook out her napkin.

Marie-Therese leaped off the sideboard, ran under the

table, and began weaving around Vivi's feet. Halfway through the meal, Sabine put down her fork and grimaced, as if she'd swallowed a bone.

"Drink you some water," Lena said.

Sabine ignored her and stared down at the road. Vivi looked, too. Shadows fell over the empty road. Way off in the distance, the lights of Valbonne cast a glow.

Lena frowned. "What you looking at, Sabine? You expecting somebody?"

"No." Sabine turned to Vivi. "Something just occurred to me. I haven't taught you how to kill."

Vivi spat out a tomato. "You're supposed to teach me how to avoid that."

"She better be." Lena shook her finger at Sabine. "I can't be having that kind of talk at my supper table. You hear?"

Sabine was still looking at Vivi. "Hemakinesis can be a defense. But you can also use it to cause exsanguination."

Vivi screwed her up nose. "What's that?"

"The victim bleeds to death." Sabine spoke in an offhand tone, as if she were asking Vivi to pass the salt. "Do you remember the breathing exercises?"

"Yes," Vivi said warily.

"When you want to kill, you hold your breath. But you also have to use your stomach muscles. You tighten them as hard as you can. You may feel the energy pass out of you, as if you'd exhaled. Remember to focus—look at the target, imagine his name, visualize what you want him to do."

"I ain't listening to this." Lena put her hand over her mouth as if she had a sour stomach. She pushed away from the table and walked back to the house.

Vivi put down her fork. "Sabine? Are you okay?"

"Perfectly."

"Good. Because I'm not killing anybody. Even if I could, and I won't, how will I practice?"

Sabine squinted at the road. "You never know when an opportunity will turn up."

Vivi's chest felt tight. If her mom knew about this, she'd freak out. "I don't want to blow up someone's chest."

"Don't be silly." Sabine's face tightened. "Chests can't explode. If you aim at the ribcage, you'll rupture the aorta—but even I can't do that. At least, I don't think I can. It's much easier to cause a cerebral hemorrhage. Just focus on the target's eyes or nose."

"I can't believe you're teaching me how to murder people."

"Self-defense is part of your training. What if someone attacks you?"

Vivi drew back.

Sabine's face softened. "I'm speaking of hypotheticals, of course."

"Well, that's a relief. Because it's creepy how you keep looking at the road. Like you're afraid a vampire might drive up."

"I've had a bad feeling all day."

"Then why are we still here? When Mom gets paranoid, we pack our bags and move."

"Flight is a perfectly acceptable reaction to fear. As long as it isn't your only response. One day you might not be able to run. You will have to fight."

"Fight who?"

"Anyone who wishes to harm you. Don't let moral

turpitude get in the way of survival. Your opponent certainly won't be concerned with ethics."

Vivi's mouth opened. She'd never heard Sabine talk this way. "Maybe I accidentally made a vessel burst in your head today. Because you're acting like you've had a stroke."

"I hope not." Sabine darted another look at the road. Headlights cut two cones of light on the dark pavement. The car snaked around a curve, then sped past Sabine's gated driveway and disappeared over a hill.

"Stop it," Vivi said. "Cars come down this road all the time."

"True."

A twisty feeling moved in Vivi's chest. "Should I pack my suitcase?"

"No. I don't want you to worry." Sabine reached under the table and lifted the cat. "I don't know what's wrong with me tonight. We won't need to leave Valbonne for a while. We'll be safe."

But they weren't.

CHAPTER 37

Sabine

VALBONNE, FRANCE

A nightmare awoke Sabine at two A.M. She sat on the side of the bed, her heart pounding, pajamas stuck to her back. It was the same horrid nightmare. The same confusing images. A shattered balcony door. Blood in a public restroom. More blood in a driveway. A blond woman standing outside a house.

But the house looked eerily like this one, Sabine thought. The Valbonne manse had a distinct look, with arched windows, periwinkle shutters, and vines running up the stone walls. The weathervane atop the pergola was adorned with a copper gargoyle. And the driveway curved down to a tall, scrolled iron gate.

Sabine rubbed her eyes. How did these violent images mesh with the peace in this household? She needed to look for patterns, to think with a physician's cool detachment.

Marie-Therese was curled up at the foot of the bed, so Sabine eased off the mattress and opened the balcony door. The night air smelled of lavender, cypress, and over-ripe plums. She stiffened as a car drove slowly past the house. The vehicle backed up, red taillights blinking, then pulled into the driveway. The head-beams shone against the iron security gate. Sabine's pulse slammed in her ears, and she gripped the terrace railing.

GO AWAY. She held her breath, then slowly released it.

The headlights retreated. The car backed into the road and drove in the opposite direction. The taillights glided down the road and dipped behind a hill.

The smell of plums vanished, too.

Think, Sabine. She tapped her index finger against her lips. Should she wake Lena? Vivi was a seasoned traveler and would not ask questions. In an hour, the three of them could pack the car, drive to the Nice airport, and wait for the first available flight to Paris. No, the shattered door had felt like Paris, and the bloody restroom had felt like London. Where could they go? Some place she hadn't dreamed about.

Vivi's training had gone well, but the self-defense aspects couldn't be completed in good conscience. Not with living beings. It was one thing to Induce portly tourists to eat a salad rather than palmiers or an apricot tart—Sabine had been right there with Vivi, monitoring her pulse and respiration, making sure the tourists were safe. It was another to make an innocent person have a nosebleed, or worse.

Teaching the theory of advanced hemakinesis was akin to reading about brain surgery in a textbook and then trying to drill through the skull of a breathing patient. Last night, she'd given Vivi a crash course, but she'd only frightened the child. And scared students seldom retained information.

The headlights returned, moving crookedly down the road. Was it the same car or a different one? A drunk driver, perhaps? She began to breathe slowly. Then she cast an imaginary net over the car and tried to pull in the thoughts of its occupants.

A black tangle spun up, raw and sexual. Sabine's head jerked back. She counted four men and one woman. The woman was pleasuring the driver. The other men were aroused and impatient.

Sabine jerked the net away. She had no way of knowing if the people in the car were college students, tourists, or murderers. Most likely, they'd drunk too much wine and weren't dangerous.

The car lights swerved to the right, straightened for a moment, then swung left. A screech of tires echoed, and the car stopped. The headlight beams glowed like a predator's eyes. Finally the car did a U-turn and drove north, moving faster and faster, the taillights skimming over a hill. Then the road went dark and still as a painting.

Sabine crept back to bed, but she couldn't sleep. She chewed her thumbnail, trying to remember where she'd put the melatonin. She lay in bed until the sky was the color of an oyster shell. She got out of bed and checked the road again.

Empty.

She looked past the hills, toward Valbonne. Above the town, the early morning sky resembled melted pewter. Her slippers brushed over the wooden floor as she paced in front of the fireplace before sitting on the bed. The bedroom was suffused with a gray pallor, lending a graveyard aura to the white walls and beamed ceiling. Her bedroom was the only white room in the house—the paleness had always soothed her, but now it felt menacing.

I need color, she thought. She rolled off the bed, opened the maple armoire, and pulled out a purple caftan. She lifted the cat, then tiptoed down the hall, past Vivi's closed door and past Lena's open one, with its piles of cookbooks, rag rugs, and green Murano vases. When Sabine got downstairs, she paused in the living room. Last year, she'd painted this room a muted shade of apricot, and the walls seemed warm and womblike. Lena had been so pleased. "Your hurt places are starting to heal," she'd said.

Sabine knew different. Her décor was a textbook example of Freud's iceberg metaphor. Her apartment in Paris represented the ego and superego; but the Valbonne house was pure id, the childish part of Sabine. Just beyond this room, she saw the green-and-apricot kitchen, with its tiled backsplash and copper pots. Paisley curtains hung over the cupboards, and messy heaps of dishes poked out. The disorder stilled her mind.

She turned back to the apricot living room, and her gaze stopped on the bookcase. She set down the cat, pulled *Elemental Kinesis* from the shelf, and carried it to the sofa. She opened the book, flipped past the hemakinesis chapter, and stopped on the electromagnetic section. Vivi could manipulate the thoughts of others with skill, but new talents were developing.

The other day in the garden, the girl had demonstrated an aptitude for phyllokinesis, a capacity for influencing plant life, though influencing was a mild description: Vivi had made grapes burst open.

Sabine tapped her fingernail against the book. Vivi's powers were inconsistent with case studies of other hybrids, which were admittedly few, but still. The girl sometimes had precognitive dreams, but she lacked telepathy. When a young hybrid demonstrated three psi skills, it indicated the presence of other, latent talents, such as pyrokinesis, hydrokinesis, or biokinesis. The ability to control fire and water was uncommon, and she'd never read about a case of biokinesis, which was the ability to rearrange DNA. Vivi was an uncommon girl, and it was impossible to know when, or if, these skills might emerge.

She set the book aside and went to the kitchen. Marie-Therese trotted behind her, letting out indignant meows. Sabine poured kibble into a bowl. The sun was coming up, staining the room with pink light. She shuffled to the window. The road was still empty, but it resembled a coiled black snake.

By the time Vivi and Lena came downstairs, Sabine had prepared breakfast. No cream puffs or brioche, no mascarpone or *marmellata*. She served *caffè latte*, a mixture of espresso and warm milk, along with fruit.

Vivi stared down at the food, her lips forming a rumpled line. "Can't we have a frittata?"

"The brain is sharper with caffeine and complex car-bohydrates," Sabine told her.

They went to Grasse, as promised, and Sabine started to calm down. They bought fruit in the market, then came home. She and Vivi spent the rest of the day working—the girl had succeeded in bursting dozens of tomatoes and eggplants.

Despite the success, tiny seeds of dread took hold in Sabine's mind. The hairs on her arms prickled, and she felt slightly nauseated. It was the same apprehension she'd experienced in medical school, when she'd run up the stairs to ICU for a code blue.

After the sun went down, Vivi and Lena went to the kitchen to make chocolate-dipped strawberries. Sabine and Marie-Therese stayed in the apricot-colored room, resting on the sofa, watching television. Sky News was full of gloom. A man had been tortured and murdered in a Heathrow restroom. Authorities in Paris were still puzzled over a recent home invasion that had resulted in a fire and six deaths.

The reporter moved on to another story, but Sabine kept staring blankly at the screen. The seeds inside her chest grew into hard, green knobs. It hurt to breathe.

From the kitchen, the phone trilled in three short bursts, indicating that a car was at the gate. If Sabine pressed 2, the gate would open.

"Don't open the gate," she called.

Lena appeared in the doorway, clutching a red dish-towel. "I didn't. But they got it open somehow."

Sabine lifted the cat and got off the sofa. "Take Vivi and Marie-Therese upstairs and hide."

Lena took the cat and ran back to the kitchen. Sabine got up and opened the front door. Behind her, she heard footsteps creaking on the stairs. Vivi was asking if she'd done anything wrong, and Lena made soft shushing noises.

Sabine walked down the curved path. A full moon lit up the upper part of the driveway. Car lights swept around the curve, and a dusty white Audi stopped at the edge of the walkway. A woman got out, the wind stirring her short blond hair. She wore a tan linen jacket and dark slacks. Her pretty face held no emotion. Her thoughts were black and twisty.

"How may I help you?" Sabine called, folding her arms. Her eyes narrowed as she remembered the car she'd seen last night. Was this the same woman who'd pleasured those men? No, surely not, Sabine told herself. She had no logical reason to connect the two women.

The blonde flashed a badge and tucked it inside her jacket, giving a teasing glimpse of a holster.

"I'm from the Grasse Police," she said. Her accent was definitely not French. Nor did she have the demeanor of an officer.

"Yes?" Sabine looked past her. The four men stayed in the car: a driver with bushy black hair; three men with buzz cuts in the backseat, their shoulders pressed together.

The blonde smiled. "Caroline Barrett asked me to find her daughter. There's been an accident."

"I'm sorry to hear it. What kind of accident?" Sabine's gaze sharpened. Should she take out the blonde now? No, first she should disable the men.

"We've been instructed to take Vivienne to her mother," the blonde said. She put her hand on her hips, and her sleeve pulled up, showing the top curve of a black infinity tattoo, a green snake twisted in the loops.

Sabine smiled, but her brain was rapidly assembling facts. The blonde had no telepathic skills, and she was struggling to hide her thoughts. The name Tatiana Kaskov floated up.

Breathing in and out, Sabine pushed out an Inductive thought.

Relax, Tatiana.

The blonde smiled. Her hand slid off her hip, and then she looked back at the Audi and waved to the men. When she turned back to Sabine, she frowned, as if she were disappointed.

"We're in a hurry," she said.

Sabine punched another thought at the woman. *You're at the wrong house, Tatiana.*

The blonde's forehead tightened.

Sabine punched harder. *Wrong house. Go away.*

The blonde sucked in a breath. Her eyelids fluttered. "I'm at the wrong house?"

"Yes." Sabine tensed her stomach muscles, and she felt a whoosh push away from inside her head. *YES.*

The blonde took another hitching breath, then spun around, as if unseen hands had wrenched her shoulders.

Sabine drew in her breath, held it, and sent out another burst. The air around her seemed to warp and ripple, like the oily film that rises from a charcoal grill. Then the blonde's head jerked forward. Her hand went to her face.

She looked back at Sabine, blood running through her fingers.

Turn around. Get in your car. Lock the door.

Sabine shifted her gaze to the driver and aimed a thought in his direction. *Unzip your trousers.*

The driver looked down at his lap. The Audi's rear doors opened, and the other men got out. They were lean, bronzed, and dark-haired. White T-shirts. Loose-fitting sweat pants. Tennis shoes. Slung around their hips were black nylon gun holsters.

"Tatiana?" called a man with clipped brown hair.

The woman, Tatiana, leaned over and propped her hand on her knee. Blood streamed out of her nose and pattered onto the gravel. She clamped her other hand over her nostrils and took a mincing step toward the car.

"What is wrong with me?" she cried, blood forking down her wrist, skating between her knuckles.

The driver didn't look up; he kept staring down at his lap. A man with a ponytail hurried away from the Audi and squatted beside Tatiana.

"Are you all right?" he said in heavily accented English.

"Obviously not," she snapped.

He peeled off his T-shirt and held it to her nose. A dark dampness spread over the fabric.

Tatiana was sobbing, blubbering to herself.

Blubbering in Russian, Sabine noticed. She drew in a breath. The night air reeked of blood and ketones; but she wasn't afraid. Long ago, she'd learned how to control her response to fear, and her mind was alert and dispassionate. She tightened her stomach muscles, trying to decide if she should Induce all of the intruders at once, imploring them to leave, or if she should use hemakinesis. Induction sped up the metabolic rate and eventually caused fatigue. Vampires weren't always affected by projection. Hemakinesis had few side-effects. She could do all three, but it would be imperative to keep the energy flowing, the way a one-woman orchestra keeps the music playing, and that was damned hard. She needed to stop wasting time and make a decision.

Definitely hemakinesis. Sabine focused on the pony-tailed man beside Tatiana.

His head jerked. As he got to his feet, blood oozed out of his eyes and nose. He screamed and put his hands on his face. Behind him, a bow-legged man stepped away from the Audi. Sabine blasted him. He halted, then rubbed his ear on his shoulder, leaving a stain on his shirt sleeve. She zapped him again. His lips parted, as if he were trying to speak, then he dropped straight to the ground.

The man with clipped brown hair walked in front of the car, his forehead puckered, and shouted something in Turkish.

Sabine saw into his mind. He liked little girls.

That bastard. Sabine opened her mouth wide, then sucked in a harsh breath and held it; she tightened every muscle in her body, then sent out a burst of energy.

The man's feet left the ground, and he fell back onto the Audi's hood. His left tennis shoe kicked out the head-light, and glass tinkled to the gravel. Blood jetted from his eyes, nose, mouth, and ears. He slid down, leaving a red streak on the white hood, then fell to the driveway and didn't move.

Sabine shut her eyes, breathing in and out. She pushed a gentle thought at Lena. *Put Marie-Therese in a closet. Bring Vivi downstairs. Run out the back door. Hide in the vineyard. Go!*

When she opened her eyes, she saw two silver Peugeot vans pull into the driveway and glide through the open gate and up the hill, gravel pinging against the fenders like bullets hitting a steel door. It was too dark too see inside each vehicle, so Sabine cast an imaginary net over both. She counted ten men, five in the first van, five in the second. All human.

Too many, she thought, the back of her neck prickling. At least they were mortal, which meant they would be easier to disable. She could project an illusion—the humans brain was so receptive—but she could project only wasps, and not for long. It required sustained focus, and she had the others to worry about. But she had to try.

Her gaze swerved back to the ponytailed man who'd helped Tatiana. He had stopped howling, but his eyes were still bleeding. He was stumbling around the Audi, both hands extended, a stain spreading down the front of his T-shirt.

Tatiana was digging her shoes into the gravel, trying to get to her feet.

"What is happening?" she screamed, the cords on her neck taut and reedy. Her lips and chin were dark red and glistening, as if she'd dipped them into a freshly gutted deer. She stood, legs wobbling.

The silver Peugeot vans were halfway up the driveway, so Sabine knew she had to work fast.

Tatiana, get in the front seat. See to the driver. He is waiting for you. He wants you. As Sabine let out a breath, the air roiled and shimmered.

Tatiana was wrenched backward, hard. Gravel spun away from her shoes, but she quickly regained her footing.

Meurs, pute, Sabine thought. She wanted this whore to die painfully. She sent another burst at the woman's belly.

"It hurts," Tatiana said, wincing. A blush spread in the V of her crotch. She crept back to the Audi, ignoring the dead man, who lay sprawled beside the front tire. She got into the passenger seat.

Sabine watched the silver vans roll to a stop behind the Audi. The doors opened and men in Hawaiian shirts got out. Each top was a different color, but the pattern was the same: parrots, oversized flowers, and palm fronds. The men were big-boned and muscular, with pale eyes, buzz cuts, and sunburned faces.

Project the illusion. A droning sound hummed in Sabine's head, as if freshly hatched wasps were trapped inside her eardrums. She visualized thousands of stinging insects, then projected this image at the men in the floral shirts.

"What the fuck," one of the men said. The others scattered away from the vans, cursing and stamping the ground, their hands swatting the empty air.

Americans. Sabine looked past their conscious thoughts, into their memories. It was like spinning a dial on a radio, a mishmash of static and music, but the same words rose up. Paramilitary. Blackwater. Iraq. Afghanistan. Post-Katrina New Orleans.

The driver in the second van got out, his hand sliding inside the waistband of his shorts, as if he were reaching for a gun. He resembled the others: a navy, parrot-strewn Hawaiian shirt, nondescript eyes, buzz haircut, athletic physique. The breeze lifted the edge of his shirt, and Sabine saw a belt holster. He grabbed a man in a red floral shirt. "What the hell are you doing?" he yelled. He didn't get an answer and flung the man away. Muttering to himself, he strode past the Audi and glanced through the passenger window. His eyebrows slanted together and he stumbled back, his sunburn turning a deep purple-red. A pulse beat in his neck as he walked around the Audi's blood-streaked hood, then his gaze passed over the bodies in the driveway. His eyes hardened as he looked at Sabine.

"What happened to these people?" he called. He reached into his belt holster and pulled out a gun.

Sabine hit him with an aggressive wallop. He dropped to his knees, and his mouth opened wide. His expression resembled the screaming man in Edvard Munch's painting. He coughed. Blood dribbled over his lips, then he coughed again, and a bright red gash spurted into the air. Another burst came out of his mouth. He hit the ground, and a dark puddle spread out him.

Sabine caught her breath. She'd aimed for his lungs, but she'd struck the aorta. And she'd failed to keep projecting imaginary wasps. The other men in Hawaiian shirts were starting to calm down, muttering to each other. Their broad As and dropped Rs reminded Sabine of her old Harvard professor.

These were humans from Boston? What about that Turk? Who had hired this crew?

A man in a blue Hawaiian shirt let out a hoarse cry and pointed toward the vineyard. "There's the girl!"

He vaulted over a low stone wall and charged into the darkness. A man in a yellow shirt followed him. They were gone before Sabine could collect her thoughts. She'd deal with them later.

She looked back at the Audi. Tatiana was still in the front seat, and her head was moving above the lap of the driver, whose mouth was wide open, showing the glint of silver fillings in his back teeth.

Sabine moved her gaze to the Peugeot vans. She projected more wasps at the men. They let out whoops and veered into the grass, their shirts filling with air.

A high, girlish scream came from the vineyard. Sabine turned toward the sound. She saw two small figures running down the rows, racing in and out of shadows. The Boston men were behind them.

Sabine pulled in a breath and grunted. The blow hit the men, but they were too far away to feel the full impact. They stumbled, then kept going. As she climbed down the hill, she stepped into a hole. She wrenched sideways, and pain twisted up her ankle.

As she pulled her foot out of the hole, she lost her balance and tumbled forward, over and over, dirt and grass filling her eyes and nose. She rolled over a ledge, arms wheeling, and then she was flying.

CHAPTER 38

Vivi

Vivi ran through the dark vineyard, angling in and out of the rows. She could hear Lena's footsteps behind her. A shadow cut in from the side, and then a big hand snatched the back of Vivi's shirt. Her collar pushed against her throat, crimping her airway.

"Let her go, you fat pig," Lena yelled, then she bit the hand that was holding Vivi. A hoarse cry rang out. The hand released Vivi's shirt, and she slid to the ground. She looked up. Lena was going after a man who wore a yellow Hawaiian shirt. She boxed his ears, then kicked his shins.

"I'll whip your ass proper," Lena said.

A man in a blue floral shirt rushed in from the other direction and aimed a red dot at her face.

"Run," Lena said.

Vivi got to her feet.

A *pish-pish* noise slammed through the dark, and then Lena clutched the side of her face. She fell over backward and didn't move.

"Lena!" A burning smell rushed up Vivi's nose. She gulped air and held it deep in her lungs. Then she hurled a thought at the blue-shirted man.

DROP YOUR GUN.

His fingers sprang open, and the red dot danced over the vines like a bee. A dark line curved from his ear, and he clamped his hand over it.

"Ow, ow," he said, then bent over double. The man in the yellow shirt grabbed Vivi from behind and tossed her over his shoulder.

BLEED, YOU ASSHOLE!

He kept running, his warm breath hitting her neck. *He's not a vampire*, she thought. She tried to Induce him again, but she was hyperventilating. He carried her up a hill, over the low, stone wall, to the driveway. He set her on the ground but held on to her wrist.

"Let go," she yelled. She tried to wrench away, but he jerked her back.

She looked over her shoulder. Bodies were sprawled on the gravel. A blond woman walked up, her face smeared with blood, her hands fisted at her sides. Her pants were dirty, as if she'd spilled wine in her lap.

"We've got her, Tatiana," said the man in the yellow shirt.

Tatiana's eyes narrowed as she pulled Vivi out of the man's grasp. "You little bitch. You'll pay for this."

"Pay for what?" Vivi cried.

The blonde's fist shot out. Vivi's head whipped backward. Her eyes blinked open wide, a whoosh of air flew out of her mouth, and a burning pressure spread through her cheek. Never in her life had anyone hit her. She bent over and vomited on the blond woman's shoes.

The woman drew back her fist again. The man in the yellow shirt caught it.

"Hey, leave her alone," he said. "She's just a kid."

"Then get her the fuck out of my sight," the blonde said.

Vivi gulped in a lungful of air and held it. She focused on the blonde's face, squeezing her stomach muscles as hard as she could. A bright ribbon curled out of the woman's ear, her eyelids flickered, and then she plopped down on her butt.

"Where are the other bitches?" asked a man in a black floral shirt.

The blonde woman stared at the ground and didn't answer.

Another man in an orange shirt walked up, brushing his hands erratically through his cropped hair, as if bugs were crawling on his scalp. "Micky shot one of the dames," he said. "He can't find the other. She ran off."

Run, Sabine. Run as fast as you can. Vivi felt tears run down her cheeks. *Lena, don't you die.*

The man in the yellow shirt touched Vivi's shoulder. His face was sunburned. "Come on, kid."

She put her hand on her aching cheek. A sour bubble pushed up in her throat, and she thought she might vomit again. If she got into that van, she would never see her mom.

"I'm gonna be sick," she said.

The man backed off. She pretended to make a gagging noise, then sprinted off into the dark, racing down the hill, curving toward the vineyard.

"Hey! Get your ass back here," a deep voice yelled.

She ran down a grassy row, pumping her arms, her chest tight. She felt a man's thick arms close around her legs, and then she slammed to the ground. Her lungs flattened.

"Stupid kid," the man said. He cuffed her hands behind her back. She heard deep voices above her. A beefy guy in a pink flowery shirt squatted beside her, holding a hypodermic needle. She felt a stabbing pain in her arm.

STOP, LET GO, STOP.

Her vision blurred. She tried to hold her breath, but she couldn't. She didn't have one drop of air in her lungs. The vineyard seemed to melt, rushing down the hill, flowing into a broad purple river. It swept her off her feet and pulled her beneath the surface.

CHAPTER 39

Caro

VILLA PRIMAVERINA, ISLA CARBONARA
VENICE, ITALY

I stood on the terrace, watching the lights in St. Mark's
Square. It was a warm August night, and the inverna, the
south wind, caught my hair. I wore a long blue dress, the
color of Jude's eyes. He'd been on my mind. I could see
the distinct *M* of his upper lip, and the brown specks in
his left iris. I remembered how he would walk up behind
me and slide his hand under my blouse, his fingers cool
and firm.

Are you still my girl? he'd say. *For now*, I'd answer.

The terrace doors stood open, and I heard Raphael
talking to his chief security guard. I turned.

"What did you find out?" Raphael said, pacing in front
of the French doors.

Signore Dolfini sat in a chair, looking down at a

clipboard, yellow Post-it notes jutting from the notepad. He was in his early forties, lean and small-boned, his face flushed from the sun. He wore boating shoes, white shorts, and a T-shirt printed with ITALIA SOCCER. At his feet was a box crammed with manila folders.

"Tatiana Kaskov was born in 1956," Dolfini said, peering down at the clipboard. "Studied ballet. Kicked out of three boarding schools, including one in Paris."

"Do you know why she was expelled?" Raphael said.

"She slept with an instructor at one school. There was talk of grade inflation. I'm still waiting to hear about the other schools." Signore Dolfini flipped a page. "Her father was a St. Petersburg physician. Worked at City Hospital No. 40. Deceased. Shot in the head. A robbery. Tatiana was sent to a boarding school in Amsterdam. The ballet lessons ended. Two years later, the mother was murdered."

Raphael stopped pacing. "How?"

"Her throat was cut. To the bone." Dolfini flipped another page. "Tatiana gave part of her inheritance to the state. Attended Moscow State Linguistic University. Worked at the Soviet consulates in Washington D.C. and East Berlin. Slept around. A lot."

"*Pompinos?*" Raphael said, using an unflattering word for fellatio.

"*Si, si.*" Dolfini lowered the clipboard and pulled a thick file from the box. "It gets worse. She was involved in smuggling—guns and black diamonds. Her name is still on an Interpol watch list. She disappeared in the post-Soviet era."

"And she's still off the grid," Raphael said. "We need to find her."

From the hallway came the pounding of footsteps. Signore Dolfini's two daughters ran into the room, their long, pink organza dresses churning around their ankles, ribbons streaming from their light brown hair. The littler girl bumped into a gilt settee, and it toppled.

"Nicci, stop chasing your sister," Signore Dolfini called, clapping his hands. "Viola, apologize to Signore Della Rocca."

"*Mi scusi*," the younger girl said, then giggled.

"*Signorina Nicci, non preoccuparti, sii felice,*" Raphael said as he caught the taller girl. *Don't worry*, he'd told her. *Be happy.*

She giggled as he lifted her into the air. He set her down, and the little sister stretched out her arms.

"*Tocca a me!*" she cried.

Raphael picked her up. "Ah, Signorina Viola, you are getting so big."

Dolfini's cheeks turned scarlet as he apologized for the disruption, but Raphael smiled. "*Un bimbo che non gioca, felicita ne ha poce,*" he said. A child who doesn't play has little happiness.

The girls hugged Raphael. "We love you, Signore," they said.

"Who wants cake?" he asked.

"We do," they said, hopping up and down in a pink organdy swirl.

"Maria?" Raphael called, turning toward the kitchen. "Two lovely ladies need cake."

I turned back to the water and spread my hands on the railing. I remembered what Walpole had said about Tatiana. And Parnell had slept with her. She'd been on that

expedition, and chased my husband. Had she stolen his
wedding ring? Or had he taken it off? I did not want
to brood on something that had happened a decade
ago, and I pushed those unhappy thoughts out of my
head.

From inside the house, I heard the Dolfini children
talking in excited voices, and I remembered when Vivi
had been young.

Oh, Vivi, I thought. *If only I had given you sisters and
brothers.*

Our constant traveling would have made it harder with
two children, but Jude and I would have managed. And
Vivi wouldn't have been alone.

I was still thinking about her when Signore Dolfini
and his daughters walked through the shadowy garden,
toward the boat dock.

Raphael strode onto the terrace and put his arms
around me. I detected an intriguingly different smell, a
clean, lemony-orange scent with a trace of rosemary. Then
I realized he'd changed his cologne—he always wore
Acqua di Parma when he was at Villa Primaverina. It was
the same fragrance that Jude had worn. For a moment, I
felt disoriented, and I stared at the dark lagoon. I was
breathing in layers of history, all of those long-ago
moments with Jude and Raphael.

The Dolfinis' boat chugged away from the dock, and
the spotlight fanned across the dark lagoon. The horn
tooted, then the boat angled toward Venice. I pressed the
back of my head against Raphael's chest.

"*Sei l'amore della mia vita,*" he said.

"You're the love of my life, too," I said. The inverna

rushed over the terrace, stirring my dress and filling me with all kinds of longings.

"It will stop blowing at midnight," Raphael said, smoothing my hair.

"I'm enjoying it." I put my hand over his. "I also enjoyed watching you with Signore Dolfini's daughters."

"Nicci and Viola are the eldest," he said, his voice holding a lightness, just a hint of laughter. "He has two babies at home. Luisa is four. Bettina is six months."

I turned and put my arms around his neck. "You'll be a loving father."

"When the gods are willing." He bent down to kiss my wrist, and his hair brushed over my arm, cool and silky.

"I can't wait for them, Raphael." I held his gaze while the wind moved around us, pushing my hair into his. He picked me up and carried me straight to his room. While he swallowed Benadryl tablets, I unbuttoned my dress and dropped it on a chair.

"*Sei bellissima,*" he whispered, pulling off his shirt.

I didn't feel beautiful, but I did feel his love. He walked up to me. I kissed his palm, inhaling him. God had granted me two great loves, and I did not want to be undeserving of that blessing. I would love this man for the rest of my life.

———

Raphael's phone trilled through the dark bedroom. He reached across me, toward the table, and lifted the receiver. "*Si?*" he said.

I heard Beppe's excited voice, but I couldn't make out the words. I pulled up on my elbows, frowning. Raphael's butler was famously coolheaded in emergencies. I'd seldom heard him speak above a bass-baritone, but now I heard a tenor, edged with a falsetto. Something was horribly wrong. Had the vampires found us again?

A shape moved beneath the covers, and I jumped. Arrapato's dark head popped out from beneath the blanket. I pulled him against me.

"Did she say what happened?" Raphael asked Beppe.

She? I blinked. The intruder was female? A sudden vision of the French designer whirled behind my eyes. Or maybe Gillian had finally arrived.

"Show them to the terrace," Raphael said, then hung up.

Them? I swallowed. Now I was hoping the angry-eyed designer had arrived. She was preferable to the nebulous *them*. Raphael rose from the bed and picked up our clothes, tossing them over his shoulder. His silence worried me, and I tried to peek at his thoughts, but I bumped into an obsidian slab.

I stroked Arrapato's head. He looked up at me and sighed.

Raphael put on his trousers, then handed me the blue dress. I slipped it over my head, then I stared up at him, waiting for him to explain. We'd never pressured or wheedled each other. Maybe that was one reason we were so compatible, but I couldn't take the silence another second.

"What's wrong?" I said.

He knelt beside the bed and took my face in his hands. "Sabine is here," he said.

We rushed to the terrace. Through the open doors, I saw the lights of St. Mark's Square.

"Caro," Sabine said. She pushed away from the railing. A wide piece of tape stretched across her nose, and her eyes were bruised. Her hands and knees were raw and scabbed. From the ground, a Sherpa bag emitted meows, and Marie-Therese pushed her face against the mesh panel.

"We're so sorry," Lena said. She stepped forward, one side of her face bandaged. Beppe and La Rochenoire stood at the other end of the terrace, their arms folded, expressions grim. Maria was there, too, and her eyes were swollen, as if she'd been crying.

No, no, no. I put one hand on my chest, my heart thudding against my palm. My vision blurred. "Where's Vivi?"

Raphael came up behind me and folded his arms around me. Something broke inside me, a quick, final sound like the crack of a dogwood branch.

Lena began to weep. "They took her," she said, barely moving her jaw, like someone who'd just had dental surgery.

Sabine stepped forward. "Be strong," she said. "Vivi was kidnapped."

CHAPTER 40

Vivi

SUTHERLAND, SOUTH AFRICA

A rhythmic *whap-whap-whap* noise roared in Vivi's ears. She was lying on a metal floor, her hands and feet bound, cold air blowing all around her. She lifted her head. A door of some kind stood open, and daylight poured in like clear water. Beyond the door was a bench. Four men in uniforms were sitting on it, earphones clamped over their heads, a steel wall curving behind them. Way up front, two men in black helmets sat in a cockpit, dials spread out in front of them.

I'm in a helicopter? She grimaced, trying to remember how she'd gotten there, but the din sliced through her mind, leaving torn images. A vineyard. The coppery smell of blood. Bodies in a driveway.

"Hey," she yelled at the men.

They didn't seem to hear her. She tried to get up, but her hands and feet were latched together. A man rose from the bench and made her lie down. His mouth moved, but she couldn't hear what he was saying. He had food in his teeth, and his breath smelled like an ashtray. Another man walked up and stuck a needle in Vivi's neck.

Ow, ow, that hurt. Dammit, stop doing that. She whipped from side to side, screaming as loud as she could.

The man shouted something, his lips moving over his dirty teeth, and then he put a smelly finger over her mouth.

She nodded. He wanted her to shut the hell up. *I'll be good, mister.*

She pressed her lips together, but some part of her kept screaming, the sound rising from her pores like a vapor. Maybe the man had given her another shot. Maybe he hadn't. She thought maybe he had.

The floor tilted beneath her. Through the open door, she saw a rumpled ocean and boats. Or was she dreaming? Because her eyelids wouldn't stay open. She felt the tug of gravity, then let herself fall.

———

Vivi awoke in stages, like a swimmer moving out of deep, black water, pushing through the rippled blue, toward the luminous surface. She opened her eyes and blinked, taking in her surroundings. It was nighttime. A dashboard cast a glow across the front seat of a big van; she was sitting up, her shoulders wedged between two men. The driver had a buzz cut and a square face. He wore a camouflage uniform and shiny boots. So did the man on her right.

Who were they? Why couldn't she remember anything? Her thoughts rose up in waves and went still. She tried to wipe her eyes, but her wrists were caught behind her back. Her ankles were bound, too.

The van hit a pothole, and Vivi keeled toward the steering wheel.

"Oopsy-daisy," the driver said. "She's tippin' over, Dave."

The man named Dave caught her shoulder. "There you go," he said.

Their voices moved above her head, slow and sticky as sugar water, reminding her of how Gillian talked. The Southern way.

"Where am I?" she asked.

"In a van," the driver said.

"Yes, but where?"

"South Africa."

"Africa?" She blinked. "How'd I get here?"

"On a broom. How d'ya think?" The driver chuckled.

"Hang in there," Dave said. "We're almost to the compound."

"What compound?" she asked.

"No more questions, kid." The driver mashed his lips together.

I've got to Induce these men and run. She inhaled, swallowed, and tightened her belly. Then she shoved a thought toward the driver. *Stop the van. Let me out!*

The driver swatted at the side of his face, as if shooing a mosquito. He lifted his arm and wiped his ear on his sleeve. "My ears are popping like the dickens," he said.

"Mine ain't," Dave said. "Chew you some gum. That'll help."

"Nah. I'll be fine."

Something's wrong, Vivi thought. *I hit him hard, and he's still driving.*

Her cheekbone throbbed, and one of her eyes felt smaller, like it was swollen, but she couldn't remember how she'd gotten hurt. She forced her eyes to stay open and looked out the windshield. The headlights poured two bowls of light onto a gravel road, but she couldn't see anything beyond that because it was too dark.

The van stopped in front of a tall wire gate. Barbed wire was coiled around the top, and floodlights spilled down, brightening dead weeds and more barbed wire. Two men in berets ran out of a little house and pulled open the gate. The van rumbled through, the headlights bouncing over the rutted gravel road.

"Goddamn vampires," the driver muttered.

"Copy that," Dave said. "Soon as I'm finished here, I'm headed back to Afghanistan."

"Anyplace beats this shithole," the driver said.

Lights fanned around a one-story, tan concrete building. A tall fence circled it, and men with guns stood outside. The van stopped, and the driver shut off the engine. Dave lifted Vivi off the seat and carried her on his shoulder, as if she were no heavier than a winter jacket.

"Catch you later," he told the driver. Then Dave put her onto a wide veranda, through double doors, into a lobby. It was poorly lit, filled with cold, red air. He set her down, and her knees collapsed.

"I got you, honey," Dave said, lifting her up. She craned her neck, looking for exit signs, trying to remember the layout.

Two men in uniforms waited at the end of a long hall. One man was short and wiry, and a thin mustache was sketched over his mouth. The older man had bushy salt-and-pepper hair. A hospital gurney stood behind them.

Soldiers, Vivi thought. Was she in a military hospital?

The driver put her on the cot. Her hands and feet were still bound, so she rolled onto her stomach, slid off the gurney, and scooted under it. The soldiers dropped to their knees and reached for her. A hand clamped over her face, and she sank her teeth into his palm.

The man howled and jerked back, shouting in a strange language, one that sounded like exotic music.

The gray-haired man laughed and said something musical, too, then put a strip of tape over Vivi's mouth. His hazel eyes circled her face, and then he looked up at Dave. Vivi had forgotten that he was still there.

The gray-haired man looked angry. "She is bruised," he said in lilting English. "Mustafa will be angry."

Dave stepped backward, his boots clicking on the tile floor. "I didn't do nothing. Her face was like that when she got to the airport."

"Let me go, damn you!" Vivi screamed into the tape, arching her back. The men put her on the gurney and hooked straps around her chest and legs. Vivi shrieked as loud as she could, thrashing against the restraints.

The men bent over her and spoke more music. Then they got on either side of the gurney. Air waffled over her as they wheeled her around a corner, past a water fountain, into an elevator. The man she'd bitten sucked his palm. She tried to remember every detail. His hair was cut so short, it resembled a brown swimming cap. His mustache was the same color. A diamond stud winked in his left ear.

The gray-haired man stared straight ahead. Both of them gave off a fruity stink.

I'm in an elevator with two vampires, she thought. If she kept screeching, they might bite her. She pressed her lips together. The elevator lurched downward.

How can we be going down? Vivi wondered. This was a one-story building. Were they going to a dungeon? Oh, jeez. Maybe they had a torture chamber. Maybe these were the prophecy freaks. She'd always thought those guys were stupid. Or something her mom had made up to make Vivi march in step. If only she'd listened. At the thought of her mom, pain sliced through Vivi's chest.

They can't keep me, she thought. *I'll Induce their blood-sucking asses and turn them into shark chum.* Except. . . she hadn't Induced Dave. And she'd only made the driver's ears pop. Maybe something was broken inside her. No, she was a Barrett. And Barretts didn't break or give up. She focused on the mustached vampire and punched a thought toward his head.

Unstrap me.

He kept sucking his palm. Vivi looked at the gray-haired vampire and slung out another thought.

Pull the tape off my mouth.

He stared straight ahead. *Why can't I Induce him?* Vivi thought. *Shit, shit, shit.*

The elevator door glided open, and the vampires steered the cot into another hallway where the air seemed colder and redder. They passed by a glassed-in room where a man in a blue scrub suit sat in front of computer screens. Each screen showed a flickering image. Of what, Vivi couldn't tell.

At the end of the hall, a door hissed open. The vampires pushed Vivi's gurney into a tiled room that smelled like pine disinfectant. A man in surgical attire came out of nowhere and leaned over her. His brows were dark and tiny, as if dabs of icing had been smeared on his forehead. A paper shower cap covered his hair, except for two dark, grizzled clumps that jutted out of the elastic rim, fizzing over the tops of his ears. He peeled the tape off her mouth.

"Hello, Vivienne," he said. "I am Dr. Hazan."

His voice was more musical than the soldiers, floating above him in the crimson air, but his breath was gross, stinking of ketones.

Another freaking vampire, she thought. And he knew her name. At least he'd taken off the tape, but she wasn't beholden to his ass. She tried to wrench herself loose, but the straps were too tight.

"How are you feeling?" he asked.

"Super. Couldn't be better." She swallowed, and her throat clicked. She saw a door behind him, but a security camera sat above it. Was there another exit? Her mind was just starting to get clear again. Maybe if she kept the doctor talking, she could get more info.

"Is this a hospital?" she asked.

"No." He lifted a syringe, and the sleeve of his lab coat pulled back, showing an infinity tattoo on his wrist. It was similar to Raphael's, except a green snake looped inside the figure-eight.

She shrank back, tugging at the bonds. "I don't want a shot."

"You will feel a stick. Then you will sleep, yes?" He pronounced *then* like *din*.

Vivi looked away as pain stabbed through her arm. *Ow, dammit. That hurt.* She felt tears seep from the corners of her eyes, slide down her temple, and catch in her hairline.

Dr. Hazan moved around the gurney, looked down at her face, and scrutinized her with unblinking eyes. He touched her swollen cheek and made a *tsk*ing sound.

"Hey, Doc?" She lifted her head. "Why is everything so red? Is it for germs? Or is this a red-light district?"

A smile broke over Dr. Hazan's mouth.

Her teeth began to chatter. "I'm so c-cold. Can you turn up the heat?"

Dr. Hazan left. A moment later he returned with a blanket and spread it over her.

"Thanks," she said. A swirly feeling moved behind her eyes. "Am I on a submarine? Is that why the light is red?"

"No, this isn't an ocean," Dr. Hazan said.

"Oh, that's right," Vivi said, or thought she said. She knew exactly where she was: in the ground with a bunch of fruitcake vampires.

PART SIX

TEAR IN MY HAND

CHAPTER 41

Raphael

VILLA PRIMAVERINA, ISLA CARBONARA
VENICE, ITALY

The helicopter touched down on the landing pad, the blades flattening the terraced gardens around the villa. Dr. Nazzareno climbed out with a nurse. Beppe escorted them to Raphael's dark, windowless master bedroom.

"No, I don't want a tranquilizer," Caro said. Her upper eyelids were puffy, and her nose was running.

Dr. Nazzareno sat on the bed and spoke to her in Italian. Caro began to hiccup, her body jolting with each spasm. Finally she let him sedate her. After he and the nurse went upstairs to check on Sabine and Lena, Raphael climbed onto the bed. He held Caro's shaking body, smoothing her damp hair, telling her he would find Vivi. But his words had sounded feeble.

After Caro fell asleep, Raphael kept holding her. Oh,

he loved her so. Beppe opened the door and said another visitor had arrived. Raphael pushed back Caro's hair and kissed her cheek, then he eased off the bed and went upstairs. Signore Dolfini was waiting outside the drawing room. "The Venice police pulled Gillian Delacroix's body from the Grand Canal this morning."

As Dolfini described the injuries, Raphael walked to the terrace window and spread his hands against the dark pane. Behind the glass, the lights of Venice burned under the dark sky. Raphael felt pressure building behind his eyes, but he could not break down.

On the other side of the room, Sabine was arguing with Dr. Nazzareno.

"I'm fine," she kept saying. "I'm a physician, too. I'd know if I needed an X-ray. I broke my nose, not my skull."

"You should be in the hospital," Dr. Nazzareno said, then straightened his wire-framed glasses. He was a portly man with dark eyes and a full beard.

"I'm not going." Sabine sat on a plush white sofa, her legs jutting out like a child's, her face swollen and bandaged. "Check on Lena. Her skin has a purple cast. Something is wrong."

As Dr. Nazzareno turned away, Sabine slid off the sofa and walked over to Raphael.

"I just remembered something," she said. "Tatiana Kaskov had an infinity tattoo. A green snake was coiled around the figure eight. Salucard forbids any cabal to alter their tattoo. Why would a cabal deliberately modify this symbol?"

"I don't know." Raphael pushed back his sleeve and

pressed his finger against his tattoo. "I will find Tatiana and deal with her. I will bring Vivi home."

"How is Caro holding up?" Sabine said.

"Not well." Raphael glanced away, wiped his eyes, then turned back to Sabine. Her whole face was scratched and bruised. "Dr. Nazzareno is right. You should be in a hospital."

"I'm more worried about Lena."

"She's lucky to be alive," Dr. Nazzareno called, bending close to Lena. "The bullet passed through her cheek."

Lena moaned. The right side of her face was puffed out like a chipmunk's.

"I'm surprised the gunman didn't finish you off," Dr. Nazzareno's nurse said.

"I ain't no fool," Lena said. "I played possum."

Dr. Nazzareno's nurse held up a mirror.

"Lord have mercy," Lena said. "Put that damn thing down. If I want to see ugly, I'll watch *Night of the Living Dead*."

She sat up suddenly and clutched her left arm. "Doctor, I don't feel too good," she said. "My heart is jumping out of rhythm. And it feels like a hog is sitting on my chest."

Five minutes later, Sabine and Lena had been tucked into the helicopter with Dr. Nazzareno, headed for the hospital. Raphael walked down to his bedroom. His heart sped up when he saw the empty bed. The bathroom door was closed, and he heard the blunt, repetitive sound of water pounding against tile. He opened the door, and steam blew into his face.

Caro sat in the corner of the shower, her chin pressed

to her knees, her nightgown wet and transparent, her skin showing through the thin cotton fabric. Her hair hung in wet, ropy curls. She didn't seem to notice when Raphael sat down beside her.

His shirt and trousers were drenched in seconds. He sat absolutely still, water pouring off his shoulders, spilling into the space between him and Caro. He shifted his leg, and she jerked.

"It's just me," he whispered. "Do you want me to turn off the water?"

"Not yet."

"You'll get sick."

She shook her head. "You don't have to stay."

"I'm not leaving." *I love this woman. As long as it takes, I will be here for her. I will never leave her alone. Never.*

"I can't get through this," she said. "I can't lose her."

"You won't. I will bring her back."

She leaned against him, her fist clenched. He opened her hand. A clear bead of water rested on her palm, as if she'd caught a teardrop. Then it broke loose and ran across her half-moon scar.

It took him a few moments to regain his composure. Now he knew why Caro was in the shower. She'd gone behind a waterfall the night Philippe and Vivienne had died. How much more loss would the gods cast down? Had the gods never loved? "Caro, I will find Vivi."

She pressed her lips together and didn't answer.

"Do not give up," he said. "I *will* find her. I'll hire an army, I'll buy every gun in the world, all the grenades, all the firepower. If it means my own death, I will find Vivi. I promise you, I will bring her home."

He drew her closer, until their cheeks were touching. Pressure was still forming behind his eyes, the weight of grief and defeat. His stomach muscles tightened as he tried to hold in the last bit of self-control. No, he couldn't break down. He had to be strong, or Caro would think it was hopeless.

But I can't hold back, he thought. Because when you love a woman, everything you feel becomes a river, one that flows between you and her, and its power is beyond a man's control. He held her, water rushing around them, his tears running into hers.

CHAPTER 42

Vivi

PATIENT CONTAINMENT AREA—LEVEL 2
AL-DÎN COMPOUND
SUTHERLAND, SOUTH AFRICA

Vivi awoke in a place that was glazed with cold, crimson light, and for a moment, she thought she'd fallen into a maraschino cherry jar. But she was in a narrow bed. Someone had untied her hands and feet and dressed her in a blue scrub suit. She sat up. The room was square and windowless, bigger than a doctor's exam cubicle, with a steel door at one end. No furniture to speak of. No pictures on the walls. A security camera with a blinking red light hung from the ceiling.

A shiver ran through her, and she lay back down. Her teeth began to click, as if the coldness of the room had somehow moved inside her. She felt harder and meaner and also numb.

She'd been kidnapped by men in Hawaiian shirts. A

badass blond lady had slugged her. Lena had gotten shot, and Sabine was missing. Then soldiers had taken Vivi to South Africa, into an underground building where vampires were in charge.

I want my mom.

Vivi's lip quivered. What was Dr. Hazan going to do to her? Give her another injection or drink her blood? Could she escape? She rolled into a ball and pressed her mouth against her knee. A warm, wet patch spread over her skin. Now she understood why her mom had been afraid, why she'd kept moving from place to place. Some part of Vivi had always known the truth.

It's all my fault, she thought.

The metal door buzzed open. Vivi pretended to sleep, but she watched the door through a crack in her eyelashes. Dr. Hazan walked in, his lab coat giving off the smells of disinfectant and fruit.

"Vivienne, time to wake up," he said, tugging at her arms. "It's morning. Mr. Al-Dîn is coming to see you."

She pretended to snore. Whoever Al-Dîn was, he could wait. The shithead.

"Up, up, up," Dr. Hazan said, forcing her into a sitting position. She held her breath, squeezed her tummy, and wrinkled her forehead. Oh, she wanted to make Dr. Hazan go away.

Dr. Hazan, let me out of this place!

He kept gripping her shoulders. She glanced furtively at him. No blood. Not even a broken blood vessel in his eye.

"The diazepam should have worn off by now," he said. "If you don't cooperate, I will give you another injection."

"No more shots. Jeez, I'm awake. Barely." Vivi rustled up a fake yawn.

Dr. Hazan melted against the wall when the door buzzed open again. An old, baldheaded man shuffled into the room, gripping a metal walker, his leg wobbling violently. He wore a long purple robe, and his right-hand pocket hung low, the fabric bulging and twitching, like a cat was trapped inside. On his feet were leather slippers, the toes curled up like a jester's hat. An IV tube snaked from his arm up to a clear plastic bag, and the bag hung from a tall pole. The mustached man she'd bitten stood beside the pole. He moved it forward each time the old geezer took a step.

"Fadime?" the geezer said. "Help me sit in that chair." He spoke in heavily accented English, adding a *d* to "that."

"Yes, sir," Fadime said. He let go of the pole and took the geezer's arm. Dr. Hazan moved away from the wall, pulled the chair close to Vivi's bed, then hurried out of the room.

It took an eternity for the old man to get settled. His eyes were reddish gold, and his lashes were so dark and thick that for a second Vivi thought he was wearing makeup, but he wasn't. That was a relief.

As he got nearer, Vivi saw that he wasn't old. No wrinkles. No jowls. No liver spots. But he'd been in a bad fight. Bruises and purple splotches covered the backs of his hands, and more ugly marks ran under the sleeve of his robe.

"Who are you?" she asked, trying to sound braver than she felt.

"Mr. Al-Dîn," he said. "My friends call me Mustafa. Welcome to my compound."

You're not my friend, she thought. "Am I in Africa?"

"Sutherland. Near Cape Town." Perspiration was beaded on his head. Someone was in charge of that, too, a man with long blond hair that hung down like a broom. He swept a white cloth over the geezer's face.

Vivi tilted her head. "Are you a vampire, Mustafa?"

"Yes."

Just as Vivi had suspected. And he could call this building a compound, but it was really a giant coffin. She scooted away from him. "Are you gonna hurt me?"

"No, no, no. Not me."

He was lying. Why else had he stolen her from Sabine and Lena? Why had those men kidnapped her? Where was her mom?

At the thought of her mom and Raphael, pain twisted through her belly, and she wrapped her hands around her waist. She felt a tear slide down the side of her nose.

"Do you have a question?" Mustafa asked, lifting his hand. His fingernails were clipped short, ridged like seashells.

She wiped her mouth. She had so many questions, she didn't know where to begin. "How long have I been here?"

"Not long." Mustafa leaned closer, studying her face. "How did you get that bruise on your cheek?"

Vivi swallowed. "A blond lady hit me."

A muscle worked in Mustafa's jaw. "Was her name Tatiana?"

Vivi shrugged. "I don't know."

Mustafa turned to Fadime. "Where is she now?"

"In her quarters, sir."

"Detain her."

"Yes, sir." Fadime bowed, then went out of the room, leaving the door open. The big, blond-haired man went out and began pacing in the hall.

Vivi rubbed her eyes. "Why did you kidnap me?"

"A long story." Mustafa tilted his head. "First, I have questions. When my people arrived in Provence, the woman who was keeping you had some type of power. She killed my men."

"What men?" Vivi asked, keeping her face slack.

"Who was this doctor you were staying with?" Mustafa persisted.

"I don't remember."

"You are a poor liar."

"Dr. Hazan gave me a shot, and now my brains are fried."

"I am sorry," Mustafa said.

"Why is this place underground?"

"Because I paid the architect to build it this way. It took four years. Lots of bribes."

He spoke slowly and clearly, but she was distracted by the way he shaved the letters off the front of some words, anything with a "*th*" sound. *This* sounded like *dis*, and *the* sounded like *de*.

"Do you know why the S.A.L.T. telescope was built in Sutherland?" he asked.

Vivi shook her head. "What does salt have to do with a telescope?"

"S.A.L.T. is an acronym for South African Large Telescope." Mustafa smiled. "Sutherland has the darkest night sky in the world. We have a little telescope upstairs. Maybe if you are good, I will let you see it."

His pocket was still twisting and writhing. He cupped his palm over the bulge, and the fabric went still. "Oh, Bram. You are tickling me," he said.

Vivi saw an infinity tattoo on his wrist. It was just like Dr. Hazan's, with a green snake looping through the curves.

Mustafa opened his pocket, and a furry head popped up. The animal was sable, with a long torso, a pink nose, and two shiny eyes, each one circled by a white bandit's mask. He wore a tiny diamond harness.

"What's that?" Vivi asked.

"My ferret," Mustafa said. "His name is Bram. He wants to know if you have any questions."

"You can read his mind?"

"No." Mustafa grinned at the ferret. "But I like to pretend. Don't we, Bram?"

"Can you read minds?" she asked.

"No. I don't need to. I am smarter than everyone in this building."

Vivi didn't believe him for a second. *Asshole*, she thought, then watched his face. His expression didn't change. She swallowed. "Why is everything red?"

"You are speaking of the light?" Mustafa asked. "An illness has made my eyes sensitive. Even the faint glow of moonlight causes my skin to burn and my vision to falter."

"What's wrong with you?" Vivi asked.

"I caught a disease in Africa. A long time ago."

"I thought vampires didn't get sick."

"Some of us are susceptible to the hemorrhagic fevers. I was infected with Marburg Virus. It is similar to Ebola, which I'm sure you've heard of. Do not be scared. I recovered from the virus. But it left me with a hematological disorder. A stem cell leukemia. The doctors say I will be dead soon."

"I'm sorry," Vivi said, her voice cracking. "But I want to go home. My mom is probably freaking out."

"Mothers are like that." Mustafa rolled his eyes, chuckling. "Always worrying."

"When can I leave?"

Mustafa's forehead wrinkled. "Leave? But you just arrived."

"My mom is a very nervous person. And she has powerful friends."

"I am more powerful. I get what I want. And I want to keep you." He patted Bram.

Vivi brushed tears off her face. "You don't want me. I'm a brat. Nothing but trouble."

"A prophecy says you will bring the vampire race into the light."

Holy shit. He was one of those freaks. "You've got the wrong person. I'm not mixed up in that damn prophecy. I can't read minds. I can't do anything."

"Your modesty is charming." He smiled. "My scientist will be here in a moment. He will help you understand why I brought you here."

Bram crawled inside the cuff of Mustafa's sleeve. A bulge appeared in the purple silk, then moved toward the old man's shoulder. A pink nose appeared and sniffed the air. Bram slid out of the robe and curled up beside Mustafa's neck.

The door buzzed. A man in a wheelchair rolled into the room, his arms corded with muscles. His legs were tiny, no bigger than baseball bats, and two bony knees jutted up beneath his blue scrub pants. His eyes were four shades darker than the scrubs. A dark brown ponytail fanned over his left shoulder. His chin had a cleft, and dark stubble ran down his neck. Two armed guards pushed in behind the wheelchair.

Mustafa's gaze roved from the ponytailed man to Vivi. The man in the wheelchair looked at Vivi, then stared at Mustafa.

"Why am I here?" he asked.

"I want you to explain to this girl how a quarter vampire's blood will allow me to walk in daylight."

The man turned to Vivi. He stared without blinking, his chest rising and falling, a vein pulsing in his neck. He swallowed, then pursed his lips.

What a loser, she thought. Whatever he had to say, she didn't want to hear it.

Mustafa smiled. "Yes, it's her," he said. "Ignore her hair coloring. Look at her eyes. They tell the true story."

"What story?" Vivi said. "You people are nuts."

The man in the wheelchair kept staring at her, his eyes filling. He put his hand over his face and shook his head.

"What's your problem?" Vivi said.

The man lowered his hands, tears spangled in his lashes, his chest sawing up and down. "Meep?" he said. "Is that you?"

CHAPTER 43

Jude

PATIENT CONTAINMENT AREA—LEVEL 2
AL-DÎN COMPOUND
SUTHERLAND, SOUTH AFRICA

Jude pushed his wheelchair toward the girl's bed, his heart thudding. Was she really Meep? After all this time? "Vivi?" he said, then wiped his face.

Her eyes narrowed. "I've never seen you in my life."

"You know him, Vivienne," Mustafa said. "You do not remember."

Jude couldn't stop staring. Her eyes were blue, with brown chips in her left iris. He should have recognized her right away, but the hair had confused him. It jutted up in short, auburn tufts. None of the Barretts were redheads, and Caro's family had been blonds. But now that he was closer, he realized the color had come from a bottle. A home dye job. A disguise, most likely, one that hadn't worked.

"Quit looking at me like that," Vivi said. "It's rude."

"I'm sorry," Jude whispered, his gaze circling her face. How long had Mustafa's brutes been chasing her? What about Caro? *She would have fought Mustafa's men, and they would have killed her. Unless . . . had they brought her here, too?*

Jude's stomach pitched. He breathed through his mouth, trying to steady himself.

"Try to relax, Dr. Barrett," Mustafa said. "You've wanted to see your daughter. Here she is."

Jude darted another glance at Vivi. Her cheekbone was bruised. Blood rushed into his head, spilling heat behind his eyes. He turned to Mustafa. "Who hurt my daughter?"

The Turk's smile faltered. "Dr. Hazan says it was a minor contusion."

Hold it together, Barrett. He faced Vivi. She was perched on the edge of her cot, staring at the floor as if it were a minefield.

"Vivi, I know you must be in shock," he said. "I am, too."

She looked up. "Mister, I don't know who you are, but I'm *not* your daughter."

Jude angled back to Mustafa. "May I have a few minutes alone with her?"

"No, Mustafa," Vivi shouted. "Don't leave me with him."

Jude drew in a breath. So this was the plan, to turn him into the enemy.

"You do not want to be with your father?" Mustafa asked.

"My dad got lost in a jungle." She glared scornfully at Jude. "I don't know this guy."

Mustafa ran his finger down Bram's fur. "All right, Dr. Barrett. You have ten minutes."

"Please, sir," Jude said, hating the groveling sound that crept into his voice. "Can't we have more time? I haven't seen her since she was three."

Mustafa lifted the ferret. "What should we do, Bram?"

The ferret wrinkled his nose. "Gabir?" Mustafa called over his shoulder. The man with broom-like hair appeared in the doorway. "Give the Barretts ten minutes."

Bloody wanker, Jude thought. How could ten years be explained in ten minutes? Mustafa was playing with his captives, throwing them together, waiting for them to clash.

A smug look came over Mustafa's face. "Vivienne, at eighteen hundred hours you will join me in the banquet hall. I will send escorts. Do not be late."

Vivi pointed at Jude. "Will he be there?"

"Did you hear me invite him?" Mustafa said. "I think not."

"What are you gonna do at this banquet?" Vivi's eyes narrowed. "Eat me?"

"Not tonight." Mustafa winked.

After he left the room, Jude glanced up at the surveillance camera. He had to get closer to Vivi so their voices wouldn't be picked up. He wheeled toward her, moving in at an angle.

She scooted away from him, moving to the opposite side of her bed, and pushed her shoulders against the wall.

"It's okay, Meep," he said. "I won't hurt you."

"Who are you?" Vivi asked. "What's your name?"

"Jude Barrett."

"Sure, and I'm Kate Middleton. Shall I give the queen your regards?"

She was spunky like Caro.

"We need to talk quietly so the camera won't hear," he whispered. "How is your mother? Is she safe?."

"She's fine." Vivi chopped her hand in the air, as if indicating the subject was closed. Then she drew her knees to her chin. "How do you know my mom? Who are you really? One of those prophecy chumps?"

"No, of course not. I did everything I could to protect you from them. Oh, Meep. How can I convince you?"

"You can't." Her gaze flicked over him. "And don't call me Meep."

The backs of his eyes prickled. "I didn't think I'd see you again. You were three when I left for Gabon. You had brown pigtails."

"Why are you pretending to be my dad?"

He leaned closer. "Because I *am*. How can you explain the brown bits in your iris?"

Vivi shrugged.

"I'm your father, truly I am." He wiped his eyes with the back of his hand.

"You're a vampire. I can smell it on you."

"I'm sure your mother explained."

Vivi looked away.

"She did it to save my life," he said.

She gave him a side-eye glance. "Why are you in a wheelchair?"

"I got hurt in Gabon."

"But you're a vampire. Why haven't you healed?"

"We'll discuss that later," he said.

"I'm through talking." Vivi put her hands over her ears.

How can I protect my daughter? The issue wasn't her skepticism. It was her safety. Mustafa would keep her alive until a serum was made from her blood. Jude could delay that process, but he was worried about something else. Level 2 containment was staffed by men, humans and vampires who seldom saw a woman. All of those wankers would have access to Vivi's room. His daughter would be brutalized.

"I know you don't want to talk," Jude said. "But I'm curious. Does Raphael still have that bad-natured dog?"

Vivi lowered her hands. "What's the dog's name?"

"Arrapato. It means horny."

"Anybody could have told you that." Vivi looked past him, toward the door, then met his gaze.

"Your grandmother gave the dog to Raphael a long time ago," Jude said.

Vivi gave him a searching look. "If you were my dad, you would've called me and Mom a long time ago."

"Oh, Meep. I wanted to. I tried to escape from Gabon, but Mustafa's men shot me in the back and brought me to South Africa. I've been his prisoner all these years. No outside communication was allowed."

"Why would he want you?"

"I'm a biochemist. He forced me to work in his lab."

She looked at the door again.

He followed her gaze. "Forget it, Meep. You can't escape. You won't make it to the elevator. They'll catch you."

She rubbed her eyes. "I don't want to talk anymore. I'm tired. That stupid medicine is making me woozy."

Jude's jaw tightened. They were drugging her? Goddamn their souls to hell. "Don't take anything they give you. Spit it in your food."

"They stuck me with a needle," she said.

A burst of knocking came from the door. From the other side, Gabir called, "Thirty seconds, Dr. Barrett."

Jude's throat clenched. "Vivi, don't let Mustafa trick you. Don't mention your mother. He's smart and egotistical. Get him to talk about himself."

She shrugged.

The door opened, and Gabir appeared in the doorway.

"Be a brave girl," Jude told her. "We'll talk soon."

She didn't reply. As he wheeled out of her room, she called, "Wait."

He swiveled the chair around, tires scraping over the tile. "Yes?"

"Before I was born, my mom saw something in a cave," Vivi said. "Do you know what she saw?"

She's almost over the shock, he thought. *Now she's starting to analyze what I've said.*

"Let's go," Gabir called, stamping his feet.

Jude kept staring at Vivi. "We were in the Gilf Kebir. We saw cave paintings."

"Of what?"

"Mermaids." His voice sounded far away, as if it had come from that cave.

Vivi's lips clamped together. Just before she turned away, he saw tears pooling in her eyes.

"Time's up, Doc," Gabir said.

CHAPTER 44

Vivi

After Dr. Barrett left Vivi's room, a redheaded guy in scrubs walked in, carrying a breakfast tray. Earphones dangled around his neck, music blaring out. Vivi recognized the music. Snow Patrol was singing "Run."

Jeez, what an oldie.

"Good morning," he said. As he put the tray on her bed, his body gave off a gust of acetone. Vivi darted a glance. He looked too young to be a vampire. And how had he ended up in this underground prison?

He held out a tiny white paper cup. "Here's your meds."

"What kind are they?" she asked.

"Benzos. They'll calm you down."

She took the cup, and two blue pills skated on the

bottom. The guy was watching her. He had pimples and green eyes.

"How long have you been a vampire?" she asked.

"Five years."

"Then you know Dr. Barrett."

"I guess."

"Tell me about him."

"Nothing to tell. He keeps to himself. I gotta get back to work. Take your meds."

Vivi dumped the pills into her mouth and worked them under her tongue. Then she lifted the water glass and pretended to take a sip.

The guy glanced into the empty cup and walked out of her room.

Vivi looked up at the camera. How would she spit out the pills if Mustafa's spies were watching? Ignoring the bitter taste in her mouth, she reached for her tray. She brought a teacup to her lips and spat out the pills.

Is Dr. Barrett really my dad? she thought. She peered into the cup, as if the answers could be found in the melting blue pills. Bit by bit, the liquid took them apart. If a mighty benzo could be dissolved by something as ordinary as tea, then she shouldn't give up hope.

Be water, Vivi.

CHAPTER 45

Jude

BIOMEDICAL UNIT—LEVEL 3
DORMITORY C
AL-DÎN COMPOUND

That afternoon Jude wheeled into Dormitory C. He was the only resident. The others were dead.

He guided his chair past a row of empty beds. As he touched each mattress, he whispered a name.

"Aiken, Turner, Griffin, Randolph, Yang."

Aside from Dr. Hazan, who was curiously exempt from Mustafa's wrath, Jude was the last scientist in the Al-Dîn compound. The moment the daylight serum was finished, his cot would be just as empty as the others, stripped and sanitized, his remains thrown into the incinerator—or worse.

How had Mustafa made the connection between Vivi and the antibodies? Jude had spent the last decade shifting the focus of his research from the antibodies to the bats' daylight gene. He'd skewed results, contaminated the cell cultures, and sent countless mice to early graves.

Never mind how Mustafa found out. She's here, and I've got to find a way to save her.

Ever since he'd returned from Vivi's room, he'd worked on an escape plan. First, he would continue to delay the research. That would buy time. Then he'd have to find a way to put Vivi in the air duct. When she was safely inside, he could release the bats from their chamber. They would take out Mustafa, his staff, and the mercenaries. Then Vivi could climb up to the ground level, crawl out, and run like bloody hell. He wouldn't come out of this alive, but he could save her.

Where is Caro? Jude's throat ached. Vivi had said she was alive, but where had she been during the kidnapping? How did Vivi know she was safe?

His bed stood in the corner, a trapeze bar dangling over the mattress. He steered the chair toward it and angled next to his night table, which was piled with books and papers. He put on the brake, then leaned down and raised the metal footrest. One at a time, he lifted his feet to the floor. He didn't bother to hide his movements from the security camera. Months ago, before Dr. Yang had died, he'd distorted the lens with Vaseline, and no one from central command had shown up to investigate.

Jude slid his feet across the floor, his toes soaking in the coldness of the tiles. Numb patches were still scattered on the ball of his left foot, but his right leg was strong. He gripped the sides of the chair and stood.

Three seconds went by. Five seconds. Ten. His knees wobbled, and he lunged for the trapeze bar. He caught it, and tendons bulged in his forearms. He worked out every morning in the gym, and his upper body had never been stronger. He eased himself onto the bed, then let go of the bar and stared at his hands.

These are my only weapons, he thought.

He'd almost gotten his legs back, and ironically Mustafa had been responsible.

Ten years ago, shortly after Jude had arrived in Sutherland, the Turk's leukemia had gone into a T-cell blast crisis, signaling the end-stage of the disease. Tatiana flew to Beijing and kidnapped Dr. Yang, a human geneticist, and ordered him to perform gene therapy.

Yang had caused a disturbance when he'd arrived at the compound. His IQ was 180, and he used his intelligence as a tool of chaos. He was proud and feisty, prone to temper tantrums. Few scientists on Level 3 had dared to complain about their working conditions. If they didn't cooperate, they were threatened with beatings, water-boarding, isolation, and starvation. The men always became docile after they realized that harm would befall their families.

This leverage didn't work on Yang. He complained about the frigid temperature, the reddish light, the Turkish food, the hardness of his mattress. He set off the fire alarm, opened the mice cages, and turned on the water valves in the restroom; it took a week to pump out the water. Every night he picked the lock to the employee's lounge, where soft drinks and bottled blood were dispensed in a small Coca-Cola machine, and he stole Fanta, Sprite, and Coke, passing over the Coke Vanilla, his least favorite. On his last raid, he saw that the racks had been refilled with blood. Even the vanilla cans were gone. He leaped onto the machine and rocked it back and forth until it collapsed on top of him. He'd spent a week in the infirmary with a broken collarbone.

He'd become a hero to Jude and the other scientists. When Yang eventually wandered into the main lab in the Biomedical Unit, everyone applauded. After a cursory inventory, he sent hourly memos to Mustafa, demanding and receiving experimental drugs and world-class equipment. Jude had never been talkative, but once he'd gotten to know Yang, everything rushed out: Caro, Meep, São Tomé, Gabon, the bats, the toothed fish, Tatiana, the monoclonal antibodies, his escape, his paralysis, his determination to protect his daughter, and his prevarication with the research. He even told him about the experiments he'd done during his human years. He'd discovered R-99, the Resurrection Gene, which exists in the immortals' unique stem cells. True, his research had involved mice, but it had almost gotten him killed.

Yang was less revealing. He had once played polo, but he'd become a workaholic. He lived in a luxury high-rise apartment and drove a BMW. His wife, Ji Li, had been six months pregnant with their child, a son, when Tatiana and her team had shown up at Yang's lab in Beijing.

"Maybe if I save the Turk, I can go home," he said.

"They won't let you," Jude said.

"Yes, they will," Yang said. "You will see."

They settled down to work, assembled the cutting-edge equipment, and reversed Mustafa's blast crisis. In return, Yang expected a one-way ticket to Beijing, but he was ordered to find a cure for the Turk's leukemia, which kept edging toward the end stage.

Yang retaliated. His weekly lab reports were long and obtuse, crammed with arcane terminology and insulting descriptions of Mustafa's blood and bone marrow. Twice, the guards put the doctor in solitary confinement. The hijinks resumed. Yang went through his repertoire—grievances, floods, fire alarms, mice running along the walls—but the results did not please him, so he shut down the compound's computer network with the ILoveYou virus. Meanwhile, Jude kept working with monoclonal antibodies, distorting the research.

A decade later, every scientist was dead except for Jude and Yang. They referred to themselves as Robinson Crusoe and Friday. When they weren't in the lab, they played poker, Angry Birds, and solved word puzzles.

This past year, Yang began amusing himself with T cell trials, supposedly for the Turk's benefit. That was when it got interesting. T cells were supreme cutthroats, the immune system's equivalent of British MI6 assassins; these cells had a license to kill, so to speak, but they had to be programmed. Mustafa's T cells had to be taught how to kill his cancer, and then they became "natural" killer cells, as scientists called them.

But Yang cultured his own T cells, knowing these "natural" killer cells would be destroyed by Mustafa's immune system. Yang would gleefully transmit photographs up to the Turk, showing off his "progress," then was unapologetic when the treatment failed.

Escape dominated his thoughts. He believed that

Mustafa's obsession with daylight was the only thing that held the compound together. When the Turk died, Yang would walk.

"You can walk with me," Yang said.

"They'll kill us. Or make us work," Jude said.

Yang made a fist. "We *will* get out. Even if the bastard Turk does not die, we will escape."

"I'd just slow you down," Jude said.

Yang shook his head. "I'm going to help you walk again."

He rubbed Vaseline over the lenses of the security cameras, and then they waited for someone in CC to show up. A week went by. Two weeks. A month.

"Mustafa's men are asleep at the wheel," Yang said. "But we are awake."

He jammed the lock on the laboratory doors, then harvested stem cells from Jude's bone marrow. He induced them to grow into long strands of glial neural cells. At three-week intervals, he injected them into Jude's spine. After the first treatment, a splotchy feeling returned to his groin. His bum itched during the second, and by the third, he felt the coldness of the tile floor beneath his feet. "Three more injections," Yang said, "and we'll be home with our families."

But Jude never received those treatments. One day in July, Mustafa's men took the scientist away, and he never returned. Jude had heard screams rising from the large animal containment center, which was just in the next corridor. The janitor had told Jude what happened—Yang had been taken into the bat chamber.

Now, Jude heard footsteps outside his dormitory, and he cleared his mind. His door opened, and Tatiana walked in. "You decent?" she called, her voice echoing. "Because I'm not."

"Get out of my dorm," he said.

"Don't be territorial." Her hand fluttered over her hair, sweeping back her bangs. As she stepped forward, her short, black chiffon dress stirred above her knees. She wore black ballet slippers, and they made a scuffing noise as she moved over the tile.

"Why are you here?" he said, his voice cold. "Shouldn't you be clubbing baby seals?"

She smiled coyly. "Speaking of babies, your daughter is beautiful. She has your eyes."

His stomach muscles tensed. Tatiana had seen Vivi? She'd probably orchestrated the kidnapping. "Did you bring her to the compound?"

"No, of course not. I've been in London."

"She's got a bruise on her cheek. Who hit her?"

"One of the mercs. I executed him."

Jude stared past her, toward the empty cots. The red light reminded him of an aggressive vine, twisting down from the ceiling, forking through the air, rooting into the floor. How had Mustafa connected day-walking with the genetics of a quarter vampire? Jude remembered that long-ago briefing in Gabon when Lenny had told the scientists about the monoclonal antibodies. His paradigm for Project Daylight had been unassailable, but Jude wanted no part of it. He hadn't known how, or if, he would make it out of Gabon, but he'd never guessed that he would end up in an underground lab, quashing and obfuscating the research. His lab partners were dead. Who had revealed the deception?

He brought his gaze back to Tatiana. "How did Mustafa find my daughter?"

"It was an accident." She assumed a ballet position, her heels pushed together, toes pointed outward.

"Accident?" Jude said.

"Vivi wouldn't even be here if you hadn't confided in Yang," she said.

A grinding sound echoed inside Jude's head. "What does a dead scientist have to do with my child?"

"Everything." She swished her dress. The gesture made him think of kudzu tendrils slithering across a field, stealing up power lines, and squashing mature trees, an insatiable force that coveted every object in its path. "What about Yang?"

"He betrayed you. You're lucky that he told *me* what you were doing. If he'd gotten to Mustafa, you'd be dead. Even I couldn't have saved you."

Her words coiled around him, looping around his chest, squeezing out his air. "I don't understand."

"Yang approached me with a deal. He would reveal your secrets—including vital information about Project Daylight—if I'd let him return to Beijing. Of course I wouldn't have allowed it. But he never doubted my word. His naïveté was greater than his intelligence, which was exceptional. He told me about your daughter's monoclonal antibodies—and that's what Mustafa needs to block the reaction to sunlight. Yang had a theory that your daughter would have the RH1 gene." Tatiana paused. "Just like the bats."

More vines knotted around Jude's ribs, forcing him to exhale. "When did Yang cut this deal?"

"You're really asking how long Mustafa has been looking for Vivi, aren't you? Here's the timeline. Yang cut the deal in June. He died in July. Now it's August."

"It didn't take you long to find her."

"Me? No, I refused to get involved. But before Yang died, he tried to tell Mustafa what you'd done. I saved you—again. Mustafa believes that Yang deceived him."

Jude's mouth went dry. Yang's need to escape had set off a catalyst.

"Not many people fool Mustafa," Tatiana said. "I have, but I'm a woman. You're the only man who conned the great Turk."

"Yang did."

"He was an amateur." She laughed. "He was weak. He offered to have sex with me. He wasn't my type. I like integrity and toughness in a man. What a combination. It turns me on. *You* turn me on."

He didn't want to hear it. "Why did you betray Mustafa? I thought you cared about him."

"I do. But I love you. Besides, he wasn't the same after he got sick. All those drugs put a veil over him. He talks to a ferret. I've kept his company going. When he's gone, you and I will run Al-Dîn. Until that happens, I can protect your daughter the way I've protected you."

"I won't run the company. And I never asked for your help."

"Haven't you wondered why no one came to investigate your security cameras? Or why Mustafa let you take your time with the research?"

Jude rubbed his eyes. Any second now she'd tell him what she'd done for him and what she hoped to do.

"Think about that a minute, Jude. I kept you alive. And I will get you out of that chair. I'm bringing in a stem cell specialist. Your treatments will resume, and you will rise in all kind of ways."

He lowered his head. "It makes me sick to look at you."

"I can give you so much love."

"You don't know what that word means."

"Go ahead. Hurt me with words. I will go on loving you."

"Your wants aren't the same as mine. I don't want you. I never have and never will. I love my wife. Why won't you leave me alone?"

"You were the only man who wouldn't sleep with me. That intrigued me. You had honor." She lifted her arms above her head and moved her fingers in delicate patterns. "But that is a facile explanation. The truth is serpentine. You remind me of someone I once knew. A good man. A human. He had blue eyes with little copper specks. Not quite like yours, but close. All my life I have been looking for those eyes."

"Then cut them out of me. Put them in a jar."

"I want every piece of you. I know you feel something. You're in denial."

"What I feel for you is the opposite of attraction."

He looked away before she could read the expression in his eyes. A decade's worth of guilt and regret welled up inside him. He was responsible for his choices. He'd gone to Gabon, trusted Yang, and divulged secrets about Vivi and Caro. He felt helpless.

"I have known you ten years, Jude. Longer than you knew your wife. Longer than you knew your daughter. Yet you love them more."

She paused, watching his face.

More? He rubbed his forehead, weary of her persistence. She heard what she wanted and discarded the rest. Or did she have a type of OCD?

"If you make love to me, I will get your daughter away from Mustafa." She smiled.

"I know what your promises are worth." He leaned toward his night table and swept everything to the floor. Books and papers tumbled down.

Her smile dimmed. "You don't even know your daughter."

"I know what love is."

"She's dangerous. A mutant. You don't know what I know. You won't love her when you find out what she can do."

What did that even mean? Tatiana was trying to keep him in the conversation. "She's my child."

"And she probably has the RH1 gene. No human has it. Just some stupid bats. You've got to know this won't end well." Her smile snapped back into place. "See? It hurts when we don't get what we want. You're my kind of guy, Jude. The patron saint of hopeless causes."

CHAPTER 46

Vivi

MAIN FLOOR—LEVEL 1
BANQUET HALL III
AL-DÎN COMPOUND

Vivi's mind felt clear and sharp as Fadime led her through the second-floor corridor. She stepped into the elevator, wondering if the benzos had cleared her system. One way to find out. She stared at the back of Fadime's head. She'd give him a little Inductive push. No blood or anything gross. Nothing that would alarm him.

The elevator doors closed, and he pushed the top button: 1. So they were going to the main floor? She glanced around for the camera. It was near the ceiling, aimed at the control panel. She pulled in a breath, felt her lungs expand, and sent out a thought.

Fadime, laugh.

She kept breathing until a smile cracked across his

mouth. Vivi smiled, too. The elevator dinged, and the doors opened. As they stepped out, she saw a floor directory:

The Al-Dîn Corporation Research Facility & Compound

LEVEL 1   **LOBBY**

Accounting

Medical Records

Security

Conference Room

Banquet Halls

LEVEL 2   **DORMITORIES 200–250**

Patient Treatment Area

Spa/Gym

LEVEL 3   **BIOMEDICAL LABORATORY**

Stem Cell Research

Dormitories A–C

Quarantine & Animal Containment

Fadime strode into a corridor. "You walk too slow," he called over his shoulder.

"I'm hurrying." Duh, didn't he know she was supposed to be drugged? If she acted too alert, Dr. Hazan would pump her full of mind-numbing pills, and then she wouldn't be able to Induce. And even that might not help her escape.

At the end of the hall, two massive wooden doors stood open. A brass plaque on the wall read, BANQUET HALLS.

Fadime guided her into a colorful, Byzantine chamber. The walls were tiled, and hectic patterns swarmed out. Grecian columns supported archways that led to other, exotic rooms.

She walked past a café-like room, where uniformed men sat in booths, shoveling food into their mouths. In the next chamber, she saw a long gilt banquet table, and Mustafa sat behind it. His chair resembled a throne, and his IV pole stood nearby.

"Vivienne, so nice of you to join me," he called. "Fadime, I want her to sit across from me."

Fadime led her to a gilt chair. Her gaze passed over platters of food, china, and silver flatware. Every piece of cutlery but a knife, she noticed. A forest of goblets spread out above and to the right of the plate.

"Say hello, Bram," Mustafa said. The ferret perched on Mustafa's shoulder, chewing a piece of raw meat.

"Thank you for inviting me," Vivi said.

Mustafa signaled Fadime. "I am sure Vivienne is hungry."

Fadime lifted a plate and moved around the table, spooning food from china bowls. He stopped beside a long platter where dozens of skewered meat kabobs jutted straight up from a bed of parsley, as if they'd been impaled. Here and there, the garnish didn't quite cover the platter, and white foam was visible through the green.

Fadime returned to Vivi and set down her plate.

"Smells good," she said, blinking at pitas and garlicky hummus and stuffed eggplants and meat pies and cucumbers. A lone kabob lay across the cucumbers like a sacrificial offering.

Mustafa smiled. "Save room for tiramisu and baklava. When I was human, I ate baklava every day."

Vivi remembered what Dr. Barrett had told her: Keep Mustafa talking about himself. "Sir, may I ask a personal question?"

"You may ask, but I might not reply." He lifted his hand and unfurled his long fingers. "Go on."

"How long have you been a vampire?"

"I left my human life when I was a man of thirty-two years," he said. "Until then, I served under Sultan Mehmed II. I was a *sipahi* in the Ottoman Army."

"A what?"

"*Sipahis* were the cavalry division. Not every Turk could be a *sipahi*. I was the son of a Bey, an elite Ottoman. We were the early commandos. Quite tough and brave. We went ahead of the Ottoman army and plundered before the janissaries arrived."

"What were they?"

He sneered. "The infantry. Some were bodyguards. All from peasant stock."

Like that meant something to Vivi. She took a breath. The air was pungent with a musky smell, one that she didn't associate with vampires. Was she smelling the ferret?

"I was with the sultan when we crossed the Danube and marched to Târgovişte," Mustafa said. "So many soldiers. *Sipahis, silahtars,* janissaries."

Vivi had crossed the Danube a few times herself, mainly when she visited Uncle Nigel in Prague. He was technically her mom's third cousin, a stocky man with a wide chest and blunt fingertips—probably from digging up pot sherds. His hair glistened like silver wires, framing a face that was round as a pizza pan. He collected famous quotations, and the last time she'd seen him, he'd said, "I'm not a fan of Napoleon Bonaparte, but I rather like this quote. 'Take time to deliberate; but when the time for action arrives, stop thinking and go in.'"

She felt a hotness behind the bridge of her nose, a sure sign that she was going to cry. Uncle Nigel would not want her to show any emotions to a Turkish solder. Let him wonder.

Mustafa had stopped talking. One of his eyes had gotten smaller and meaner. The ferret was watching her, too. "Am I boring you, Vivienne?"

What had he been talking about? The Danube. Romania. "No, sir. I was wondering why you went to Târgovişte?" she said, pronouncing the town's name just the way her mom had taught her.

Mustafa's face darkened, as if a hawk had passed over him, casting a long shadow. "We went to Wallachia to put an end to Kaziklu Bey," he said. "The Impaler. You probably know him by another name. Vlad Ţepeş."

A quiver ran up Vivi's spine, and she struggled to keep her face from showing any emotion. Was he talking about Vlad the Impaler? If so, Mustafa wasn't near as old as she'd thought. But that didn't matter. She leaned forward, fixing an attentive expression on her face.

"When we passed through Târgovişte, the streets were empty," Mustafa said. "The people had gone. But the smell . . ."

He broke off and reached for the platter of kabobs. "In

the distance we saw thousands of poles, too many to count. As we got closer, the stench was unbearable. Thousands of Turkish soldiers had been impaled. Our general was among them, staked higher than the others."

"So you'd be sure to notice?" Vivi asked.

"Men were staked according to rank," Mustafa said.

Vivi mulled over that a moment. Long ago, when she'd found out that Raphael was immortal, she'd watched every vampire movie she could find on Netflix. She'd read about Vlad III—the real Dracula hadn't even been a vampire. Where was Mustafa going with this story?

"So, did you fight this Vlad guy?" she asked.

"History is divided, but the truth is, the sultan retreated," he said. "Mehmed II was a brave, hard man. His temper was legendary. He understood the science of war and the science of the mind. But so did Vlad Ţepeş."

"I thought Vlad was just cruel," Vivi said. "He was smart, too?"

"No, no. You see, Vivienne, when Vlad and his brother were young, their father sent them to live with Sultan Murad II. Vlad and Radu grew up with the sultan's son. Mehmed bin Murad Khan. Better known as Mehmed II." Mustafa lifted a skewered kabob. "Prince Vlad was jealous. Such a twisted mind."

Vivi cupped her hand over her mouth. Not because she was shocked or ill, but to keep from blurting what her mom had taught her. Mehmed II had brought down Constantinople in 1453. Vivi had not been interested in the Ottoman empire, but she'd been wild about Vlad Ţepeş. She'd studied him with the care and attention that the fictional Renfield had given his bugs. The real Dracula had died at the end of 1475 or early 1476. No one knew how. But his head had ended up in Constantinople.

She dragged a pita wedge through the hummus, waiting to see if Mustafa would continue.

He looked up from the kabob tray. "Am I scaring you?"

Vivi lowered her hand. "No, sir. Were you actually in a battle with the real Dracula?"

"The sultan sent my cavalry to Bucharest. Our instructions were to bring Vlad's head back to Istanbul. But his men attacked at night, as was Vlad's custom. I was captured that December and taken to Palatul Curtea Veche, the dungeon fortress. The air stank of human waste and blood. Dogs fought over bones. I was put in chains, and Vlad kept me as a pet. I was dragged to his torture chamber."

Mustafa broke off, his chin shaking. "He committed unspeakable acts upon my flesh. Then he let his men persecute me. I barely noticed the bite wounds. They were nothing. When Vlad could not abide my stench, his men staked me. They put ropes on my ankles and tied me to horses. The blunt end of a pole was greased with hog renderings and shoved into my rectum. When the men led the horses forward, the pole went into the air. And I went with it."

Vivi looked at the skewered kabobs, then up at Mustafa.

"The blunt pole slowly worked its way through my body, ripping through my internal organs," he said. "The sharp end would have killed me too quickly."

"How did you get off the pole?"

"I wasn't the only man who'd been impaled. There were twenty of us. *Sipahis*, janissaries, some peasants. Vlad's executioner went down the row, decapitating men—they knew we would become immortal, and Vlad could not allow an immortal *sipahis* to walk in the dark. Before the executioner reached me, he went to work on a man with a large, bull neck. The blade broke—Allah's guiding hand. So my head remained attached to my body."

"And you became immortal?" Vivi asked.

"I was still transforming. But I appeared dead. The soldiers threw me and the other men into a wagon. Headless corpses were stacked on top of me, so I was somewhat protected from the sun. I was dumped in the Vlasiei Woods. I crawled to water and drank. It came right back up. Yet I burned with thirst. I drank more. Again, I vomited. I do not remember dying. I only remember waking in sunlight, and my skin was covered with blisters. I longed for water. I had never felt such powerful thirst. At night my flesh healed, and when the sun came up, I burned. I was like Prometheus."

"You poor thing," Vivi said. "How did you manage?"

"I learned to hide in the shade. I did not know what was wrong with me. But I could move around. I found a bird's nest. I had hoped for eggs, but I found three fledglings. Oh, I can still see their wide-open beaks. I bit off one's head. I had never tasted such sweetness."

Vivi drew back, her breath coming in hot spurts.

Mustafa didn't seem to notice. His eyes blazed at a spot just over Vivi's head.

"When I became stronger, I hunted more birds and

drank their blood," he said. "One night I walked to a village. I was like a wolf, attacking goats and sheep. When my full strength returned, I set out to find Vlad. I still did not know what I was. I only knew that I could not tolerate daylight, and blood was the only liquid that stayed in my stomach. I craved blood and revenge. I caught up with the Turkish army south of Bucharest. Vlad was somewhere in the hills. The Wallachians struck at night, killing hundreds, always retreating before dawn. So I waited for him. I was darkness layered in front of darkness. A memory of jagged teeth. It was a cold night, and snow blew over the hills in great drifts. I wore a white turban and a caftan, and I followed the smell of blood. Vlad could not hide. I brought his head to the sultan."

Vivi blinked, her head swimming with the words *I, me*, and *my*.

"Vlad made you immortal?" she asked.

"I do not know. So many men bit me. Including the Impaler."

"What happened to Dracula's body?"

"It is not a story for a banquet," Mustafa's said.

And the other stuff was? Vivi thought. "I'm not a scaredy-cat," she said. "I can take it."

"So can Bram." He gave an approving nod. "We like girls with strong stomachs. Perhaps we shall become friends. So I will tell you a secret. Before I severed Vlad's head, he told me what I had become and what I would have to do to stay immortal. I went blind with rage. I did something to him that history never recorded. His torso was not buried at Snagov. There was no torso. I butchered him and fed his quivering muscles to his own dogs. The bones were chewed. Scattered into the night wind."

His brow furrowed. He broke off and gazed behind Vivi. "Tatiana," he said. "How long have you been eaves-dropping?"

Vivi turned. Standing beside her was a blond woman, her black dress rustling like crow feathers. Her eyes were blue and glacial. In her hand was a toy gun, yellow-and-black plastic, like a giant wasp. *I've seen you before*, Vivi thought.

"Long enough," the woman said. "You told this mutant things that you never told me. What makes her special?"

Now Vivi recognized the voice. This woman had kid-napped her in Provence.

She hit my face, but I made her bleed, Vivi thought.

A buzzing noise came out of the gun, and two prongs flew into her chest. She barely had time to whimper before her jaw clenched and all the pain in the world swarmed into her body.

CHAPTER 47

Tatiana

MAIN FLOOR—LEVEL 1
BANQUET HALL III
AL-DÎN COMPOUND

Tatiana dropped to the rug, looped her arm around Vivi's throat, and mashed the Taser gun against it. Then she scanned the banquet hall. Fadime circled her, his diamond earring sparking in the red light. Mustafa hadn't moved from his chair. "Stand down, Fadime, or I'll break her neck," she said.

The guard fell back, his mustache quaking, as if whispering a secret. Tatiana lowered the gun, bent over the girl's chest, and removed the metal prongs. Tears ran down Vivi's cheeks, over her mouth, and slid down her chin; her carotid artery leaped against her flesh.

"Quit scaring her," Mustafa called from his chair. "She can see and hear."

"For now." Tatiana scooted closer to the girl, and cut her gaze around the room. Fadime leaned against the wall. No other guards had arrived.

"How did you get out of detention?" Mustafa asked.

"I transformed myself into fog. Like Dracula." Tatiana pinned her knee against the girl's chest, then reloaded the Taser.

"No, Tatiana!" Mustafa slid his hands across the dining table, then twisted out of his chair. A long, furry torso glided across his shoulder, claws biting into the silk. Now that Mustafa was on his feet, she could imagine him as a *sipahi*, his pointy helmet tucked under his arm, the clicking of his armour as he strode toward his war horse.

"I would have enjoyed hearing how Vlad rewired your chivalry," she said.

"Let Vivienne go," Mustafa said.

Tatiana smiled. The pleading tone in his voice confirmed her power over him. She straddled Vivi's stomach and fired the Taser again. The girl stiffened.

"The Chosen One is an impaling instrument," Tatiana said, removing the prongs from Vivi's scrub shirt. "Who wants to be first? Fadime? Get over here and drop your pants. Don't forget the butter."

"You have come undone," Mustafa said.

"You made me what I am. You never told me who made *you*. Yet you told her."

"This performance is beneath you." Mustafa's head tilted like a blade.

"Maybe you'll enjoy the encore," she said, reloading the Taser. A cold eddy shifted behind her, then a hard object pushed against the base of her skull. Fadime's blood-and-curry smell waffled around her.

"Release Vivienne," Mustafa said, his voice rising. The ferret scampered down his sleeve, and then he disappeared under the table.

"How?" Tatiana said. "I can't move. A gun is pointed at my head. Tell your little asswipe to back off."

"Your profanity is offensive to Vivienne and Bram," Mustafa said.

"Get another fucking ferret."

"Fadime, when I give the order, you will count to five. Shoot Tatiana if she refuses to obey."

"Yes, sir," Fadime said.

Heat scattered behind Tatiana's eyes. "The Prophecy Girl can witness a murder, but no one can curse?"

"Start the countdown," Mustafa said.

"One," Fadime said. "Two."

"Fine." She set the Taser on the floor, then climbed off Vivi.

But Fadime pushed the gun harder against the back of Tatiana's neck.

Her eyes began to water. What was wrong? She'd followed orders. Fadime hadn't. Yet she was being punished? She slid her gaze toward the table, trying to see Mustafa. His face was serene. Why was he still standing? How was that even possible?

"Samin, get rid of the weapon. Move Vivienne away from Miss Kaskov."

A thin, red-haired vampire rushed out of the shadows. He put the Taser in his waistband, then dragged the girl off to the side.

"Good boy, Samin. Now find Dr. Hazan. Bring him to Vivienne."

The red-haired vampire ran through the archway, his footsteps pattering. Fadime backed away from Tatiana. She let out a breath. Wiped her eyes. Forced herself to smile at Mustafa. "You look tired. Sit down before you fall."

His eyes were sharp, yet unemotional, like a hawk studying prey. He stood taller, pulling the IV tubing taut behind him. "You have not heard my good news? I am in remission."

Tatiana felt something crash inside her chest. "When did this happen? Why didn't you tell me?"

"I have not seen you in weeks." His gaze was unreadable. "My blood tests were wrong. The machine had not been properly calibrated. Dr. Hazan believes Yang had tampered with it. My white blood count is now eleven thousand, not one hundred and eleven thousand."

"What makes you think the remission will last?"

"What makes you think that *you* will last?"

"Don't threaten me," she said, nostrils flaring.

"You have ruined my dinner."

Right. The real problem was Jude's daughter.

"I'm *not* your enemy," she said. "But this girl is a miscreation. She will kill you. She is hemakinetic. So is that French dwarf who was keeping her. She bewitched Maury's guys—tough, paramilitary men. She made them hallucinate. She killed some of your best soldiers. I was injured."

"Yes, Maury told me. Did you catch the dwarf?"

"I was incapacitated."

"This is your excuse?"

"Did Maury tell you how he botched the Paris job?"

"Jealousy has torn your mind apart." Mustafa gestured at Fadime. "She looks unwell. Make her sit."

"I am not jealous," Tatiana cried. She felt her arm twist painfully behind her back, then a force shoved her into a gilt chair, and her arms fell to her sides. She knew Mustafa's strategy. He was showing Fadime that her rank had dropped. She was below eye-level. Now everyone would look down at her.

Footsteps pounded in the outer dining hall, then Dr. Hazan hurried into the room and knelt beside the girl. He gently pulled back her eyelids and checked her pulse.

"Vivienne, can you hear me?" he said. "This is Dr. Hazan, my dear. You will be fine." He caught Tatiana's gaze. "Torturing this child is most unwise. You are shameful."

Tatiana felt the balance of power shifting in the room, moving away from her. Would it go to Hazan or the mutant girl? No, it was the girl. If Mustafa was in remission, he could live another decade. Had he replaced her with Vivi? His next protégée? Out with the old, in with the new. And Jude loved the girl—that hurt most of all.

She shifted in the chair, watching Hazan fuss over the brat, dabbing a napkin over her face, telling her not to weep, she'd be fine, just fine. Tears swarmed behind Tatiana's lashes. Next chance she got, she wouldn't use a Taser, and someone would be washing the girl's brains from the wall.

"Dr. Hazan, take Vivienne to her quarters," Mustafa said.

Tatiana's vision blurred. "Why are you fussing over this girl? She is a danger to us all."

"She is courageous."

"So am I."

"But you possess great cruelty."

Why has he turned against me? Tatiana brushed the water from her eyes. He was a military genius, skilled at mind games. But once he'd formed an opinion, he never changed it. She must find another way to appeal to him. Quickly. The last time she'd been this afraid, the Berlin Wall had fallen. Or maybe before that, when she was a girl, and her father had walked out into the snowy night in a black tuxedo, and her mother had raced after him. The back of his head had splashed into the snow, like the borscht Babushka had made that morning.

"I loved you, Mustafa," she said grinding her teeth. "I love you still."

"Yes, I can see. But love is unimportant." He sat down in the chair. A scrabbling noise began under the table, then the ferret climbed into Mustafa's lap.

"I don't deserve this." She put her hands in her lap, balled up her fists, and the diamond horseshoe ring cut into her leg.

"Your voice hurts my ears, Tatiana. I want you to leave tonight. Find Vivienne's mother. What is her name? The half-breed." He flipped his hand. "Bring her to me."

Tatiana's chest tightened. Bring Caro *here*? "You're reuniting the holy family?"

"Listen to yourself. Do you hear how pathetic you sound? I will harvest the half-breed woman's eggs. Then I will obtain semen from my finest human soldiers. In vitro fertilization will produce many Viviennes. These embryos will produce the daylight serum that I want."

Tatiana draped her palm over her mouth, trying to hide the sudden downward turn of her lips. How would an uneducated Turk know about IVF? She lowered her hand. "I didn't realize you had a prodigious understanding of reproductive science."

His smile was machete-sharp. "I know about Western medicine. I have decided to produce a son with this half-breed."

"You want to breed monsters?"

"No, I am building a new world. Now that I am in remission, I will live to see the prophecy fulfilled. Vivienne will allow me to walk in the light. I will own the day and the night. I will be a modern-day Mehmed."

"A child army can't help you achieve this. Unless you drain them and make an endless supply of serum."

"They will grow. And if Vivienne dies, I will have another and another and another."

Tatiana opened her hand and stared at her palm. She sensed nothing but doom in Vivienne Barrett, a creature that ripped through the veil between daylight and darkness. A miscegenation. So was her mother.

"I don't want Caro Barrett in this compound."

"That is not your decision."

She looked up. His eyes were hard, the pupils dilated. "I want no part of that woman. I'm staying in Sutherland. Let Maury's guys fetch her."

"I do not ask my soldiers to do what *they* want."

"I was more than your subordinate."

"That time has ended."

"You're angry because I Tasered your messiah."

"Do you not understand my order? You will begin your hunt tonight. Kill the people around her, but do not harm the woman. Or you will feel my wrath. Do you understand?"

"Yes. But I don't approve."

"You do not understand your own nature. If you remain in the compound, you will hurt Vivienne. You will not be able to stop yourself. Your lack of control will threaten everything I want. I will have no choice but to remove your head from your shoulders, and Fadime will take your pieces to Level 3."

A tear caught at the edge of Tatiana's mouth. "Mustafa, please—"

He cut her off. "Either find Vivienne's mother or I will banish you from this compound. If you attempt to stay here, you will be executed. Make your choice. I will give you one minute to decide. Think carefully before you answer."

Her heart clenched. She didn't want to die. But she didn't want to fetch Caro. The last thing she wanted was to leave the compound. She'd wanted Jude from the first time she'd met him in the Gabon camp. She'd felt something stir inside her, a Freudian glitch. Jude was like her father, a man who had loved her unconditionally. Dr. Pavel Kaskov. Oh, she'd loved him. He'd praised her intellect, her spirit, and gift with languages. She'd loved his honor and the soft plunk that his boots made when he'd set them inside the front door, taking care to arrange them on the pile of newspapers that her mother, Galina, had set down with malice. Galina had killed Pavel in a jealous rage, and she'd forced Tatiana to quit ballet lessons. But Galina had paid for her sins.

Tatiana pressed her fist against her chest, feeling the erratic surges. She had not expected to find another man with a brown-speckled blue eye. Her father's jaw hadn't been square, and his chin hadn't been dimpled, but Tatiana didn't expect perfection. Jude saw only her defects, but he would see her virtues. And she would be loved. She rose from the chair.

"I'll find your breeder."

CHAPTER 48

Vivi

Vivi didn't know how long she'd slept. She lay in bed, rubbing her chest, feeling the spots. She remembered the jolts of the Taser. Pain. Rigid muscles. Angry voices. Dr. Hazan had taken her to her dorm. She'd been afraid he would give her an injection, so she acted calm and sleepy. After he left, she'd immediately tumbled into a nightmare about bats and blood.

Her door buzzed and Fadime walked in. "Put on your slippers and come with me."

"What time is it?" she asked.

He glanced at his watch, a fancy chronometer with dials. "Ten A.M."

She fit the paper booties over her feet. Now she was starting to see how things worked in the Al-Dîn compound. If you didn't make a fuss, if you pretended to go along, they would assume you were a wimp and quit watching your every move.

"Where are we going?" she asked.

"No questions." He led Vivi into the corridor, where crimson light pooled in the corners. They walked past the elevator and turned down another long hall, past a large, glassed-in room where the redheaded vampire sat in front of a computer. She followed Fadime to the end of the hall. On the steel doors, DO NOT ENTER was written in French, English, and another language that looked Cyrillic.

Fadime swiped his security card on a scanner. The doors creaked open, and he led her into a corridor that smelled of disinfectant and animal dung. The walls on both sides had glass walls. On the right, Vivi saw a concrete aisle with cages on both sides. It looked like a dog kennel, but chimps were inside the runs. Another room held little cages, and mice ran inside metal wheels.

The next set of doors made Vivi think of NASA—they were oval, made of thick metal, and posted with a warning sign: NO UNAUTHORIZED PERSONNEL BEYOND THIS POINT.

Fadime swiped his card again, and these doors made a whooshing sound and came apart like a jigsaw puzzle. They walked through, and Vivi sensed a change in the air pressure. Fadime turned to a keypad. A message appeared on the screen. *Close doors? Yes No*

He clicked *Yes*.

The doors rumbled shut behind them. Vivi's ears popped. She moved behind Fadime into a metal tunnel. Another glassed-in room was on the left. No one sat at the desks, and the computer monitors showed a twirling screen saver.

Vivi turned to Fadime. "Where is everybody?"

"This way," he said.

Halfway down the corridor, Vivi saw three small windows on the left side of the tunnel. She paused beside one, stood on her toes, and peered through the glass. It looked thick, and her nails made a dense, plunking sound as she tapped it. Was something radioactive in there? She pushed closer. The room was dark, two stories, huge and cavernous. Near the hazy ceiling, large black things hung upside down from a wire ceiling. White gunk was piled on the floor. It was spattered on the walls also.

"What's in here?" she asked.

"You ask too many questions." Fadime pulled her away from the window.

Vivi's ears kept popping, and she tugged her lobes as she walked through another set of steel doors. Two minutes later, she and Fadime stood outside a door that read LABORATORY—C.

He opened it, and cool air blew out, carrying the odor of fingernail polish remover.

"Doctor? You have a guest," Fadime called, pulling Vivi inside.

Which doctor? She thought. *Hazan or Barrett?*

"Just a moment," called a crisp, British voice. It seemed to be coming from behind a shelf, where brown jars were lined up.

Dr. Barrett pushed his chair around the shelf, the fluorescent light shining on his dark ponytail. His legs looked shriveled beneath his blue scrubs, but the rest of him looked fit. He wheeled toward her, muscles outlined in his upper arms.

Vivi glanced behind him, where a long black counter was jammed with equipment. Microscopes, empty beakers, machines, computers, and a Bunsen burner.

Is he really my dad? she thought. *But he makes me feel shy and suspicious.*

"How nice to see you, Vivi." His smile quivered at the edges.

What should she say? "Uh, yeah. Should I call you Dr. Barrett or Jude?"

"Whatever pleases you," he said. "Jude's fine."

Fadime stepped between them. "Mustafa wants a blood sample from the girl."

"Sorry?" Jude said, raising his eyebrows. "Dr. Hazan's assistant always does that."

"Not today," Fadime said. "Do not argue. I am following Mustafa's orders." He removed items from his pockets, heaping them onto a counter: a vacuum syringe with a long, capped needle; a large, floppy rubber tube; glass vials with colorful stoppers.

"I won't do it." Jude folded his arms across his chest. "Not until I talk to Mustafa."

Vivi saw a stiffness in Jude's shoulders, one that suggested he was a fighter. He couldn't walk, but she bet he was tough. She bet his mouth had gotten him into trouble with Mustafa and his rat-bastard army.

Fadime crouched so he could look in the doctor's face. "If you do not cooperate, I have been instructed to draw the girl's blood myself, and I will not use a needle."

Jude made a fist. "Now, see here—"

"It's okay," Vivi said.

"See?" Fadime said. "The girl, she is smarter than you."

"Fadime?" Vivi said. "Could you leave me and Jude alone while he gets the sample?"

He snorted and flashed a cocky look. "No."

"What about afterward?" Vivi said. "Can I have a minute with him?"

Fadime tilted his head, as if giving the matter serious thought. "No."

Vivi forced herself to breathe in and out, gathering her thoughts the way Sabine had taught her. *Fadime, give us time alone. Go in the hall and wait.*

His eyelids flickered, and then he reached for the doorknob. "I will be in the hall."

She waited until the door had clicked behind him, then turned to Jude. He pointed at her cheek. "Who hit your cheek?" he asked quietly.

"Forget it. I'm fine." If he was worried about her bruised face, he'd really get upset about the Tasering. Better not mention it.

She forced herself to breathe, and then she gave him a little nudge. *Jude, tell the truth.*

"Are you my dad?" she asked.

"Yes." His eyes filled. "You're my Meep."

She leaned forward, studying his arm. "You have a green snake tattoo like Mustafa."

"It wasn't always like this. Mustafa added the snake after he brought me here."

Vivi felt confused. "Added it? To what?"

"When I became a vampire, I received an infinity

tattoo. It's the logo for the Salucard Foundation. Raphael has one. So does your uncle Nigel." He frowned at his arm. "Mustafa was a member of Salucard. He broke away and added the snake."

"A serpent for a serpent," Vivi said. "If you spell Salucard backward, you get Draculas."

Jude smiled, and then his eyes fogged. "How's your mother? Is she here, too?"

"No. She's with Raphael."

"With him? I'm not following you. How did Mustafa's soldiers kidnap you if Raphael was around?"

"He wasn't. Neither was Mom. They were in Paris. I was in a little town in southern France. Near Grasse."

Jude's eyelids flickered. "Who was taking care of you?"

"A French doctor. A lady. Not a vampire. But she's like mom—half immortal. They're related somehow."

Jude rubbed his temple. "Is your mother still in Paris?"

"Who knows? She's like a great white shark. Always moving. But now I understand why. Try not to freak out. If Mustafa's army shows up, Raphael will beat the crap out of them."

Jude gave her a long, searching look. "How is he?"

"Fine." She stretched her arm on the counter. "Fadime won't stay gone forever. We can talk while you get my blood."

Jude tied the rubber strap around her arm. "Make a fist. There you go. I'm sorry. I hate doing this."

"I don't mind." She stared down at her arm. Blue veins ran along the inner aspect of her elbow. Jude fit a tube into the vacuum syringe, then swabbed her arm with an alcohol pad.

"You'll feel a stick," he said.

Vivi saw her blood splash into the tube. She looked away.

"I'm sorry," he said. "It'll take a moment or two. I've got to fill the lot of these tubes."

"Why do you need my blood? For a paternity test?"

"I know you're my daughter," he said. "Mustafa wants your blood for another purpose."

She turned back to him, eyebrows lowered. "What kind?"

"I can't explain right now." He cut his eyes to the door, then back to Vivi's arm. "Fadime might hear."

"Do they have security cameras in here?"

"They're broken." He leaned over her arm and replaced a blood-filled vial with an empty one.

"You talk like Uncle Nigel," she said. "The British way."

Jude glanced up. "You have an ear for dialects?"

"I guess. Mom and I travel a lot."

"That's how you got your nickname. Because you spent your babyhood in airports."

"Yeah, Mom told me." She felt another wave of shyness and looked at his his left hand. No ring. No indention in the flesh. No mark.

"You lost your wedding band," she said. "Mom still has hers. She keeps it in a box."

"Mine was stolen," Jude said.

"By whom?"

"Someone from Al-Dîn." He removed the rubber tourniquet, took the needle out of her arm, and put an alcohol swab on the puncture.

"Glad that's over." Vivi folded her arm.

"One more thing." Jude held up a long Q-Tip. "I need to swab your cheek. Open wide."

She opened her mouth. "Ah," she said.

The swab was in and out in a flash. He snipped off the end, dropped the white part into a tube, and added a liquid. "What're you doing?"

"I added lysis solution. *Lysis* is the Greek word for 'separate.'"

"No, I meant, what are you doing with that swab?"

"Oh, I'll extract your DNA." Jude nodded at the counter. "Everything is set up. A warm water bath, microcentrifuge, micropipettes, more solutions."

"Why would anyone care about my DNA?"

"Mustafa thinks—"

The door opened, and Fadime stepped into the room, looking befuddled. "Are you finished?" he asked.

Vivi was just about to Induce him again when Jude spoke up.

"No, not entirely," he told Fadime. "I'll need to run a few more tests. Bring Miss Barrett to my lab in the morning."

CHAPTER 49

Caro

VILLA PRIMAVERINA, ISLA CARBONARA
VENICE, ITALY

When I awoke, Raphael was gone, and for a moment I thought we were still in Paris. Then I remembered. Vivi was gone. I rolled into a ball and pushed my face into the pillow. I felt hollow and scraped out. A part of me had always feared this might happen. I'd tried to cast a protective net around her, the same kind my parents had drawn around me. But evil possessed a stronger force than goodness. I hadn't sent Vivi to a safe place. I'd sent her into the heart of danger.

How do you keep breathing when your child has been taken away? Was she hungry? Scared?

Arrapato wiggled out of the blanket and licked one side of my face, his tongue working meticulously. I caught his face.

"Where's Raphael?" I whispered.

Arrapato snorted. I looked at the gold cherub clock. Nine fifteen P.M. The sun had set.

I put on a black long-sleeved dress that matched my mood, then I opened the bedroom door. Arrapato stayed on the bed, licking his paws. I shut the door and stepped into the hall. Raphael's study was on the lower terrace level, under the kitchen and the main entry.

I walked down the stairs and passed through a wide hallway. At the far end, a massive walnut door stood ajar, showing another hallway. A light spilled out of Raphael's study and I heard voices—Beppe's Germanic accent, La Rochenoire's French lilt, and the softer Italian tones of Raphael and his detectives.

I didn't want to disturb them—no, that wasn't true. I couldn't be around anyone right now. I'd lost my place in this world. I turned toward the French doors. Rain forked down the glass panes. Beyond the doors, floodlights brightened the grounds. Mist crouched in the garden, lurking around a statue of Athena, stalking a menagerie of topiary animals that had been shaped and sculpted into mythological beasts. A dark shadow edged between a unicorn and the Kraken. I blinked. My saliva tasted sour and metallic. And I smelled ketones—not pomegranates or cherries, but something fetid and earthy.

My pulse bumped under my jaw. Had I suffered a complete breakdown? Would vampires dare come to Villa Primaverina? Could they bypass Raphael's small, well-armed navy?

The back of my neck tightened as I inched closer to the window. The wind shook one of the Kraken's tentacles. Further out, the island of Murano was hidden by smoke and clouds. Someone was out there, waiting and watching.

Stop being paranoid, Caro. No one is there.

I glanced over my shoulder, toward the hallway. What was keeping Raphael? I heard the faint sound of Arrapato's barks from the bedroom, and I turned back to the window. A woman stood on the other side of the glass.

I jolted.

Her hair was plastered to her head. Blue lights leaped in her eyes. She wore a black body suit and combat boots.

Tatiana. She had taken Vivi and now she had come for me.

"Open the door, Caro," she shouted.

Everything moved too fast. I stepped backward, screaming for Raphael. She lifted her boot and kicked in the door. The glass shattered and clinked to the floor. Wind blew in through the broken glass, stirring Tatiana's hair. Behind her, in the garden, I heard gunshots, and a man shouted.

She lunged through the space where the glass had been, into the room. I spun around and ran toward the doors. She beat me to them, wrenched the handles, and grabbed me. I twisted at the waist and pulled her hair.

"Cunt," she said, and shoved me to the floor. She pounced on top of me and sank her teeth into my neck. I felt a burst of pain below my ear, heard sucking noises. She was too strong, and I couldn't fight her. A memory broke through my panic. My blood might be a weapon. She could be sensitive to my hybrid antigens. I let my arms drop to the floor, hoping she'd think that I was succumbing to her neurotoxin. She would expect me to become paralyzed.

I lay still, listening to her swallow. Jude had told me long ago that vampires weren't automatically allergic to hybrids. First a vampire had to drink a hybrid's blood. During that initial encounter, the vampire would not have a physiological reaction. Because he'd never been exposed to the antigen, he would have no antibodies. But the first moment he drank a hybrid's blood, the vampire's super immune system would start building antibodies to the antigen. The next time the vampire bit a hybrid, the result could be fatal. This wasn't a theory. It was a scientific fact, like a human's reaction to bee stings, nuts, shellfish, or penicillin.

Tatiana had most likely consumed Keats's hybrid blood. If so, her own immune system would have made antibodies. The allergic reaction occurred swiftly in immortals.

I waited. She sucked my neck harder, her throat clicking, the coppery smell of blood rising up. Her body pushed hard against mine, as if she were enjoying herself. What if she hadn't drunk Keats's blood? What if she'd never been exposed to a hybrid's antigens? A fissure opened up inside me, and all of my fears rushed out. I would die.

Then she started breathing faster and faster.

I've got you now, I thought. The anaphylactic reaction was beginning. Her blood pressure would start to drop; she'd wheeze and break out in itchy hives. The more blood she swallowed, the greater the allergic response.

Drink, drink, drink.

Tatiana's body went rigid, and her boots scraped through the broken glass. She braced her hands on the

floor and rose up, my blood running down her chin. Her
pupils were dilated. Her lips had turned faintly blue; she
pursed them and released a harsh breath. It sounded like
a stick being dragged through gravel. The bitch was going
down.

I pushed her away from me, and she rolled onto her
back, banging her fist against her chest. I saw a diamond
horseshoe ring on her pinkie. She'd killed Gillian?

From the hallway, I heard footsteps. The logical part
of my brain told me to open the door, to let the men
handle it. But a blood lust welled up inside me. She'd
murdered Gillian. She'd killed my husband; taken his
wedding ring and put it on Keats's finger. She'd stolen my
daughter. She was responsible for Mrs. MacLeod's death.

Tatiana rolled over and scrambled to her hands and
knees. Her chest heaved. A thread of blood and saliva fell
from her mouth, onto the floor. Red welts were breaking
out on her face and arms.

Raphael was knocking on the door. *"Caro?"*

"Tatiana broke in," I called. "I'm okay."

As I felt my blood stream down my neck, I wanted her
to die. I kicked her ribs. A burst of air rushed through
her teeth. Another round of gunfire exploded on the
lawn.

I heard the distant sound of excited Italian voices. She
lifted her head, blinking toward the shattered French
door. "Gambi?" she called in a slurry voice. "Siphi?
Moyo?"

My heart was pumping so hard. How had Tatiana and
her killers gotten to the island? Raphael's men patrolled
the lagoon, and armed guards were posted on the boat

dock. I dug my fingers into her scalp and yanked her head back. With my other hand, I picked up a long shard of glass and pressed the pointy end against her carotid.

"Where's my daughter?" I said. I felt the glass slicing into my fingers, but I didn't let go.

She opened her mouth wide and dragged in a breath. "Fuck you."

I pushed the shard in a little deeper, and a dark string ran down her throat. "What have you done with her?"

"Goddammit, where are my men?" She clenched her teeth.

I heard Raphael and the men kicking the door, calling my name.

"Your husband fucked me." She broke off and wheezed. "He cried when we finished. And then he fucked me again."

"Where have you taken my child?"

Her gaze clouded. One side of her mouth kicked up in a grin. "I killed my mother," she said, her voice thick with phlegm. "I'm late for my dancing lessons. I should go now."

Mental confusion was part of the anaphylactic reaction. She wasn't going to tell me where to find Vivi. And unless I pumped more of my blood into her mouth, she would regain her strength and break my neck.

"This is for Keats and Vivi," I said, then dragged the glass over her throat. Blood spurted over the front of her black top. She made a gurgling noise. Her hands reached up. I kicked them away.

"This is for Mrs. MacLeod and Gillian," I said. I cut

her again. Blood hit the wall behind her and streamed down.

"This is for Jude," I carved notches on her cheeks. I felt the glass slash deeper into my own hands, but I kept going. A wet coldness seeped around my feet. Her pupils grew and grew, eclipsing the blue irises.

I'd killed her, and it still wasn't enough. I'd crossed a moral barrier. I had taken a life, and that meant I was no different from her.

I felt someone grab my shoulders. "She's dead, *mia cara*. She can't hurt you."

My hand opened, and the shard clinked to the floor. "She wouldn't tell me where Vivi is."

Raphael knelt beside me, folding his hands over mine, trying to stop the blood. "You're hurt. Beppe, call Dr. Nazzareno."

I leaned against Raphael, and my knee skidded over the wet floor. It was impossible to know where Tatiana's blood ended and mine began.

PART SEVEN

TIMING IS EVERYTHING

CHAPTER 50

Vivi

BIOMEDICAL LABORATORY—LEVEL 3
AL-DÎN COMPOUND

Two days later, Vivi was walking around Jude's lab, tracing her finger along a black counter. Her mind was alert, taking in details, but it also felt blunted. Not a benzo kind of numb, but an emotional blankness, as if all the wires in her brain had been disconnected. Inside, she felt nothing. No fear, no sorrow, no shock.

She paused in front of a huge stainless steel hood. It rose up into the ceiling.

"This looks like the exhaust fan over Uncle Nigel's stove," she said in a flat voice.

Jude looked up from his desk. "Yes, it's a fume hood. It takes smoke and chemical odors out of my lab."

He looked as if he wanted to say something else about the hood, but Vivi turned toward a stainless-steel freezer and opened the door. The bright light made her wince, and frost curled out of the shelves, swirling up into the reddish air.

"What's up with the weird light in this compound?" she asked. "Does it kill germs?"

"No." Jude wheeled away from his desk and moved along a black counter. "Colors give off energy. Blue and purple have the most. Red has the lowest. It doesn't hurt Mustafa's eyes. His disease caused him to be hypersensitive to all light."

"But he's not in your lab. Why can't you have fluorescents?"

"If Mustafa can't have light, no one can."

"That figures." She closed the freezer, and the air around her got darker. She walked over to Jude. "Are you working on my blood?"

"Yes."

"What are you looking for again?"

"Proteins."

"Like the protein in a rib-eye steak?"

"No." He smiled. "These proteins are called monoclonal antibodies. They neutralize other proteins by attacking them. Think of them as a SWAT team. They block a compound called IgE."

"What's that?"

"IgE is what causes vampires to burn when they get in sunlight."

"Why would that be in my blood? Daylight doesn't bother me."

He set a pipette in a stand, then rubbed his forehead. "A quarter vampire produces a special type of monoclonal antibodies. These are proteins in your blood—and your special MAs will allow vampires to walk in daylight."

She forced herself to breathe as she opened a drawer—it was empty—then closed it. "You're kidding, right?"

"Oh, Meep. I wish I were kidding. I've known about your proteins since you were a baby. After Mustafa kidnapped me, I tried to hide this information. But he found out. Vampires don't have MAs. However, we do have IgE—this makes us sensitive to light. And your MAs will block Mustafa's IgE. He wants to walk in daylight."

That figured, too. Suddenly she understood. "Is that why we're here? So that old poop can take a sunbath?"

"I'm sorry, Meep. I tried to keep you safe. But now he's forcing me to make him a serum out of your proteins."

"Is that what you're doing now?"

"I'm extracting your DNA." He lifted the lid on a water bath and removed a vial. "You might have a special gene. It's called RH1, the low-light gene. Vampires don't have it."

"Do humans?"

"No."

"This is getting worse and worse." She crossed her arms. "What makes you think I've got this gene?"

"I'm following orders, Meep." He transferred the vial to a large machine and closed the lid. "If I find the RH1 gene, I'll cut the DNA into fragments. And then I'll sequence the DNA code. I'll do another test. A PCR. That stands for *polymerase chain reaction*. Basically this means I'll zoom in on a portion of your DNA and copy it over and over. Then I will make a serum."

"That's a lot of trouble."

"Not really. Insulin is made in a lab," he said. "That's a drug that's used in diabetes."

"I know what that is." She looked away. In her mind's eye, a picture of Keats rose up, his hand caught in the reins as he led Ozzie along the paddock.

"Some diabetics need insulin injections to control their blood glucose," Jude said. "Years ago it was made from the pancreatic glands of pigs and cows. Now insulin is made in a lab like this one. Scientists isolate the gene that makes insulin, they spiff it up a bit, and add it to a mild strain of *E. coli*. The insulin gene begins to make insulin."

"My friend Keats was diabetic. He died."

"I'm sorry, Meep."

"He injected himself twice a day. But what does that have to do with me?"

"I'm going to study your IgE proteins and isolate the gene that makes them."

"And that's it?"

"Well, it's more complicated. I have to add a DNA enzyme and place the gene on little rings of DNA called plasmids. The spiffed-up IgE gene will be introduced into a bacteria—a mild form of *E. coli*—and the gene will make more IgE."

"Then what happens?"

"I'll do trials on mice. If they go well, I will inject Mustafa with the serum."

I hope he croaks, she thought. "If the serum works, what happens to me? Does the gene need a human body in order to survive?"

"No, the gene can function in the bacteria. But don't

worry, I'm getting you out of here." He swiveled his chair away from the desk. "You see that fume hood? It has a pipe that goes all the way outside. I will disable the motor, and then you can climb inside. It's got metal notches along the sides. Just be careful. When you get out, run."

"And then what? The compound is fenced. Guards are all over the place."

"I'll distract them."

"How?"

"We've got some huge bats on this level. They've already killed a few scientists. I'm going to release them from the chamber. They'll wipe out the compound."

Bats? She shivered. Was that what she'd seen through those little windows the other day?

"How big are they?"

"The size of a goat. Huge teeth. Claws. They'll take down this compound in ten minutes."

"But they'll be trapped on this floor with you."

"I haven't figured that out. But if I find a way, the bats will use echolocation to find their way upstairs."

"Maybe I can help. I can open the doors in the stairwells."

"You're a dandy girl, Meep. But you can't leave your dorm."

"I can try."

"No. Too dangerous. I'll find a way."

"If I get out, what happens to you? Won't the bats kill you?"

He hesitated. "No, I'll stay in my lab."

Yes, they will. "How will you open their chamber?"

"There's an air lock."

"Where?"

"In the control room. It's not staffed. Too many people have died."

Vivi felt something stir inside her chest, and she grabbed his hands. "Listen, I can help you escape."

"I don't think so."

"You need to know something about me. You asked why I wasn't staying with my mom. It's because I make people bleed. Raphael found a doctor who could teach me how to control it."

His eyes opened wide. "You're hemakinetic?"

"I can also influence thoughts. It's called Induction. Do you know about it?"

He shook his head.

She gave him a quick summary. "When I got here, Dr. Hazan gave me pills, and I couldn't Induce. I spit out the pills. And now I can do stuff. Remember the other day, when Fadime brought me here for the blood samples? He wouldn't leave. So I Induced him."

"So that's why he went into the hall." Jude rubbed his chin.

"If I can hurt Mustafa and his men, you and I can get out of here."

"No, we can't. There are thirty-eight men in this compound. Ten vampires, including myself. The rest are human mercenaries. And they're armed. I don't know how Induction works, but I don't want you to try." He squeezed her shoulder. "I'll come up with a plan. Promise that you won't do anything until I do."

She crossed her fingers behind her back. "I promise."

CHAPTER 51

Vivi

MAIN FLOOR—LEVEL 1
BANQUET HALL III
AL-DÎN COMPOUND

Three nights later, Vivi was seated in Mustafa's dining hall, listening to his stories of Vlad the Impaler. He sat in his thronelike chair, dishes spread out on the table—lamb kabobs, tomatoes, pitas, and yogurt. Silver candelabras flickered over his gaunt face as he talked about Vlad's long-suffering wife.

"Did she really kill herself?" Vivi asked.

"I did not see it happen," he said. "But I heard tales."

As he talked, his face took on an incandescent glow. She saw something else, too, a crazy spark behind his eyes, as if he were illuminated from within by his own self-love.

While Mustafa described the trajectory of Mrs. Dracula's fall and the extent of her injuries, Vivi frowned. "Why didn't Vlad turn his wife into a vampire?"

"She despised him," Mustafa said. "He killed her father."

You're gonna kill mine, too, Vivi thought. The minute Mustafa got that serum, he wouldn't need Jude or Vivi. Genes were little shit-heads that could function in bacteria and didn't need a human body. She and Jude had to escape. Could she even fit up that exhaust duct? Climb three whole stories? What if she fell? Maybe it wouldn't kill her, and she'd end up like a rat in a cage.

No, I won't be trapped.

I have to go after Mustafa right now, Vivi thought. He might not invite her to the banquet again. She remembered the Napoleon quote. The time to deliberate had ended; she needed to stop thinking and go make people bleed. This might be her last chance. She'd make the Turk bleed. Lots and lots. But she didn't want to hurt the ferret.

She was conscious of her lungs expanding and deflating. Then she slung out a thought.

Give Bram to Vivi.

Breathe, breathe, breathe. She forced air in and out of her lungs.

At first, nothing happened. Then Mustafa's forehead creased. He stopped talking, and then his hand slid up to the ferret. "You are lonely, Bram?"

YES! Bram is lonely.

It was tempting to hold her breath and give Mustafa a nosebleed, but she held back. What if he got angry? What if he knew about her hemakinesis? He'd summon Dr. Hazan, and they'd pump her full of benzos.

Mustafa handed Bram to Fadime. "Let Vivi have him."

Fadime stretched out his arms, and his jacket opened, showing a holster. He took the ferret, then hesitated. "Are you sure?" he asked.

"Yes. Do as I say." Mustafa waved his hand in a shooing motion. His sleeve fell back, showing an IV catheter taped to the inside of his wrist.

Fadime put Bram in Vivi's arms. A musky odor rose up as she petted him. He felt so cold. The way Arrapato felt. Was the ferret a vampire, too?

Mustafa was smiling. "He is yours to keep."

"Mine?"

"As long as you live, my dear."

Vivi swallowed. Her spit tasted like rust. *Don't freak out. Be calm.* She bent closer to Bram, waited a few seconds, then glanced up. "Bram wants to know how much longer that will be."

Mustafa's eyes drooped at the edges. "That depends on you. And your father."

A drop of perspiration skated down her neck. "But you will kill us, right?"

Mustafa's gaze sharpened. "Do you fear death?"

"No. And I don't mind pain," Vivi said. "Just don't hurt Dr. Barrett."

Mustafa's eyes softened, and he tilted his head. "Your spirit is impressive."

"Thanks." *Asshole.*

"You have impeccable manners, too." He lifted one finger. "But spirit and social graces will not change your father's fate if he doesn't cooperate. Make sure that he does."

Vivi felt nauseated. "Will I get to see him?"

"That is up to you. And your father."

"But, sir, I don't understand what's going on. Why am I here?"

Mustafa rested his hands on the table. "Your DNA is remarkable. It will set me free. No more red light. No more darkness. Bram and I shall walk in the noon sun."

Just keep him talking, Vivi thought. "Why can't you go in daylight?"

"Immortals are photosensitive because of an inborn error of metabolism and mast cells," he said. "An overproduction of IgE and mast cells cause us to be photoreactive. You see, in vampires, these molecules are concentrated at a level five million times that of humans. They are deposited just under the skin. When sunlight touches a vampire's skin, the reaction is blistering. And finally death."

It couldn't come soon enough for him, Vivi thought.

"I am tired." Lines cut across Mustafa's forehead. "Vivienne, I will say good night to you and Bram. Fadime, take them to the dormitory."

She ached to cry, but she forced herself to take little sips of air. She gripped the ferret, then sucked in as much air as her lungs would hold. She felt pressure build behind her eyes and nose. Then she hurled an Inductive thought.

MUSTAFA, DON'T LEAVE!

She held her breath until her throat ached.

Mustafa groaned, and the back of his head smacked against his throne. She hadn't meant to zap him that hard, but it was too late to call it back. Perspiration dotted his bald head, and his skin was ashy. He lifted a blood-drenched sleeve and turned to Fadime. "Will you fetch Dr. Hazan? Something is wrong with my IV."

Vivi exhaled, then cast a furtive glance around the dining hall. She could hear the soldiers in the other chamber. Could she get past them? How could she find Jude? She had a sudden vision of herself dying in this red place.

No, I'm not going down without a fight. She tucked Bram inside her scrubs so he wouldn't get loose. It wasn't the ferret's fault that his master was a ogre. She didn't think the soldiers would be unaffected by the sight of blood, but maybe it would be different if the blood was coming out of their own bodies. At least, that was what had happened at Sabine's farmhouse.

Samin glided out of the shadows, toward Mustafa's throne, and said something in Turkish.

Vivi lowered her chin, focused on Samin's red hair, and inhaled.

Samin, go away. Leave Mustafa alone.

Vivi felt a hot, snapping current move out of her. Samin's eyes squinched up. He clapped his hand over his ear. Then he fell to his knees and rocked back and forth.

Mustafa was wrapping napkins around his IV site. Red patches instantly bloomed on the paper. Vivi took a breath. She tossed out a small, heated wave at him.

Mustafa, you are sleepy.

Vivi stared at the old Turk, waiting. A red ribbon flew out of his sleeve and spattered on the paisley robe. His eyelids fell, and he slumped down in his chair.

Dr. Hazan rushed into the room, pushing an empty wheelchair. His eyes wobbled as he looked at Mustafa and the red-haired guard. Then he turned his gaze on Vivi.

"What is going on?" he cried. "What have you done?"

She shrugged. Dr. Hazan dragged Mustafa into the

wheelchair. A man in a white coat ran up, his black beard churning around his face.

Vivi lashed out at him. *Leave us!*

A red bubble grew out of the bearded man's right nostril. He sat down hard.

Vivi kept holding her breath until the man keeled over, blood streaming into the Persian rug. Dr. Hazan was struggling to pull Mustafa into the chair.

"Help me," he yelled at Vivi.

Go to sleep.

The doctor's eyelids fluttered, and then he fell on top of Samin.

Vivi leaped out of her chair and ran through the archway. She didn't see Fadime. When she reached the buffet tables, she paused. The soldiers stopped eating and turned. Vivi counted twelve heads.

It's me or them. They had guns; she only had herself.

She cupped a protective hand over Bram, who was shivering. Then she faced the soldiers. She focused on her respirations, then hit them as hard as she could.

Go to sleep.

A swirling force tore away from her body. Three men toppled out of their booth. A moment later, a fourth slumped to the floor. A fifth man got out of a booth, then sank to the floor.

Go to sleep.

The sixth man fell face first into a plate of hummus. The seventh, eighth, and ninth sprawled across the table, their hands knocking over beer mugs. The tenth, eleventh, and twelfth began to slump.

Go to sleep.

Vivi kept sending out pulses until the last three men fell. She had never seen so much blood. She hadn't meant to do that. A coppery stink rushed up her nose, and she thought she might be sick.

Don't pity them, Vivi, she told herself. Those men were employed by Mustafa. That meant they'd been paid to lose their ethics. Maybe one of them had shot Lena.

She ran out of the banquet hall, turned into the elevator, and punched the button for Level 3. Bram was squirming inside her scrub shirt. She had to put him in a safe place. But where?

Before the doors opened all the way, she punched the emergency stop button, then hurried to the glassed-in room. A dark-haired man sat in front of a computer monitor, playing solitaire.

He turned, frowning. "What are you doing here?"

"I'm sorry," Vivi whispered. She held her breath.

You're paralyzed.

As he fell, his chin hit the desk. Blood flew out of his mouth and splashed across the keyboard. The back of his head banged against the floor.

She opened a drawer and set Bram inside. She had no idea if Induction worked on animals, but if she kept him with her, he'd die. She breathed in and out, then sent him a little pulse.

Bram, you're tired.

The ferret yawned, then curled up, wrapping his tail around his face. Vivi bent down, making sure he was breathing. He was. She pulled off her paper slippers, tucked them around the ferret, then gently closed the drawer, leaving a gap for fresh air.

Vivi brushed tears from her cheeks. This was bad. This was evil. But Mustafa had stolen her dad. He'd stolen *her*. She squatted beside the dark-haired vampire and yanked off his laminated ID card. A key chain was clamped on his belt. She pulled it off—two keys, one large, one small.

Focus, Vivi. How long before someone figured out what she was doing? They'd come down here with guns. She couldn't make them all bleed. Her head was already throbbing, as if she'd hurt something inside her own brain. But she might have time to release the bats. Jude said they could take down the compound.

Hurry, hurry, hurry. She raced out of the room, into the stairwell, then pushed back the door and kicked down the metal stopper. She ran up to the next floor, unlocked the door, and propped it open. Her pulse thumped in her ears as she looked into the hall. It was cold and empty.

She raced up to the main level and went to the door. She stood on her toes and looked through the chicken-wire glass. Two soldiers rushed toward the banquet hall. She unlocked the door, braced it open, then sped back down to Level 3.

She was a sweaty mess by the time she reached the bottom floor. Then she ran toward the bat chamber, swiping the ID card at each junction.

The giant metal doors rumbled open. Beside them, a message floated up on the security panel.

Close doors? Yes No

She punched *No*.

Then she ran into the tunnel. A small control room was on the left. The desks were empty. A layer of dust covered the computer monitors. Across the room, she saw a rounded door, like airplanes have.

If this was the airlock, how was she supposed to open it? Maybe she should get Jude. He'd know what to do. No, the soldiers would come. She had to release the bats. She walked up to the airlock. Beside the door was a panel. A red light was glowing, and just beneath it was a large black button.

She pressed it, and the light turned green. She heard a hissing noise, and the door opened. Her ears stopped up as she stepped into a small, metal tunnel. It had a door at the other end. In between, heavy uniforms and helmets hung on the walls.

She tugged a helmet over her head—yikes, it was big. Her breath steamed against the Plexiglas. She walked toward the door. Her fist slammed down on the black knob, and the door opened with a whoosh.

A fetid odor rolled out of the bat chamber. She smelled guano and decayed flesh. From somewhere above her, near the wire ceiling, she heard clicks. If she could Induce a ferret, could she Induce a bat? If the bats killed her, it would be worth it. Mustafa wouldn't get her damn blood.

She looked at the ceiling, where the hulking shapes were beginning to stir. She filled her lungs with the nasty air, then slowly exhaled.

FLY AWAY.

It was sweltering inside the helmet. Perspiration ran down her cheeks. The air above her began to move.

You're free. All of you. Fly away. Go up the stairs.

Like a bat would know what stairs were. This wasn't

going to work. She exhaled, and the mask fogged. This was crazy. She couldn't herd bats.

Above her, a whirring noise started up. She raced back into the airlock, propped open the door to the control room, and slid under the desk, banging her helmet against the wood.

Black shapes flew out the door and veered into the hall, whirring past the windows, streaking through the red air. There were so many of them! The smaller bats flew after the adults, their echolocation clicks streaking through the air like bullets.

Vivi waited a few minutes. Then she crawled out from under the desk, threw the helmet away, and hurried out of the room. She ran past the windows of the bat chamber. She ran toward the lab, using the ID card to open the doors. When she reached Jude's lab, she started yelling. "Open up!"

The door opened and he stared up at her. "What's going on?" An alarm started blaring, the high-pitched sound slicing through the air. A disembodied voice said, "Level Three, security breach. Evacuate the compound in an orderly manner."

"We've got to hurry," she said. "The bats are loose."

His eyes blinked open wide. "Oh, my God."

The alarm kept bleating. Vivi got behind the wheelchair and pushed Jude out of the lab. On their way to the main control room, she told him what she'd done.

She parked his chair in the hall. "I'll be right back."

The dark-haired vampire staggered out of the room, dabbing his nose with a Kleenex. "Whew, did you see the bats?" he said. "Jesus Christ, the smell. Dr. Barrett? You shouldn't be here."

"You're bleeding," Jude said.

"I don't know what happened," the guy said. "I think a fucking bat hit me from behind. Hey, you really shouldn't be here. And what's the girl doing out of her—"

Vivi looked down at his ID tag. His name was beneath his photo. *Timmy Price, Technician.* She sucked in a breath, then punched out a command. Because that was what it felt like. As if she could control everything and everyone around her.

Timmy Price, shut up.

His lips clamped shut. Then they opened.

She sent out another pulse.

Timmy Price, take a nap. A long nap.

He crumpled to the ground. Vivi stepped around him and hurried into the room. She opened the drawer and lifted Bram. He yawned, showing his pink mouth. She ran back to Jude.

"Hold the ferret," she told him.

"Uh, okay." Jude tucked the animal inside his scrub shirt. "How did you get Bram?"

"We've got years to talk," she said.

Her father's ponytail jerked when Vivi pushed his chair toward the elevator. They got in, and she hit the top button. As they passed the second level, and she heard gunfire. Jude looked up at her.

"I hope this works, Meep. If we don't make it, I want you to know something. I love you."

She nodded, holding back tears. The elevator doors

skidded open. Vivi stepped around the wheelchair and peered into the hall. She didn't see any bats, but she could tell they'd been here. Blood was splattered on the floor and walls.

Gunfire echoed in the distance.

She darted back into the elevator car, grabbed the handles of Jude's chair, and pushed him into the hall. A boom sounded, and the floor wobbled.

"Jude, where's the closest exit?"

He pointed right. "Down that corridor."

They rounded a corner. A man lay face down by the water cooler, blood spilling toward his outstretched hand. His fingers curled around a Glock. The back of his skull had been torn off, and his brains glistened in the red light. Vivi felt sick, but she let go of Jude's chair, tiptoed around the pooled blood, and lifted the Glock.

She gave it to Jude, got behind his chair, and steered him down the corridor. At the far end, a tall metal door swung open, dangling from its hinges. Beyond the veranda, the night sky spun out, jammed with stars. She pushed her dad through the doorway onto a wooden veranda.

What now? She'd gotten them out of the building, but how could they leave the compound? Dammit. She walked to the edge of the veranda. Three bodies lay in the gravel road, and a dark, shining stream ran between them.

Jude pointed to a yellow Hummer that was parked at an angle. "If you can get me to the Hummer, I can drive."

She stared, uncomprehending.

"There's no time to explain," he said. "Just help me walk to the Hummer."

Walk? The poor guy had lost his grip on reality. But they still had to get to the vehicle. She pushed his chair to the edge of the veranda. "What about the gates?" she asked.

Behind her, she heard a gasp. Then a musical voice said, "Girl!"

She turned slowly, expecting to see Mustafa, but it was Fadime. His cheek was gashed, and blood streamed down the side of his face. He shuffled to the wheelchair and pointed a gun at the back of Jude's head.

Vivi's nostrils flared, and she tugged in a breath. Oh, what if she accidentally Induced Jude? Or hurt Bram?

"Put your face on the floor!" Fadime yelled at her. "Move it."

Jude reached around and grabbed the soldier's hand. The bone snapped. Fadime screamed, and his gun clattered to the veranda.

"Grab that forty-five," Jude said.

She scrambled over to the gun and snatched it.

The little Turk got to his knees, his eyes glowering, cradling his arm. A bone jutted up through the flesh, and dark blood streamed down.

"Don't move, Fadime," Jude said, aiming the Glock. "I don't want to kill you in front of my daughter."

Fadime's lips drew back, showing his teeth. "Shoot me, cripple."

"Look away, Meep."

But she didn't.

Jude squeezed the trigger. Fadime's head kicked back and he thudded to the veranda.

Down the road, toward the security checkpoint, a

fireball exploded, and flames rolled up into the darkness, sparks arcing in all directions. The veranda trembled, then went still.

Above them the air began to roar. Three lights cut across the dark sky. Helicopters? Vivi's heart began to pound. "More soldiers!"

"We'll be ready for them, Meep. Get behind my chair."

Vivi pointed at the sky. "Look. Those are Raphael's helicopters."

Each door was stamped with DELLA ROCCA, LTD.

Vivi's eyes brimmed. She crouched beside Jude's chair and reached for his hand. She was going home to her mom. And she was bringing her dad with her.

———

Daylight spilled over the compound, casting a pink glow over the helicopters. One of Raphael's men came to the door. He wore tactical gear and combat boots. His light brown hair was combed straight back.

"Vivi, your dad wants you."

She followed him inside the building, past the blood-splattered walls, into the dining hall. Mustafa was strapped to a gurney, and Jude sat beside him, adjusting the tubing of an IV machine.

"Are you ready for daylight?" he asked Mustafa.

Mustafa gritted his teeth, his face turning red.

Jude rose slightly from his chair and stabbed the needle into a rubber stopper of a small IV bag. The tubing looped across the cot into Mustafa's arm.

The Turk wrenched from side to side, trying to loosen the restraints.

"You wanted to walk in sunlight," Jude said. "Now you will. I adjusted the dose, by the way. So you'll have maybe five minutes before you fry."

Mustafa arched his back. Tears streamed down the sides of his face.

Vivi sat on the floor, petting Bram. He wrapped his paws around her wrist. "I'll take good care of the ferret," she said.

"You little bitch," Mustafa said.

Jude punched Mustafa in the mouth. A tooth flew out and clattered to the floor. Dark, smelly blood ran down the Turk's bottom lip.

Vivi felt a little trembly inside, as if she might fly apart. Had she become like Mustafa? Was her life more important than his? Maybe the difference was, she felt remorse. She didn't want to be the kind of person who hurt others. But she didn't want to spend the rest of her life hiding, either.

Signore Dolfini, Raphael's head security guy, walked up. "Are you ready, Dr. Barrett?"

"Yes." Jude turned back to Mustafa and examined the intravenous bag. It was almost empty.

Mustafa's lip curled. "Long after I am dead, you will still be a cripple."

Holding his gaze on the Turk, Jude braced his hands on his chair and rose.

Mustafa's face knotted. His mouth looked rubbery as he shaped and reshaped his lips.

"Jude!" Vivi scrambled to her feet.

He put his arm around her and turned to Signore Dolfini. "Will you please move this piece of trash to the lawn?"

"My pleasure," Dolfini said.

As Raphael's men pushed Mustafa's cot into the hall, Jude sank down into the chair. Vivi put the ferret in his lap.

"This is totally awesome," she said. "Have you been faking the paralysis?"

"No, no. It's a long story." He smiled.

From the veranda, Vivi heard Mustafa yelling at Raphael's men, calling them donkey fuckers. "Will he die?"

Jude nodded. "The light will take him."

"I want to see." She walked toward the door.

"Vivi, no," Jude called.

She turned. "I want to make sure Mustafa's gone. Or I'll always wonder."

Jude pulled in a ragged breath, then nodded. "I'll be waiting."

As Vivi stepped onto the veranda, she saw Raphael's men push the gurney across the lawn. Mustafa struggled beneath the restraints, his head whipping from side to side, hands fisted. The sun bulged over the horizon, and a crisp wind blew from the west, stirring the long grass. Mustafa stiffened his back. "Do not leave me here. My eyes are burning. It hurts. I will pay you. How much do you want? Name your price."

Vivi inched toward the edge of the veranda. The Italians parked the cot in the sun, then stepped back to the veranda.

"You are nothing," Mustafa yelled. "A wrinkle in history. But I was a Turkish warrior. A *Sipahi*."

"You are a demon," Vivi whispered.

His fists opened and his fingers clawed the air, as if trying to shred the light.

A shimmer radiated around his head. Bubbles spread across his scalp, down his forehead, over his cheeks. Mustafa began to gurgle as a deep scarlet flush rose to the surface of his skin and boiled out. Bits of flesh peeled back and floated up, wafting on the cool breeze. Sores erupted over his hands. Smoke drifted from his nose and ears. He opened his mouth, and a belch of steam curled out.

Vivi almost expected to see the restraints snap away from his body, allowing him to rise off the cot and spread leathery wings. Signore Dolfini guided her back into the building, where her father was waiting.

CHAPTER 52

Caro

VILLA PRIMAVERINA, ISLA CARBONARA
VENICE, ITALY

I spent a week floating in a drug-induced ennui where time moved in concentric circles, each one pressing tightly against the other, my past looped around the present. I perched inside the spiral, watching moments revolve: flames leaping out of a white house; Uncle Nigel leading me up the Egyptian escalator in Harrods; Jude holding Vivi on his shoulder; night wind rushing through the pink house in São Tomé. I dreamed of objects that wouldn't close: an overstuffed box, a door that refused to latch, a bracelet with a broken clasp. I dreamed of things that were lost and found. I dreamed that Jude had gone missing again, and I surrendered myself to grief.

I awoke in Raphael's bedroom, my chest heaving, my vision blurred. I tried to find a still place in my mind, and

I focused on an arrangement of seascapes that hung on the far wall. Lamplight washed over a carved desk, where my hairbrush lay next to Raphael's old rosary beads.

Maria came in later and set a tray on the bed. She tucked her wiry, gray-blond hair behind her ears. "I brought breakfast."

Enticing smells of coffee and pastry wafted over me, but I couldn't shake the ashes out of my thoughts.

"Caro, you've got to try. And you must get out of bed. You haven't moved in seven days."

"Just give me a minute." I gazed up at the ceiling. The trompe l'oeil clouds seemed different, larger and darker. I sat up, rubbing my eyes.

"I made croissants," Maria said.

She had a soft voice, infused with Germanic angles. She'd fallen in love with Beppe over a bowl of gnocchi. As a professional chef, she believed in the healing powers of food.

I pushed back my hair. "I feel dizzy."

Maria sighed. "It's those pills. Dr. Nazzareno shouldn't have given them to you."

"It's not every day that I murder someone," I said. I'd aimed for a cynical tone, but my voice held back a sob.

"It's not every day that an evil bitch gets her comeuppance," Maria said.

A cold feeling edged up my neck. I couldn't believe I'd taken a life. Now I had to live with this knowledge for the rest of mine.

Maria tore open a croissant. "I made Scotch marmalade, just the way you like it. Do you need me to do anything else? Are your hands still sore?"

"No, I'm much better."

I peeled off the bulky gauze bandage. My hands had healed rapidly. A two-inch scab ran across my left palm and dozens of tiny scabs marked my right hand. I gave silent thanks for hybrid DNA as I flexed my fingers—they were only a little sore.

The wounds had healed, but I wasn't sure that I would be quite the same. I'd murdered Tatiana, but I'd moved closer to a blurry line. How could I pull back from that line?

I glanced up. Maria looked troubled. "You acted in self-defense," she said.

Her words flowed right over me. She was loyal to Raphael, and that loyalty extended to me. Not only that, she was always impossibly upbeat, sunny, and positive. I'd never seen her crack, not even the year she'd burned the Easter ham. She just didn't have enough darkness to understand that I no longer recognized myself.

I drank a few sips of coffee and forced myself to taste the croissant. It was buttery and flaky, and I took another bite.

"It's ten A.M.," she said. "A beautiful August morning."

I sighed. It might as well be ten P.M.

"I'll get your clothes." Maria walked to the armoire.

I closed my eyes. A sense of impending doom rose up, and I knew something terrible was going to happen. I tried to shake it away, but it jerked me into a dark vault where all the clocks were ticking out of rhythm, where events and people meshed into one continuum. All the minutes and seconds and years ran together in a spiral.

Maria's voice brought me back. "Do you want to wear this dress?" She held up a pink, dotted shift.

"Perfect," I said a little too brightly. "What's been happening at the villa?"

"You'd know if you left this room." She placed the dress on the bed. "Shall I draw your bath?"

"I can manage on my own." I moved to the edge of the mattress. "Where's Raphael?"

"In the library, worrying about you," she said, a smile in her voice. "I'll tell him you're up."

After she left, I went into Raphael's bathroom. It was the size of a ballroom, with a sunken tub and pale blue tiles that ran along the edge. Fluffy white towels were stacked on a shelf. On the counter, clear jars held soaps from Grasse, France.

I drew a bath, got into the tub, and closed my eyes. The water sluiced down my thighs, a kind of baptism, rinsing away the scummy edges of the sleeping pill. Steam drifted up, fragrant with the smell of lavender.

A while later, I heard a knock at the door. I sat up, suds falling down my breasts. "Yes?"

"It's me," Raphael said.

"Come in," I called, brightening at the sound of his voice.

The door opened, and Arrapato raced into the room. Raphael followed him, looking handsome in a brown cotton shirt and white shorts. His hair fell in straight panels to his chin. I couldn't read his expression, and he wouldn't let me into his thoughts.

My stomach tightened.

I got out of the tub, and he wrapped me in a towel, knotting it over my breasts. I ran my fingers through his hair. "Are you all right?"

He kissed me before he spoke. "Your uncle Nigel just arrived."

"*Here?*" A flutter stirred in my chest. Normally I would be thrilled to see my uncle. But something felt wrong.

"How did he know where to find me?" I asked.

"I e-mailed him," Raphael said.

"Why?" I looked up into his eyes. What was going on? Was he just trying to keep me calm? The tranquilizers were still in my bloodstream, and I couldn't hold my thoughts together. I felt blunted and empty.

Raphael started to say something, but his lips couldn't seem to shape the words. Then one edge of his mouth tilted down.

"You've got that look, Raphael. Something's wrong. You're holding back."

He grabbed another towel and patted it against my shoulder. Then he led me into the bedroom. I started to pick up the dress Maria had set out, but Raphael caught my hand. I gave him a questioning look. He guided me to the bed, and we sat down on the comforter, facing each other. I put my hands in my lap and stared at my upturned palms, trying to appear calm, but my heart was racing. *Vivi is dead. That's why Uncle Nigel is here. People always come together for weddings and funerals.*

"No, *mia cara.*" Raphael lifted my hand and kissed the scabs on my palms. "I apologize. My voice has left me today. But I wanted you to be sitting down when you hear the good news. Vivi is coming home. Dolphini and his men are bringing her here tonight."

The air swirled. Long, glossy streaks were moving around me. My heart was still leaping. I let out a joyful sob and flung my arms around him. His hands tightened on my waist.

I leaned back. "She's all right?"

He nodded. "Healthy and unharmed, *mia cara*."

"Where was she? How did she escape?"

He explained how Dolfini had traced numbers on Tatiana's cell phone to a compound in Sutherland, South Africa. Raphael had assembled a team. And now my daughter was on her way home.

I'd been holding my breath while he talked, and now I let it out in a rush. "Where is she now?"

"Madrid. She can't wait to see you. Before Dolfini's team arrived in Sutherland, Vivi had prepared the way. She did a takedown of the Al-Dîn compound. She used her skills. Dolfini said she even took a hostage—a ferret. She called while you were sleeping. She wants to tell you what happened. I gave her my word."

I smiled and shook my head. So that was why he'd brought Uncle Nigel. I pressed my cheek against Raphael's. "Thank you for bringing her home."

"Anything for you, *mia cara*," he whispered.

"We'll have to plan a welcome-home dinner," I said. Now we can have only one wedding. Do you still want to get married in the garden? Uncle Nigel can give me away. And Vivi can be the flower girl."

Raphael made a tiny, choked sound. And then his

cheek felt damp. I couldn't see his face, but I knew he was crying. I cradled the back of his head, and my tears spilled down.

After a while, he pulled back, wiping his face. "There's more."

"What is it, then?"

He put his hand on my cheek, more tears glistening in his eyes. "Jude is alive. He's coming with Vivi."

A roaring sound filled my head. I slumped, as if my bones had softened. Raphael caught me in an instant and wrapped his arms around my waist. No, this couldn't be right. I'd misunderstood. Jude was dead.

Raphael's breath stirred in my hair. "He is alive, *mia cara*."

Alive. I couldn't breathe. A tumble of emotions ran together. Shock, happiness, fear, disbelief. My heart slammed against my breastbone, as if trying to punch its way out. I didn't blame it. Jude was coming here? All this time, he'd been alive?

I moved back. "Where has he been for the last ten years?"

"South Africa. Mustafa Al-Dîn imprisoned him. Forced him to work in his lab."

I remembered Tatiana's dying words. They didn't matter. He was alive. Vivi was alive. They were together. She would finally have a father. But I wasn't sure about the rest of it. I reached for Raphael's other hand. What would we do?

"One more thing, *mia cara*," Raphael said, pulling back, his eyes searching my face. "Jude was injured. His spinal column was severed, and he lost the use of his legs.

He's undergone stem cell transplants, and he's regained some use of his legs. But he's still in a wheelchair."

I felt sick to my stomach. I couldn't imagine how much he'd suffered, trapped in two different prisons, locked in a laboratory, confined to a chair. There was a long silence.

"I loved him, Raphael. I love him still. But I thought he was dead. I've moved far away from that grief. I'm not the same woman he left behind."

"Your love for him won't end," Raphael said.

"No, no. But it has changed."

Tears stood in Raphael's dark eyes. "Caro, you don't have a choice. You never had one."

This was the last thing I wanted to hear. "If I have no choices, I still pick you." I pressed my chin on his shoulder and laced my fingers through his hair. I knew every plane and slope of his body, and they felt just right to me. My hands dropped to his shoulders. I felt the hard curve and slid my hands lower, over the firm length of his arms. He was just as stong on the inside. "How long before they arrive?" I asked.

He moved back a little and tilted his watch. "Ten hours or so. Why?"

I stretched out on the bed and held out my hand. "Just hold me."

He climbed in next to me and gathered me into his arms. A tear moved slowly down the side of his nose. "I want every clock in the world to give back our time," he said, his voice filled with yearning. "I want all of those hours in Norway and Zermatt and Paris and Morocco."

"This won't be the last time we're together," I said.

But one door was gusting open, and I couldn't prevent the other door from closing, no matter how hard I tried.

"*Sei il grande amore della mia vita,*" he said in my ear. *You're the love of my life.* "In all my time on earth, I've only done one thing right. I've loved you."

I leaned into him, bound by his gravity, and no force could take me away from him.

We did little talking for the next ten hours, and what happened will stay between me, Raphael, and the gods.

CHAPTER 53

Vivi

VILLA PRIMAVERINA, ISLA CARBONARA
VENICE, ITALY

Vivi could barely contain her excitement as she leaned against the helicopter window, watching the lights of Venice recede. The water stretched out black and silky as a ball gown. The darkness parted, and a dazzle radiated from Villa Primaverina. She saw the landing pad in the lower garden, a giant white X in the center. The steps rose up past sculpted flower beds, past a stone nymph who danced in a fountain.

Everyone she loved was waiting on the front terrace of the villa, their faces upturned. She saw Beppe in a white dinner jacket, his bald head gleaming. Maria leaned against him, holding Arrapato. Uncle Nigel smoked his pipe. Raphael stood on the bottom step, the wind catching his shirt. Her mom was beside him, a mass of honeyed curls rising behind her.

Jude leaned toward the window, and Vivi saw his face crumple.

She kissed the top of his head. "It's all right, Dad. She loves you."

He pointed to his ears and mouthed, *I can't hear you.*

Soon they would be on the ground, out of this loud bird. They would be a family with a house and an address that would never change. She even had a pet. She reached down and adjusted the strap on Bram's Sherpa. She and her dad would garden at night, and her mom would smile all the time. Jude had been trying so hard to walk the last few days. He'd explained about those stem cell treatments he'd secretly gotten at the compound; they had rebuilt part of his spine, but he needed more implants. One day he would rise from that chair. But tonight, if he fell, if he even wobbled, Vivi and her mom would be right there to catch him.

CHAPTER 54

Jude

As the helicopter veered toward the landing pad, Jude remembered the first time he'd come to Villa Primaverina—Raphael's stereo had played a Nine Inch Nails song, and the red, black, and white décor had complemented the music.

Jude's eyes brimmed. How could he ever thank Raphael for taking care of Caro and Vivi?

Vivi tapped the window, and it looked as if she were saying, *Mom*.

He leaned toward the window. Lights blazed over the steps that led to the villa. Everyone was waiting on the terrace—Beppe, Maria, Nigel, Raphael. Caro looked just like she had the first time he'd seen her. All legs and cheekbones, with irrepressible hair. Oh, how he loved her.

She was looking up at the helicopter, her white dress billowing. Living without her had been unbearable, but he couldn't think about that now. He'd need to take it slowly with her. One step. A half step. Their lives had shifted and realigned, and they would shift again. Maybe not in the way he hoped. Or maybe into something wonderful.

Caro ran down the steps as fast as she could, her hair flying. He sat up a little straighter, his heart booming. Everything would be the same. She loved him. And she was still his girl.

CHAPTER 55

Caro

I waited at the edge of the landing pad, my dress foaming around my knees. Lights streaked across the water, and when the helicopter touched down, I felt dizzy. The more things change, the more they stay the same.

The door opened, and Signore Dolfini helped Vivi out of the helicopter. Then he climbed back inside and emerged with a folded-up wheelchair. My heart clenched as I watched him open it and lock the wheels. One of Dolfini's men came out of the door with Jude in his arms and put him in the chair, then Vivi pushed him away from the landing pad. As they got closer, the wind kicked up his dark ponytail. His eyes were the same porcelain blue, tilting up at the edges. I put my hand over my mouth. This was everything I'd ever wanted. This was everything

I didn't want. I'd already decided what to do. I would be on my own for a while. Let both Jude and Raphael go.

But I was wrong. Vivi locked the wheelchair. She looked as if she'd grown two inches, but she was so thin.

"Mom!"

She dove into my chest. I hugged her as hard as I could. She hugged me, too. We swung from side to side. Finally, she pulled away. "Look who I brought home for supper."

Jude's smile widened. "Sorry, I'm a bit late."

"A bit," I said. Long ago, I'd realized that we might never have tranquil days, but right now, as I looked into my husband's eyes, I found a quiet place inside me.

He grabbed the side of the chair, arms trembling, and slowly rose. I threw my arms around him. I felt him lean into me, and then he put his hands on my waist. I felt the cool rush of his breath against my neck. Then I felt him wobble, and for a moment, I couldn't tell who was holding on and who was letting go.

He let out a breath and sat down hard in the chair. His hands slipped around my waist, and then he turned me around, so that I was facing the villa, and pulled me into his lap. He pressed his chin against the back of my head.

"You're still my girl," he said.

I knew he was waiting for me to say the words, our litany, but my throat clenched.

Vivi sat down on my lap and put one arm around Jude, one around me. I couldn't seem to pull in a breath, as if the whole lagoon were caught in my chest. The wind kicked up, and my hair streamed across my face.

I pushed it out of my eyes. Raphael stood at the bottom of the terrace, washed in golden light from the villa. He rubbed his eyes, leaving a damp sheen on his cheeks. I felt a sudden longing to run back to him. His lips parted, as if he'd released a sigh, and his thoughts brushed through me. His expression was caught somewhere between grief and yearning. I held his gaze and pulled him deep inside me, out of the night, into a sun-drenched place. His eyes brimmed with knowing.

Raphael, I will always love you.

Always, mia cara. *Always.*

I owe a debt of gratitude to everyone at Berkley, including my editor, Faith Black; my copyeditor, Amy Schneider; and Lindsay T. Boggs, my publicist. Nancy Nicholas checked my French (all mistakes are my own). I will always be grateful to Ellen Levine for believing in these vamps from the beginning, when no one else did. Love and thanks to the in-house biochemist, Tyler West, and medical/genetics expert, Dr. Will West.